# TIMELESS SHADOWS

# J. A. Ferguson

## TIMELESS SHADOWS

Published by ImaJinn Books, a division of ImaJinn

First Printing April, 2000

ISBN: 1-893896-07-2

PUBLISHER'S NOTE:
This book is a work of fiction. Names, characters, places and incidents are products of the author's imagination or are used fictitiously. Any resemblance to actual events or locales or persons, living or dead, is entirely coincidental.

Books are available at quantity discounts when used to promote products or services. For information please write to: Marketing Division, ImaJinn Books, P.O. Box 162, Hickory Corners, MI 49060-0162, or call toll free 1-877-625-3592.

Cover design by Patricia Lazarus

**ImaJinn Books**, a division of ImaJinn
P.O. Box 162, Hickory Corners, MI 49060-0162
Toll Free: 1-877-625-3592
http://www.imajinnbooks.com

# Dedication

For Allison Kelley,
who has made my job so much easier
that I actually had time to write this book.
Thanks for all you do, Allison, and your friendship

# Note from ImaJinn Books

Dear Readers,

Thank you for buying this book. The author has worked hard to bring you a captivating tale of love and adventure.

In the months ahead, watch for our fast-paced, action-packed stories involving ghosts, psychics and psychic phenomena, witches, vampires, werewolves, angels, reincarnation, futuristic in space or on other planets, futuristic on earth, time travel to the past, time travel to the present, and any other story line that will fall into the "New-Age" category.

The best way for us to give you the types of books you want to read is to hear from you. Let us know your favorite types of "New-Age" romance. You may write to us or any of our authors at: ImaJinn Books, P.O. Box 162, Hickory Corners, MI 49060-0162. You may also e-mail us at: authors@imajinnbooks.com.

Visit our web site at: http://www.imajinnbooks.com

# Prologue

## Castle Braeburn, Scotland - 1619

*They were within the walls.*

*Steel clashed. Men shouted, then screamed with their last breaths.*

*The little girl ran to cling to her mother's skirts. Mam's fingers trembled as they brushed the little girl's hair back from her face.*

*"It is time," Mam said.*

*The dark-haired woman kneeling by the window, her hands pressed together, interrupted her keening prayers. "Take care, milady. Before you begin, ask yourself if this risk is one you are willing to take."*

*Mam bent to frame the little girl's face with her trembling hands. Furrows the little girl had never seen puckered Mam's mouth. Dampness lined her cheeks, but the tears did not dim her earth-brown eyes. "I must," she whispered. "I must send her away. It is the only way to save her."*

*The little girl threw her arms around her mother. "I want to stay with you."*

*"You cannot." She gently untangled the little girl's arms from around her shoulders. Looking past her, she said to the other woman, "I must do this. They are here. They have killed my bairn's father and will suffer none of his blood to live. I will not stand by and watch them spill innocent blood."*

*"'Twill be your death to abide here a moment longer, milady," moaned the woman.*

*"My end is assured, for my death sentence was signed the day I wed. I will save my bairn."*

*The little girl shook her head. There had been too much talk of death. So many had marched away. None had returned, save for the enemy.* "I want to stay with you, Mam."

*Her mother kissed the little girl's cheek and whispered,* "I will be with you when you need me, my beloved bairn." *Rising, she said to the other woman,* "Leave us."

"Milady, you need to remember well what I told you to say. I can remain to help you."

"I remember it well. Leave us."

"If you speak a single word wrong, you may doom the child instead of saving her. Let me remain and help you."

"I know well what I must do and say. Flee, Gertie, before you face your death, too."

*The little girl thought Gertie would protest again, but she bowed and left. When Mam held out her hand, the little girl put hers in it.*

"Trust me," *Mam said.* "I do this for you. You will like where you go. I promise you that. Everything will be as I wished it could be here for you."

"Come with me, Mam."

"No, for there is no place for me here on this earth without your father. I pray you may one day regain what is rightly yours and reap vengeance on those who have destroyed our family, but, if not, I wish you to be safe and loved." *Kissing the little girl on the cheek, she lifted her onto the high bed. The scent of her perfume, fresh and free like a mountain brae tumbling down a burn, caressed the little girl.* "Lie down and close your eyes."

*The little girl obeyed, then sat when something struck the door. Without a glance toward the door, Mam pushed her back into the pillows. Reaching up, she pulled from over the window a branch twisted with ivy. The savage thump came again. Mam placed the rowan branch with its pointed leaves and white, star-shaped blossoms in the little girl's hand.*

"Ne'er forget," *Mam whispered.* "Ne'er forget your birthright and your fate, wee one."

*Another thump. The door cracked. Shouts reverberated in the corridor.*

*Desperation filled Mam's voice as she repeated over and over words the little girl could not understand then said once more,* "Ne'er forget."

*Wood shattered, but the sound came as if from the depths of a dream. The little girl screamed as darkness consumed her...*

"Baby, baby, it's okay." Warm arms surrounded her.

The little girl opened her eyes to look up into a shadowed face. "Mommy!" she cried, leaning her head on her mother's shoulder.

Her mother turned on the light on the night stand. "Is it that bad dream again?"

"Uh-huh."

"You must forget it."

"I'm not supposed to."

"Who told you that?"

"She—"

"She who?"

The little girl wiped her eyes and whispered, "I don't know. I thought it was you, Mommy."

"I'm not in a dream. I'm right here." Her mother looked past her to a silhouette in the doorway. "And there's Daddy right there. We won't let anything happen to you. Do you believe that?"

The little girl nodded.

"Then you must promise me something."

"What, Mommy?"

"You've got to forget the bad dream. Will you?"

"Yes."

"Promise?"

The little girl nodded again and squirmed back between the wrinkled covers. As her mother kissed her, turned off the light, and went to the door, leaving it ajar so the glow from the nightlight oozed into the room, the little girl gripped the bedspread with its dancing teddy bears to her chin.

The door closed, but she heard her mother's anxious voice. "Kenny, I think we need to get her some professional help. I'm scared it's the memories of the accident."

"We can call someone tomorrow." His sigh flowed down the hall to the little girl. "Poor kid! Who knows what she saw? It'd be better if she didn't remember until she's old enough to deal with it."

"First thing tomorrow morning, I'm going to take down that picture in her room."

"Picture?"

"Of that stupid castle. It seems to disturb her."

Daddy's voice softened to a low chuckle. "How can a picture of a castle in Scotland bother her? You know how she loves pretending that she's a princess in that castle. Honey, you're getting too upset over this. We'll take her to see the doctor, and he'll help her forget."

The little girl shuddered as, through her mind echoed, in a voice that was as familiar as the nightmare, *Ne'er forget.*

# ONE

## Castle Braeburn - 1644

The great hall of Castle Braeburn was every bit as magnificent as he had anticipated. *And it was his.*

Colin MacLachlan strode across the stone floor. Fisting his hands on his waist, he looked up at the dusty banners hanging from the rafters four times a man's height above the tables. The thick timbers were darkened by smoke from the trio of fireplaces ringing the room. A pair of iron chandeliers hung over the plank tables, each one more than twenty feet long. Pewter was scattered about, warning that his arrival had surprised the residents of Castle Braeburn.

Good, let them be upset from their Royalist complacency. God had given neither them nor their king a divine right to rule Scotland. Let them pay the price for daring to claim even a grain of its soil. If good fortune was with Colin MacLachlan, all the English would be chased from the Highlands back to their own country where they would be welcome to fight their wars against their king until not one of them remained.

"'Tis fine, Laird MacLachlan, no doubt about that."

Colin laughed as he clapped Jackie Kilbride on the back. His friend, who was more than a head shorter than he was, deserved to share this moment. They had fought together and starved together and nearly died together. Now they would enjoy this castle together.

"Aye," he said as he walked to the ornate chair set in a place of honor at the head of the longest table. A lifetime of hard work and daring had culminated in this victory. He ran his hand across the intricate carving on the chair's back—on *his* chair's back. The seat was covered with a purple velvet cushion, unlike the hard benches along the sides of the table.

Spinning, he looked at his men who were gathered at the other end of the table. He raised his hands and shouted, "Ale, my lads! Ale for all of us!"

A roar of appreciation met his order. The men scattered to the kegs set by the doors. As the pungency of ale filled the hall, Colin smiled. The campaign had been long and the weather chill in this autumn of siege and war. A few days at Castle Braeburn would suit them well.

Jackie held out a golden goblet which was encrusted with gems. "Drink Stanton's ale with his own gold, laird." He gave a wicked laugh. "Stanton can use it no more."

Tapping the goblet against Jackie's pewter one, Colin said, "My thanks, my friend. Having you at my back has brought me to this day instead of being dead and buried long ago."

"I remain at your back, laird." His pudgy cheeks were flushed with fervor, but his nose wrinkled. "The treachery of Royalists reeks within these walls."

"That odor shall not be with us long. This stronghold belongs to our clan once more."

Jackie spat on the floor. "Let those who would steal MacLachlan land lie unmourned beneath the earth. This is now the castle of Laird MacLachlan!" His last words rose to a bellow.

The other men echoed it with the clatter of pewter and calls for more ale and food to be brought. One started an insulting song about the Royalists, and the others joined in, each line becoming more lewd than the one before it.

Colin drained the ale from his goblet. He pulled his *claidhmor* and climbed onto the table. He shouted, "*Fortis et fidus!*"

His men cheered their clan's motto. Holding the broadsword up in both hands, he sliced the rope connecting the largest banner to the rafters. The Stanton family crest crashed to the floor in a cloud of dust. Too long it had hung here. Now it had fallen, like the man whose family had stolen this castle from its rightful laird.

Colin smiled. The vow he had made when he was little more than a bairn had been fulfilled today. The English invaders had sent his father and so many others on the low road to death. Colin had pledged to see English blood spilled in return. Through the years, he had waited for this moment. Now he, who had the strongest claim on this castle, for his father was a many times removed cousin of the late laird's father, held Castle Braeburn.

"Send that banner to the flames," he called. "Let it feel the fires of Hell as all Royalists shall."

Renewed shouts filled the hall, echoing wildly up into the rafters and setting the birds nesting there to wheel about the roof. Someone splashed more ale into Colin's goblet and held it up to him. He raised it as the huge banner was dropped onto the flames on the largest hearth.

A furtive movement caught Colin's eye. His hand went for the knife at his side as the cups clinked around him again. Cautiously, he turned and stared at the door to his left. Who was the woman standing in the doorway?

She was no common serving wench, for her gown was of the finest light green satin. Lace edged the low, square neckline and peeked from beneath the full sleeves. Forest green velvet bows accented her slender waist, and the single strand of pearls at her throat drew his gaze to the curves hidden so enticingly. Her hair, which was as ruddy as Jackie's, held no more curl than his own. Instead of being layered in ringlets about her face, it curved gently on her bare shoulders.

A lady! But there should be no ladies of the Englishman's blood still alive within these walls, and the last laird's family were long dead.

He stared at her. Her face was pretty enough to urge a man closer, but not so beautiful that she would daunt a suitor. Her brown eyes were wide...and she was smiling.

Smiling? Stanton's daughter would not smile when her father's enemies were making themselves welcome in his castle. His daughter, if he had one, would be pale with grief at the news of Stanton's death within the same hour as his two sons. No, she could not be the lone survivor of the Stanton name in Castle Braeburn. Then who was she?

As she gathered up her skirts, raising them farther from the floor than he had thought a lady would, he was treated to a glimpse of slim ankles. When she aimed her smile at him, every muscle along his body tightened. Too long he had been at war. It was time to savor the rewards of his victories. He smiled back at her as he wondered if her lips would be sweet or as bitter as betrayal.

He stepped down from the table. With his foot on the bench, and the tip of his *claidh-mor* against the floor, he called, "Come in, and acquaint us with your name."

His men's voices halted as if they had been frozen in a midwinter blizzard. A low mumble came from them when they turned to see the woman in the doorway, but Colin heard appreciation in the sound.

He held out his hand, but, instead of hurrying forward to press it to her forehead as she knelt before him, she exclaimed, "Kilts!" Laughter filled her voice when she came into the great hall, a gray-haired serving woman at her heels. "You're all wearing kilts. Cool!"

Colin frowned. He had been unsure what the reaction would be to his arrival, but he could not have imagined this. Her words were so odd. "Are you Stanton's daughter?"

"I think...Just a minute." She turned to the old woman, who whispered something to her. With a grin, she added, "I'm not a Stanton. I'm a Gordon."

"Gordon?" He scowled, wondering what she wished to gain with her transparent lies. "No Gordons remain in Castle Braeburn."

"As you can see, there is at least one." Her lips twitched as if she were trying not to smile. When her nose wrinkled, she asked, "Did something die in here? It smells like an outhouse."

He ignored her insults that mirrored the ones fired too often at the Scots by the king's men. Seeing her smile, he scowled. She would have no reason for merriment if he discovered she was lying. Quietly, he asked, "What is your given name?"

"Ashley."

"Come here, Ashley."

The old woman did not look at him as she murmured, "'Tis Lady Ashley."

*Lady Ashley!* That was absurd. No one of the laird's blood could have survived Stanton's massacre here more than two decades ago. She must be a bastard, who hoped in the midst of chaos to claim what should never be hers. He would be wise to dismiss her, but, he decided with another smile, there was no need for hurry. He liked looking at this lass, and he would enjoy looking at her much more intimately.

She glanced up at the rafters. "What happened to the other banner?" Her eyes grew wide when smoke billowed from the hearth as the velvet burst into flames. "You're burning it? Do you think that's such a good idea?"

"Without question." He never had been as sure of anything as he was of his victory over Stanton. All signs of the accursed Englishman would soon be banished from Castle Braeburn.

"But it must be so valuable."

"Not to me."

She looked at him again. "Does Mr. Campbell know you're burning it?"

"Why do you speak that name so lightly, milady?" He caught her elbow and pulled her closer.

Surprise stole across her face, then, again inexplicably, she smiled. "Oops, I forget. You're probably sworn enemies, aren't you?" She turned to the old woman, drawing out of Colin's grip as if he were no more of a threat to her than a piece of straw on the floor. "What year did you say this was supposed to be?"

Jackie edged closer, frowning. "My laird, the lass is daft."

The old woman rushed forward. Dropping awkwardly to her knees, she hid her face in Lady Ashley's full skirt. A moan burst from her lips before she cried, "Milady, you must greet Laird MacLachlan and thank him for freeing us from our imprisonment."

"Really? Imprisonment?" Lady Ashley asked.

"By whom?" Colin demanded.

The old woman whispered, "By Lord Stanton, my laird. You have freed us. We are so grateful."

Before Colin could reply, Lady Ashley reached out and gripped his sleeve. Rubbing the fabric together, she whistled softly. "This is the coarsest wool I've ever felt. I bet you're glad you don't have to wear it all the time."

"Milady!" the old woman moaned again. Pushing herself to her feet, she added, "You must welcome Colin MacLachlan, who claims the title of laird of Castle Braeburn."

"All right." She dipped in a slight curtsy. Her eyes glittered with amusement. "Welcome, Colin MacLachlan, who claims the title of laird of Castle Braeburn." She laughed softly.

His irritation at her peculiar behavior was becoming a slow-burning anger, the kind that filled him in the moments before the call to battle. He would not be made to look like a fool by this woman. "I have come to take what is mine."

Throwing out her hands, she said, "My lord—"

"*Laird*," whispered the serving woman frantically.

"Sorry," Lady Ashley whispered back with a smile. "My laird, it's all yours."

"Milady," gasped the old woman, "do not give him what is not his."

"Really?" she asked.

Colin locked eyes with the serving woman, but she looked hastily away as he demanded, "Not mine? Who, pray, claims this castle?"

He did not wait for the old woman to answer. Instead he turned back to the lass who called herself Lady Ashley. He caught her at the waist and pulled her to him. Shock filled her eyes, but no fear. She was either courageous or deranged, as Jackie suggested. Whichever she was, she also was a soft, perfumed delight in his arms. A man could lose himself in the promises within her sparkling eyes, but he must not.

"The Marquess of Argyll has granted me this castle and all within it, milady," he said in the low tone his men would know meant he was furious. She must learn that as well. "If you have been a prisoner here, you should be grateful that I have freed you."

"Grateful?" When his arm tightened to bring her soft curves up against his chest, she added in a whisper, "Don't get carried away with your role."

"Carried away? Is that what you wish?" He bent and, putting one hand under her knees, lifted her into his arms. When she cried out in surprise, he added, "I would like to see the laird's rooms, milady. Will you show them to me?"

She shifted in his arms, then faltered when his fingers slipped along the enticing curve of her waist. "Put me down! It's hard enough to breathe in this outfit as it is."

"Is that so?" He laughed, ignoring the soft moan of dismay from her serving woman. "Then there is nothing to do but get you out of it."

"If you'll put me down, I'll do that right away."

Colin thought he could be no more shocked by anything this woman said or did, but he was. When she wiggled, trying to stretch a low-heeled shoe toward the bench, he said, "Let me help, milady." He set her on her feet and reached for the topmost hook at the back of her gown.

"Are you crazy?" she gasped as he opened it and found the next.

"Not I."

She smiled, shocking him more. "I guess you were the surprise promised to me." She bent toward him and whispered, "Just a couple more hooks here are far enough for this game, but don't get any idea about the ones in the front. When this is all over, if you want to get something to drink down by the loch, I can give you a few pointers on—"

"You talk too much, woman."

"So I've been told." She gave him a saucy smile. "So what are you going to do to shut me up, my laird? Send me off to the dungeon or—"

She gasped as he pressed his lips to the curve of her neck. Her pulse leapt beneath his touch, and an answering throb erupted through him.

He tugged her to him, his lips claiming hers. Only a fool would deny himself the pleasure of this pretty woman, and Colin MacLachlan was no fool.

Her hands rose to push against his chest, but he pinned them between him and her supple body as he tasted her lips, savoring how they warmed beneath his. When her fingers uncurled along his doublet, rising to edge along his shoulders, he deepened the kiss to sample every sweet flavor waiting for him. She shared each breath with him while the rapid beat of her heart caressed him.

As he sprinkled eager kisses along her face, another gasp grazed his cheek. He groaned with the craving he had submerged during so many weeks of fighting. Twisting his fingers through her hair which was as fiery as her mouth, he stared down into her delicately carved features. Who was she? At the moment, he did not care. She was in his arms and willing.

"That was nice," she murmured as a slow smile edged along her lips. "I bet you get a lot of practice in this job. You can kiss the women and get paid for it, too. Not a bad deal."

"Bad deal?" He scowled. "Of what do you speak, milady?"

She slid out of his arms. "Of you, my lord—I mean, my laird." She walked her fingers up his sleeve and draped her hand over his shoulder. "What did you need to land this job? Just rugged good looks and that great accent?"

"Milady," cried the old woman, "watch what you say!"

"Aye," growled Jackie. He slammed his mug of ale onto the table. "Watch your tongue, woman, or you shall lose it." The crack of his hand against her cheek resounded through the room.

Lady Ashley reeled back, holding her hand to her face. Her eyes narrowed, and she took a step forward. Her serving woman grasped her sleeve. She shook it off.

With a laugh, Jackie raised his hand again.

"Jackie!" snapped Colin. "Don't—"

"No!" shrieked Lady Ashley.

Her voice vanished beneath Jackie's stunned shout as she seized his arm. Suddenly Jackie's legs were swinging up in the air. He crashed to the floor at the lady's feet.

Colin stared in disbelief from his friend to Lady Ashley who whispered in amazement, "It really works." With a chuckle, she put one foot on Jackie's chest and raised her clenched fist over her head.

Laughter rumbled from the other end of the table. Colin flashed a scowl at the rest of his men as Jackie rolled away and jumped to his feet, his hand on his knife.

Colin began, "Milady—"

She poked at Jackie's nose and said tautly, "If you ever touch me again, I'll show you what else I learned in self-defense class." Turning, she walked back to Colin. "If I were you, I'd make sure I had a good lawyer before I let him out of his cage again. I don't know about your laws here, but, if he'd hit me like that in the States, I could sue you and get everything in this castle, including the shirt off your back and the skirt off your butt."

He was not sure which outrageous statement to respond to first. He never had seen a lady—or anyone—take down an opponent with such ease. What Royalist trickery was this?

"Your threats are worthless! You shall have nothing!" cried Jackie.

Colin grasped his friend's hand as it rose again. "Enough. This is no way to treat Lady Ashley."

"That's right," she replied. "Listen to your boss. But, first, take a bath. You smell as bad as whatever stinks in here."

Jackie growled incoherently.

Ashley Babcock paid him no mind. Her head still rang with the blow she had not expected. If Castle Braeburn always treated its guests like this, it was no wonder she had not seen any of the others this morning. Only she had been stupid enough to get caught up in whatever this charade was supposed to be.

When the shorter man edged toward her, she cried, "Touch me again and—"

"Enough from you, milady," the tall man, who called himself Laird MacLachlan, ordered.

"Enough from *you*, too!" she fired back. "I've had enough of all of this."

"But I have not."

A finger under her chin tilted her head toward him. "Leave me alone!" she spat, stepping back. She held up her hands as Jan had taught in the self-defense class at the community center. "Back off, buster!"

His elbow knocked her hands aside as his finger became a strong hand that cupped her chin, forcing her to look into the cold blue eyes of Colin MacLachlan. Unlike the others, he was clean-shaven. An ebony beard would have diminished the sharpness of his high cheekbones and narrow nose. His square jaw warned, needlessly, of his stubborn nature.

"I am sorry you suffered Captain Kilbride's hand, milady," he said. "It was my intention to see that you are not abused as long as you obey me."

"I said 'Enough already!'" She tried to jerk her face away, but his fingers were as unyielding as steel. "Let me go, and I'll pack and be out of here as soon as the bus comes around."

"Bus? What is that?" He did not give her a chance to answer as his black brows lowered in a forbidding scowl. "No matter, milady, for you shall not be leaving Castle Braeburn until you answer a few questions. The first is: Who are you?"

Ashley put her hand on his wrist. "Please let me go."

"You shall not leave Castle Braeburn."

"I don't mean that. Please let go of my face. It hurts."

For a long moment, she feared he would not release her. Then, with a nod, he drew his fingers away. Just as she was about to breathe a sigh of relief, he tipped her face so he could see the spot where the other guy had slapped her.

"Who are you, lady fair?" he murmured.

She shook her head. "How much longer is this going to go on?" When he frowned at her, she sighed. "All right. I'll play along a while longer if you keep that brute away from me." She glared at the short man who was muttering something. "Next time, I'll make sure he gets more than the breath knocked out of him. He'll be singing soprano." She was not sure if any of the other techniques she had learned would work, but she was not going to let him hit her again.

"Captain Kilbride shall not touch you, milady. You have my word on that."

"Your word?" This had been fun until Captain Kilbride had gotten slap-happy, but, if they wanted to continue, she would play the fine lady to the hilt. "What value does your word have, Colin MacLachlan?"

"Milady," whispered the old woman, "take care what you say. Heed the necessity for caution."

"Caution? Why?" She laughed and pointed to Captain Kilbride. "Is he the best of your lot? He can't even hold his own against me." When Colin MacLachlan stared at her, speechless, as she took the offensive in this battle of words again, she smiled. "You ask me who I am. I shall tell you, Colin MacLachlan. I am Lady Ashley Gordon of Castle Braeburn."

"Impossible! All of that name here are dead."

She walked to stand behind the fancy chair, the very one that had first caught her eye when she entered Castle Braeburn last night. "As you can see, you are wrong. And let me warn you, Colin MacLachlan. You may think you have won, but your ragtag army will never see Bonnie Prince Charlie on the throne of England."

"Prince Charlie?" Fury straightened his eyebrows across his forehead. "'Tis no prince, but a king we battle, milady. We would never raise our swords in the defense of any traitorous Stuart king who has tried to force the Church of England down our throats. Charles Stuart forgot his origins when he ascended the throne."

Ashley faltered. "Wait a minute. Aren't you fighting against King George to put Bonnie Prince Charlie on his grandfather's throne?" When the strange looks were shot at her, she snapped, "It'd help if you guys would let me know what war you're supposed to be fighting."

"*Supposed* to be fighting?"

Rushing to take Ashley's arm again, the gray-haired woman turned to Colin MacLachlan. "She is troubled by the sudden changes in her fortune, my laird. Forgive her. She has not been herself today."

"Step aside, old woman, or her fortune will be only bad." Colin tugged Ashley from behind the chair. "What game do you play, milady? You know as well as I that the year is 1644. Why do you pretend someone named George rules England? No one rules England now, for the whole of the country is a battleground between Charles Stuart and his Parliament." He searched her face. "Are you mad, milady?"

"1644? The English Civil War?" Ashley tried to remember what she knew of that period. King Charles had lost his head to his Puritan enemies. When that had taken place and what had happened after it, she was not sure. Everything she had learned in school about the 17th century had focused on the colonization of America.

Turning to his men, he shouted an order in a language she did not understand before adding, "Take your lady from me, old woman. I shall send for her later. Have her mind as clear as her brown eyes, for I wish to hear the truth on her lips of how she claims to have survived Stanton's tenancy of this castle. Warn her to speak the truth, for, if she continues with her lies, she shall die."

When Ashley hesitated, wanting to know how much longer this play was going to last, the old woman pulled on her arm in desperation. She took a step toward the door, then paused. She stared at the men in the room. There must be more than forty. Who were they? Mr. Campbell had said last night only about two dozen people worked at the castle.

What was going on here? Uneasiness pricked her as she stared at the smoking remains of the banner on the open hearth. It looked no different from the others which Mr. Campbell had bragged were more than 400 years old.

A rumble of laughter brought her gaze back to Colin MacLachlan. No one would taunt him for wearing a skirt, for the kilt snapped with every step he took as he talked with the other men. Its red background and navy and green plaid were dulled by wear. A stain ran along the left sleeve of his wool doublet that was as black as his hair.

Blood!

She clenched her hands at her sides. *What was going on here?* From the moment she had opened her eyes this morning, she had been swept up into this. She had been greeted by this old woman and offered a lovely gown to wear. With the old woman's help, she had dressed up to be part of whatever entertainment Castle Braeburn offered its guests during their stay. The old woman had babbled about needing to come down to the great hall, and Ashley had thought some sort of play would take place here. Was it a reenactment? Now she was not so sure. *What was going on here?*

Bile was bitter in her mouth as a man hobbled forward. His right leg was gone, replaced by a chunk of wood. When he turned to speak to one of his comrades, she could not keep from staring. It was not just a costume. His leg was really gone.

"Milady, we must not linger."

She looked at the old woman. The old woman's round face was crisscrossed by a riverbed of wrinkles, and fear filled eyes that were a paler blue than the laird's. Her layers of clothes were tied together at the waist. Her skirt draped back to reveal petticoats. A wide collar came nearly to her thick waist and dropped to her elbows. A heavy piece of cloth covered her gray hair.

*Just like the costumes at Plimoth Plantation*, Ashley thought. If she let herself get enmeshed in this, she might start believing it all. A shudder raced through her. Closing her eyes, she took a deep breath. In Massachusetts, they had created the 17th century so vividly with historical interpreters who never went out of character.  Mr. Campbell could have copied the idea here, although she was surprised the tour guide had said nothing about it.

And...her fingers touched her aching cheek.  She never had heard of anyone being hit at Plimoth Plantation.  Something was not right here.

"This is crazy.  How long does this go on?" Ashley asked.

The old woman flinched.  "I know not, milady.  Pray that the laird will be merciful and allow us to live in spite of your strong claim on this castle."

"Allow us to live?"  She bent down and drew off the shoes that pinched her toes.  "I've had enough of this."

The gray-haired woman glanced over her shoulder.  "Please, milady.  We must take our leave without delay.  If the laird were to notice we have not obeyed his commands..."

Nodding, Ashley lifted the heavy hem of her skirts.  She had thought it would be exciting to wear such a costume when she put it on, but the bodice was laced with something that cut into her on every breath and the skirts threatened to trip her.  She wiggled her toes.  At least, they did not hurt any more, but the floor was as cold as a freezer.

"This way," the old woman urged.  "Hurry."

As they went through the low door, Ashley looked back.  A mistake, she realized, as her gaze locked with Colin MacLachlan's.  He smiled and raised his goblet in her direction.  Taking a slow drink, he continued to hold her in his powerful stare.  Sensation swarmed over her with the memory of his barely leashed passion when he had kissed her.

He set the goblet on the table and took a single step toward her.  As if they possessed their own mind, her feet sped her away along the stone corridor toward the stairs.  She raised her gown higher and called to the old woman.

"What is it, milady?" she asked, struggling to keep up.

"I don't care what's going on here.  I want you to find my bags and my stuff.  I'm getting out of here right now."

The old woman put a gnarled hand on Ashley's arm.  "Milady, that is impossible.  Where would we go?"

"We?  I don't know about you, but I think those guys are a couple of gallons short of a full tank."

"What?"

*Didn't these people ever go out of character?*  "They are crazy!  I'm getting back on the bus."

"Bus?" she asked with the same puzzled expression Colin MacLachlan had worn.

"I've had enough of this. Tell Mr. Campbell it was interesting, but enough is enough."

"Campbell?" She pressed her hand to her full bosom. "Milady, if you know a way to contact the Campbells, speak it now. They may be our salvation."

Ashley rolled her eyes. She was beginning to think she was the only one here who was *not* mad. "Just get my clothes and my bags."

"Yes, milady."

Hurrying up the stairs, Ashley shook her head. This was all too much. She had had enough of this castle which was damp and cold even in the middle of the summer. She hoped tonight they would be staying at a hotel with a hot tub and room service.

A rumble caught her ears. It must be windy or...The bus! Was it leaving without her? She did not want to be left behind in this crazy place. She paused on the landing to look out the window to make sure her bus was still in the parking lot.

Amazement riveted her to the floor. Where the parking lot should be, a row of low buildings clung to the side of the hill. The gift shop by the gate had vanished. The loch and the high wall were the only things still where they were supposed to be.

And it was spitting snow!

How could it be snowing? It was July. Even in the Highlands, it did not snow in July!

Was it trick glass? Maybe the scene was just a very realistic painting. Almost too realistic, because the loch ruffled with the wind and shadows of clouds raced across it. Was it some kind of virtual reality? A hologram? She banged frantically on the window.

"Milady, take care. The glass is brittle, and it might break." The old woman reached up and unlatched the window. "If you wish to see out..."

Cold wind surged in, and Ashley backed away from the window. Snow mixed with rain and pelted the deep sill. Looking out into the storm, she stared at the courtyard.

"Where have the parking lot and gift shop gone?" she gasped. "Where has *summer* gone? And where have I gone?" Slowly turning to stare at the old woman's frightened face, she whispered, "I should not be wondering where I am, should I? I should be wondering when."

# TWO

Ashley sat on the hard bench in the bedchamber where she had woken up what seemed a lifetime ago. Or had she woken up? Could this all be a dream...a nightmare? She shivered as she stared at the fire crackling on the hearth. It burned fiercely, but its heat could not reach the coldness inside her. Nightmares had haunted her all her life. But none of them had been like this. What had happened to her?

Yesterday, everything had been as it should be. She had been halfway through her tour of the Highlands. Her mother had left money for this trip in her will when she died four months ago. Mother had hoped to come with Ashley to Scotland after Father's death, but she had become ill.

Tears pricked her eyes, and she tried to blink them away. Ashley's taking this trip had been incredibly important to Mother...and to her. One of Ashley's earliest memories was finding a photo postcard of Castle Braeburn among the souvenirs her parents had brought back from their honeymoon in Scotland. She had begged to have the picture hung up in her room. She had loved looking at it and imagining herself as the fine lady who lived there. The castle had played a part in her dreams and in her nightmares.

Those nightmares were what Mother hoped would be laid to rest by this trip. Ashley almost laughed out loud. This trip had *become* the nightmare, as horrible as the pain that surrounded the three years of lost memories before she had come to live with her adoptive parents. She recalled nothing before the accident that had left her an orphan. Her childhood fantasy of Castle Braeburn had been twisted inside out, because she now apparently *was* the lady of this castle.

Her hands clenched in her lap. Yesterday, her biggest problem had been trying to figure out a way, before she went home to Springfield, to tell her best friend Sally that she and Sally's brother Mark had broken up after their third date. The only thing she and Mark had in common was wanting to make Sally happy. Yesterday, she had wanted adventure and escape from her everyday troubles. Today, she had found escape by becoming enmeshed in madness.

No, she was not mad, although, until she had seen the snow drifting over the bare ground, she had comforted herself with the thought that everyone else was. The facts spoke for themselves, even though she did not want to believe them.

This was not a dream. Even in her worst nightmare, she had not suffered a slap that left her head aching like this. The pain rippling along her skull was the one thing that made her believe this was real.

But if this headache was real...then, somehow, and she had no idea how, she had been dragged back in time. Nothing that had happened yesterday had suggested she was about to step blindly into an open shaft of time and arrive here and now.

The tour of Castle Braeburn had been very much like the others she had taken in the past five days since her arrival in Edinburgh. History, real and legend, was mixed to entertain the tourists. The only difference was that she had had the chance to speak with the castle's owner, Niall Campbell, in the great hall. Even then, they had spoken of nothing more unusual than the glorious chair which he had called the "laird's seat." They had laughed over the changes in Scotland since the castle had been raised by the loch. He had urged her to get a good night's sleep because the staff of Castle Braeburn had a surprise for their guests in the morning.

Everything had been just the way it was supposed to be until she woke this morning. Even then, she had guessed that the dress being brought to her was part of Mr. Campbell's *surprise*. The surprise was on her, because what she had thought to be a reenactment seemed to be the real thing.

None of this made sense.

Ashley looked up as the old woman, in her pacing, crossed once more between her and the hearth. "Tell me again," she said quietly. "My father was laird of this castle?"

"Yes, until he was betrayed by one within these walls and was slain by Lord Stanton, the most despicable man who ever lived." The old woman dabbed at her eyes with the corner of her muslin apron.

"And Lord Stanton?"

"The baron is dead, if Laird MacLachlan's men are to be believed."

"But if Lord Stanton is my father's enemy, Laird MacLachlan must be my ally."

"Laird MacLachlan will try to steal from you what is rightly yours. I have not hidden you in the kitchen, telling everyone that you were my dead sister's child, all these years just so that another might claim your birthright."

Ashley frowned. If Lady Ashley had worked since her childhood in the castle's kitchen, where was that person now? None of this made any sense. Her hands clenched in her lap. When the dress rustled, she touched it and asked, "Where did you get this gown?"

"From the trunk your mother hid to await you at the time when you could reclaim what is yours. You know that, milady, for I have shown it to you when we both despaired that this day would ever come." She dropped to her knees before Ashley and clasped her hands. "Milady, I beg God that you might escape this confusion which has unsettled your mind. We have waited so many years for this moment, vowing to see that your family and allies did not die in vain. You must not let it slip through your fingers now."

Rising, Ashley put her hand on one post of the massive canopy bed. The blue velvet curtains and gold tassels brushed her icy fingers. She was certain the old woman was right about one thing. The methods of dealing with the mentally ill in the 17th century were probably as barbarous as Colin MacLachlan.

Her fingers fisted on the carved wood. It would be so much easier if she did not need to deal with Colin MacLachlan at the same time as she was trying to figure out how she had gotten here and who exactly everyone was supposed to be. To figure out who *she* was supposed to be. When she had thought Colin MacLachlan was an actor hired to play a Highland chieftain, she had been amused by his imperious assumption she would obey his commands and delighted by the sexy swagger of his kilt. And his kiss had taken her breath away. It had been all for fun and meaning nothing. Or so she had thought.

Now...

She wished she had some idea of what now was. What did she know for sure? She was not dreaming. This, especially the dull thud in her head left by Captain Kilbride's hitting her, was too real. Colin MacLachlan's breathtakingly dangerous kiss had been real, because the sensations still resonated through her, warning her that she might have been a fool to let him kiss her when he could really want her dead. The castle was also real, for she never had had a dream that stank like this place did.

*Just like you'd expect a castle to smell in 1644.*

She tried to ignore that taunting voice as she fought to sort out what she knew. There must have been a battle where the Englishman who had stolen this castle was killed. Too much was still too confusing.

"Let's start at the beginning, Ellen," Ashley said. "I'm Ashley—"

"I am *Ella Marshall*, and your name is Lady Ashley Gordon." The old woman raised her chin in weak defiance. "Ne'er again must you hide that truth, milady." She buried her face in Ashley's skirt. "Milady, as you stand here in the rooms that are yours once more, I beg you to look into your heart and find the courage to face what is ahead of you."

Ashley pulled her skirt away from Ella. Putting her hand on the old woman's quaking shoulder, she whispered, "I'm trying."

"You must. Already you have seen that Laird MacLachlan is not pleased that your claim on Castle Braeburn is stronger than his. You must not give him another reason to slay you."

"I know." As much as the snow clinging to the mullions in the window, Ella's vehemence brought a cold shiver of reality to Ashley's center. Reality? How could this be real? It was more like a dream.

No, she knew what a dream was, and this was a nightmare! She had hoped to escape nightmares by coming here, but they refused to relinquish their hold on her. Could she really die lost in time?

She looked around the room again. A ball of fear burned within her as she noted the electric fixture had vanished from the wall. She touched the stones where the door to the hallway should be. Slowly she drew back her fingers. This wall had never been broken to provide rooms for Mr. Campbell's guests. Wrapping her arms around herself, she turned. The unaccustomed fullness of the skirt flapped against her legs.

She did not doubt this was the same room she had gone to sleep in last night, despite the many small changes. A tapestry of a gathering of ladies in a garden hung where there had been a photograph of the front elevation of the castle. A candle stub sat on the stone mantel next to a metal box. Neither had been there when she went to bed.

The niche in the wall by the window was familiar, but instead of a pot of flowers, a book with an embossed cover stood in it. From across the room, she could read its title. *The Book of Common Prayer* belonged to the Church of England. She shivered as she recalled Laird MacLachlan's rage when he spoke of King Charles trying to ram his religion down the throats of the Scots.

"Forgive me, Ella," she said as the old woman came to her feet. "I can't concentrate today. This has all happened so quickly." Clichés might work best until she had a few more answers.

"Of course, milady," Ella replied so swiftly Ashley guessed she was taking the right tact. "I understand your grief. Only because Laird Colin MacLachlan insists on taking what has been awarded to him by the Marquess of Argyll are you in a position to beg for what is yours."

"The marquess?"

"Lord Argyll! Archibald Campbell! Milady, you must be able to think clearly before you next meet Laird MacLachlan. Laird? He dares much to claim what is yours." She made a sign in the air which Ashley did not recognize. "May they burn in the depths of the Pit for all eternity."

Laird MacLachlan had reacted so strongly at Campbell's name. She had not been sure if that clan would be his allies or hers. Her allies? She was not part of this war.

Ella continued, "Fear not, milady. There are those within these walls who shall support your claim against Laird MacLachlan, if he will not acquiesce. Those who survived the bloodbath that took the laird and your mother will not wish to see another outsider claiming Castle Braeburn."

"I'm glad," she said, for she guessed that was what Ella expected. Each explanation only brought more questions, but she must not ask the one that haunted her.

How had she been brought to this time? And why? The people here appeared real. The castle appeared real. The year was 1644. Everything was exactly right. Except for her. She should not be here.

Yet she was, and something must have brought her here. It could not be just random. What had changed in Castle Braeburn? Colin MacLachlan!

Everything came back to that arrogant man. She had met his type before at Lourie Construction where she was a construction project estimator. Those men wore designer suits and carried attaché cases, but this so-called laird was just like them. They were hungry for power and the wealth it brought, unprincipled in gaining it, uncompromising in seizing success.

She went to the window and stared out into the storm. He scared her. More than anything else, she was frightened of Laird MacLachlan and how alive he had made her feel when he drew her into his arms. If she were alive now, she wondered what she was in her own time.

A sudden warmth, like a spring breeze, slipped over her shoulders like a blanket. No, it was more like an embrace, a familiar welcome in this place where nothing else was familiar. She wrapped her arms around herself, longing to hold in the comforting warmth, but it did not come from within her. A whisper brushed her ear.

"What?" she asked.

"Did you speak, milady?"

Ashley frowned. The soft voice, if it had been a voice, was not Ella's, which quivered with fury and fear. There had been no words, just the knowing that someone dear was close to her. She shut her eyes and held her breath. Was it the future reaching out to her, luring her back to her own time?

Fingertips grazed her cheek. She opened her eyes and whirled to see a sparkle reflected on the dull stone wall to her left. Rushing to the wall, she reached out to touch the light.

It was gone.

"What is it, milady?" Ella hurried to her side. "What is amiss?"

"I'm not sure..." She ran her fingers along the wall. The plain, gray stones were chilly, and no sign of any sparkle remained. Someone *had* touched her. She was as sure of that as she was of...

She fought back hysterical laughter. What *was* happening to her? First she was surrounded by things that should not exist, and now she was looking for things that were not there. She needed answers. There was too much to learn too quickly. But she must learn it before she betrayed herself. The price of being deemed mad in this century could be death.

A knock on the door brought a low moan from Ella. "Do not answer it, milady," she whispered as Ashley went to the door.

"If you want to get it—"

"Mayhap if we are silent, whoever it is will go away."

Ashley sighed. "I doubt we can escape more trouble that easily." She started toward the door.

Ella gasped, "I shall answer it, milady. You must not forget your place within this castle now."

*What was my place before? The kitchen maid? Or the daughter of the laird of this castle?* She could not ask that question, for it would condemn her as surely as the others that filled her head.

"Gertie!" cried Ella. "What are you doing here?"

Ashley looked past the serving woman and locked eyes with a tall, slender woman who wore a black shawl over a dress that was a lighter gray than Ella's hair. The woman possessed an elegance which did not match her simple clothes. Her ageless face was strong rather than beautiful, but it was a face that would not be ignored.

The woman pushed Ella aside, striding into the room as if it were hers. Her eyes, which were as dark as her hair, widened with surprise.

"What are *you* doing here?" Gertie asked, raising an arm that was covered with silver bracelets and pointing at Ashley.

Ashley would have liked to answer that, but she could not. She was grateful when Ella piped up, "That is no way to speak to milady."

"Milady?" asked the tall woman. She squinted, then her eyes popped open wide. "'Tis you, Ashley Gordon!" With a derisive laugh, she said, "You have changed much."

"You know me?"

Ella grasped Ashley's arm and drew her back. "Do not heed her, milady. Gertie Graham is a witch woman."

"There's no such thing as a witch," Ashley retorted, then wished she had stayed quiet. Her answer brought a wild laugh from Gertie even as Ella sketched the air with her fingers in the same strange pattern she had made before. Was it a symbol against witchcraft? This was all crazy.

"Ella Marshall," Gertie said with another laugh, "you need not appear so shocked. That cannot be the most outlandish thing your lady has said today."

"How—?" Ella shrank back against the bed. "You are a witch woman to know what has happened when you are not about."

Ashley put her hand on Ella's arm and said, "Calm yourself. She just made a guess. It was luckily the right one, for she got the reaction from you that she wanted. If she hadn't, she would have tried another tact so quickly you still would have been astounded."

Ella whispered, "Milady, they say—"

"Only the rumors they've heard, and rumors are usually wrong," Ashley said.

Gertie sat on the bench where Ashley had been watching the fire. "See, Ella? I told you she would say things even more remarkable...and mistaken."

"What do you want?" Ashley asked.

"To speak with you, milady." She glanced at Ella, who cowered away once more. "Alone."

Ashley dampened her lips. She could not doubt Ella's fear, for it had stripped her face of all color, but Gertie Graham was not who frightened Ashley. Quietly she asked, "Did Laird MacLachlan send you here?"

Gertie's laugh did not match her hard expression. "He is the reason I am here, but he did not send me."

"Are you his ally?"

"I am your ally, milady."

Ella fell to her knees and grasped Ashley's hands. "Milady, do not heed her. She lies with the ease of a serpent."

Gertie stood and settled her shawl about her shoulders. "If you do not wish to speak to me, milady, I shall take my leave. You have traveled far to speak with me today, but I can wait. I have time. Do you?"

"Traveled far?" asked Ella with sudden heat. "You know nothing, you old witch woman. She has lived all her days within these walls."

"Has she?" Gertie looked at Ashley. "Have you? Do you recall days when you slaved for your father's murderer within these kitchens, or do you recall a place far beyond the wide water where you lived a very different—?"

Ashley gasped. "Go, Ella! I will speak with her alone."

How did Gertie know about her journey back in time? Was this just another lucky guess? Cold sifted through her again. The woman could not be a witch...not really! But Ashley should not be here in the 17th century. None of this made sense.

"Milady," began Ella.

"Go, but wait right outside the door." She glanced at Gertie. She needed some answers. "Come back in about five minutes. Whatever Gertie Graham has to say to me, she can say in that amount of time."

She thought Ella might balk, but the serving woman nodded. Backing out the door, Ella drew it closed behind her.

Ashley took a steadying breath as she turned to face the tall woman who had made herself comfortable on the bench. Quietly she asked, "What do you want?"

"Want, milady?" She gave another of her rusty laughs that did not fit with her elegant form. "I do not come asking a boon of you. Rather I have come to answer your questions."

"What questions?"

Gertie touched her temple and smiled. "The questions that even now are swirling through your brain, milady. The questions you dare ask no one, for you fear to speak them would label you as insane. The questions of how you came to be in this time."

Ashley gripped bedpost and whispered, "How—I mean, why do you think that?"

"I was here in this very room when your mother sent you into the future to protect you."

"That's absurd," she retorted. Had Laird MacLachlan sent this woman as a ploy to persuade Ashley to betray herself? She could not trust him, and she certainly could not trust this woman.

"Is it?" Gertie flung out her hands, the silver bracelets on her arm jangling. "You see the truth before you, milady. Once you knew this castle well, for you were the pampered daughter of its laird, his only heir. Then the English came to separate your father from his head and your mother from her life as your clan's blood washed over the stones in the courtyard."

Ashley slowly sat on the steps by the high bed. No memories stirred in her head, but the scene Gertie painted was horrible. Here, in this time, war was personal, aimed at destroying an enemy and all his family and allies.

"Ella tells me I have been here in the kitchen since then."

"But you haven't." Gertie chuckled. "Your mother was determined you would be safe in another place and another time."

"How could I be somewhere else if Ella believes I was here? Where is the woman who is the real Lady Ashley?"

"You are the real Lady Ashley. That the others within these walls believe you spent your childhood as a kitchen drudge must be part of your mother's spell." A frown stole across Gertie's face. "I had no idea that she had conceived such a broad plan to protect you. She must have learned more than I had guessed."

"But this is the 17th century. You all should be talking like characters in a Shakespearean play, and I don't. No one has noticed anything odd about the way I speak, except for a phrase or two here and there."

"Your mother planned very well." Her scowl deepened. "Very, very well. She put many safeguards into her spell so your return would be seamless."

"You want me to believe," Ashley whispered, "that my mother conjured up a spell to send me as a child into the future? That the same spell has persuaded everyone that I never left Castle Braeburn and that I belong here in this time? That is ridiculous."

"Believe as you wish, milady, but 'tis the truth. I know it well, for 'twas I who gave her the spell that saved you from your father's foes."

"You gave her the spell?"

"Aye, as well as the way to bring you back."

Ashley knew her face was as pale as the snow beyond the window. "You're crazy!"

"Am I? *You* are here, milady, and I can tell you why. Lady Stanton, the late baron's wife, practiced the dark arts, the ones I disdain." Gertie shivered and drew her shawl more tightly around her shoulders. "When she fled from this castle in the wake of her husband's death, I have no doubts she put a curse on this castle."

"Are you saying that I am the curse she put on this castle?"

Gertie's smile widened, and she patted Ashley's arm. "No, not you, but that curse must have reached out to where your mother hid you to draw you back here."

"I don't understand!" She had wanted to say those words so often, but got no comfort from them now.

"The spell I gave your mother would keep you safe until one of the blood was needed to protect those of your clan and this castle from its greatest enemy. I had thought you would return swiftly, for who could imagine a greater threat than the English lord? You did not. You returned only now. Why? To face this castle's greatest enemy."

"Colin MacLachlan!"

Gertie nodded, her eyes glittering as brightly as the candle. "You have your father's wisdom as well as your mother's beauty, milady." Standing, she reached under her shawl. "I am finally able to return this to you."

Ashley gazed at the gold locket which caught the candlelight until it seemed to have a glow of its own. She nodded when Gertie told her to take it. Slowly she raised her hand to cup the locket that spun on its simple chain.

She blinked to clear her eyes as she held it in her palm. Opening the round locket which was etched with vines, she stared at the two tiny portraits within it. The man she did not recognize, but the shape of the woman's face matched her own.

"You know what you must do," Gertie said with unsuppressed excitement.

"What I must do?" Ashley repeated.

"You have been brought back to fulfill your destiny. You must claim your legacy."

"How?"

"Destroy Colin MacLachlan!"

# THREE

"She is mad, my laird."

Colin smiled at Jackie as they entered the rooms that he had been told were the laird's. His friend was furious, so furious, every red hair in his beard was pointed in a different direction. He might resemble a ruddy hedgehog, but he would not roll into a ball and let trouble pass him by. Jackie Kilbride looked for trouble, reveling in it. Colin could not recall the number of times he had reined Jackie in from running headlong into disaster. Even now, they must be cautious in securing the castle.

"I am not so certain of that." He poured wine from the dusty bottle that had been brought, on his orders, from the cellars to the antechamber of the laird's bedchamber. This was a good sign, for the servants must be pleased to have a Scot as laird once more instead of an English interloper.

The room with its high ceiling and grand expanse of floor offered privacy, but no comfort. The English who had fled before Colin's arrival had stripped the castle of its best furniture and carpets. No doubt, the furnishings filled some cottage, for none of the English had been allowed to get far before the sword of vengeance halted them.

Motioning for Jackie to help himself, he took a sip of the wine, then grimaced. Malmsey was too sweet for his taste. He would have preferred a sack with more bite.

"Mad she may be, but, if the woman truly is Lady Ashley," Colin said as he sat on a simple bench beside a table which was too large to get through the door, "my claim on Castle Braeburn has no merit."

"She cannot be a Gordon from Castle Braeburn. All of Gordon's family died when Stanton came here."

"So we believed." He twisted the goblet in his fingers and frowned. "She seems to be a very odd lady. You saw her serving woman. She was as shocked by her lady's behavior as you and I."

"It could be just another ruse to hide the truth."

"Mayhap, mayhap not." He chuckled. "However, I think you wish you could hide the truth of how she knocked you from your feet with such little effort."

"Trickery!" he cried, his face reddening nearly to the shade of his hair.

"No doubt," Colin said, "but a trick, even you must admit, we would be wise to learn."

Jackie shook his head, a smile trickling through the hairs of his mustache that drooped thickly over his upper lip. "You seem much taken with the fair Lady Ashley, my laird."

"Curious only." He leaned back against the table. This room suited him better than English luxury, for it would not be right for him to become too accustomed to a comfortable life. He was, as he had always been, a warrior in the battle to make Scotland free. Setting his wine on the table, he stared at the animal heads mounted above the oak doors on either side of the immense fireplace. "You must agree that she is a most intriguing woman."

"So satisfy your curiosity. Take her to your bed. Once she is naked before you, she will be able to hide few secrets from you."

"A tempting idea."

"But?"

He frowned at his friend. God's breath, but Jackie could be witless at times. Colin had fought too hard for too long to let lust betray him into folly just when all he wanted might be within his grip. "I must know the truth. If she is Gordon's heir, I owe her liege duty, even though I need to entangle my life with a lady laird no more than I need an English king ruling Scotland."

"I did not speak of entangling your life with hers." He arched a red brow. "I spoke of entangling her body about yours as—"

"Enough!" Colin took a deep drink of the sweet wine. He could not afford such thoughts when there were too many tasks awaiting him here. He must set the watch along the outer wall as well as make an inventory of provisions for the winter and see to the repairing of weapons and men. Those tasks could not be postponed.

Rising, he opened one of the doors by the hearth and peeked in. The room was bare. Stanton's office? Mayhap, for Lady

Stanton would not have been willing to leave any of her husband's papers behind when she had tried to reach England.

Curse England! If the English had stayed within their own borders, Colin would not have grown up without a father while he watched his mother fade away from the drudgery a lady should never suffer. He had had a taste of vengeance, and he wanted a feast.

"The war is not yet won, Jackie."

"Nothing should happen until the weather warms. You know Argyll believes that English blood is too thin and flows too swiftly from wounds in our winters."

"I hope he is right, but we must be ever-vigilant for Royalist treachery." He reached for the other door.

"So what will you do with the lady?"

Colin's answer was lost in a shriek as he opened the door. He stared down into the wide eyes of the woman who called herself Lady Ashley. As she backed away a step, he looked past her to the ornate bed that nearly filled the chamber.

"What are you doing here?" she cried.

"I would ask you the same, milady." He allowed himself the slightest of smiles. "If 'milady' is a title you justly deserve."

"Get out!"

He scowled as he heard Jackie's chuckle. He would not be ordered about like a stableboy. Grasping her hand, he drew her out into the huge antechamber and closed the door before her shocked servant could follow. He wished to speak to this lady without the old woman helping her find the proper answers.

"*These*, milady, are my rooms as laird of Castle Braeburn. I shall stay or leave as I choose."

"Then stay, but release me. Please." She slid her hand out of his and whirled to reach for the door.

Colin halted her by putting his hand over hers on the latch. With a cry, she pulled away. Her eyes, which were as deeply brown as raw earth, stared up at him as she pressed back against the door.

He frowned. She was frightened now as she had not been when she came into the great hall. If she were as mad as Jackie believed...No! He refused to believe that. Something was amiss here, but not with Lady Ashley's wits. Of that he was sure, for her gaze was sweeping the room, seeking another way to flee.

Throughout the Highland glens, the tale of the beautiful Lady Fia Gordon had been sung like an ancient legend. She had not deserted her husband when he was slain by Lord Stanton. Instead,

she had died at his side. Along with their daughter, it was said.
Yet this lovely woman now claimed to be that child. If she had
not been slain, where had she been hidden? He must know the
truth while Argyll decided who rightly held the castle.

Holding up his hand, he smiled. "You should not rush away
before we have a chance to become better acquainted, milady.
Your grandfather was my father's cousin, many times removed.
We may be among the last of our sept alive. It behooves us to
know each other better." He glanced over his shoulder at Jackie.
"You shall find us eager to listen to your tale."

"Yes," Jackie said, taking a deep drink of his wine and
wiping the back of his hand across his mouth, "do come and spin
us a story which will entertain us. We need a good laugh."

"Jackie," Colin cautioned quietly before adding, "Milady,
forgive Captain Kilbride his sense of humor. He is seldom in the
company of a real lady."

"And I am not now." Jackie sat on the bench and grinned at
her.

Ashley took a steadying breath. More than ever, she must be
careful what she did or said. Any action, any word, any glance
could betray her. Until she knew more, she would be wise to
continue to battle Laird MacLachlan with whetted words as she
had in the great hall. Such words might be her only weapon, but
she must wield them with care. Even though he might respect
courage, she guessed he would not allow her to pass a certain line.
She wished she knew what that line might be.

*Destroy Colin MacLachlan.* Gertie's voice continued to echo
through her head. This was all crazy! She should not be here.
She should not be facing this handsome man who, if she believed
Gertie and Ella, wanted to kill her. None of this made sense. She
did not believe in witches and witchcraft, but...

Wiping her clammy hands on her skirt, she raised her chin so
she could meet his eyes. They were bright with amusement. Not
only amusement, she realized, when his fingers curved along her
elbow.

She edged away, knowing she must get away so she could
have time to sort this all out. "Don't worry about him, my laird.
I wouldn't expect anything else from one of your warriors."
When she saw Laird MacLachlan's eyes narrow, she realized how
her words could be misunderstood. She had been speaking of
Captain Kilbride's acerbic sense of humor, nothing else. "No,
that's not what I meant—"

"Let me cut the vixen's tongue out for such words!"

Her breath caught as she stared at Captain Kilbride. His hand was on his knife, and his lips were straight with fury. He might ridicule her as much as he wished, but she must not speak an insult to his laird.

Laird MacLachlan lifted one hand. Captain Kilbride's fingers quickly released the knife and clasped behind his back as he muttered, "Whore!" just loudly enough so she could not fail to hear it.

Ashley bit her lower lip as she fought the fear rising within her throat. This exchange told her more than anything else had about the dark-haired man who held her life in his hands. Obedience without question was something he expected from his men.

And from her? As she looked at him again, Laird MacLachlan smiled and held out his hand once more.

"Milady," he said.

Although unsure what he wanted, she set her fingers on his. His smile broadened when they trembled on his palm. He gripped her hand and drew her gently away from the door.

Captain Kilbride pulled out the bench from the table as Laird MacLachlan said, "Milady, if you will sit..."

"If you'll tell me," she replied, "what you plan to do with this castle."

He seized her arms and shoved her onto the bench. Gripping the seat, she stared up at him. His eyes were slits once more. Had she pushed him too far?

When he caught her chin between his thumb and forefinger, he brought her face up toward him. His eyes glowed like the hottest embers as he whispered, "Choose your words with more care, milady. Jackie is not the only one among my men who would gladly see you bedded and dead."

"*Bedded and dead?* Are you crazy?" Ashley started to stand, but he held her in place easily with a single hand. This had gone on long enough. She wanted to get out of here. "I'm not interested in your fantasies."

"Fantasies?" He plucked at the lace on her sleeves. "It takes very little imagination to think of a worthy way to spend time with you, milady, when you dress so enticingly. Each time you move, the gentle sway of your skirts rustle with whispers of satin and starched petticoats. You sit here, and I can enjoy a beguiling view of your soft curves."

She crossed her hands over the deep neckline of her gown. When he slipped a single finger beneath the uppermost one, he slowly lifted her hand to his mouth. Holding her gaze with his, he tipped her hand over and pressed a searing kiss into her palm. A gasp puffed from her parted lips as he lowered her hand and held it against the bare skin above her gown. The moist heat of his mouth branded her.

"My laird," she whispered.

He smiled. "Aye, that is what I am. Your laird. Do not forget that, milady."

Captain Kilbride's crude laugh broke the spell Laird MacLachlan had cast with his seductive touch. Pushing Laird MacLachlan's hand away, she folded hers primly in her lap. She tried to slow her ragged breath, but her heart thudded against her chest when she saw the icy calculation in his eyes.

He was using every means he had, including that fiery kiss, to gauge her weaknesses, seeking any way he might defeat her. She wanted to tell him he could have Castle Braeburn and everything in it, but she feared such a surrender would mean her death. If she died here, would she wake in her own time? Or would she be dead then, too? She needed answers. She needed a chance to think. If she did not have to concentrate on guarding every word to protect the truth, she might be better prepared to contend with Colin MacLachlan.

She nearly laughed at that thought. He would be her match under any circumstances—in his time or hers. As he walked around the table to pour a goblet of wine, his kilt again accented his assertive motions. His brawny legs hinted at the strength coiled within him. For the first time, she wondered how long he had been fighting along the crags of the Scottish hills.

When he held out the goblet, she carefully took it without letting her fingers touch his. "Thank you," she whispered.

"I hope this brings some color back to your cheeks."

Captain Kilbride sat on a deep sill. "Looks as if she has no more life than a corpse, doesn't she? Like the corpses of *all* the dead Gordons."

"Jackie, no more about that."

Ashley was unsure if she or Captain Kilbride was more astonished by Laird MacLachlan's soft admonition. Holding the wine goblet, she watched as Laird MacLachlan pulled a heavy chair next to hers. He leaned one elbow on the table and put his other hand on the back of the bench. When she tensed as he surrounded her, he smiled, but his smile was as cold as the floor had been beneath her bare feet.

"Why do you want to talk to me?" she asked.

"The others within these walls have taken an oath of fealty to their new laird," he answered as he lifted a strand of hair away from her shoulder. Rocking it between his fingers, he murmured, "If you wish to know the truth, milady, few were averse to having Castle Braeburn governed by a Scot once more. Many, however, are now concerned about what will happen to their lovely lady." He brushed her cheek with her own hair.

"Yet they pledged fealty to you?"

"Before you appeared in the Great Hall. I suspect many of them wish they had waited, so they could make their pledge to you, the supposed daughter of Gordon. You are well loved here, milady. Many of them accept the tale that you are Gordon's bairn returned from the dead."

Pushing the hair away from her face, she chose another of the vague answers which had served her well. "People believe what they want to."

"Whether it be the truth or not."

"I *am* Ashley G-Gordon." She stumbled over the last name, but both Gertie and Ella had agreed on this one important fact. She was Ashley Gordon, only child of the murdered Scottish laird of Castle Braeburn. She wanted to shout that that was impossible, but she no longer was sure. "Nothing you say or do can change that, my laird."

He smiled. "I can almost believe you speak the truth."

"My laird!" cried Captain Kilbride. "Do not be taken in by her lies."

Holding up his hand, Laird MacLachlan said, "Heed my words closely. I said *almost*." His icy gaze returned to Ashley. "Your quick wit suggests you have needed to hone it well against the bumbler Charles Stuart sent here, proving his unworthiness to hold his throne."

She was delighted with the change of subject. Even though she knew little of the politics of this time, she would rather speak of anything but herself. "What do you expect? Charles did nothing to keep from losing his head."

"Losing his head?" He pounced on her words. "Do you know something of the fate of that fool?"

Ashley shoved aside his arm and stood. As she had in the great hall, she put a chair between her and the intense fire in his eyes. How stupid could she be? Already she had said the wrong thing. King Charles must still be alive.

"Milady?" Laird MacLachlan prompted with a serenity she could not believe.

She had to give him an answer. Praying she was devising the right story, she whispered, "I only meant his men's panicked flight from battle." She prayed there had been a battle with the king recently.

"The king's lords ran like peasants at Newcastle!" Captail Kilbride jumped down from the sill. Raising his glass, he crowed, "Drink to the coward who calls himself king!"

Laird MacLachlan stood, but did not answer his friend's toast. "I am sure you will excuse Lady Ashley and me now, Jackie, while we talk."

"Talk?" He drained his goblet and set it loudly on the table. Grinning broadly, he walked toward the door. He opened it and laughed. "I trust you will enjoy your *conversation*, milady, although the only word Laird MacLachlan wishes to hear from you is 'yes.'"

As the door closed, Ashley said, "He has to be the one with the idea of bed and dead. He certainly has a one-track mind."

"One-track, milady? I do not understand."

She shook her head. She had done it again. She must watch every word instead of thinking how the candlelight danced with a blue radiance off Laird MacLachlan's hair, with a fire that was brighter than the gold pin holding his doublet closed. "It isn't important."

"True. What is important is that your household has taken an oath of fealty to Laird Colin MacLachlan."

"Before I made my claim."

"Yes."

"And you expect me to do the same?"

He pulled the chair from between them. Catching her shoulders, he jerked her closer. "What I want from you is not exactly the same."

"If you think I'm going to sleep with you, you're mistaken." She was risking his fury, but she had to draw the line somewhere, too.

"You mince no words, do you?"

"I know the fact that I'm here threatens your claim on this castle. Being diplomatic would be easier if I knew I was going to be alive tomorrow."

"You have a month at least."

"A month?" She was torn between being grateful and terrified. When his fingers traced an aimless pattern across her shoulder, she tried to pull away.

"Aye." The word brushed her cheek as he bent toward her. "The Marquess of Argyll has spoken often of how he admires the courage of those you claim to be your parents. He would not appreciate that I had you killed without allowing you to present your appeal to him. With the war, I suspect it will take at least a month for my message to reach him and return here."

"You have already sent him a message?"

"Victory goes to those who grasp it, milady. By the time a pair of fortnights have passed, we should learn his decision."

"And then? Will you leave if he decides to accept my legitimate claim?"

He stepped away. "I would not be so certain that he will decide in your favor, my dear Lady Ashley."

"But—"

His cold smile returned, and his eyes became as dark as thunderheads. She gasped as he drew a line across her throat. "If he decides you are lying, he shall simply remove your pretty head from your slender shoulders."

Ashley stared at him, then, with a soft cry, whirled away. Going to the window where Captain Kilbride had been sitting, she stared out. She sought any sign of her own time, anything to give her hope there was an escape from this. There was nothing.

1644.

It was inconceivably far back into the past. New York was still New Amsterdam, and, in Massachusetts, the Pilgrims were struggling to exist. No telephones, no electricity, no indoor plumbing, no almost everything.

When, from the corner of her eye, she saw Laird MacLachlan's hand on the wall by the window, she closed her eyes and tried to gather what strength she had left. Fatigue washed over her. She had made mistakes already; she must not make another. "It's so beautiful here. Everyone should be able to live here in peace."

"Strange sentiments for the daughter of a warrior." The breath of his words rustled her hair.

"Really? I don't think so. I have no use for war when it brings so much grief to so many."

"Lady Ashley, you are as wise as your father was reputed to be."

"Thank you." That was a stupid answer, but she had no idea what else to say.

His hands slid along her shoulders as he turned her to face him. He kissed her lightly on the tip of her nose.

"What did you do that for?" she asked, fear surging through her again.

"Would you rather I kissed you here?" He skimmed his lips across her cheek. "Or—?"

"No, that was fine, my laird."

"Merely fine?" He laughed. "You shall call me Colin, and I shall call you Ashley, for 'tis a name which lilts on the tongue as easily as my eyes dwell on you."

"Are you suggesting that we become friends?" Ashley walked to a bench by the fireplace. Although she was certain he would follow, always standing between her and the closest door, she must put some distance between her and his strong, firm hands which were so gentle on her. "One question you need to answer before you answer that is: How do I know *you* are who you say you are?"

"Me?"

"Any fool could raise a small army and take advantage of the chaos here in the Highlands."

"True, but I do not worry that the marquess will doubt my claim, for I have fought at his side, and he knows me for the man I am," he said as he sat on the bench. He grasped her hand and pulled her down beside him. His left arm slipped around her waist as his right fingers brushed her cheek lightly.

She shook her head as his mouth lowered toward hers. She did not dare to sample his savage kiss again. As his hand splayed across her back, his fingertips resting on her bare shoulders, she could not breathe. Even the slightest motion would graze her against his chest. If a phantom of the past seduced her, would she give up all chance of returning to her own time? To let herself be caught up in the fierce emotions of this century might tie her more tightly to the past.

That was absurd. But everything was absurd now, especially her longing to sample his kisses again. She must halt this.

He smiled as she tried to stand. "Do not flee, pretty one. We have yet to settle this matter."

"It is settled. I don't want you touching me!"

"On this, I am certain you are lying." His broad hand stroked her jaw as his fingers combed through her hair.

"No, I can't do this!" she cried as she pressed her hands against the breadth of his chest to keep his mouth from hers.

His fingers were like steel manacles around her wrists as he drew her hands away. Struggling to escape, she could not. She was no match for his strength. She turned her head to avoid his mouth.

"Do you think you can stop me?" he whispered.

She looked up at him. "I shall try."

"I know. 'Tis unfortunate for both of us." His sibilant words brushed her skin. "We could have had a most enjoyable pair of fortnights." With a sigh, he released her wrists.

Her breath was uneven as she slid away on the bench, fighting to regain her composure. He was far more dangerous than she had suspected. When his gaze caught hers, she realized nothing had changed with him. He still was seeking any way he could to twist her to his will. Any kindness he showed her was just an act. Didn't he think she would remember this if the marquess decided in her favor?

*In her favor!* She was getting sucked into this madness. If this was not real—

The bench screeched as Colin stood, sending a new pain through her aching head. Quietly he said, "You are excused, milady."

"Colin, if—"

"You are excused, milady."

Ashley tried to guess what she had said to bring on this abrupt dismissal. If anyone should be angry, it should be she at his assumption she would melt in his arms. Not that she could blame him, she had to admit, because she had done exactly that in the great hall. That had been fun. She had believed it was just a game. Now, if she was to believe what was in front of her, it *was* a game, a very deadly game where she knew none of the rules. "I don't know what I said that—"

He took her arm and brought her to her feet. "I told you that you were excused, milady. Begone."

"After you tell me what I said that has upset you."

"I am not your servant, milady. You give *me* no orders."

"It wasn't an order. Just a request. If we have to be here together for the next month, you must extend me some courtesy."

He took her hand and lifted it to his lips. The chill from his kiss was as cold as his eyes as he murmured, "I have granted you the greatest courtesy of all, milady. I shall allow you to live as long as I deem your life worthwhile to me. Jackie has suggested I can end this with your death. Do not persuade me to heed his counsel."

She backed away. He meant his words, each of them. Lulled by his jests and trying to avoid revealing the truth, she had forgotten he was a Highland barbarian. He had come to the castle with the blood of his enemies on his clothes. He would slay her with as little regret.

"Milady!" he called as she opened the door to her bedchamber.

She must find another room far from here right away. She could not be so close to him, for keeping space between them would be the smartest thing she could do now. "Yes?"

"I await your pledge of fealty."

"But if I do that..." She shook her head as another pulse ached through it. Ella had been as insistent about this as Gertie had. She had to trust them, because she could not trust Colin MacLachlan.

He came toward her and ran a fingertip along the chain of the locket Gertie had given her. As he slipped a finger beneath the locket that rested over her heart, she tried to step away. He gripped her arm, holding her next to him with no sign of effort.

"And what is this, milady? You were not wearing it before."

"A legacy from my parents."

"Is it now?" He drew the knife from his belt.

She took a deep breath to scream, but it exploded out in a squeak as he used the tip of the knife to open the locket. He lifted it so he could examine the tiny faces. When he raised his eyes to scan her face, his smile was taut.

"Congratulations, milady," he said quietly. "You have planned this well to have these miniatures made to confirm your resemblance to Lady Fia Gordon. However, a portrait cannot swear testimony to the marquess about your true birth." Letting the locket fall back against her, he ran his finger along her shoulder once more. "I await proof of your fidelity to the one presently named laird of Castle Braeburn."

"But, my claim—"

"Will be heard and dismissed."

"Until then, I'll acknowledge you as Laird MacLachlan, but not laird of this castle." She took a steadying breath, praying this madness would end, and she could return to her own time. Yet she could not cede herself completely into his control, because she had no idea how long it might take to find her way back to when she was supposed to be. *Unless this is where and when you're supposed to be.* She ignored that taunting thought. "And you shall acknowledge me as Lady Ashley—"

"Lady Ashley only." He folded his hands behind him. "It is yet to be seen if you are Lady Ashley Gordon."

"All right. I can live with that."

"That is also yet to be seen," he said with the smile that chilled her. He was enjoying this, she realized with a shiver. He was savoring every moment of his victory over the English Royalists and now over her as each word he spoke reminded her how powerless she truly was.

Ashley took a step backward toward the sanctuary of her room. She wanted to close the door and break his cool stare's hold on her.

"The least you could offer me is a curtsy as you leave," he continued. "Even if you truly are Gordon's legitimate child, you owe me such a courtesy as a member of your clan."

Ashley nodded and whispered, "All right." After all, what did it matter if she gave in on this one thing? She must keep herself alive until she could find a way out of the 17th century. She started to curtsy.

*No! You cannot bend your knee to this Scottish cur!*

Ashley clapped her hands to her head as the howl rang through her. Her voice? Had she spoken aloud? Or was it only in her head? She heard another shout. Who was talking? She could not tell. Was she really mad? Had this all been just a delusion? The floor came up to swallow her as all thought vanished into that primitive scream.

# FOUR

Ella pressed her hands over her mouth and backed away from the bedchamber door as it opened to reveal Laird MacLachlan holding a senseless Lady Ashley in his arms. What had he done to Lady Ashley? Without speaking, he pushed past Ella and set the lady's limp form on the bed.

When he reached to remove Lady Ashley's shoes, Ella surprised herself with her own temerity by stepping forward and saying, "I shall tend to her, Laird MacLachlan."

"Does she have spells like this often?" he asked.

"Spells?" She nearly choked on the word. Lady Ashley had not told her any of what Gertie Graham had said to her, but Ella knew the witch woman had disturbed her lady, because Lady Ashley had been oddly silent. The laird's daughter had never been one to babble incessantly. Still, she had not said a single word until Laird MacLachlan opened the door.

Would Laird MacLachlan be as fearful of Gertie Graham as Lord Stanton had been? The Englishman had not dared to denounce Gertie Graham as the witch she was. Instead, he had given her free entrance into Castle Braeburn whenever she wished. Mayhap that would all change now that Laird MacLachlan was here.

Ella was startled at the pleasure that thought brought. She had not guessed that she would be happy about anything with this upstart laird who dared to claim what was Lady Ashley's.

"She fainted in the other room," said Laird MacLachlan. "Does she do that often?"

"Nothing like that has happened before, my laird." She placed her lady's shoes on the floor and halted herself from asking what the laird had done to cause her lady to take leave of her senses like this. Every effort Ella had made to listen through the thick door had been for naught.

"'Twas odd. It..." He reached up and touched the branch woven through the rings holding the bed curtains in place. "Is this rowan?"

"Aye. Milady's mother always had it above milady's bed when Lady Ashley slept here as a child. It was a habit I kept during the time I hid her from Lord Stanton."

"But rowan is for the MacLachlans, not the Gordons."

"True, the Gordons use ivy, which is why the rings are carved to look like ivy, but milady's mother chose this for Lady Ashley."

Puzzlement eased the hard lines of his face. "I have many questions for you—"

"Ella, my laird," she said softly.

"And many more for your lady." He fisted his hand on the bed post. "Let me know when she awakes."

"Aye, my laird."

"As soon as she awakes."

She nodded, wanting to look away from the icy determination in his eyes. She could not. As he walked out of the room, she whispered, "I pray you are not more of a threat to milady than that accursed English lord."

***

*"—the English lord who will see the blood of all our allies spilled."*

*Ashley recognized that voice. Gertie Graham! Opening her eyes, she stared at a woman who was Gertie and yet she was not. She looked much the same, but seemed as tall as the towers on the west corner of the castle.*

*Glancing down, she realized the floor was shockingly close. She must be a child. Was she the child who had been banished from this time? Or was this just another dream? Another nightmare like the ones that had haunted her childhood?*

*"Calm yourself," another woman answered. "What shall happen cannot be halted. I can save only my bairn."*

*Ashley sought the face of the woman who was speaking. Was this person the Lady Gordon who had died beside her husband when the English overran Castle Braeburn two decades before? She could not see the woman's face, for it was lost in the shadows beneath a hooded cloak of unrelieved black.*

*When she was picked up and set on a high bed, Ashley knew what would happen next. This had been part of the nightmare that had filled her nights endlessly. Now it had returned to plague her again.*

*But was it only a nightmare? She no longer was certain of anything.*

*Warm fingertips brushed her forehead, and her eyes widened. She recognized this sensation, this gentle, welcoming sensation, because it was the same one she had experienced when the sparkle of lights glittered on the wall of her room at Castle Braeburn. Closing her eyes, she listened to the murmur of the voice. Was it the one that had rung through her head when she knelt to Colin? No, this one was kind and loving, not filled with hate.*

*She did not understand the words, but the tone comforted her as nothing ever had. As the voice swept her away from fear, she let it cradle her like beloved arms. Here, she was safe. Here, she would not forget what she must always remember. Here, no one could do anything—*

"—to you, milady."

The words burst into Ashley's head as if a volume control had been turned up. Amazed, she discovered she was no longer asleep. She was awake and walking along a hallway in the castle—the castle that Colin MacLachlan claimed was his.

The young man walking beside her was familiar, although she knew she had never seen him before. Or had she? She recognized his dark hair and honest, brown eyes that gazed down from his gawky height. He was Davey Beaton, who had warned everyone within these walls of Colin's arrival.

Her forehead furrowed. How could she know that? *She* had not been here when Colin arrived. Yet she could recall Davey rushing through the castle, shouting about what he had seen from the top of the wall.

In disbelief, she realized that she could remember other things about Davey Beaton. She recalled kindnesses he had done for her when she had to conceal the truth of her birth, a secret he had known because Ella was his great-aunt. As well, she remembered how she had joked with him while she sat by the hearth in the kitchen and how she dabbed away his tears of joy when the tidings of Lord Stanton's defeat and death reached the castle.

How could she know these things? She shivered as she recalled Gertie telling her that Lady Fia Gordon had created a spell that caused everyone to believe Ashley had never left Castle Braeburn. No, she did not want to believe that she was now caught up in the spell also, recalling the past that the others believed was real. Yet this *knowing* of what had been might help her survive this century.

"Milady, did you hear what I said?"

Surprisingly, she did. She could remember hearing him just as she remembered waking this morning in the bedchamber that Ella had insisted was Lady Ashley's and dressing in the chilly room. She could remember Ella's words of warning that she should remain in bed after fainting yesterday. She could recreate it all from her memories, but she had not done it. Or had she? All she could recall for certain was walking here with Davey just now. Where did the nightmare in her mind end and the waking one around her begin?

Forcing aside those questions she could not answer, Ashley said, "I heard you, Davey. Thank you for your fealty, but I am willing to wait to learn of the marquess's decision of who should hold this castle."

"If that is your wish, milady."

"It is." She smiled gently, knowing that he had hoped she would ask him to risk his life to be a hero. "You can serve me best, Davey, by being patient and asking others to be the same. My time to claim Castle Braeburn will come. Never fear."

"Aye, milady." He bowed before racing away, his long legs making quick work of the long hall.

She was glad that Davey was willing to be put off a while longer so she could sort all this out. She understood his anxiety to claim what had been taken from the Gordons by Lord Stanton, especially after what Stanton had done to Finlay Ballard last year.

She froze. Into her mind came the image of the pompous Lord Stanton who had tried to wipe out all hints of Gordon loyalty in Castle Braeburn. Lord Stanton stood in the main courtyard. Around him screams sounded, but he wore an imperious sneer as he looked down his aristocratic nose at a woman who was on her knees before him. Then he struck her and turned to speak with his two sons.

Ashley's hands clenched at her sides. Between the two, Stanton's sons had never conceived one logical thought, but both had been determined to steal the virginity of every lass in the castle. It had taken all of her wit and Ella's to foil their plans for her.

Many people had gathered around the open area, but she could only remember those four and the man who was shrieking as he was tortured...

"No!" she whispered, trying to shut out the memory. She did not want to see the torment used to punish a man who had taken food from the kitchen to feed his ailing granny who lay in one of the cottages near the loch. She shuddered.

Ashley leaned her head against the chilly wall. What was happening? She was assuming what must be Lady Ashley's memories. Had something Davey said triggered them? No, it must be the dream. Yet, that did not explain why she had woken from it to be here in the corridor. She could recall her own life in the future, but, like a transparency, another set of memories were overlaying hers with scenes of a life she had not lived. Maybe these memories were another part of the spell Lady Fia placed on this castle.

"But there are no such things as witches and spells," she whispered.

"Good morning, Ashley. I must say that you look much better this morn."

At Colin's voice, Ashley stiffened. Had he heard her? Her words might damn her in this superstitious time. She glanced around and realized she was nearing the door to his rooms, along the corridor that led to the front stairs. She could not snarl at him for stalking her when she was so close to his private chambers.

She turned and gave him her coolest smile. "A good night's sleep can work wonders."

"So I have heard." He rested his hand on the wall beside her. When she started to step away, he put his other hand on her elbow.

His touch was amiable, but she suspected his fingers would become a vise if she tried to walk away before he was ready for this conversation to be over. Never could she allow herself to forget that he was a man who was used to getting what he wanted, by violence. Her eyes widened when she saw fresh blood on his sleeve.

"What have you done now?" she whispered in horror.

He looked down at his sleeve. "Put your mind at ease, Ashley. I have not been attacking your allies, who should be mine as well. I have been visiting my men who were injured in the battle to send the English Royalists to a premature grave. One of them needed the surgeon's attention, so I helped."

"You have many talents, I see." Ashley tried to reconcile this ruthless man with one who obviously cared so much about his men.

"And more that you have not seen." He smiled as his gaze slid along her. "Do you dress so provocatively to tempt me to do what you already know I wish to do?"

She followed his smiling gaze and gasped. This light blue brocade dress was cut even lower across her breasts than the other gown had been. She must have been out of her mind to choose it. *But I didn't choose it!*

She would treat him with the same cool indifference that had worked well in the construction office when some guy stepped over the line. Raising her chin, she said, "I can honestly say I haven't given you more than a passing thought this morning."

"How odd, when you have not been out of my thoughts since I reached Castle Braeburn." His fingers glided along her bare arm beneath the sleeve that reached just below her elbow. When they reached her hand, he took it and raised it to his lips.

Her other fingers curled into a fist as he scalded a kiss into her skin. What arrogance he had! He thought he could persuade her to do as he wished simply by seducing her. That his plan could work if she was not careful irritated her even more.

"Are you ready to show me around Castle Braeburn this morning, Ashley?" he asked.

"Show you around?" She gulped. Her tour with Mr. Campbell had been short, because he had promised to give her a tour of more of the rooms in the morning.

"Why are you hesitating? Do you have something to hide?"

*You bet I do!* She must not say that, but how could she show him around this castle when she had not seen much more than the great hall and the passage near her room? Even as she thought that, room after room appeared clearly in her mind, from the stillroom beyond the kitchen to the chapel with its windows overlooking the loch.

"Why would I hide something from a clansman?" Ashley returned, determined not to let him browbeat her. "Although I don't recognize your claim on this castle, I am grateful that you are here to stand between us and our enemies."

He smiled. "That is the first truly wise thing I have heard you say." He offered his arm.

She started to put her hand on it, then pulled back as she grimaced at the blood on his sleeve. It was still damp.

With a laugh, he loosened the brooch holding his plaid to his shoulder. He tossed it to her as his plaid fell away. She caught the silver pin while he pulled off his bloodied shirt and called to a servant to bring him another one.

Ashley stared. She could not help herself. The muscles she had sensed beneath his clothes were strikingly carved across his naked chest and along his arms. If he had been living in her time, he would have been the star of the Highland Games, tossing a caber like a toothpick. Or he could have made big bucks posing for underwear ads and traveling to shopping malls to sign autographs for screaming teenage girls and their mothers.

When the servant returned with a wrinkled shirt, Ashley looked away. She was acting as bedazzled as one of those kids. Colin MacLachlan was great looking, but he wanted her in his bed and then executed. She could not forget that. He had not denied that he agreed with his buddy Jackie Kilbride.

Colin took the brooch from her and hooked his plaid in place without comment. Surely if he had seen her staring like a gape-mouthed teenager, he would have made some comment. Instead, he simply held out his arm again.

"Milady?" he asked with impatience.

Putting her hand on it, Ashley was not surprised when he clamped it to his arm with his other hand. Never did he let her forget who was in control here. She had dealt with people who had to have everything their way. She just hoped what she had learned would be useful in dealing with a 17th century control freak.

"What do you want to see?" she asked, trying to keep her mind on anything but his broad chest. "The kitchens—"

"Can wait until later. I wish to see the armory and the walls, Ashley."

"There are others who know more about those things than I do."

His smile grew chilly again. "Do not mistake me for a fool. I know well that others have greater knowledge of the castle's defenses than you, but I thought you would be interested in the opinion of the man who leads those who stand between you and your enemies."

Ashley only nodded, stung by how easily he tossed her own words back at her. She would never mistake him for a fool.

Never.

\*\*\*

Colin gazed up at the crenelated walls. He could not have imagined that he would be grateful to that English dog, but Stanton had kept the walls strengthened and in good repair. No doubt, Stanton had feared being overrun in this isolated glen. But one question remained with no answer. With these strong walls to protect him, why had Stanton come out of the castle to meet his enemies?

"Is there a water gate?" he asked.

Ashley—How easily her name filled his mind!—looked up from where she had been running her fingers along the wall. An expression of amazement vanished from her eyes, but he was sure he had seen it.

"Did something about the wall startle you, milady?" He frowned. She acted as if everything within the castle was a surprise for her, but claimed to have lived here all her life. She was lying about something. He was not sure what.

She shook her head. Her smile was forced, he could tell, for her eyes became dim. "If you want to see the water gate, we need to go toward the loch."

"It opens onto the loch?"

"Of course not. That would allow someone to slip through it." Astonishment flashed across her face, although he had not heard her say anything unusual. A woman who had been raised in this castle and hoped one day to claim it should be well aware of its strengths and weaknesses.

"You know more about defending this castle than I might have guessed," he replied quietly. "Who taught you? Not Stanton. He would not want his enemies to learn how to defeat him."

"It's nothing but the obvious." She looked away from him again. She had been avoiding his eyes all morning. "A small stream comes beneath the wall before continuing to the loch, but it's enough to provide water for the castle if it is put under siege."

He frowned. "A stream can be easily blocked."

"It comes from a spring beside the wall. Any men who tried to block it would be cut down easily by those on the wall."

"I am impressed, milady," he said as he brushed his wind-blown hair back out of his face, "by your grasp of military matters."

"Thank you."

"Who taught you?" he asked again.

At her flinch, he wondered why his simple question seemed to disturb her so greatly. She did not look at him as she replied, "I learned by observation and heeding what was said when others did not realize I was listening. No one expected a kitchen lass to be interested."

"Something I should keep in mind."

"Yes."

He chuckled at her cool reply. "You have intrigued me about this spring. Will you show it to me?"

She nodded and walked into the wind that blew between the mountains rising nearly straight up from the shores of the loch. This glen was a narrow strand around the water. Although it broadened out beyond the castle, the mountain ridges provided an outer wall that could be easily defended. Why *had* Stanton left these walls to meet the Scots in the wide glen beyond those hills?

"If Stanton had had some of his skilled English bowmen there and there," Colin said, pointing to the rock faces, "we would not have been able to defeat him."

"That was just what I was thinking."

He gave her a superior smile that he had already learned she found so exasperating. "I know. Your face hides very little, Ashley."

"Then you should not be so distrustful of me."

"How can I trust the one who would wish to see me denied what I have rightly won?" He laughed as they crossed the uneven ground that was dropping down toward the level of the water. "You need not say that this castle may not be rightly won."

"Then I won't."

Colin chuckled at her acerbic answer. Even though she could not hide her fear of him or the fact that she concealed more secrets than she revealed, she was not able to control her sharp tongue. Gordon had been renowned for his wit, so, if Ashley was truly his daughter, she might have inherited that from her father.

He continued to be baffled by this lovely woman. He had long prided himself on being able to judge accurately anyone he encountered. Now he was confounded by this woman who called herself Lady Ashley Gordon. For a lass who claimed to be raised in a kitchen, she was too educated. She was frightened of him, but offered him as little respect as a chieftain would a young warrior who had not yet proven himself in a raid. She seemed embarrassed by the cut of her bodice, yet held her skirt high above her ankles as they crossed the courtyard. If she was Gordon's heir, she was like no other lady he had ever met. If she was not, then she must die for her audacity of trying to steal what was his.

He suspected the Marquess of Argyll would be asking the questions Colin already had asked. The marquess would be as unsatisfied with the answers Ashley had offered. Somewhere, the truth was hidden. He needed only to find the key to unlock it, and he would understand all of this.

He would find it. He must. He had worked too hard, struggled for too long, given up too much not to savor the victory now that it was his. No woman, be she laird's daughter or strumpet, would stand in his way.

"Milady!" came a call from the stables.

Colin frowned as a man waved to her. Hume was once again in charge of the stables, a position he had held when Gordon lived. The bent man had been forthright in his loyalty to the Gordons, including Ashley.

"Your allies risk much with such a show," Colin said, watching for her reaction.

Her eyes sparked as she waved back to the man. "It has never been a crime to be friendly, has it?"

Colin laughed. This was not the answer he had anticipated, although he should have known the unexpected was to be expected where Ashley was concerned. "Jackie would say it was worthy of death."

"He doesn't think of much else, does he?" She stopped and faced him. "It is a shame that he and you have worked so hard and risked so much to get to this point, but that you can't enjoy it because all you can think of are enemies lurking in the shadows ready to leap on you."

He flinched as she nearly echoed his thoughts. How had he betrayed himself? He must not allow it to happen again. "Mayhap because that is the truth. Montrose and his men are coming in this direction. They would be happy to destroy any ally of Argyll's."

"But they will march over the mountains into this glen, not sneak up on you."

"I did not realize you were a student of warfare as well as the lessons you learned in the kitchen."

Again her face bleached, but she returned stoutly, "How can anyone live in the Highlands and not know something about battles?"

"True." He took her hand and tugged her toward the sluice that cut off a narrow triangle of the courtyard near the wall. Wide enough for a pair of men to stand there to repel any fool who dared to climb over the wall here.

As the water chimed out a hushed song on its way through the narrow, rock-filled passage, he stroked Ashley's palm with his thumb. Color flashed up her face, emphasizing each beguiling angle. It would be so easy to heed Jackie's suggestion to take this pretty lass to his bed. Yet, if there was even the slightest chance she was Gordon's daughter, he must offer her the respect she denied him.

If not...He could not hesitate to make her pay for her crime, not even long enough to savor the delights she displayed so shyly.

She pulled her hand out of his as she bent to touch the edge of the sluice, much the same as she had the wall, and he frowned once more. She had a peculiar way of running her fingers along everything as if she could not believe what her eyes were showing her.

He was further startled when she said, "This is poorly made." She pointed to the wall where an opening was lined with iron bars offering a view of the loch below. "Look at how the mortar is crumbling around the top of the bars."

"You show rare insight into masonry."

She glanced at him, then away. Again he saw the flash of fear that warned he had said something that frightened her more. What could there have been in that compliment to unsettle her?

"I have some experience in building," she said in a voice barely more than a whisper.

"I thought you worked in the kitchen while you hid from Stanton."

Instead of answering him, she squatted and reached for one of the bars. "Look. The bars are so loose that—" She cried out as the bar broke free, and she rocked back against him.

He caught her, but her momentum knocked them both to the ground. Before he could enjoy her against him, she pushed herself out of his arms and struggled to her feet.

"Are you all right?" Ashley asked as she brushed dirt from her gown. How many more ways could she humiliate herself today? She held her hand out to Colin. "Let me help you up."

"You, Ashley?" When he looked from her hand to her face, she knew she had done something wrong again.

"You *are* my clansman," she said. That had worked before. Maybe it would now. "The least I can do is give you a hand up."

He gripped her hand, but came to his feet alone. "How do you fare, Ashley?"

"I'm okay."

"You are what?"

"Fine." She pulled her hand out of his before he could feel her fingers fist in frustration. "That's just a saying I used to use in the kitchen."

"A bizarre one. O-K. That seems to mean nothing."

"It was a child's game. Didn't you make up silly things when you were a little boy?"

He put his hand on his knife in the waistband of his kilt. "I seldom had time for games when I was a child. I had to learn the skills that would enable me to gain my vengeance against Stanton and his fellow Englishmen who had tried to destroy my family."

Sympathy lashed Ashley, but she knew better than to speak it. Colin would not appreciate what he would deem as pity. His life of deprivation would have been hers if she had remained here.

*Are you beginning to believe all this nonsense?* She wished her own common sense would be quiet for just a few hours. She was here, and she had to assume that everything Gertie had told her was true. Gertie had been in her nightmare, both now and during her childhood, although Ashley had not recalled that until today.

"You wanted to see the armory, too?" she asked, hoping her question masked her uneasy thoughts. "It's behind the stables."

"Lead on."

She almost giggled, but bit her amusement back. Colin was not quoting *Macbeth*, although he had every bit of the self-assured determination of Shakespeare's doomed Scot. She shivered at that thought. If Colin was as bent on amassing power as Macbeth, then she could be the one who was doomed.

As they walked to the stone building set near the wall where it could supply defenders, Ashley answered Colin's questions about the castle as completely as she could. She was surprised to learn that Argyll's Covenanters did not hold a strong position in the Highlands. Quickly she learned that Montrose, whom Colin had mentioned before, fought for the king.

"And he is headed this way?" she asked, not hiding her shiver of horror.

"He is after Argyll, but the marquess's allies are his prey as well." Colin's smile sent another icy shudder along her. "I am sure you agree with me, Ashley, that Montrose shall have Castle Braeburn only when he has slain the last soul within these walls."

"I hope it doesn't come to that."

He glanced up again at the mountains beyond the walls and nodded. "I doubt if it will. This glen would take him far out of his way on his route to capture Argyll. More likely, we shall be called to defend the passes on the other side of those mountains." Lowering his gaze to her, he gave her another dose of that frigid smile. "Why do you look so despairing, Ashley, when my absence could give you the very chance you need to take control of this castle?"

Again she decided not to answer. She opened a door in the low building and walked into the dank, windowless room. A door allowed in very little light to warm the stone floor beneath a pair of crude tables and empty weapons racks.

Colin shook his head. "This is an unbelievable disarray. It may take weeks to make this armory usable again." He walked to where a musket leaned against the wall. Lifting it, he sighted it on the far wall. With a grimace, he placed it back on the floor. "The barrel is so misaligned that it is worthless. Where are the other weapons?"

"Lord Stanton's men took them."

"All of them? It looks as if he did not expect to return to defend the castle," Colin said as he dropped a rusted blade onto a dusty table and walked toward her. "Once Stanton fell, his men fought as if they had no heart. They allowed themselves to die upon our swords like—"

"Don't!" Ashley placed her hands over her ears. "I don't want to hear your gruesome war stories."

His finger followed her jaw in a sweet caress, but his eyes burned with bloodlust that warned he would fight anyone or anything to hold onto what he had won here. "Forgive me, Ashley. You have spoken so plainly of the defense of this castle that I had not guessed you would be uneasy about hearing of the battle that allowed me to claim it."

Moving away, she picked up the tattered remains of the feathers left by the fletcher. "I don't want to hear about the battle, although I am glad that Stanton took his stand past these walls instead of inside."

"Where those you care for could have been killed?"

"Yes." She wrapped her arms around herself. "Although many here believed it did not matter who won. If Stanton had been the victor, our imprisonment would have continued. If you won..."

"You believed I would have you all slain." He put his hands on her shoulders. "If you had been a man, Ashley, I might have had no choice but to slay you."

"If I were a man, Stanton would have beaten you to it." She stepped away.

His laugh sounded hollow in the empty room. "Then it is your good fortune and mine that you are a woman." He held out his hand in a silent command for her to come with him.

Ashley trembled again when they entered the keep and Colin opened another door. "Why do you want to see the dungeons?"

"You aren't curious about who might still be down here?" He plucked a candle from a sconce by the door.

"No." She ducked to miss the cobwebs that hung with years of dust from the low ceiling. A stench assaulted her senses. Beneath her feet, the uneven and broken stone risers disappeared into the darkness beyond the candle's flame. Slime which shone blackly threatened to snatch her footing from her. There was no railing, so she slid her fingers along the filthy wall. She pulled them back and shook them with disgust.

"I am surprised to find these dungeons so unused, Ashley." His voice echoed, warning her that the space was cavernous. Dankness oozed through her leather slippers as the candle's flame flickered with some breath of air which was not strong enough to ruffle her hair. "I had thought Stanton would have found many uses for his cells."

Swallowing the sickness rising from her stomach, Ashley said, "He preferred more *modern* methods, as he called them."

"And what did you call them?"

"Torture."

"A criminal deserves to pay for his crimes."

"Maybe, but innocent people don't. Lord Stanton delighted in flogging, branding, and dismemberment for the most menial crime."

Colin's face was shadowed, but from his words, she suspected it was twisted with abhorrence. "I have heard tales of the brutality here, but I did not want to believe they were true."

"They were." She did not want to recall more scenes like when Finlay Ballard had been put to death, but others haunted the edges of her mind, flickering about like bats swirling on a night's breeze. She was usually grateful for the knowledge that she had been given as part of Lady Fia's spell, but she wished she could rip these images out of her memory and throw them away.

"You are very brave to come here then."

Ashley looked at him. In the light cast by the single flame, his hair shone with a blue-black glow. "Why should I be afraid to come here? Lord Stanton is dead, so I need not fear him. There seems to be no one alive here but you and me."

He placed the candle on the floor and pulled her into his arms. "You stand between me and my claim for this castle." He smiled as his hand settled on her throat. "I could imprison you here, and no one would dare cry nay."

"You are wrong. There are those who believe I am the rightful holder of Castle Braeburn," she whispered, knowing she must not lower her guard to him for even a moment. Then he would strike out at her like the savage he was. "There are those who would gladly slay you upon seeing you threaten me like this."

"Mayhap, but they are far from here above us. What is your freedom worth to you?"

"This isn't funny." She tried to pull out of his iron-strong arms. "Release me! I don't have to suffer your abuse."

"I have no intentions of abusing you, pretty one." He chuckled even as his mouth descended toward hers.

"No!" she cried, her fear of his kiss luring her to surrender strengthening her. She leapt back.

Her foot struck the candle. It skittered across the floor, and she moaned in horror as the flame was extinguished on the damp floor.

Colin's voice was calm. "Can you find the taper? It must still be near your heel."

She nodded, then realized he was as blind as she was. "Let me try." She stretched her hands to sweep the floor. Her finger was scorched by the hot wax on the wick. She cried out, her voice twisting through the dungeon.

As if he could see, Colin took her hand and raised it to his lips. When his knee brushed hers, she discovered he was squatting next to her. Humor laced through his voice as he asked, "Can I assume you found the candle?"

She scooped it up, careful to hold it at the base. "I always do things the hard way."

"So I have seen." He chuckled as, with a flint, he relit the candle with an ease she knew she would never be able to copy. He motioned toward the stairs. "Shall we continue our tour of the castle, Ashley? On the morrow, I would like you to show me what awaits in the village and along the braes outside the walls."

"As you wish."

He smiled as she put her hand on his proffered arm. "I look forward to the day when you speak that answer to another question. Then the candle will not be doused, for I would delight in seeing every pleasure you have for me."

"I am your clansman's daughter. You should not be thinking such things of me."

"Who better to think such things of than a beautiful woman who is here with me?" His finger traced her cheekbone, sending a thrill through her. "I have seen that you are wise, Ashley, so the day is coming when you must admit the truth of how you, too, want what we could share."

"Don't hold your breath waiting for that to happen." She snatched the candle from his hand and rushed up the stairs, not caring if he tripped in the dark. She had to worry more about him tripping *her* up when he discovered the truth.

If only she knew what it was.

# FIVE

"You've got to be kidding!"

Colin followed the sound of laughter into the stables. He was not surprised to see Ashley, not only because he had recognized her warm voice but because of the odd words she so frequently chose. At first, he had guessed this isolated castle had developed its own cant, but no one else used the peculiar phrases she did.

Her arms were folded in front of her, hiding the beguiling curve of her breasts, but he could admire the determined line of her upraised chin. Her dark green dress that had a modest inset of lace above its neckline could not conceal her stubborn stance.

Facing her was Hume. The white-haired man wore a puzzled expression, one that Colin had become increasingly familiar with, after seeing it on many faces within these walls and wearing it on his own when confronting Lady Ashley Gordon.

*Lady Ashley Gordon!*

Colin wanted to curse his own thoughts. Simply because he had come to admire her knowledge of this castle and her insight in ways to defend it and—most undeniably—her captivating curves, that was no reason to start believing what might be an intricate lie created by an illegitimate daughter.

He strode past the stalls, many of which were empty. "What is the problem?"

"That." Ashley pointed to the saddle on the back of the horse.

"'Tis a fine looking side saddle, milady. Why is it a problem?"

Her pose faltered for a moment as her gaze slipped away from his. Then she met his eyes steadily again as she said, "I have no interest in using something that Lord Stanton purchased for his wife from the blood and sweat of my father's people."

He looked at Hume, who was now listening with the hint of a smile. "Is there another sidesaddle?"

"No, my laird."

"Then, Ashley," Colin continued, "you will have to use this one."

"Quite to the contrary." She gathered up her skirts and strode out of the stable. "I would rather walk."

"Walk?"

She did not turn to offer him the courtesy of an answer.

Hume chuckled. "She reminds me much of her mother. Lady Fia knew her own mind quite well and seldom was strayed from what she thought unless presented with good reasons to."

"That I have seen." Colin continued to watch Ashley hurry toward the keep as he added, "Have my horse saddled."

"Aye, my laird."

Colin went to the door. Leaning his elbow on the frame, he wondered why Ashley truly had refused to use the saddle. He had not wanted to denounce her as a liar in front of Hume, who clearly was loyal to her. But Ashley had been lying. She had moved her personal possessions to a set of rooms that, he had learned, had belonged to Lady Stanton. That proved she was not averse to using what Stanton's wife had used.

"My laird?"

At Hume's voice, Colin turned and took the reins of his horse. He thanked the stableman before mounting. Patting Leal on the neck, he murmured a greeting to the horse that had served him so well for the past year.

"What of Lady Ashley's horse, my laird?" asked Hume as Colin dipped his head to ride out of the stable.

"It seems that she has no interest in riding today." He would not beg her to journey around the loch with him, even though he would have appreciated her knowledge of the tenants and their ways.

"I would say quite the opposite."

When Hume laughed again, Colin looked out to see Ashley rushing toward the stable. She was looking back over her shoulder as if the dogs of hell were nipping at her heels.

He set his horse to cut her off. When she did not change direction, he grasped her arm and yanked her up to sit behind him. Her arms gripped him around the chest. He smiled as he turned toward the gate, waiting for her fury to explode around them.

"Thank you," Ashley said, resting her head against his back.

"Thank you?" He would have as soon expected her to acknowledge his claim on this castle as to say those two words just now.

"You saved me from having to speak to Gertie Graham."

"Who?"

Ashley looked back over her shoulder to see Gertie standing in the courtyard near the kitchen doorway, scowling at them. Maybe Ashley had been a coward to scurry off like this, but she had not wanted to face Gertie. Everything Ella had told her while Ashley's things were being moved yesterday suggested that Gertie truly was a witch. Ashley's own nightmares confirmed that Ella was right.

Yet she could not speak the words that would focus a witch-hunt on Gertie. Lady Fia must have trusted Gertie, for, if Ashley were to believe her dreams held an element of truth, Gertie had been in the room when Ashley was sent into the future. Gertie had spoken of teaching Lady Fia what she needed to know to save her child. If not for Gertie, Ashley might have died here along with her family.

"Gertie Graham," Ashley said quietly. "She lives beyond the walls. She is bothersome, and I wished to avoid her."

"Odd, for I had thought you wished to avoid *me*."

"Why would you say that?"

"Because of the silly tale you spun for Hume in the stable. Why didn't you want to ride with the sidesaddle?"

Ashley sighed as he turned the horse onto the road ringing the loch. She should have known that she could not fool him with that silly excuse. Maybe it was time for some truth. It was a risk, but she was tired of lying. "I don't know how to ride with a sidesaddle."

"You don't know—?" He looked over his shoulder and drew in the reins, so the horse slowed to a walk. With a curse, he added, "This is uncomfortable."

"Then let me change that." She slid off the horse.

"A good idea." He reached down and, grabbing her at the waist, lifted her onto his lap. "Much better."

"I'm not surprised you think so." She started to slide off again, but halted at his laugh.

"Continue that wiggling, Ashley, and you shall persuade me to do something you may find much more pleasing than sitting here."

"You are assuming much."

He pressed his mouth over hers. When she shivered with the yearning that careened through her, he pulled her even closer. She fought her body as it tempted her to soften against him. Her fingers climbed his arm to his shoulder as he leaned her back onto his other arm. Cradling her nape in his broad hand, he deepened the kiss until her uneven breath mingled with his.

"'Tis no assumption," he murmured as the horse shifted beneath them, "when 'tis a fact."

Ashley was not sure how she would have answered if the sound of other hoof beats did not come from behind them. When Colin lifted her from his lap and let her slide to the ground, she saw Hume walking toward them with another horse.

"I thought," the old man said with a knowing smile, "you might find this more suitable, milady. However..."

Grabbing the reins of the horse which wore a regular saddle, she said, "Thank you, Hume. This would be much, much better."

"I warned you, my laird." The old man chuckled to himself as he went back toward Castle Braeburn's main gate.

"Warned you about what?" Ashley asked as she led the horse to a downed tree. Stepping onto the log, she mounted with less trouble than she had expected in these wide skirts.

Colin only smiled before saying, "Ashley, we have much to see today. Shall we go?"

This time, Ashley knew exactly what she wanted to say. However, to voice her frustration with Colin and Hume and everyone else in this time would be stupid. Instead, she simply nodded. She suspected she would find out what Hume meant...when Colin could turn the words' meaning to his best interest. She sighed. This might not be a pleasant ride.

***

Ashley watched Colin closely as they rode along the loch. He could not hide his pride in what might still be his. Nor could she blame him. The hills were steep as they rose to the bare-faced cliffs, but closer to this end of the loch, the land had a gentle roll that was perfect for growing crops. Hearing a distant sound, she looked up at the hills and saw sheep grazing along them, each a white dot against the verdant green.

"It is magnificent, isn't it?" Colin asked, warning her that he had been appraising her reaction as she had his. "This must be the part of creation God made last. He practiced on the rest of the world. Here is perfection."

Keeping her horse to a walk, she laughed. "When did you become a poet?"

"It surprises you that I can speak of something other than battles?"

"Yes, if you wish to know the truth."

He drew his horse closer to hers. "That is because, Ashley, you only see me as a warrior."

"You're a chameleon."

"There is nothing changeable about me."

"No?" She pointed to his black cloak that he wore over dark breeches and a fawn-colored doublet with embroidering along the front. "You have changed your feathers."

He laughed. "Aye, you are right. When I first arrived here, I was dressed as a warrior. Today you see me as a gentleman riding with a favored lady by his side."

When she flushed at his unexpected compliment, he chuckled again. She grimaced. She must be careful not to respond to his flirting.

They rode toward a cluster of cabins clinging to the strand. The thatch-covered cottages had no windows, but people stared unabashedly at them from the doorways and yards. Ashley guessed they were surprised to see her riding with Colin. They must learn, as she was, that staying alive in this time required more compromises than she had ever suspected.

Compromises? Ashley smiled as she turned her horse into one of the grassless yards. Why hadn't she thought of this before? The best way to halt Colin's attentions to her was to turn them toward someone else, someone who would welcome them.

*Take care.*

She did not bother to look about, because she knew that that voice was within her. But whose voice was it? She wanted to shout that question, but bit it back as a man came around the edge of the house at the edge of the hamlet to see who had arrived.

The balding man could not mask his shock as he dropped to one knee and put his fingers against his forehead. "Good day to ye, milaird." As if an afterthought, he added, "And to ye, Lady Ashley."

"You are?" Colin asked as he jumped down from his horse.

"Lundy, milaird."

"Rise, my good man. 'Tis too fine a day to spend on your knees watching the last of the summer's bugs."

"Thank ye, milaird." The man came to his feet slowly. "Do ye need hay for yer beast?"

"No, I think I..."

As Colin's words faded into silence, Ashley followed his gaze. She stared at him as he watched a woman emerge from the shadows within the house. She did not have to look, for his expression of awe warned her who was stepping out of the house.

Lilias Lundy had hair of golden sunshine and a form like a statuesque Grecian sculpture.

No one spoke as Lilias sank to her knees before him, her hand pressed to her chest, so he could not fail to notice her full curves. Ashley was not the only one awaiting Colin's first words, she realized. Mr. Lundy was watching closely, a hint of a smile curling along his lips. No wonder, her conscience—for what else could that soft voice be?—had warned her to take care. She should have considered that there were consequences beyond giving Colin someone else to trifle with. If his daughter found favor with the laird, Lundy's already fearful prestige near the loch would be enhanced. Many men had garnered a fortune or power because they had daughters to trade for gold and favors.

"Lilias Lundy," murmured the woman who was still on her knees, her voice as soft as the breeze tickling the top of the loch.

"Do rise, Lilias." Colin offered her his hand, bringing her to her feet. She was taller than Ashley, for she stood nearly eye-to-eye with him.

Lilias gave him a smile that could define come hither. "Thank you, my laird." When her father cleared his throat, she said, without taking her gaze from Colin, "Good day, milady." She brushed her lustrous hair back over her shoulders. "May I offer you something, my laird?"

Even though Ashley fought to restrain her laugh, a bit of it escaped.

Colin turned to her. "Is something amiss?"

"No, just some dust in my throat, I think."

His eyes slitted, and she knew he did not trust her quick answer.

Before he could ask another question, Lilias said, "I have fresh milk that will take the dryness of the road from your throat, my laird."

"That might help." He reached up and grasped Ashley by the waist to swing her down off her horse. He set her on the ground with a thump.

She scowled at him. Her irritation was wasted, because he turned back to thank Lilias for the two tin cups she held out to them.

Trying not to think how many germs could be on the tin and in the warm milk, Ashley took a cup. She sipped and smiled at the sweet taste of fresh milk. Walking to the stone wall at the edge of the loch, she gazed out at its aquamarine waters. Near the shore, the forest darkened the reflection. The light breeze was ruffling the surface into miniatures of the mountain ridges around them.

When an arm slipped around her shoulders, she was so startled she almost dropped the cup. Colin raised his mug and smiled as he said, "You are admiring the view as if you never saw the loch on a sunny day before."

"I have looked at this loch for as long as I can remember." That was the truth, because the postcard of Castle Braeburn hung on her bedroom wall had had a view of the loch on a day as glorious as this one. "I just never have grown accustomed to its beauty."

"It is splendid."

"God's perfect creation," she returned.

He arched an eyebrow and laughed. "If only you would heed as closely everything else I tell you." Not giving her a chance to retort, he asked, "Have you finished your milk?"

"Yes."

"Did it help your throat?"

"My throat is fine now."

Smoothing her hair back from her cheeks, he said, "Then let us continue on our ride."

"I'm in no hurry if you want to enjoy the view here a while longer."

"That is most kind of you, Ashley, but..." He took her cup and set it on the wall. "I believe I have seen enough here for now. Shall we ride on?"

Although she wanted to ask him what he thought of Lilias, she just nodded. Colin MacLachlan was a complex man, and she must heed that little voice that warned her to take care. Most of all, she must be cautious not to let him too close, for then that little voice might be silenced beneath the heavy pounding of her heart.

He helped her onto her horse, so he could not have seen the withering glare Lilias shot in his direction. Lilias must be furious that he had not accepted her unvoiced invitation. Wanting to tell Lilias to have more patience, Ashley again had to swallow a chuckle. Patience was something she needed, too, to help her through this 17th century maze.

"You look pleased with yourself," Colin said. "What are you plotting now, Ashley?"

Her reply faltered when his hand slipped from her waist to rest on her leg. Tingles, heated and frightening, swept across her skin. No, she did not want to be dazzled by his touch. Let Lilias have him! Mixing her life up with this man would be insane.

She grasped the reins and slapped them against the horse. Colin jumped back as she sent the horse speeding out of the cottage's yard and along the loch. When she heard a shout behind her, she slowed the horse. She could not flee from this any more than she could flee to the future.

Colin drew even with her. His frown knitted his brows together. "Do you want to explain trying to run me down?"

"No, because I did not try to run you down."

"Then what—?"

"Can't we just enjoy this pretty day and forget everything else?"

He reached across to put his hands over hers on the reins. "You know that is impossible, Ashley."

"Nothing is impossible if you want it badly enough." When he regarded her with amazement, she asked, "Why are you staring at me like that?"

"I had not anticipated hearing from your lips my own words that I have repeated often to Jackie and the other men." His smile returned. "But I should not be surprised, for you clearly want the impossible of claiming Castle Braeburn as your own."

"Better you should say I have already done the impossible by surviving long enough to claim what was my father's."

With a laugh, he set his horse to a faster pace. He motioned for her to try to catch up with him.

Ashley shook her head. Colin MacLachlan *was* the puzzle. One minute arrogant, and the next teasing. She followed him as the sun rose higher to warm the day and make last week's snowstorm a distant memory.

As they rode along the far side of the loch, Colin took the lead. He selected a path which wound at a gentle angle along the hill climbing up out of the water. Leafless trees surrounded them, and leaves crunched underfoot.

He looked back and smiled at Ashley. She had not answered his question about what she had been scheming in the farmer's yard, although he suspected he knew quite well. He had to admire the woman she had selected to intrigue him. Lilias Lundy was a rare beauty with a sensuality that would garner a reaction from a dead man. Mayhap later, he would call again at Lundy's farm. Later, but not today, for one thing Ashley had not considered was that she was the woman who intrigued him most just now.

He swung down from the saddle as they reached a glade halfway up the brae. "Ashley, shall we take a rest?"

"Yes."

When she did not move, he said, "I will gladly assist you down."

Her laugh was unsteady. "I'm still not accustomed to this treatment." She leaned forward to put her hands on his shoulders, then pulled them back. "You aren't going to jar every tooth in my head again, are you?"

"You could trust me just once, Ashley."

"I would be a fool to believe that."

With a chuckle, he grasped her at the waist and plucked her from the saddle. "Aye, you would."

He held her suspended, her feet above the ground, as he watched emotions flash through her volatile eyes. When he shifted, she gripped his shoulders. Slowly he lowered her to the ground, drawing her up against him as her toes touched the earth.

She stepped back from him, but her hands shook as she drew them off his shoulders. When she started to reach for the horse's reins, he put his finger under her chin and tilted her face back toward him.

The view of her soft lips nearly undid him. He could think of nothing but tasting them, as he had thought every night he had slept at Castle Braeburn. Or tried to sleep, for the memories of her soft breasts against him when he had arrived to claim the castle refused to be forgotten.

"You trusted me once," he whispered.

"I never—"

"You trusted me the first time I pulled you into my arms."

All the color fled from her face. "That was a mistake. I didn't know then...I mean...It was a mistake."

Colin frowned. He had seen this horror in her eyes too often, but he did not know what caused it. She was hiding some secret that frightened her to the very core of her being. That frightened her more than his attempt to prove his claim on the castle did. She was so courageous about everything else, so he did not understand this.

He reached for a bladder on the back of his horse. "Something to drink?"

"Yes. Thank you." She uncorked the container he handed her. Tilting it to her mouth, she took a hearty drink.

He chuckled and caught the bladder as it dropped from her fingers. With her hands over her mouth, she coughed.

"Why didn't you warn me?" she cried. "That's horrible!"

"Now, Ashley, that is no way to speak of fine whisky." He held it up and drank. "Mayhap 'tis an acquired taste."

"It's not one I wish to acquire."

"Then you may enjoy this more." He reached behind the saddle and lifted off a rolled blanket.

She backed away a half-step. "Colin, I think we should return to the castle."

"Without something to ease our hunger?"

More desperation filled her voice as she reached for the saddle on her horse. "Yes."

"I brought food for our midday meal. Will you let it go to waste?"

Ashley paused and closed her eyes. Colin was taunting her again, playing on her fears that he brought to life with such ease. How could she blame him for that when she was such a ready victim for his jests? She wished he would play his games with Lilias or some other woman and leave her alone.

He walked up the hill to a flat area. As he spread the blanket on the ground, he motioned for her to join him. She knelt at the very edge and said nothing as he unwrapped the packages of food. Taking a slice of thick bread, she placed a piece of the cheese and some roast beef on it. She folded the bread and lifted it to her mouth.

"What are you doing?" he asked.

"I'm eating my sandwich."

"Your what?"

Ashley knew she must not falter. Why hadn't she thought that sandwiches might not have been invented yet? Forcing a smile, she said, "It was something I made while working in the kitchen. I didn't always have time to eat my meal sitting at a table. I wrapped it in bread so I might eat it while working." She watched his face, wondering if he would swallow her lie along with his food. "It's good this way. You might want to try it."

"And trust you?"

She shrugged. "That's your choice."

He did not move for a long minute, then rolled some meat and cheese into a slice of bread. His eyes lit with appreciation as he took a bite.

"So it's good?" she asked.

"Hush, woman, and let me eat!" He quickly finished the sandwich and reached for another piece of bread. "This may turn out to be a good day. Fine food, pleasant company, and a day unlike any we shall have until the new year arrives. I could grow to like this."

"You are a laird. You should be able to live your life as you wish."

"I was not raised in luxury." He twirled a leaf between his fingers. "After my family's holdings were destroyed by English raiders, I lived on a farm that was not so different from one of those down in the dell."

"The farmer in the dell?" She laughed. "Forgive me, Colin. Simply an off-hand thought."

"You seem filled with such off-hand thoughts, as you call them."

She knew he hoped she would be honest with him, after he had revealed a bit of his past to her. Instead, she said, "Ella despairs at my sense of humor."

"It is vexing at times."

"I'm sure." She took the cup he handed her and smiled when she discovered it contained water. Sipping, she said, "I wonder how many more days we shall have like this before the heavy snows begin."

"Not many." He leaned forward, folding his arm on his drawn-up knee. "It is clear that Stanton cared nothing for his tenants. I look across the loch, and I see byres in disrepair and fences that would not keep in livestock. There is so much to do before the weather worsens." With a sigh, he gave a terse laugh. "Our ride today has shown me how much work waits to be done."

"Lord Stanton cared only for the wealth he could garner from these lands, not about the people." Ashley quickly took another drink. Again that was something she should not know, but she did. She could no longer tell which memories were real and which were not. Maybe they all were real, but some of them were not hers.

"Finally."

"Finally?" she repeated, wondering if she had missed something else he had said.

"Until now, you have been very forgiving of the English beast who tried to slay all of your father's blood." He cupped her chin and brought her face toward him. "The hatred in your voice now convinces me more than anything else that you might be telling the truth about being Gordon's daughter."

"I am!" *Or so everyone tells me.* That thought had been most definitely her own, seeping up from her despair.

"Mayhap you are." His hand slid around to her nape before his fingers combed up into her hair.

"Colin, you shouldn't—"

His lips brushed hers before he whispered, "You are as brave as Gordon's wife, and as beautiful."

She had to put a stop to this. She could not let him kiss her again. He tempted her too easily.

Pushing herself to her feet, she stooped and gathered an armful of the brown leaves. She tossed them over his head. He sputtered as he wiped dust from his eyes. She sidestepped his swipe at her skirts and raced down the hill.

Ashley listened for his footsteps as she tried to keep from falling on her face. This gown was not designed for running. As she reached the horses, she paused, discovering that she could hear nothing but her rapid breathing. It was not like Colin not to give chase.

"Colin?" she called. "I'm leaving. Are you going to ride back to the castle with me?"

No answer came back.

Ashley hesitated. What prank was he playing now? Her hands clenched. Maybe he was not playing a prank. He could have slipped on the steep path. She hurried back to where they had been sitting. In disbelief, she stared at the empty blanket. Where was he?

"Colin! This isn't funny!"

Again no answer.

She opened her mouth to call out his name again, but a terrified squawk emerged as hands encircled her waist.

"Were you, by any chance, looking for me, Ashley?" The deep growl sounded like thunder against her ear.

"Colin! Where have you been?"

"Watching you." He twirled her to face him. "Your concern about me is most surprising...and most gratifying."

"You have the biggest ego in the world!"

"The biggest what?"

Arching her shoulders, she snapped, "Just let me go! I'll walk back to the castle."

"Not yet, Ashley," he murmured, his voice growing husky.

Her retort faded as his eyes became amethyst with desire. As his arms slid around her to bring her to him, his lips caressed her cheeks in a slow circle which ended on her mouth.

He put his arm under her knees. Lifting her to his chest, he slowly explored her mouth. Her hands clenched on the front of his doublet as he carried her back to the blanket. As easily as if she weighed no more than one of the leaves, he knelt and leaned her back on the wool. His cloak dropped forward to envelop her in a soft twilight. Leaning over her, he deepened his kiss until she gasped against his mouth. She could not resist the caress of his breath, and her tongue delved into his mouth to savor each slippery surface.

He raised his mouth away from hers. "You are bold, Ashley."

"Does that boldness remind you of my father or my mother?" she asked with a soft laugh. "Every other thing I do or say brings them to mind for you, although you deny who I am."

"It reminds me that I prefer your lips beneath mine rather than aiming fierce words at me." With a laugh, he captured her mouth once more.

She knew she should push him away, that she was asking for more trouble when she had too much already. Yet, her arms went around his shoulders. She moaned with the growing need as his lips slipped along her cheek. When his tongue teased the curve of her ear, she drew him even closer. He followed the line of her pulse along her neck.

With her lips hungering for his kiss, she started to draw his mouth back to hers. She froze as she heard a soft sound and discovered Jackie Kilbride standing beside the blanket. With a cry, she tried to push Colin away. His hands tightened on her.

"No!" she cried. "If *this* is your idea of fun, I don't want any part of it. Not you or him!"

"Him?" Colin half-turned to see Jackie watching them with a taut smile. Coming to his knees, he put his hand on Ashley's shoulder to keep her from moving. His voice was as rigid as Jackie's expression as he asked, "Why are you here?"

"Argyll has sent a messenger to you, Laird MacLachlan." He aimed his most superior sneer at Ashley. "I would not have intruded on your fun if I had not believed that the message was urgent."

"Go, and tell the messenger I shall be there posthaste."

"Aye." Jackie laughed sharply. "I am sure the tidings will justify this intrusion. After all, a whore can always be yours if you make the price worth her time."

Ashley edged from under Colin's hand, but he caught her as she jumped to her feet. "Milady, do not send Jackie head over heels again. He could get hurt on this brae if you flipped him here."

"I have vowed that she will not have a second chance to work her trickery on me." Jackie scowled. "Mayhap you should vow the same, my laird." He stamped down the hillside.

Colin sighed as Ashley continued to struggle in his arms. Faith, she should understand that Jackie's words were aimed at getting just this reaction. "Calm yourself, Ashley. There are larger matters to consider."

"Argyll," she whispered, sagging against him.

"Aye, Argyll."

"Do you think he has made his decision already? It hasn't been much more than a week. You said the message would take a month to return."

"We cannot know what tidings the messenger brings until we return to Castle Braeburn."

She stepped away and put her hand on his arm. "And if he decides in your favor, what will you do?"

"With you?" He drew his arm away. "On this matter, as with any other, I will obey my chieftain's orders." When she started to turn to go down the hill, he halted her. "Ashley, if he decides in your favor, what will *you* do?"

"I don't know." She wrapped her arms around herself and shivered. "I honestly don't know."

He nodded and held out his arm to her. As she put her fingers on it, she wondered what awaited them at Castle Braeburn. Whatever it was, it threatened to destroy one or both of them.

# SIX

When Ashley handed her horse's reins to Hume, the old stableman did not meet her eyes. She understood why when she walked into the keep. Fear stank in the air. By now, everyone in Castle Braeburn knew the messenger's identity and who had sent him.

Colin said nothing as he led her to the door of the antechamber that connected his rooms. Pausing by the door, he asked, "Do you wish to hear this, too, Ashley?"

"Yes, I want to."

"Your courage is admirable. Continue to be brave."

She walked beside him, her right hand on his arm, her left hand knotted in a fist. She kept her head high, determined no one would guess the breadth of her terror. When he opened the door, he graciously motioned for her to precede him.

Ashley entered the large chamber. The last time she had been here had been the day both she and Colin arrived at Castle Braeburn. She stared at the messenger who might be the harbinger of her death. The state of his clothes and the fatigue etched into his young face told of his many hours of riding without a break. His message must be as important as Captain Kilbride had said.

Panic strangled her until a gentle hand settled on her shoulder. Comfort seeped to every inch of her. She turned to smile her thanks at Colin, but he was not behind her. No one was. Her eyes widened when she saw the sparkle, like vagrant starlight, congealing on the wall next to her.

"Colin, do you see—?"

He brushed past her, acting as if he had not heard her while his attention focused on the man bowing to him. "You come from Argyll?" he asked.

The man nodded. From beneath his cape, he drew a rolled page which he handed to Colin.

As Colin scanned the single piece of paper, Ashley looked from him to the glitter on the wall, but it was gone, along with its solace. She had enjoyed this warmth in her nightmare when her mother—when Lady Fia Gordon—sent her child from this time to the future. Was that sparkle what was left of the lady? It was impossible, but everything here was impossible.

"So I am to do nothing now?" Colin demanded, drawing her attention back to him. His scowl was venomous as he let the paper close with a snap. "Why did the marquess send me a message to tell me what I already know?"

"The message was given to me by the marquess's nephew," the messenger replied, glancing at Ashley quickly, then away.

"Which one?"

"Harry Campbell, the baron."

"Lord Campbell?" gasped Ashley as memories burst into her head. Harry Campbell had come here, it had been rumored throughout the castle, to try to persuade Lord Stanton to set aside his loyalty to King Charles and join the Covenanters. He had been as unsuccessful at that as he had been in coercing her into his bed. Stepping around the chair, she asked, "You do Harry Campbell's bidding?"

"The baron is his uncle's aide, Lady Ashley," the messenger said. All color washed from his face as he looked uneasily at Colin as he spoke her title. He quickly recovered and added, "Lord Campbell's words are the words of the marquess."

"His words are the words of evil. He wears the somber cloak of the Solemn League and Covenant and does the devil's work! Lord Campbell's a—"

"Enough, Lady Ashley!"

She spun to see Colin's fury, warning that she had overstepped herself. As she had when last she stood in this room, she was inundated with emotions that were not her own. The hatred frightened her, but she could not halt herself from saying, "'Tis nowhere near enough, Laird MacLachlan! I do not pledge my allegiance to a cur who will bury everyone in his determination to become as powerful as his uncle." Her laugh sounded strange in her ears. "I would not obey him when he thought he could bed me, and I vow that I shall see this castle brought to ruins before I shall obey him now."

"Lady Ashley! I said enough!"

She stared at Colin's rage as she struggled to hold onto her identity. Putting her hands to her head, she wanted to claw out the voice in it that had taken control of her. This anger was not hers, but the words spilled from her lips. "Laird MacLachlan—"

"Enough, Lady Ashley!" He seized her arms.

Closing her eyes, Ashley quelled the uncontrollable hatred within her. She swayed and leaned against Colin. His touch had broken the grip of the malevolence. When she spoke, the words she whispered were her own. "Help me, Colin."

"Help you?" He pushed her to sit in a chair. "If I and my allies are your enemies, you should have no interest in me aiding you."

"You aren't my enemy." She could not explain what had happened without divulging the truth. That she could not do. She was afraid he would think she was truly mad. Or he would believe her and send her to burn as a witch.

He motioned for the messenger to leave. The startled man hurried out of the room.

"Colin, what did the message—?"

He whirled to face her. "It said nothing. We are to wait for word from the marquess who has other things to concern himself with that he deems more important than you or me."

"That *Lord Campbell* deems more important."

"Do not disparage Harry Campbell to me, Ashley. His uncle is my chieftain in this battle against the king." He slammed his fist against the wall at the exact spot where the sparkles had disappeared. "This losing battle."

"Losing?" She came to her feet. "What has happened?"

"Why do you care?"

She grasped his sleeve as he started to walk past her. "This affects everyone's life in the Highlands." She hesitated, then said, "Colin, I'm sorry for what I said. I was—I was upset."

For a long moment, she feared he would throw her apology back into her face. Then he said, "You know that the Royalists under Montrose have been harrying the Covenanters throughout the Highlands. Campbell has no time to deal with you while he suffers one defeat after another."

"And you are angry because he didn't invite you to be a part of his next battle?" She shook her head. "You can keep your death wishes. I don't want any part of a suicidal foray."

"What is it that you want? Not an hour ago you were warm and soft beneath me. Now you are spitting at me like a snarling cat."

"I want this madness to end!"

"It appears it may soon." He walked toward the door. Holding it open, he said, "I am sure you will understand when I say I think it would be better if you take your dinner in your rooms. I find I don't want to be reminded of your words here."

"Colin, I said I was sorry. Lord Campbell...He upsets me."

"So I have seen." His voice, if possible, grew even colder. "I bid you a good evening, Ashley."

"I shall remain in my rooms." She was glad to agree. Maybe, in her rooms, she would be able to sort out all of this.

He caught her arm. "Tell me, Ashley, why do you have rowan over your bed?"

She faltered at the sharp question. "Rowan?"

"The branches laced through your bed. Your servant tells me that you have always slept under rowan. That belongs to the MacLachlans, not the Gordons."

"I don't know." She was so glad to speak the truth.

"Ella tells me that your mother put it there among the ivy when you were young, and Ella continued the tradition after the Gordons were slain."

"I don't know." She hurried to add when his eyes became as dark as thunderheads. "Colin, I honestly don't know. I was so young when my mother was slain by Lord Stanton. If Ella does not know, why would you expect me to?"

"You don't find it odd?"

"I find everything odd now." Again that was the truth. "Will I see you at breakfast?"

"Yes, for I shall be here instead of at Argyll's side." He sighed as he looked at the door. "I fail to understand why I am ordered to remain at Castle Braeburn when my men and I should be fighting Montrose."

She put her fingers on his wool sleeve as frustration flared in his eyes. "This is Lord Campbell's work. He doesn't want you showing him up. You must have heard the stories of what has happened before. When Carleton MacLaws advanced quickly in Argyll's favor, he met his end in what was deemed a hunting accident."

"I know of what you speak. Campbell was in Edinburgh when MacLaws was killed."

"Believe what you will, but don't trust Harry Campbell. He'll be looking for a way to destroy you, Colin." She sighed, wishing she could persuade him to heed her. But how could she when she could not even trust her own memories? Where did reality end and madness begin?

"Why are you warning me when you would have no one to contest your claim if I were not here?"

"Don't you understand? If Harry Campbell is involved in this, if you die, so will I."

*** 

Ashley sat on the wide windowsill in her bedchamber and watched rain run along the uneven glass. The weather had taken a turn as dreary as her spirits. Cold oozed past the casement, and she stood.

She never had been so aimless. In the past week, she had explored all of Castle Braeburn. Now she had nothing to do but worry. Before Ella had left to visit a sick friend in one of the cottages by the loch, she had whispered a warning that not everyone in Castle Braeburn was happy with the current situation. Some wanted Laird MacLachlan to renounce his claim.

Ashley wished she could ignore these hints of insurrection, but she could not. How would she get Colin to listen to her? He had not said more than a greeting to her in the past five days.

With a sigh, she went to the table that was set opposite her bed. This room was far bigger than the room where she had first slept. Clearly, Lady Stanton had not wanted to endure the coziness of that room, so she had chosen this expansive suite of rooms.

The bed was draped with white curtains that were embroidered with gold thread, and the pair of tapestries on the wall would have been envied by any museum. Beyond the bedroom were an antechamber that Ella called a reception hall and a very rustic bathroom. Ella might call it a garderobe, but Ashley thought of it as the outhouse. This seemed to be the height of 17th century luxury.

Right now, she would rather have a Swiss army knife to get this drawer open. Maybe there was something in it to keep her mind off the troubles around her. She slipped her fingers inside and discovered a book with papers bunched around it was jamming the drawer. Rising, she scanned the room, trying to decide what she could use to release the jam.

When the door opened from the antechamber, she was amazed to see Colin's servant Ramsey White. He seemed to be a valet, but she had heard him addressed as *An Gille-copain*, which Ella told her meant cup-bearer. That title did not fit him as well as *An Gille-coise* fit Captain Kilbride. That translated as henchman, which she thought was perfect for the short man and his endless schemes.

Ramsey was in his middle years with hair to match his name. His face was etched with lines that suggested he was more accustomed to smiling than the uneasy expression he now wore. As his fingers toyed with his plaid, he bowed in her direction. Unlike Captain Kilbride, he treated her with respect.

"Come in, Ramsey," she said.

He entered, but did not close the door. "Pardon my intrusion, milady. My laird wishes you to attend him in his office."

Grasping her thick skirt, Ashley lifted it so she could walk. She wondered if she would ever get accustomed to these long dresses. She would give just about anything right now for a pair of jeans, a t-shirt, and some sneakers.

The corridor was filled with people hurrying in every direction. She was pleased to hear the lingering notes of someone's song as well as a happy laugh from around a corner. Those sounds had vanished the day Lord Stanton came to claim Castle Braeburn. It was amazing that anyone here remembered how to laugh.

The door to Colin's rooms was open. Crossing the antechamber, she knocked on the door she knew led to the laird's private office where he would receive reports from his tenants and advisors.

"Come in," Colin called.

A welcome she had not imagined washed over her as she opened the door. Memories pelted her. Early memories, for she could remember playing here while her father worked. He had been gone from the castle so often that, on the rare occasions when he was here, she had wanted to spend all her time with him.

Ashley's eyes widened as she noted how little had been changed in the office. Why hadn't Colin gotten rid of a portrait of King Charles and a painting of the Stanton family seat in Yorkshire? Because he had no time to remove it, or was it that he did not realize the insult it was to see these still here?

*'Tis because he cares for no one but himself.*

*No!* she argued to the voice in her head. *You aren't going to cause trouble for Colin and me again. Go away.*

A pain seared through her as the hatred faded. She closed her eyes, then opened them to see Colin regarding her with astonishment from where he sat at the desk. With her head aching, she gave herself the pleasure of saying, "I must have been foolish to expect a gentleman to rise when I came into the room."

"*Gentlemen,*" he corrected, gesturing to where Jackie Kilbride lounged on the windowsill.

Ashley knew her dislike of Jackie Kilbride was all her own, not from that despised voice she could not identify. Since he had interrupted her and Colin on the brae, she had tried to ignore his gloating. She looked back at Colin and crossed her arms in defiance. When her expression did not waver, Colin stood and signaled Captain Kilbride to come to his feet also.

The redhead shook his head. "I shall be damned before I jump up every time that daughter of who knows what bootlicker enters a room." He leaned back and put his dusty boots on the table.

"It doesn't surprise me that you'd recognize a bootlicker, Mr. Kilbride," she fired back. "You're so low, you'd have to crane your neck up to see the top of anyone's boots."

"*Captain* Kilbride!" He leapt to his feet and took a threatening step toward her, pausing when Colin held up a hand.

Ashley smiled. "How kind of you to rise when I enter the room, Captain."

Colin laughed, before saying, "What do you want, milady?"

"You tell me. You sent for me."

"I did?"

"Ramsey came to tell me you wanted to speak to me."

"I am afraid there has been a misunderstanding." His smile returned. "I mentioned I wanted to discuss some matters with you, but I intended for that conversation to take place at the evening meal."

He picked up a paper from the desk, and Ashley guessed she had been dismissed. As she saw Captain Kilbride move toward the door to open it for her, she said, "Colin, I'd like to discuss something with you."

"And what is that?" He glanced up, obviously surprised she had not done as he wished.

She hesitated as she looked at Captain Kilbride. To speak of what Ella had told her about the unrest in Castle Braeburn might set this volatile man off. That would cause even more problems. She had to say something, but what? Not sure how else to answer, she said, "I'm bored. Can't you give me something to do?"

Captain Kilbride gave a derisive laugh. "I think she is offering you an interesting proposition, my laird."

"I doubt that," Colin said as his lips quirked. "What do you want to do, milady?"

"I'm not sure."

Again Captain Kilbride snickered. "Would you like some suggestions?"

"Jackie!" Colin growled. Exasperation remained in his voice as he added, "I shall give to you, milady, the duties of running the household within Castle Braeburn."

"The whole household?"

"Yes, all within the keep while I focus my attention on the matters of its defense. You have experience within the kitchen, so you should have no trouble overseeing the rest of the household."

"I guess so." What did she know about running a castle? Again, in answer to her unspoken question, memories burst forth, showing her what she needed to do.

"That should keep you busy," Colin said.

"It should." She faltered again, then knew she could not wait for Captain Kilbride to take a hint and leave. This was too important not to be said. "Colin, I wanted to speak to you on behalf of the men who remained loyal to my father, but survived Lord Stanton's tenure. They are afraid they will be called traitors."

"Are they willing to be faithful to the oath of allegiance they have taken to their new laird?" Colin asked, his calm tone warning of the strong emotions he kept in tight control.

"I have been assured they will honor it until a decision is made about the rightful holder of this castle."

"Words mean little. 'Tis easy to say one thing and mean another in your heart."

She leaned on her hands on the desk. "Colin, if you ever want peace within these walls, you must learn to trust these men. They have suffered greatly for the past twenty years. Most of the people here have proven they're willing to accept you as long..." She lowered her gaze.

"As long as I do nothing to hurt their beloved Lady Ashley?"

"Yes."

He reached across the desk and put two fingers under her chin. Bringing her face up, he smiled, but his voice was taut as he asked, "So you think you are as valuable as this castle? If I give you back to your people hale and unharmed, they shall offer me their fealty. At least temporarily. Few have such a price affixed to their lives."

"And fewer are worth it!" Captain Kilbride added.

Ashley whirled from the desk and glowered at Kilbride. Although she wanted to spit an insult back at him, she said, "I've done what I came to do. Good day, Colin."

She went to the door. Opening it, she smiled when she heard Kilbride's muttered curse. Her smile faded. Colin would not allow this battle of wits to go on. Either she or Captain Kilbride would be the victor in this power struggle. She did not want to think of what would happen if she lost.

***

Colin looked up when he heard soft footsteps coming toward his office door. His lips quirked. 'Twas good that Jackie had gone to oversee the work in the armory. His friend's antipathy toward Ashley was no longer amusing. In fact, it was downright tiresome.

His smile disappeared when he realized the footfalls did not belong to Ashley. The tall woman was not young, although no hint of gray lightened her ebony hair. Her dark eyes narrowed when she looked around the room.

"You are alone?" she asked.

"It would appear so." He came to his feet, trying to repress his irritation that Ashley had not returned...and his irritation that he had been so hopeful that she would.

"Things can be very different from what they seem, Laird MacLachlan."

"If you came here to tell me what I already know, you are wasting your time as well as mine."

She flinched, but drew her shawl more tightly around her shoulders. "I am Gertie Graham." Her tone suggested he should recognize her name.

He did, for he recalled Ashley's dismay when she spoke this woman's name. *Bothersome* had been her description of Gertie Graham, but he suspected that was a tepid term for this woman whose eyes were as cold as the loch's waters.

"Yes?" he asked.

Again she started at his voice that was as frigid as her gaze. "I thought you might wish to know what I know, Laird MacLachlan."

"And what is that?"

"That your claim on this castle is doomed."

Colin was torn between laughing and scowling. He chose the latter because he wanted to put an end to this conversation immediately. "It would seem you are privy to information that no one else knows."

"Now you are beginning to understand." She laughed. "Heed me, Laird MacLachlan, and you may live to see the day when this castle is yours. Ignore me, and you will suffer as have those before you who dared to claim Castle Braeburn."

"You speak in cryptic riddles."

"Mayhap, but there is nothing cryptic about insurrection, is there?" When Colin did not answer, she laughed again before saying, "Now that I have your attention, Laird MacLachlan, mayhap you will be interested in what else I have to say."

"Mayhap."

"And mayhap you will remember that 'twas Gertie Graham who told you of it."

"I do not forget my allies."

"Nor your enemies?"

"Never my enemies."

Gertie Graham smiled as she sat on the windowsill where Jackie had been perched earlier. "Then, Laird MacLachlan, you shall forget nothing of what I am about to tell you, for I am about to tell you the names of your most treacherous enemies."

\*\*\*

The kitchen was vast, surprising Ashley, even though she had memories of the long years of working here and trying to stay out of everyone's sight. The ceilings of all four rooms were blackened with smoke as were the stone walls, especially around the hearths that were so tall Colin could have walked through without bending his head. People scurried everywhere, giving the kitchen the appearance of an ant hill.

In the midst of it all, Ashley sat at a well-worn table. Beathas, the chief cook, set a plate of scones in front of her, and Ashley took one. They would be delicious.

Beathas was a rawboned woman. Sweeping her white hair back from her forehead which was beaded with sweat from working at the half-dozen hearths ringing the room, she smiled and pushed a glass of warm milk toward Ashley.

"Tell me, milady," Beathas said, "what is disturbing you."

Ashley scanned the kitchens. No one else was within earshot. She was not sure whom she could trust, although Ella had told her more than once how often Beathas had saved Ashley from being discovered by Lord Stanton. "It's Charlie McAllister. I hear he's saying—things."

"Which everyone has heard, milady. He vows to rid Castle Braeburn of the laird. He hates anyone who denies that you have the best claim here."

"Do you think it would help if I talked to him?"

"To the laird? He is so bemused with you, he might allow Charlie to use him as a target if you asked."

She laughed, but when Beathas did not, she asked, "You're joking, aren't you?"

"About being a target? Of course." She glanced around, then lowered her voice. "Milady, don't you know what everyone else knows? The laird is fascinated with you."

"He's fascinated with solidifying his claim on Castle Braeburn." She put the scone on the table. "Should I talk to Charlie McAllister? I don't want anyone getting killed when only the Marquess of Argyll can settle this."

"If you go to Charlie, he shall think that the laird forced you to. That will make him even more unreasonable. Let the laird handle it."

Ashley's smile became more genuine. She leaned her elbows on the table, letting the full lace on her sleeves drop onto it. "I just want peace here. I'm tired of the tales of all the bloodshed."

"If that is true, you are in the wrong place, milady. There can be no place where the ground has absorbed more blood then the Highlands." She put her hands on the table and rose. "I must tend my gravies. Do not fret. It will come to be as it is meant to be."

Ashley stood and picked up the scone. "Thank you for listening, Beathas. I need good friends now."

"You have more friends than enemies, milady. Just open your eyes, and you shall see that."

While she went to her rooms, Ashley pondered Beathas's words. She had not guessed that she had so many allies, but she suspected Colin had. That would explain why he had sent word to the marquess so quickly. She wished she had not let Ella talk her into demanding that her claim be heard. If she was stuck in the 17th century, keeping things simple would have been better.

"Nothing's simple," she muttered as she opened her door. She called to Ella, but apparently Ella had not returned. Ella must have been delayed with her visit with her friend.

Ashley wondered who had placed her best gown on the bed. Picking it up, she sighed. It would not be easy to dress all by herself. If she could not reach the small hooks, she would have one of the serving lasses help her. She chuckled. She had quickly become accustomed to having a maid.

Drawing off her dress which was dusty from walking through the castle, she reached into her armoire for her light green robe. She wrapped it around her. Graceful lace outlined the deep neckline which showed off the top of her chemise. Forest green braid curled along the bodice and down the front of the skirt that was split to show her petticoats. When she walked, it flowed like sea foam across the floor.

She sat at the table and tilted the mirror, so she could see herself in its tiny surface. She knew a mirror was a luxury in this time. She picked up a comb and began to smooth her hair. When she had spoken of curling it, Ella had been so aghast at the thought of such vanity before the Covenanters, she had not made the suggestion again.

When the door opened, she did not turn. "How's your friend, Ella?"

She gasped when fiery lips caressed her nape. Her gaze met the laughter in Colin's eyes that were reflected in the mirror. As his fingers slipped along her shoulders, the dressing robe loosened. She held it closed, not wanting him to guess how easily it could open.

"What do you want, Colin? You should knock before coming in here."

His chuckle brushed her skin in an invitation to pleasure as he picked up the comb and ran it through her hair. "How beautiful your hair is, Ashley. Like fired gossamer." He grinned more broadly. "And to answer your question, I shall knock only when I wish. Castle Braeburn is my home."

"And mine!"

"Nay, for you are, while I wait to hear from the marquess, my guest."

"Even as a guest, don't I deserve some privacy?"

Dropping the comb, he slid his hands from her shoulders to her elbows and back. "Mayhap, but you shall not be a guest much longer."

Ashley stared at her own eyes in the mirror. They were dark in her pallid face. "Not much longer? Have you gotten another message from the marquess?"

"No."

"Then what has changed?"

"You, for you shall not be my guest when you are my wife."

She turned on the bench to face him. "Your wife? Are you insane?"

"Mayhap, but 'tis your choice, Ashley." He bent toward her. "I have learned that your allies have devised a plan which compels me to decide your fate. Now." Running a single finger along her cheek, he murmured, "To kill you would mean explaining your death to the marquess. Not a pleasurable prospect, so it would be better if you show that you are very accepting of your new laird."

Ashley stood and tightened the sash around her waist. "No."

"No?"

"What don't you understand? I don't want to marry you."

He seized her shoulders and tugged her into his arms. She stiffened as his mouth caressed her ear while he whispered, "Pretty one, if your father had lived, you would have been married to assure the future of Castle Braeburn. You shall do the same now."

"No!"

His lips traced a blazing line along her neck. "We can have fun together. Remember your delight when I held you by the loch?"

She pushed herself away. "I'm not going to marry you. I don't love you, Colin MacLachlan!"

"I do not love you, either!" He gathered her back against him. "What I do love is staying on this side of the grave. I have learned that your allies plan to slay me some night while I sleep. If I must stay awake to be on guard against them, I need something to keep me from sleeping. Why not you?"

Ashley was insulted and tired of being used. Maybe this was how things worked in the 17th century, but not for her. A slow smile slid across her lips. Two could play this game.

Slowly she edged out of his arms. When his eyes narrowed, she knew she was risking his wrath, but she went to her bed and picked up her gown. With her back to Colin, she untied the sash on her dressing robe.

As she shrugged the robe off her shoulders, he asked, "What are you doing?"

"I have to get ready for supper."

She faced him, amused by his shock. Her chemise fell past her knees, and her legs were covered by fine, white stockings. On any beach in her own time, she would have been overdressed. Maybe she could use his shock to put an end to this. "As we're betrothed, it shouldn't bother you to see me like this."

His gaze hungrily followed the lines of her body as he stepped toward her. He ran his hand over her bare shoulder. "Ashley," he whispered huskily as he drew her into his arms.

Her breath clogged in her throat. She had intended to laugh at his lust and shame it, but she could not spit the harsh words in his face. All she could do was delight in his touch.

"Pretty one," he murmured as his fingers tangled in her hair, "do not be foolish."

He tipped her head to bring her mouth to his, then bent her back to deepen the kiss. As he teased her softening lips, she ceded her mouth to him. His tongue's unhurried stroke against hers fascinated her, and she savored the taste of whisky which flavored his mouth. When his fingers encircled her breast beneath the lace, she dissolved to become part of the passion.

Her hands glided up his back, splaying across its breadth. When his finger teased the tip of her breast, she slipped her fingers beneath his doublet to stroke his bare back. He moaned with eager longing against her mouth.

Suddenly he stepped away. She did not understand why until she heard the watch calling the hour from the wall. Taking her hands, he kissed one, then the other. "Ashley, take care that you do not tempt me while you try to twist me to your desires. Remember this. I have very strong desires for you already." He brushed her lips with a light kiss before going to the door. His smile returned. "Do not forget that I have asked you to be my wife. It must prove that I want you in my bed, for there are limits to what even I will do to hold this castle."

She did not answer as his gaze moved along her once more. The heat racing through her veins was of embarrassment. He was right. Trying to humiliate him like this had been stupid.

When the door closed behind him, Ashley sat on the steps to her bed. He had wanted to make love with her here. He had wanted to, but he had not. She did not know if she should be happy that he had stopped or sorry that he had not continued. The only thing she was sure of was that she never had met a man as dangerous as Colin MacLachlan.

# SEVEN

As the evening meal began, Colin took Ashley's hand and brought her to her feet at the raised table in the great hall. She knew they were heading for trouble. Why was he being such a fool? Flaunting his plans like this was going to add to the hatred brewing among those who refused to accept him as the rightful laird.

All sound vanished as every eye turned in their direction. She clenched her hand, digging her nails into Colin's palm, but he smiled.

"I wish you to know," Colin called, his voice echoing in the high rafters, "that Lady Ashley has agreed to marry me one week from tomorrow."

She glanced at him, shocked. He had not said anything about the ceremony taking place. Why was he delaying? Eight days would give Charlie McAllister's men time to stew in their anger. Was Colin out of his mind? Or maybe she was. No matter how she tried to convince herself that he had not made love with her earlier because he cared for her, she knew it was not true. He had no interest in anything but keeping himself alive and securing his claim on Castle Braeburn.

When she tried to pull her hand out of his, he growled a warning and turned her to face him. In his eyes, an obsessive glow dimmed anything she had seen in them before. He *was* mad just like everyone in these blasted Highlands. Why had she ever wanted to come here? She almost laughed as she remembered how many times she had dreamed of being the lady of this castle. Now her dream—her nightmare—was exacting its vengeance, for Colin was willing to destroy her along with her allies.

The hall was as silent as a mausoleum. She shivered at that thought. Would he slay her if she refused to cooperate? She would be a fool to risk finding out.

"I am sure," Colin continued into the silence, "that all of you will share Lady Ashley's and my joy."

Captain Kilbride stood on the other side of Colin and lifted his glass. "A toast to Laird MacLachlan and his bride. Long life, my laird!"

Ashley recoiled from the triumph in Captain Kilbride's smile. This had been his idea! She should have guessed. He had been babbling about *bed and dead* from the day he arrived at Castle Braeburn. Using her to betray her father's men reeked of his manipulation.

Her shoulders sagged. It did not matter whose idea it had been. Colin was willing to force her into his bed to make sure he could claim the castle. By taking her as his wife, it did not matter how the marquess decided. Castle Braeburn would be Colin's.

A glass shattered by a doorway to the kitchen. A serving lass cried out, "No, milady, do not give yourself to him so he can take what is rightfully yours! If—" The girl was surrounded by several of Colin's men who herded her from the hall.

Ashley took a step to halt them, but Colin hooked his arm through hers, holding her in place. "Release me!" she hissed.

"Stay here, Ashley."

"Colin, if they hurt her, I—"

He gripped her face in one hand. "Silence, milady."

Trying to pull away, she retorted, "I shall say what I wish—"

"When I wish to hear it." He lowered his voice to a whisper as a rumble of rage raced around the room. "She shall not be harmed. I am not concerned with the opinion of one lass. 'Tis the ones who will act upon such thoughts who concern me."

"Then stop this!" she answered as quietly. "Can't you feel the hatred? It's going to explode."

She moaned as his voice rose again. "Nay, milady, 'tis I who shall explode when you give yourself to me as my wife." He stroked her cheek.

"Don't touch me like this!"

"Would you rather I touched you like this?" His fingers swept down toward her breast.

No! He must not make what had been so sweet another part of his scheme to force her to surrender the castle...and herself to him.

She raised her hand, but he caught her wrist before she could defend herself as she had against Captain Kilbride. When he leered at her, she wondered if some demon had possessed Colin MacLachlan.

A bench scraped the floor as it was shoved back. Charlie McAllister, a broad man whose face was scarred from battle, jumped to his feet, his hand on his knife. Several other men stood, too.

Colin ignored him as he ordered, "Give me no orders, woman. My wife shall be subservient to me as you acknowledge my claim on Castle Braeburn."

"Don't be stupid!" she shot back, looking from his superior smile to McAllister's fury. "Can't you see what is happening here?"

He pulled her up against him. His arms were a vise as he kissed her savagely. Her cry of betrayal was muted beneath his mouth.

When he released her, she rocked back on her heels. Her fingers rose to her bruised lips. "Leave me alone!" Her voice broke. "Why are you treating me like this?"

As his fingers sifted through her hair, he said so lowly only she could hear, "Because I must."

"No, you don't have to do this."

"If I want this castle, I must."

She wrenched herself away and cried, "I hope you and this castle rot in Hell, Colin MacLachlan!"

She shoved past him and strode across the hall toward the door closest to her room.

"Lady Ashley!" Colin shouted.

She kept walking.

"Lady Ashley, I would speak with you."

Closing her eyes, she took a deep breath, but did not slow.

"Lady Ashley, I would speak with you *now*."

Behind her, she heard steel being drawn. She could not let this hall become a battleground as it had the day her father had died. Turning, she saw every man on his feet, each one holding his *sgian-dubh* at ready. The small knives shone in the torchlight.

Colin forced his gaze from Ashley's face, although he would have enjoyed admiring the stubborn tilt of her chin even while furious tears glistened in her eyes. Swiftly, he noted which men glared at him and which were amused by his decision to solve the problem of who should hold the castle by marrying Gordon's daughter. He cursed silently. McAllister had more men allied with him than Colin had guessed.

"What do you want, Laird MacLachlan?" she asked, her voice sharp with fury.

Jackie elbowed him and laughed. "I thought that was obvious."

Another rumble of anger rushed through the hall like a great storm wind. Knowing he must stop it before it swept away all he was trying to hold, Colin shouted, "You have my leave to depart, Lady Ashley."

A flush stained her pale cheeks as she dipped in an insolent curtsy. Rising, she left without looking back. He heard her rapid steps along the passage.

Dropping into his seat, Colin called for a pint of ale. Thank heavens, Ashley was wise enough to know when to react and when to be silent. He glowered at Jackie. Why was his *an gille-coise*, a man he thought he could trust no matter what, acting like a consummate fool?

He sipped his ale as he listened to the uneven conversation in the hall. Good! The explosion, as Ashley had deemed it, would not happen here in the great hall tonight. He had wanted to make certain of that, so he had pushed the anger to the brink to judge its strength.

The astounding sound of a laugh jolted Colin. He glowered at Jackie who sat back and crossed his feet on the table.

"She is a very good ally, even though she does not want to be on our side," Jackie said quietly, so the servants bringing food would not overhear. He chuckled again. "Do you think she will be as fiery in your bed?"

In a voice he had never used with his friend, he said, "Be silent, Jackie, or I swear I shall break your jaw!"

With a curse, Jackie picked up his mug of ale. He did not speak again.

Colin sighed. He had thought, of all around him, Jackie would understand what he was doing, but he knew Jackie did not understand.

Not at all.

***

Ashley stormed out of her room. She could not endure Ella's whining about the wedding plans any longer. What did her maid expect her to do? She had already told Colin she did not want to marry him, and that had not changed his mind in the past week. If she had tried to put a halt to the hurried plans for a grand wedding in the castle's chapel overlooking the loch, she was not sure what Colin would have done. She no longer could guess how he would react to anything.

She had made her biggest mistake when she had thought Colin would behave like a civilized man. He was a 17th century Highlander. He had won the right to claim Castle Braeburn by slaying his enemies and exulted in that triumph. Now his victory was over her. His priorities were clear. He would marry her because he could use her to solidify his claim on this castle. If only she could get out of here and go back to her time! Then she would be able to forget him.

Who was she kidding? She could not forget his beguiling kiss and magical touch, no matter how many centuries lay between them. Not that she had savored either since the announcement of the wedding. She seldom saw Colin, and, when she did, he was as indifferent as if they were strangers, although he often watched her with an odd expression she could not decipher.

As she walked down the stairs, not sure where she was going, but just wanting to get away from all the talk of weddings, she swore under her breath when Captain Kilbride popped out of the shadows at the lower landing. He had not been the least bit reticent, taking every opportunity to show how he was looking forward to the ceremony.

"Good morning, sir," she said, moving to step around him.

He blocked her path. "You can address me as *Captain* Kilbride, milady, or as *an gille-coise*."

"Forgive me, but I can't see you as a captain leading these heathens. With your bandy legs, you would be trampled." She eyed him up and down. "Now as a henchman? Yes, that fits you and your sick ideas."

"Insult me, but it shall not change the truth."

She gave him her coolest smile. "Did you think I was insulting you? I thought I was speaking the truth."

As his face became as vivid a shade as his hair, he grasped her arm. "You may play games of words with me, but that is not what the laird will expect from you tomorrow night."

"That is none of your business." She tried to steady it, but her voice trembled.

With a laugh, he shoved her back against the wall. At her groan of pain, he smiled and turned to walk up the stairs. When he reached the upper landing, he called, so loudly it could be heard through both corridors, "Sleep well in your maidenly bed tonight, milady. Tomorrow night, you will learn what Colin MacLachlan demands from his women."

"Damn you," she whispered. "Damn both of you!"

"Milady?"

Ashley whirled. Seeing compassion on Davey Beaton's young face, she pushed past him. She did not want anybody's pity. She wanted to put an end to this madness. She hurried out into the sunshine, far from everyone.

For the first time, she realized it must have snowed overnight, because the courtyard was dusted with white. She shivered. She should go back inside because she was not wearing a cloak, but she did not want to face Captain Kilbride or Ella or Davey...or Colin.

She was walking toward the stables before she quite realized what she was doing. The memories that were hers and were not hers reminded her that Hume could be counted on to have a good shoulder to cry on. The old stableman had offered her one several times when she had been growing up, constantly apprehensive as she lived under Lord Stanton's rule.

"Hume?" Ashley called as she entered the twilight stables. It was not much warmer in here. She shivered and stamped her feet on the crackling hay.

Looking about in bafflement, she heard only the animals in their stalls. Where was everyone? The stables appeared deserted. That was impossible. There was always someone working in them.

Footsteps sounded behind her. Before she could turn, she was seized from behind. A heavy arm around her waist tightened to keep her from taking a breath to scream. A sweaty palm covered her mouth.

Disgusting material was stuffed in her mouth. She fought not to gag as a bag was slipped over her head. Someone picked her up, surprisingly gently. Her hands were caught and held as she tried to pull the bag off her head.

She was carried out into the cold. The wind cut through the bag to chafe her cheeks. They entered another building, and she was placed on her feet.

Ashley pulled the bag off and stared at a stone wall. It could be any outbuilding within the walls of Castle Braeburn. When the gag was untied, she was turned to look across the room.

A score of men dropped to their knees. Horror knotted her stomach when she saw Charlie McAllister among them. These were the men who refused to accept Colin's possible claim on the castle. A few women were gathered at the far end of the room, but she paid them no mind as she asked, "What is the meaning of this?"

"Forgive me, milady, for such rough treatment," McAllister said as he rose. The others followed like dancers in a chorus line. "We must speak to you and did not wish to be overheard."

"So you abducted me?"

Kneeling, he raised her fingers to his forehead. "We are yours, milady. Once we belonged to your father, but he was laid low by English duplicity. We do not wish to see his daughter forced to share her bed with a man who claims what is rightly hers."

"No more bloodshed." She pulled her hand away. She glanced at the walls of whatever shed they had commandeered. Nothing told her which one it was. "I want no part of what you've planned."

His servility disappeared as he rose to tower over her. Venom deepened his bass voice. "Does your Gordon blood grow thin, milady?"

"Laird MacLachlan is our clansman."

"Then why would he force you into this marriage?"

Ashley faltered on her answer. She had asked herself that so many times over the past week. If Colin would accept her as an equal, they could figure out a way to keep peace within the walls of Castle Braeburn. She could not guess why he wanted to bring the war here. Had he become so inured to battle that he knew no other way?

"Will you docilely go to Colin MacLachlan's bed?" McAllister persisted.

"I don't want to marry Colin MacLachlan!"

McAllister smiled. "Then say the word, milady, and—"

"Heed me," Ashley said. Bloodlust distorted the faces of these men, astounding her because she had not guessed they would raise their swords against their own clansmen. This did not make any sense, but what *had* made since she had arrived in Castle Braeburn? These men must be stopped. If not, the castle would be destroyed along with everyone within it. Softly she asked, "Am I your lady? Do I have your fealty?"

"Of course," came McAllister's immediate response.

"Will you do as I say? Will you follow me as you followed my lord father?"

A cheer answered her. Looking at their eager faces, she knew they were waiting for her to give the order to begin the battle that would leave Colin's allies' corpses fit only for ravens.

"Speak to me of your loyalty," she said in the same quiet voice. "Are you mine? Do you follow my lead?"

McAllister knelt once more, his men following. Bowing his head before her, he repeated as if it were an oath, "We are yours, Lady Ashley Gordon. We follow you to the death."

She nodded as if to acknowledge an indisputable fact, but fought to keep her shoulders stiff so they could not see her shiver of disgust at the vow. *To the death* would not gain them anything but a grave. Hoping they would obey her, she said, "Then I tell you it is my wish that you do nothing now."

The men began to protest, but McAllister raised his arms for silence. Coming to his feet, he asked, "What hold does MacLachlan have on you, milady?"

"He is our clansman."

"He dares to claim what is yours." He eyed her up and down.

"Which I have told the Marquess of Argyll in a message that was sent to him the day after Laird MacLachlan's arrival."

"Are you sure that it was given into the hand of the marquess himself?"

"Yes," she said, although she was not certain of that. To admit the truth might add to McAllister's fury. "We must await his decision."

From beneath his doublet, McAllister pulled a sheath. He knelt and held it up to her.

Ashley gazed at the weapon. Its blade, hidden by the leather covering, must be ten inches long. When he placed it in her hand, her fingers curled around the haft. A fury that was frighteningly familiar gripped her, threatening to smother her.

She raised the knife over her head as words poured from her lips. "To the memory of my father and to Lady Ashley Gordon who will rule Castle Braeburn!"

A roar of excitement answered as the men surged to their feet. It froze her heart in the middle of a beat, but she cheered along with them. She wanted to silence her voice. It refused to obey her.

*Go away!* she cried in silence.

*When you have done what you must do*, came the horrid voice within her.

Ashley winced as the shouts ached through her skull along with the exultant laughter that she had heard when the voice took control of her before. *No! Go away!*

"Tell us how to serve you, milady!"

She glanced at McAllister. She fought her lips, but felt her smile dissolve into the sly expression of a cat on the prowl. She drew the long blade from the sheath, letting it flash in the motes of sunlight sneaking through the boarded windows.

"Let the wedding ceremony take place." She waved aside their protests. "Hear me! Think of Laird MacLachlan coming to his bride. As he presses her to his bed, she shall press this into him."

Ashley slashed downward. The blade caught her full skirt and tore it. The men cheered, and she looked from her ripped skirt to them...and beyond. Her gaze was caught by Gertie Graham's dark eyes which were crinkled with laughter.

Gertie was at the back of the room with the women who were shouting along with their men, but Ashley noted that none of the women stood too close to Gertie. That the woman Ella claimed was a witch was mixed up in this did not astonish Ashley, because Gertie had made her opinion of Colin known the day Ashley was returned to Castle Braeburn.

*Was returned?* Was she beginning to believe this nonsense about witchcraft? The laughter rose to a shriek in her head.

Slowly she lowered the knife as she put her other hand to her forehead. As the knife crossed between her eyes and Gertie's, a more vicious pain riveted her and the laughter faded. Horror filled her. What had she done? *She* had not done anything, but, if she tried to explain that now, she would be deemed mad.

Maybe she was not alone in her madness. The men were laughing in jubilation at her words. With a shudder, she knew Colin dying in his wedding bed appealed to these men.

McAllister did not join in the jests. Quietly he ordered, "Hide the knife, milady, before you return to the keep."

"Where would I hide it?"

His laugh was tight, and she saw his eyes burned with the same intensity as Gertie Graham's. "Put it in your garter."

"Turn your back," Ashley said, because she knew they would expect that.

McAllister repeated her order to his men. Obediently they turned away.

Ashley lifted her skirt and petticoats. Her skin crawled as she slid the sheath beneath the ribbons holding her black stockings in place. Her hands clenched as she fought to control her heaving stomach. Somehow, without betraying these men, she had to warn Colin.

A blindfold was wrapped over her eyes as she straightened. McAllister said softly, "Say nothing, milady. It would be too dangerous for you to know where we meet."

"Don't you trust me?" she asked, pulling down the cloth before he could tie it.

"'Tis MacLachlan we do not trust. We do not trust him not to put you to torture to force information from you."

"Colin wouldn't do that to me!" When she saw the disbelief on the men's faces, she argued, "He knows he has to wait to hear from the marquess."

"Be that as it may," McAllister said, "we ask that you cover your eyes. Where we are is something no one beyond our small number from the stables must know."

"But you let Gertie Graham in."

"Gertie Graham?" He spat a curse. "She is not welcome here."

Ashley turned and said, "No? She is back there..." She scanned the room, but Gertie was gone.

"You are mistaken, milady. That old crone would find no welcome here."

She had seen Gertie. She was certain of that...Or was she? When she had looked into Gertie's eyes, she had been in the hold of that hateful voice. She pressed her hands over her fiercely beating heart. That voice rang only in her head, and now maybe it was making her see things that were not truly there.

When McAllister held up the cloth, she let him tie it around her head. The trip back to the stable was quick. She was placed on her feet, but the blindfold was not untied. As she heard footsteps receding, she undid the knot and tossed it to the floor.

She was alone.

Ashley went out into the courtyard, but saw nothing amiss. With a shiver, she hurried into the keep and up the stairs. She had to hide this knife until she could think of a way to dispose of it. As she rushed along the upper corridor, she heard her name called.

Clenching her hands, she turned to meet a cool blue gaze. "Yes, Colin?"

He walked toward her until he stood so close that she had to bend her head back to see his eyes gleaming in the candlelight. He bent to kiss her cheek. "So cold? Have you been outside?"

Fearful he had someone spying on her, she said, "I went to the stables. With all the work for the—the—"

"The wedding?" he supplied with a laugh.

"Yes!" His attitude was intolerable. "I've been very busy, Colin, to insure this unwanted wedding is a success."

His hands rested on her shoulders. Easily he drew her closer. Although she wanted to ignore his strong muscles, they exerted an intoxicating attraction she could not deny. "Unwanted? What makes you say that?"

"You don't want to marry me! I don't want to marry you."

"You are half right. Being married to you, Ashley, would not be the worst fate a man could know."

She fought to keep from laughing, but it was impossible. "You're a most unromantic bridegroom."

"Am I? I must remedy that."

His arms swept around her. Slowly his mouth lowered to hers, so slowly she thought she would shout out her frustration. She wanted him to kiss her.

With eager desire, he sought to relearn every secret inside her mouth. Far deeper within her, the pulse accelerated. Her eyes closed in soft surrender when his lips burned along her neck. As he bent her back to enable him to follow the lace of her gown's neckline, she moaned in unfettered yearning.

"Colin!" she gasped as his mouth explored the curve of her breast above her chemise. His moist tongue created a luminescence in her.

With a soft chuckle, he teased her ear. "Is that romantic enough for you? 'Tis no more than a sample of all I wish to do when you lie in my arms tomorrow night."

Stepping back, she whispered, "Colin, there still is time to stop the wedding."

"You do not wish to marry me?"

"No."

"Or enjoy what we could in the laird's bed?" When she faltered on her answer, he laughed. "At least, you are being honest about that, *belovit*."

"Do not call me that."

"Would you rather that I show you how I would be loving you?"

"Colin, you know this is wrong."

"Is it?" He smoothed the shoulders of her dress back into place.

Until then, she had not noticed how he had drawn it along her arms with his eager kisses. As her gaze rose to meet his, he brushed her lips with a fiery kiss. The need for more swept all other thoughts from her head.

"Pretty one," he breathed into her hair. "Pretty one, look at me."

She opened her eyes as she stroked his cheek. "Yes?"

"Remember that I do as I must, pretty one."

"As you must?" Coldness sank through her as she heard how his voice had changed from gentle to hard. "What—?"

He pushed her roughly against the wall, and his mouth clamped over hers. Raising her hands, she turned her face away. "Colin! Stop! You're hurting me!"

The savage sound returned to his laugh as he recaptured her mouth. He held her wrists in one hand while his other slid along her neckline. She stared up at him and wondered what had happened to the sweet caresses of moments ago.

"You dare to order me?" he snarled.

She tried to pull away, but the wall kept her from escaping him. With a growl, he shoved her aside, an expression of revulsion on his face. She started to whirl away. Her foot caught in her ripped skirt, and she dropped to her knees. She waited for Colin to speak, but, as his gaze moved past her, she looked over her shoulder to see a man walking rapidly away. She could not see who it was, but, from Colin's taut face, she guessed he knew.

"Go to your rooms, Ashley," Colin ordered with a sigh. He held a hand out to her. "Let me help you to your feet."

"I don't want your help!"

"Take it, Ashley."

She considered disobeying, but put her fingers on his hand. She tensed as he brought her to her feet. Pain raced along her right hip. As she pressed her hand to it, she felt his hands on her skirt. She gasped and edged away, then realized he was brushing dirt off it.

"When did you rip your gown?" he asked as he held up the tattered material.

She did not dare to hesitate. "In the stable."

"Is that so?" His eyebrows drew together. "Would you like to try another lie?"

Her frustration became a rage that was all her own. Stepping around him, she spat, "Go to hell, Colin MacLachlan!"

Colin watched Ashley race away. He had wondered if she would understand what he meant. It seemed she did not. A brand of sorrow burned through him with the power of the passion she created within him.

With a soundless sigh, he turned toward the stairs. There were plans he had to see were completed before the wedding ceremony tomorrow. Everything must be perfect. If not, Ashley would suffer the most, and he doubted if there would be anything he could do to prevent it.

# EIGHT

Ashley stood before the small mirror in her bedchamber. The warm color of her deep blue dress contrasted with the iciness in her middle. She touched the pearls strung through her hair which had been brushed until it captured the glow of the fire on the hearth. No white gown, no veil, no flowers, no groom who loved her. No wonder she did not feel like a bride.

Why had Colin decided to wait so late in the day for this wedding ceremony? Maybe it was some bizarre Scot custom. Or, and her fingers locked together so tightly they hurt, it was because he did not want to chance anything happening before he could bring her to the privacy of his rooms down the hall.

She touched her lips. His kisses thrilled her, and his touch beguiled her into believing he might truly care about her. When she was in his arms and he murmured of his desire for her, she longed to satisfy the passion they could savor.

"But not like this!" she whispered.

Walking away from the mirror, Ashley gazed out the small spot on the window that was not covered with frost. The glimmering of the stars was bright. Somehow she had thought Colin would stop this before now.

He had not.

She would have to marry Laird Colin MacLachlan, a man she did not know, a man who baffled her. She had thought she knew all about men from working with them at the construction company. Colin confused her more with every passing day. He treated her sweetly when they were alone, but, when others were near, he was cruel. Which man was the true Colin MacLachlan?

*Ashley, you know the truth.*

She spun around. No one else was in the room. That was no surprise, for the voice was the one that was as gentle as a passing breeze's caress and only in her head. Seeing the sparkles dancing in the middle of the room, she sat on the steps to the bed.

She closed her eyes. *I don't know the truth. I am so confused.*

The answering laugh was melodic. *That is because you are thinking with what you learned in your other life. You must look through the eyes of the woman you are now.*

*I don't know that either.*

*You are Ashley Gordon, beloved daughter.*

*I was Ashley Babcock until just a few weeks ago.*

*You are Ashley Gordon, beloved daughter.*

Shaking her head, Ashley opened her eyes. The sparkles nearly filled the room, although none touched her. It was as if she had been lifted up to become a part of the star-encrusted night. She raised her hand and watched the sparkles flow around it. She smiled at the sensation that reminded her of minnows nibbling against her toes in a stream.

*Who are you?*

The sparkles gathered together and vanished.

She jumped to her feet and called, "Come back! I didn't mean to frighten you away. You don't need to answer if you don't want to."

"Milady?"

At Ella's startled question, Ashley whirled to look at her astonished maid. Ella's face was damp with tears, but her eyes were wide.

"Who are you talking to?" asked Ella.

"Myself," she lied.

"Yourself? You were awaiting an answer from yourself?"

"Pay no mind to me at the moment. I am distressed." That was most certainly the truth.

Ella nodded, and Ashley wondered if she could ever submerge her curiosity as Ella had. The old woman said, "He sent me to tell you that the time has come for the ceremony, milady."

Ashley walked toward the door, pausing to stare at the sheathed knife on the table by her bed. Over it came the image of Colin's face coming closer as she waited for the joy of his mouth on hers. She winced as she imagined her hand sweeping down with that knife toward the man who brought her so much pleasure amidst this madness.

"No, I can't!" she whispered.

"You cannot marry him?" Ella asked in a shaking voice which was raw with grief. "I know that is the truth in your heart, but—"

"No, I don't mean that."

"Then, what do you mean, milady?"

"It isn't important." She squared her shoulders. "Smile, Ella. How many times have you told me that I should have a husband to make me happy? Now it seems that I shall have one."

The old woman bit back a sob. "This is not how I imagined you marrying, milady."

"Nor I." She sighed. "There is no sense lurking here. If we are late, it might make matters worse."

"Milady, if you take this..." Ella picked up the knife and handed it to Ashley. "Put it in your garter, so you might have it for later."

"You expect me to slay Colin?"

"Your father and mother never shied away from what they had to do."

Ashley wondered why Ella's voice sounded so odd. She had guessed that Ella would be appalled at seeing this knife in her lady's hand. "Nor will I shy away," she said. She slipped the knife under her gown. It would stay there until she could find a way to get rid of it.

"Then you should not shy away from Charlie McAllister's plan."

"McAllister? How do you know of that?" Her heart threatened to stop beating. If Ella had heard of the plot, had Colin?

"Do not ask, milady." Ella closed her eyes as two more tears ran along her face.

Ashley took pity on her maid and asked no more questions as they walked to the chapel, which was set into the wall above the loch. She had peeked into it during one of her explorations of the castle with Mr. Campbell, but had not visited it in this time. It was a simple room with a few stone pews set in front of a raised altar. No stained glass blocked the view of the loch.

As they went through the hallways, she saw nobody else, but suspected the shadowed doorways hid many silent observers. Not many of the household had been invited to attend the ceremony. Everything had been arranged to assure that she would not be able to stop this marriage from taking place and being consummated.

The plain wooden doors of the chapel were thrown open. Music sifted out, surprising her. She had not guessed that Colin had arranged for anything but a minister and the needed witnesses.

A lone figure waited by the door. With easy insolence, Captain Kilbride bowed as he moved so Ella could go inside. Then he stepped in front of the door again and said, "Good evening, milady. 'Tis a fine night for a bride to become a wife."

She gave him her coldest smile. If she was being forced to marry this man, she would not have hesitated to bring that knife to their bed. Captain Kilbride would be satisfied with nothing less than degrading her completely.

He held out his arm. "Milady?"

"If you will step aside, I will enter."

"The laird has requested that I be your escort as your father, whoever he might be, is not here to do so."

"No, thank you."

"I misspoke. 'Twas not a request the laird made, but an order." He grabbed her hand and pressed it to his sleeve.

Ashley knew she would be a fool to argue further. This was one fight she had no hopes of winning. Maybe later... "I suspect this wedding was your idea."

"I wish I could say that it was, although I was the first to suggest to the laird upon our arrival that letting you sleep alone was silly."

"If it was not your idea..." She gulped, unable to speak the words that clogged her throat. She had wanted to believe that Colin did not despise her so, but she had been wrong. He would do anything to obtain the best claim on this castle.

As Captain Kilbride drew her through the doors, a haunting melody roiled along her sense. Bagpipes! She had always loved their untamed songs and, as a child, had looked forward to the Scottish bagpipe and drum corps performing in Fourth of July parades.

Had that been her childhood or someone else's? She looked toward the front of the chapel and swallowed her moan. If she married Colin tonight, all chances of holding onto that part of her which was Ashley Babcock might be lost. She heard gasps from the congregation as she stopped between the two rows of stone pews.

She could not risk being stuck in this time forever. Her childhood wish to be a princess in this castle had been perverted by the reality surrounding these men who would do anything to obtain their wishes.

Captain Kilbride tugged on her arm, and she began to walk again by his side. She had to marry Colin, for she knew of no way to stop it. Until she could find a way to go home—

*You are home. See the truth around you.*

Ashley closed her eyes as the warmth that accompanied that voice enfolded her like loving arms. The comfort was precious, but she wished the voice would stop talking in riddles. Castle Braeburn might be home, but the truth wore many guises within it.

A hand took hers, and that warmth deepened into a flame. She opened her eyes to look up into Colin's sapphire eyes. The heat that was coursing through her seemed to have its source deep within them.

*See the truth around you.*

"Good evening, milady," Colin murmured as he placed her hand on his arm and drew her up to stand beside him by the raised altar.

"Good evening." There was nothing else she could say. The time to demand that he explain why he was doing this had passed.

As the thin minister picked up his book to intone the wedding service, a cold finger jabbed into Ashley's side. She glanced down and bit back a shriek. The end of a long barreled pistol pressed into her gown, hidden by the thick lace at Captain Kilbride's wrist. Her gaze rose to his innocuous face. No one looking at him would guess he would slay the bride if she balked.

Jackie Kilbride grinned with triumph as Lady Ashley's face blanched. He was determined that she would not forget her part in this charade. As he had joked with his men, he would live up to his name—Kill bride—if she did not cooperate now. She had been too compliant this week, and he did not trust that.

When he had mentioned his distrust, Laird MacLachlan had laughed. "Ashley? Faith, Jackie, she is so confused, she does not know if I want to marry her because I cannot sleep for thinking of having her in my bed or simply to make sure Argyll has an easy solution to this dilemma of the claim on the castle."

"And which is the true reason you have asked her to be your wife?"

The laird's gaze had grown icy cold. Jackie had seen that expression too many times to let it daunt him as it did others, but he knew better than to continue an argument when that frozen fire seared the laird's blue eyes.

And Laird MacLachlan had never answered that question.

With a silent curse that was out of place in the chapel, Jackie shoved the pistol viciously into the tender spot beneath Lady Ashley's ribs. He knew he was hurting her. He had not missed Laird MacLachlan's admiration of this woman while Jackie escorted her along the aisle. If the laird had been caught within her spell, his craving for her could destroy them all.

*Damn woman!*

Ashley bit her lip as Captain Kilbride muttered something under his breath. She could not cry out her pain, or he might fire that gun. She looked at Colin. His strong profile did not give her any clues if he knew what his friend was doing. If he sensed her gaze on him, he did not acknowledge it. He appeared to be listening to the minister as if the words of the wedding rite were ones he had never heard before.

A sliver of fear cut into her as the minister turned to her and began to read the wedding vows. When Colin brought her to face him, the pistol dug into the center of her back. She stared at the design on the plaid draped across Colin's chest. His fingers under her chin brought her face up. As the pastor asked if Colin would love and protect her through sickness and health, through bad times and good, Colin's blue eyes twinkled.

"Do I promise to love her?" A strange fervency entered his voice. "Till death do us part."

Fear strangled her. His words were a threat.

"Lady Ashley?" prompted the minister.

She broke out of her terror to ask, "What?"

Colin answered, "Milady, he asks you to answer 'I do.'" His eyes burned into her. "Tell him that you promise to love and succor me until the day you die."

She looked from Colin to the minister. If she replied as Colin wanted, her life would be enmeshed with his forever. Since her arrival here, she had learned how long forever could be. She watched Colin's eyes change to an angry gray, and the gun's barrel stabbed into her back.

Stepping away from Captain Kilbride, Ashley spat, "No! I won't marry you!"

She heard a click.

Colin pushed her away as his hand slashed down, knocking Captain Kilbride's gun aside. "Do not be a fool, Jackie!" Turning, he grasped Ashley's shoulders. "And you should not be a fool either. Marry me."

"No! I won't marry you!"

A cheer seconded her defiance. The men in the back pew leapt to their feet. Charlie McAllister stood in front of a dozen men. Their muskets were aimed at Colin, an easy target on the altar.

Screams echoed as the few guests dove for safety beneath the pews.

Ashley stared at the men. By refusing to obey Colin, she had played into McAllister's bloody hands.

"Move aside, milady," McAllister called. "We shall make sure he never touches you again!"

"You can't shoot him!" She raised her arms. "Lower your weapons!"

"Move aside, milady," he repeated in a colder voice.

"No, you can't—"

"Move aside, milady, or you shall die as well." He stared past her to Colin who had not moved. "He has bewitched you, milady. You are no true daughter of Gordon if you plead for this cur's life." The men raised their guns as McAllister shouted, "Move, milady, before I count to three."

She could not obey. Her feet were soldered to the steps by her terror.

"One—two—"

Pain swelled through Ashley as she was thrust to the floor. A scream burst from her before her breath was squeezed out by someone lying atop her.

The second sharp explosion of gunfire resounded. She hid her face against the floor as she tried to breathe. As the last shot faded into silence, she wondered if the person atop her was alive or dead. Her stomach threatened to revolt at that thought.

The heaviness shifted, and a hand jerked her to her feet. Hastily she brushed her dress back down along her legs, then looked up to realize Colin had been pinning her to the floor. Seeing the holes in the altar behind them, she knew he had saved her life.

"Colin—" she began.

"Not now," he ordered through clenched teeth, then shouted orders. He leaned on her, his arm across her shoulders becoming an iron bar.

At the back of the chapel, several of Colin's men bent toward the floor. Ashley shuddered. McAllister's men must be dead. Again her stomach twisted.

Involuntarily she gasped in pain as Colin tilted her face up again. His eyebrows on his surprisingly pale face came together as he handed her a handkerchief. "You have blood on your chin, Ashley. You do not want it to drip on your pretty gown."

"Thank you." She winced as she placed the cloth over the scraped area.

"Are you otherwise injured?"

She shook her head, not trusting her voice.

Although she wanted to ask him the same question, for his face was growing grayer, he did not give her a chance. He turned to Captain Kilbride. "Jackie, your men did a fine job."

"Aye, they did well. Thank you, Laird MacLachlan." He pointed at Ashley. "Shall I rid you of *her*?"

Colin shook his head, wincing. "I shall see to Lady Ashley myself." After giving Captain Kilbride orders to clean up the chapel, he thanked the minister.

The clergyman rose from behind the altar. "You are quite welcome to my assistance whenever you require it, Laird MacLachlan."

Colin followed the minister's gaze to Ashley's drawn face. Fury strengthened him when he saw the blood on her face. Pain erupted along his right leg, like a stroke of lightning beneath his flesh, but he forced himself to stand straighter. "You might want to say a few words over the dead. There shall be no wedding."

Ashley's eyes widened with astonishment. Like an angel she was. An angel...His eyes tried to focus as he fought the shriek of a high wind rumbling in his ears to comprehend what the minister was saying.

"I understood that from the beginning," he heard the minister say. "Curse these madmen!" He shook his head with despair as he stared at the altar that was pockmarked with bullet holes.

"Thank you for com—"

Ashley cried, "Colin!" as he sagged against her. Her knees buckled. He groaned in agony. She wrapped her arms around him, but fell to the floor beneath him.

Captain Kilbride leapt over a pair of pews and called for help. Ripping off his plaid, he draped it over Colin. As the other men helped him lift Colin, who was senseless, to a pew, he ignored Ashley. She knew he did not care if she was hurt or not.

With her hand on another bench, Ashley stood slowly. Every muscle protested. Shaken, she could not stifle her moan when she saw blood on her gown. It must be Colin's, for it stained her skirt where he had been against her.

She tried to shove through the crowd encircling Colin. The men abruptly stepped aside. She stared at the gun that was again in Captain Kilbride's hand. He pointed it at her as a woman screamed at the back of the chapel.

Ashley did not move. If she reached for the knife in her garter, he would fire.

"You have played my laird false for the last time!" Captain Kilbride snarled.

Colin commanded in a strained voice, "Put the damn gun away, Jackie. 'Twas not her fault I was too slow."

Ashley wanted to rush to him, to find out how badly he was wounded, but the hammer on the gun clicked back when she moved.

Captain Kilbride said, "My laird—"

"Put it away, Jackie." Colin cursed under his breath as he tried to sit and failed. "I think it would be a good idea if you help me out of the chapel. I do not want the good pastor to hear what I shall utter when the doctor fishes this lead from me."

Reluctantly Jackie lowered the gun and turned to his men. "Take the laird to his rooms."

"A moment," Colin said. He looked up at Ashley. "Do not greet, *belovit*."

"'Greet?'" she whispered, as she knelt by the pew.

His laugh was a shadow of its customary thunder. "Do not cry. I shall be fine."

"Only if you see the doctor. We can talk later, Colin. Get yourself taken care of first."

"Aye." He placed his hand against her cheek, and she put hers over it.

She stood aside when Captain Kilbride tugged on her arm. He could not hide his outrage at his laird's clemency, but he ordered, "Take care, my lads, with the laird." He followed the men, but paused as he reached the last pew. Facing her, he smiled. "I hope you have made a good bargain with the devil, milady."

Her voice quaked as she asked, "What do you mean?"

"Attempted murder will send you back to Hell where you belong."

"I did nothing wrong."

"I shall see you dead!"

"Colin knows I was not—"

He laughed. "Mayhap he does, but, if the laird dies, I vow that you shall not live to see his successor."

# NINE

When Captain Kilbride stormed through the chapel door, Ashley started to follow, then dropped to sit on a pew. Her trembling legs refused to hold her. And there was no need to hurry. She would not be welcome in Colin's rooms.

"Come, milady. You must get out of that bloody dress."

She looked at Ella and nodded. Pushing herself to her feet, she gripped the back of the pew as she looked around the chapel. All the witnesses had fled, and the only sign of the ceremony was the ruined altar.

Was this disappointment she was feeling? Impossible! But how else could she explain the emptiness that ached inside her? It might be the residues of her fear, or it might be sorrow that the ceremony had been interrupted.

*Are you out of your mind?* she asked herself as she went with Ella back to her own rooms. She did not want to be married to that arrogant, overbearing Scot. Yet, she could not ignore that she was beguiled by his kisses. How much more thrilling would his touch have been in his bed? *You are out of your mind. That's for sure.*

*See the truth around you.*

Ashley did not bother to look for the speaker, for it was the gentle voice in her mind. Even if she saw the sparkles that accompanied it, she had no energy to ask the questions she did not want to face while Captain Kilbride's fury still resonated through her. Colin had been shot in the leg, she guessed from the blood on her dress. That would not be a fatal wound...in her time. In this time, she was not so sure. If Colin had not pushed her aside, she might be hurt worse or dead.

That McAllister had threatened to shoot her, too, had been a shock. She had not thought he and his men hated Colin so much that they would risk murdering her as well. It showed her how little she understood the men of this era. Her lessons were becoming more costly.

In her rooms, Ashley drew off her gown. She reached for her dressing gown, then froze. Where was the knife that had been stuck in her garter? If it had fallen out, Captain Kilbride might find it. He would quickly discover McAllister had given it to her.

"I wish I had left it here," she murmured.

"Left what here?" asked Ella.

"That damned knife you told me to take with me."

Ella stared at her with an expression of disbelief. "I do not know what you are speaking of, milady."

"But you said..." Ashley let her breath sift out through her teeth. This confusion was becoming too commonplace. It was as if the castle's whole household were still caught up in the spell supposedly cast by the late Lady Gordon. She pulled on her dressing gown and shivered. Maybe it was.

Ashley paced as she waited for water to be brought to clean her bloody hands. When Ella tried to talk to her, she motioned the old woman to silence. She did not want to answer questions about the knife. She wanted to know how Colin fared. She strained to hear the knock that might bring tidings.

The door opened, and she spun with anticipation, but it was only a maid carrying a canister of warm water. The girl did not look at her as she put down the container and hurried away.

"Come here, milady," Ella said as she dipped a cloth into the water and wrung it out.

Ashley nodded, but froze as footfalls neared her door. They hurried past.

"Ramsey will send word to you, milady. He is a man of honor and knows that you are fretting."

"Maybe I should go and check for myself."

"No!" Ella dropped the cloth and gripped Ashley's arms, startling her. "You must not give the laird any reason to slay you when Charlie McAllister has offered him too many already."

"I knew nothing of Charlie McAllister's plans to bring guns to the chapel."

Ella glanced toward the door, then lowered her voice. "But you knew of Charlie McAllister's discontent."

"Yes."

"That is enough to condemn you in many eyes, milady." Picking up the cloth, she dabbed at Ashley's chin. "Take care, for there are some here who would gladly see you as dead as your father."

"Who?"

"You know." Ella's eyes narrowed as she made that strange symbols in the air.

"Gertie Graham?"

"Hush, milady."

Ashley stepped away before Ella could finish washing the blood from her face. "Gertie helped my mother send me—" She clamped her lips shut.

"Send you where? You have never lived beyond these walls."

"Send me to you for safety," she improvised, hoping she was right.

Ella nodded with a sigh. "That is true."

Closing her eyes, Ashley said, "I should redress right away in case—"

The door crashed against the wall. Captain Kilbride swaggered into the room.

Icily, she demanded, "Yes, Captain?"

"The laird wishes to see you."

"He's alive?" She smiled and clasped Ella's hand.

"You act very happy for a woman who tried to get him murdered," Captain Kilbride said.

"If you would use what little brains you were given, you would know I don't wish to see Colin dead."

He stepped closer, his eyes cutting into her. "Why? Because you love him?"

Ashley edged back and bumped into the steps to her bed. Even if she knew the state of her puzzled heart, she would not speak of it to *this* man. She walked to the window and looked out at the snow falling gently from clouds that had swallowed the starlight.

He chuckled. "You have no answer? Where is that quick wit my laird raves about until I think I shall go daft? Mayhap it is true that Lady Ashley Gordon has fallen in love with the man who wants to deny her this castle."

"My feelings for Colin are none of your business. Nothing you say or do will change them."

"You misunderstand." At his triumphant laugh, she whirled to look at him. "Love him. Give him your heart. Give him whatever you wish. Then I shall enjoy it even more when the marquess banishes you to the prison you deserve. It shall be amusing to see you broken when you are taken away from Castle Braeburn in chains."

Appalled, she said nothing. She wanted to see how Colin fared. She reached into the clothes press to pull out another dress.

Captain Kilbride seized her wrist and twisted her toward the door. At her cry of pain, he said, "I said the laird wants to see you now, Lady Ashley."

"I'm not dressed to go about the castle. Give me a few minutes, and I—"

He laughed. "The laird wants to speak to you *now*. 'Tis time you learned to obey Laird MacLachlan."

When he pulled on her arm, Ashley did not balk. She wanted to discover how Colin was doing, but she was tired of being ordered about by this pipsqueak with a bad attitude. She did not speak to Ella who stood to one side. The maid wrung her skirt and whispered prayers for her lady's safety as Ashley went to the door. From Ella's expression, that added years to her face, it was clear she expected never to see her lady alive again.

Ashley walked calmly by Captain Kilbride's side. She would not give him the satisfaction of seeing her fear. If she let him think he had frightened her, she would never be able to bluff her way out of a confrontation with him again.

Opening the door to Colin's rooms, Captain Kilbride pushed her inside. Her eyes blurred with tears of happiness when she saw Colin standing in the middle of the large room.

"Colin!" she cried. "You're up!"

He stepped out from behind an ornately carved chair. Bloody bandages swathed his right leg from below the knee to past the hem of his kilt. His face was still a peculiar gray beneath its bronzing. He held tightly onto the chair, letting it support him.

"Come in. Sit down." He pointed to the chair next to where he stood. When she did, he added, "Jackie, I wish to speak to Lady Ashley privately."

"Are you sure?" Captain Kilbride glowered at her, and she returned his frown.

He smiled. "Do you doubt that I cannot subdue this lass if she decides to make more trouble? I shall speak with you later."

The captain nodded, saying nothing. Silence settled on the room when the door closed behind him.

Ashley stared at Colin. She longed to ask how he was doing, if he was okay, what the doctor had said. When she met his blue gaze, she saw that his internal strength had not diminished. His face might be lined with pain, but he remained determined to hold this castle.

When a smile eased across his lips, she could not keep from smiling back. He held out his hand, and she put hers in it. He raised it to his lips. His kiss was a succulent fire that raced through her, melting the ice of her fear.

"Did my summons interrupt you, Ashley?" His gaze slipped along her. "You look most deliciously undressed."

She pulled her dressing gown closed at her throat. When she saw his gaze drop, she realized her bare legs were visible where her robe had come open. She flipped one side over the other, and he chuckled.

"You would be a gentleman not to notice," she said primly. Although she had shown off more of her legs in a pair of shorts when she had been Ashley Babcock, his eager reaction disconcerted her, reminding her how she had been about to marry him such a short time ago.

"A gentleman would be a fool not to notice and express his appreciation of such a lovely sight."

In spite of herself, she wanted to smile. He might be using compliments to twist her to his will, but she longed to be in his arms...no matter the price. No! She must not be a fool.

"I was getting cleaned up, but Captain Kilbride was most insistent that I come here immediately." Drawing her hand out of his, she asked, "How is your leg, Colin?"

"'Twill be fine. I may not be fit to dance at the wedding party, but I will recover."

"What was the doctor's opinion?"

His nose wrinkled. "Doctor? Why would I send for a doctor for this?"

"You were shot!"

"Aye, I do recall that." He laughed, but the taint of pain colored the sound. "I do not need him bleeding me and telling me not to rush my recovery."

"Rush your recovery? You should be in bed!"

With a smile, he sat facing her. "I might have been in bed by now if McAllister had not tried to stop our wedding." His smile vanished. "Before you ask, they are dead."

Ashley hid her face in her hands. "I told them not to be foolish. I thought they would heed me."

He drew her fingers away. "When you promised to take care of me yourself?"

"I don't know what you mean."

"Do not lie to me. Not now, Ashley."

At his entreaty, she looked into his face. It was as hueless as it had been when he had his arm around her in the chapel. Paying no attention to his protests, she stood and went to the ewer by the door to his bedchamber. Soaking a cloth, she wrung it out. She placed it on his forehead. Sweat shone on his skin, and she suspected he had strained himself more with his efforts to appear unhurt.

She massaged his temples and along his neck to his shoulders which were taut with pain. She wished there was something she could offer to him to ease it, but nothing was available in this time.

"Colin," she murmured, "at the risk of having you snarl at me again, I think you should be in bed."

He leaned back and relaxed under her ministrations. "I cannot. This castle is seething with rumors. It needs a strong laird to secure it."

"It needs a laird who is alive."

Colin gazed into her eyes which were above his. The sensation of looking up at her was odd and somehow pleasing. "Is that how you truly feel? Is that why you did not put an end to me with the knife McAllister gave you?"

Stepping away, she drew a chair close to his. He winced as its legs scraped the stone floor. She sat and asked, "How do you know about the knife?"

He reached beneath his plaid and drew out the long knife in its sheath. Tossing it onto her lap, he smiled when she recoiled. "I plucked it from beneath your garter, Ashley, when you were beneath me on the chapel floor. If Jackie had seen it before I did, I doubt I would have been able to waylay him from cutting your throat with it." He ran his finger along the leather sheath, then tipped up her chin. "I knew that, if you were unwise enough to bring it to the chapel, I had to find it before he did. He does not suspect that you had that most interesting conversation with McAllister out near the stables."

"You knew about that?" She gulped and drew back away from him. "Why were you spying on me? I thought you trusted me more than that."

Colin was amazed to see hurt on her face. At his lack of trust? Amazing! He had not guessed she would worry about what *he* thought after tonight. Then he realized she must not suspect the truth of why blood now stained the chapel floor. In so many ways, she was as innocent as a child.

"I do trust you, Ashley," he said with a sigh. "I assume that does not offend you."

"No, but I assume you do not mind that I find that hard to believe at the moment."

He chuckled in spite of the pain ricocheting through his skull like a rock careening down a brae. "I understand you put on quite a performance for McAllister and his comrades."

"You never said anything about that meeting."

"I would have been foolish not to have a spy among men who refused to acknowledge that nothing would change while you and I await the marquess's decision."

"I feared what they planned." She clasped her hands as her face blanched. "It was horrible to hear their anger, but I felt so sorry for them. They had endured much in hopes of seeing Lord Stanton defeated."

"And you hoped to appease them by promising to see me dead?"

"Yes, I had promised to kill you when you—after the wedding."

He laughed when color soared up her face. What a strange woman she was! She sat before him dressed in barely more than her chemise, yet she could not speak of the pleasure he would have been quite happy to share with her if she were willing and he was not wounded. He noted that her robe had gaped again to reveal her slender legs. It took all his strength not to reach out his fingers to trace them from ankle to thigh.

Pushing aside that tantalizing thought as his hands fisted on the arms of the chair, he said, "Like me, McAllister knew you could not slay me."

"You are right. I could not kill you or anyone."

He placed his hand against her cheek, although he glanced again at the enticing curves of her legs. "You need not worry about this deception any longer."

Her dark eyes grew wide. "Deception? What deception?"

"Our wedding. I planned the whole ceremony because I was certain that McAllister would not allow it to be completed and would reveal that he is a traitor even to you."

"You mean you never meant to go through with the wedding?" she gasped. "Why did you let me think—?"

When Colin laughed, Ashley stood, clenching her hands at her sides. This was all a jest for him, a way to secure his hold on the castle. From the beginning, he had played with her as if she were a toy to be enjoyed and then tossed aside when the Marquess of Argyll selected him to hold the castle.

"Would you have allowed McAllister and his allies to continue with their deranged plan if I had told you the truth?" Colin asked.

"They were loyal to my father."

"They said that, but I have it on good authority that McAllister was one of Stanton's favorite henchmen."

Ashley put her hand to her forehead as another of the memories that she should not have pulsed out. She had been quite young the first time she saw Charlie McAllister come out of Lord Stanton's office, smiling. Even then, she had known enough to slink back into the shadows so he would not see her when he was where he should not be. She should have remembered that before. She rubbed her forehead. What else hadn't she recalled that could now betray her? Somehow she had to find out. Maybe Ella would help her fill in the blanks.

"Then why," she whispered, "would he have claimed to be my father's ally now?"

"Because he needed your father's allies to stand beside him. They must not have guessed his double dealing." Colin caught her hand and folded it between his. "You are the most credulous woman I have ever met. And the most incredible woman I have ever met."

She ignored his compliment. He might be using it just to twist her to his will...again. "I was not part of their stupid scheme. If I were going to kill you, Colin MacLachlan, it would be slower and more painful than a ball through the heart!"

"Should I have my food tasted? Or shall I find a viper in my bed?"

"That is all you shall find from me in your bed!"

Ashley yanked her hand away and went toward the door. She wondered why he could not be honest with her just once. Then she feared he *was* being honest. He wanted her. She saw that in his eyes and savored it in his touch, but he wanted this castle more.

Hearing him awkwardly getting to his feet, Ashley did not turn. She whispered, "Why do all of you use me as if I have no feelings of my own?"

"What do you mean, pretty one?"

She faced him, watching his studied steps while he came toward her. "'Pretty one'? If I were as old and ugly as Hume, would you have treated me as well as you have?"

"I vowed to protect the claim of my clansmen to this castle before I ever saw you." He laughed, then flinched as if the sound hurt. "I must admit it might have been easier if I had not discovered how you hold a man's eye and taunt him in his fantasies."

"What did you tell me? That my father would have exchanged me in marriage for power?" She laughed coolly. "Maybe, but I would have known that he chose my fate with hopes for my best interests at heart. You use me to get rid of your enemies without caring how I feel about it."

"I did what I must. I always shall."

"So shall I." She raised her chin. "Don't forget that, Colin."

"I shall not. Nor will I forget how much I want this." He pulled her closer, his mouth capturing hers before she could protest.

Her resistance sifted away as he cradled her head in the crook of his arm and explored, bit by bit, the contours of her mouth. The tip of his tongue traced the circumference of her lips as if testing to determine if they would taste as sweet as he hoped. At the far corner of each side, he placed a tender kiss.

When her hands slid along his arms to encircle his shoulders, his embrace tightened so she rediscovered his powerful muscles through the thin material of his shirt. His mouth imprisoned hers beneath it, but she had no longing to escape. She could not fight the desire which urged her to touch him.

His hands stroked her back in rhythm with his lips, which were slipping to brush her throat with a heat that softened her in his hands. Her breathless sigh of delight was magnified by the high ceiling to surround them with her yearning to know more of the rapture he created deep within her.

"Ashley, pretty, delicious Ashley," he whispered in her ear. She had no chance to answer as he recaptured her lips. Their breaths strained and melded in a fierce storm of desire. He drew back enough to whisper, "Be mine, *belovit.* That you do not want the pleasure we could share is a deception that must come to an end."

Ashley ripped herself away from him before she told him yes. How stupid could she be? No wonder he thought she would come willingly to his bed. Each time he pulled her into his arms, she softened like ice cream on a hot summer afternoon. Turning on her heel, she rushed to the door.

"Ashley, wait!"

She threw the door open, but froze when she heard a crash behind her. Whirling, she moaned. On the floor, with his hand outstretched toward her, Colin lay in an enlarging pool of blood.

She ran back to drop to her knees beside him. "Colin!"

Only a groan answered her. That sound stripped away everything but terror. All his schemes, all her uncertainty vanished. She had to get help to stop this flow of blood, or Colin would die.

# TEN

Ashley stared at her scarlet fingers. She ran to the door. "Ramsey!" Seeing someone in the shadowed hall, she shouted, "Find a doctor! Bring him here as soon as you can."

She raced back to Colin's side. Kneeling beside him, she cautiously rolled him onto his back. She pulled one of the pillows from the window seat. Gently she lowered his head back onto it.

While he was unconscious, the stiff line of his jaw had softened slightly, but agony branded his face. She longed to smooth the seams of pain from his forehead. Taking a deep breath to strengthen herself, she drew back the vermilion bloodstained hem of his kilt.

She picked up the knife that McAllister had given her. A fury that threatened to devour her tightened her fingers around the haft. She stared down at Colin's slowly rising chest. If she drove the knife into it, she would never have to be humiliated by him again. She would be free of his arrogance.

*No!*

Ashley did not know if she screamed that aloud or only in her head as she flung the knife across the room. Looking at her fingers, she shivered. That knife! It was filled with hatred and evil. She rubbed her hands together. Before she arrived at Castle Braeburn, she would have laughed away such thoughts about witchcraft. She no longer was so sure.

Reaching across Colin, she drew his *sgian-dubh*. The short blade would be perfect for her task. She carefully slit the bandage on Colin's leg.

"Oh, no!" she gasped. The reddened skin around the hole warned that nothing had been done to prevent infection. She pressed the bandage back over the wound to stanch the blood and fought not to be sick. How could she help him? None of the antibiotics she had taken for granted would be available in the 17th century.

"Get away from him!"

Ashley stood as she heard Captain Kilbride's fury. Without Colin conscious to protect her, she feared she could not convince Captain Kilbride to let her live. If she died, Colin might, too. She steadied her trembling fingers and turned to face him.

Captain Kilbride's lip curled in rage as he stared at the bloody knife in her hand. "Have you succeeded in killing him?"

"He is hurt. He needs a doctor's help." She forced herself to ignore the gun that was aimed at her.

"Get away from him."

"Let me do what I can to help until the doctor gets here."

"Move aside!"

"He is going to die, Captain Kilbride! He needs help!"

"Move aside! Or I swear I shall shoot you."

Ashley watched in horror as his finger reached for the pistol's hammer. With a satisfied smile, he drew it back.

"Stop!" Ramsey's shout filled the room.

Colin murmured something unintelligible, and Ashley knelt again to put her hand on his head.

"Oh, no!" she whispered again. His skin was clammy, a sign she knew that he was struggling to fight the infection that might already be swirling through him.

"Milady?"

She glanced up at Ramsey. His face was as drawn as his laird's.

"What can I do, milady?" he asked. "Shall I have some men move him?"

"No. Bring blankets. He needs to stay warm. Where can the doctor be? How long will it take for him to get here?"

Ramsey frowned. "Do you really want a doctor here?"

"Yes! I have sent for him."

"The doctor will probably want to saw the laird's leg off."

"No! That's barbaric!" She took a steadying breath and added before anyone could reply, "Send for Ella. She can help."

As Ramsey started for the door, Captain Kilbride ordered, "Stop!"

"Captain, milady wishes me to—"

Ashley cried, "Go, Ramsey! Now!"

"Stop!" Captain Kilbride ordered, his face florid with rage.

Standing, Ashley wiped her hands on her dressing gown. "Captain Kilbride, you accused me of trying to kill Colin, but you

may be the cause of his death if you continue to be pig-headed."
She waved to Ramsey. "Go! And hurry!"

"Aye, milady." Ramsey rushed out of the room.

"You have gone too far this time, Ashley Gordon!" snarled
Captain Kilbride.

"We can fight together to save Colin," she said quietly, "or
we can fight each other while he dies. Which will it be?"

The soldier did not reply as the room filled with servants who
rushed to Ashley for instructions. She could not ignore his
scrutiny. If she did one thing wrong, she knew he would not
hesitate. He would kill her.

Warm blankets were brought and placed around Colin.
Ashley sat on the floor beside him, holding his hand. Every few
minutes, she sought his pulse. The beat was no longer as steady
as it had been.

When Captain Kilbride was called from the room, she let her
shoulders sag. Blast that man! He had no more sense than a rock.

Another man rushed into the room, shoving aside those in his
way. He was gaunt, with eyebrows that seemed to be reaching for
his hairline. He was dressed all in the black, and he aimed a
fierce scowl at Ashley.

"Move!" he snapped.

"Who are you?" she asked.

"The doctor from the village."

"You?" She stared at his filthy hands and frowned. "Let me
get you some water to wash up in."

"Later! Now I must do my work."

"Don't cut off his leg," she whispered.

"I know what I am doing. Will you let me do it?" Opening
his bag, he reached for a jar. He withdrew a brown, slimy object.

As he started to place it against Colin's leg near the wound,
Ashley grasped his narrow wrist. "What are you doing?" she
asked.

Fiercely, he wrenched his arm away. "He must be bled. The
bad humors within him will be sucked out by this leech."

"No!"

"I am a doctor. I wish to see Laird MacLachlan live. Do
you?"

"Would I have sent for you if I had wanted him to die?"

He scowled, his eyebrows lowering. "Then let me do as I
was trained to do."

Ashley rose and walked toward where Ella stood beside
Ramsey. It appalled her to leave Colin in this man's hands. What

he was doing could hurt Colin more. If only she could tell him what she knew! But she could not explain how she had that knowledge.

Suddenly she whirled. Running back, she fell to her knees and plucked the leech from Colin's leg. It stretched out far longer than she had guessed it could. It popped off, leaving a tiny red incision on his leg.

The doctor cursed, then shouted, "Now see here, Lady Ashley—"

"Out!" She took his bag and shoved the jar and the leech into it. "He has lost too much blood already. You shall not take the last drop from him! Leave."

"He must be bled, or he will lose the limb and die."

"He will die if you suck every last ounce of blood out of him. Go!"

The doctor hesitated. No one else spoke. With a bitten-off oath, he stood and walked away without another word.

Ashley called, "Ella! Ramsey!"

They hurried to her.

Not giving them a chance to ask a question, Ashley dropped her voice to a whisper. "Is there someone else who might be able to help him?"

"I would be glad to, milady," came a woman's voice from behind her.

Ashley whirled to discover a stranger behind her. The short woman was bent with age beyond even Ella's, and silver-white hair drifted from beneath the dark wool shawl draped over her head and along her simple gown.

"Who are you?" she asked.

"I am Wynda Thompson, milady. I know how to heal those who have been hurt."

When Ashley glanced at Ella, her servant looked quickly away. Why? She took Ella's arm and drew her aside. "Tell me what you know of this woman," she whispered.

"I know nothing of her, but what is murmured along the loch." Ella wrung her apron and still did not meet Ashley's gaze. "She keeps to herself."

"Does she know how to heal?"

"It is possible."

Ashley searched her mind, trying to resurrect the memories of the times she should not be able to recall. Nothing came forth about Wynda Thompson. Turning, she started to dismiss the woman, then faltered when she saw the old woman kneeling beside Colin, looking at his wound with an expression of concern.

The old woman took Ashley's hand, drawing her closer. "The bad humors are within him already, milady, but it is possible to scatter them once more."

"How?"

"If you would agree, I will ask a lad to go to the bakery and find some cobwebs that are lingering in the corners."

"Bakery cobwebs?" she repeated. The old woman must be insane.

Wynda nodded. "The cobwebs will hold the wound closed, and ones from the bakery, especially when the bread has been recently set to rise, are the best for healing."

Ashley sank to her knees beside the old woman. Maybe Wynda Thompson was not mad. Penicillin came from bread molds. It was possible that those same molds would catch upon the sticky strands of a spider web.

Putting a vein-lined hand on Ashley's, the old woman said, "You can trust me, milady, as your mother did before you."

"My mother?"

"A dear soul who did not deserve the death she received." Her hand rose to cup Ashley's chin, and a warmth like when the sparkles filled the room washed over her. "I know you are confused, milady, but the truth will be revealed to you when the time is right."

"If you know the truth..." She looked back at Colin when he groaned. "Help him, please."

"I shall try." Heaving herself to her feet, Wynda called for what she needed.

Ashley remained by Colin while a lad ran to obey Wynda's orders. When a hand settled on her shoulder, she looked up and smiled weakly at Ella. Then, she stood, too.

"Ella, we will need a needle from your sewing box as well as thread to close the wound once Wynda has tended to it. Get some water boiling on the hearth and make sure the thread goes in it for at least five minutes."

"In the water?" Ella's forehead rutted. "It is clean, milady. I would not reuse thread for your gowns."

"I know, but do as I ask."

Ella's baffled expression was shared by all of those in the room as Ashley supervised the boiling water and then held the valuable needle in the flames until it glowed. Although wanting to assure Ella that the needle would be replaced if it was ruined,

Ashley said nothing. She was not sure if a needle could be found in the Highlands during the war, but she knew that she condemned Colin to death if she let his wound become more infected.

"Thank you, milady," Wynda said, holding out her hand for the needle. "I will sew up the wound."

"After you have had your hands disinfected."

"What?"

Ashley did not bother to explain the word none of them would understand. Taking a bottle of whisky from a nearby table, she poured it over the threaded needle and her hands before dousing Wynda's.

"Alack!" moaned Ramsey. "Why are you wasting good whisky the laird could be using for his recovery?"

"Trust me," Ashley replied sharply, handing the needle to Wynda. "I learned about the importance of putting whisky on your hands years ago, Ramsey. Trust me to know what I am doing."

Her tone must have been more astringent than she had guessed because no one spoke as Wynda knelt to tend to Colin's wound. Again a hand settled on Ashley's shoulder, bringing comfort with it. She savored the warmth, but kept her gaze on Wynda. If she looked back, she knew what she would see. The sparkles which would swiftly disappear. She wanted to keep the solace for as long as it would stay.

*See the truth around you. Seek among those around you for the truth.* The words were as gentle as the fingertips upon her shoulder.

Wynda halted as she was taking another stitch to close the wound on Colin's leg. She looked about, and her eyes widened when they met Ashley's. With a nod and a smile, she bent to her task again.

Ashley wanted to ask the old woman if Wynda had heard the voice, too. She bit back her questions as Wynda continued to sew. She could not betray herself. Not now, when she had so few allies.

Through all of her work, Colin did not wake. He groaned with obvious pain, but remained lost in it.

"Where is the doctor?" Captain Kilbride bellowed as he stormed into the room.

Ashley rose as Wynda did not pause in her work on Colin's leg. Folding her arms in front of her, she said, "The doctor left. Wynda Thompson is helping him."

"Left?" Captain Kilbride jutted his chin toward her. "I heard you sent him away."

"Then why are you asking why he isn't here?" She turned to watch as Wynda directed several men to carry Colin into his bedchamber. His arms drooped lifelessly toward the floor.

Captain Kilbride grasped her elbow and twisted her back to face him. "If you have killed him..."

"He is breathing. You can check for yourself."

"I will."

"Good, but do not get in Wynda's way." She slid her arm out of his grip.

"I shall do as I wish when—"

Again she turned her back on him. She saw dismay in Ella's eyes, but kept her head high as she said, "Ella, tell Beathas I want broth brought. Beef or chicken or whatever she has. A potful so you can keep it warm here on the hearth. Ramsey, have the lads bring in more wood. I want this room warm, so Colin does not take a chill."

"Very wise, milady," Wynda said, wiping her hands on her bloodstained apron.

Ashley looked up at the high ceiling. "It may be impossible to heat this room much above freezing if the temperature dips as it has the past few nights."

"Winter attacks more cruelly than an enemy."

"Yes." She stared at Wynda, wondering what this woman was hiding. Wynda Thompson seemed to know so much.

"Milady," the old woman continued, "have kettles brought. They can be filled with embers and set close to the laird. That will keep him warm."

Taking the old woman's hand, Ashley squeezed it. "How can I thank you?"

"Save his life. He is meant to be here at this time." Wynda added nothing else as she walked away, herding the others ahead of her out of the room.

Ashley wanted to run after her and ask her to explain, but Captain Kilbride spun her to face him again. Before he could say anything, she pulled her arm away and picked up Colin's wrist. She checked his pulse before setting his arm across his slowly moving chest.

"Ramsey, more pillows," she called.

"What for?" asked Captain Kilbride.

"Ramsey," she ordered, ignoring the soldier, "please get as many pillows as you can find."

Colin's servant ran as fast as his aged legs could carry him to gather pillows. She placed one under Colin's head. The others went beneath his injured leg to elevate it.

She nodded her gratitude, then turned to meet Captain Kilbride's furious scowl. "I think Colin will live if..." Again she could not explain the need for keeping the wound clean, so she simply added, "If you wish to play the hangman, now is the time."

He started to laugh, then frowned again. "You are serious, aren't you?"

"I don't want to die. I don't want Colin to die, either. I cannot help him recover if you intend to look over my shoulder and countermand every order I give."

"So you are ready to pay for a crime the laird is sure you did not commit?"

Ashley could not hide her shock that he was willing to admit that Colin trusted her. "You may be closer to the truth than even I thought, Captain Kilbride. I care what happens to Colin. I care very much."

He opened his mouth to answer, then closed it. Without another word, he walked out of the room.

Ramsey put a comforting hand on her arm and said, "Milady, it is not easy for a man like Captain Kilbride to own to his mistakes. Give him time."

Ashley pretended to be comforted, but the warmth from the sparkles had vanished when Captain Kilbride had come back into the chamber. Her life depended on a man who hated her and hated that his commander had not slain her weeks ago.

But that must not matter now. All she should be thinking of was seeing Colin's clear gaze again. Only then, would she believe he would live.

***

Days passed as Ashley waited for her wish to come true. Through bouts of delirium Colin mumbled incoherently, through hours when fever burned until his skin was a flame beneath her fingers, through prayers and applications of an herbal paste Beathas brought from the kitchen, Ashley seldom left his side.

Again and again Ramsey urged her to rest. Although she was swaying on her feet, she resisted. She reclined on a bench and catnapped between attempts to reduce Colin's fever with cooled cloths.

Each morning, she went to the great hall and shared the unchanging news. From the long faces staring back at her, she knew his men did not expect him to recover. The residents of

Castle Braeburn could not conceal their fear, for they had no idea who might try to claim the castle if Colin MacLachlan died.

Late during the fifth day after the disastrous wedding ceremony, Captain Kilbride asked to speak to Ashley alone. She wiped her hands on the apron she wore over a work dress that Ella had brought.

"We can speak in the main chamber without disturbing Colin," she said. "Ella, call me if there is any change."

"Of course, milady," Ella replied.

Ashley was shocked when Captain Kilbride helped her to a chair. Grateful, for she was exhausted, she asked as she sat, "What is it?"

He sat opposite her. "Will Laird MacLachlan survive?"

"I hope so."

"Has there been a change?"

"No." She sighed. "Right now, he is holding his own against this infection. Damn that doctor! If only he had washed his hands first."

Captain Kilbride frowned. "Wash his hands? Why? He was being sensible to wait until he was done." Raising his own hands to halt her retort, he said, "What has happened matters little. I have come to tell you that I have received orders for Laird MacLachlan to appear at the Marquess of Argyll's side with a force from Castle Braeburn. The marquess shall not be pleased to learn Colin MacLachlan is unable to fight, and I am there in the laird's stead. I shall take only the men that can be spared from the castle's defense."

"That is wise. When news of Colin's condition seeps beyond this valley, it might mean danger for Castle Braeburn."

"Or for you, milady. Montrose is a sneaky bastard. He could well try to wrest this dale into his control."

"But with Colin unconscious, who will be in charge of the castle?"

He smiled. "Why, you, milady."

"Me?" Ashley squeaked.

"Who else?" He laughed, but she heard little humor in the sound. "Aren't you in charge now? You have been overseeing the castle while the laird oversees you." He stood. "I must go, milady."

"Have you left for Colin the information of where you plan to travel and your expected return?" As he frowned, she rose, too. "Captain Kilbride, the information is not for me. Colin will have many questions when he awakes. Write it all down and leave it with someone you trust."

Reluctantly he nodded. "And you will send reports to me of the laird's condition?"

"Of course."

He turned to leave.

"Captain?"

"Yes?"

"Take care of yourself." She smiled. "Colin would be angry if you did something foolish like getting yourself killed."

"Aye, the laird would be most put out. He would dig my carcass from my grave to berate me." Taking her hand, he bowed over it. "Take care of him, Lady Ashley."

"I will."

With a swirl of his kilt, he was gone. Ashley dropped back onto the chair. Days ago, hours ago, Jackie Kilbride had been her foe, eager to see her dead. They had become reluctant allies fighting for Colin's life. She wondered how long this alliance would last.

***

Three days after the men left from Castle Braeburn, Ashley was sitting by Colin's bed as she had almost every hour since the wedding. A hand settled on her wrist. Colin's grip was weak, but the electric shock which raced through her remained strong.

"Colin!"

He motioned for her to lower her voice. "What did you give me to drink? I have never had such a painful head."

"The shot you received was not in a glass."

"What?"

Instead of answering the unanswerable, she ran to throw the door open. "Ramsey, Ella, he is awake."

"Praise the Lord!" cried Ella, dropping to her knees with a fervent prayer.

Ashley laughed at Colin's startled expression that Ella was grateful for his recovery. "Many things have changed," she murmured as she placed a damp cloth against his forehead. "You shall hear all about it when you are feeling better."

He reached to pull the cloth off, but she halted him. His eyes widened in his haggard face. "How long?"

"Eight days."

"That long?"

She gave him a sympathetic smile. She wished she could tell him how she could empathize with his disorientation at having time evaporate without warning. She must kept locked in her heart that the time she had lost could be measured in centuries rather than in days.

Taking a bowl from Ella, Ashley watched as Ramsey tilted up his laird's shoulders so Colin could sip the warm liquid.

"Thank you, *belovit*," Colin whispered as he sagged back into the pillows again. His eyes closed, and he was asleep.

For a long moment, Ashley stared at his face that had eased from an anguished strain. Burying her own face in her hands, she released the tears she had withheld for more than a week. Colin would live. As soon as he had touched her, she had been sure, for she had sensed the undiminished determination within him.

A hand under her elbow brought her to her feet, and she was steered to the door. It took too much energy to lift her feet, so she scuffed them along the uneven stone floor. When she realized she was being guided out of Colin's rooms, she murmured, "No, I must—"

"No, milady," Ramsey said, and she realized he was following them out of the bedchamber. "Let Ella take you to your rooms. Rest. You cannot help the laird if you are ill."

"Come, milady," Ella seconded. "Ramsey will send for you as soon as the laird awakens."

"'Send?'" she repeated numbly. "I told Jackie Kilbride that, when Colin awoke, I would send him the news immediately. You must—"

"'Tis the third hour past midnight." Ella chuckled. "The message will wait until sunrise."

Stubbornly, Ashley turned. "Ramsey, will—?"

"Go!" His smile contradicted his harsh tone. "I will alert a messenger to go to Captain Kilbride. As soon as the laird awakes, I shall send for *you*. Go and get the rest you deserve."

Knowing they were right, Ashley allowed Ella to assist her to her rooms. Her stomach grumbled, but she ignored it. She was hungry; eating would take too much energy now. She did not bother to undress. Falling into her bed, she fell asleep as quickly as Colin had. For once, she was not overwhelmed by nightmares. Mayhap they had vanished along with the threat to Colin.

***

The sun glared into the room, pouncing on Ashley's closed eyes. She smiled as she saw a fire burning on the hearth. Hurrying across the cold floor, she stood close to the hearth as she stretched strained muscles.

When the door opened, she knew Ella had been listening for her. "Good morning, Ella."

"Good *afternoon*, milady."

"Afternoon? You were to wake me when Colin woke up."

She smiled. "He just has. Ramsey sent a message for you."

Ashley rushed out. She almost collapsed, but locked her knees in place. She was not going to be slowed down because she was still tired.

She ran along the hall and into Colin's chambers. She was amazed to see him sitting on a bench with his leg propped out in front of him.

"Milady, I have been awaiting your call," he said, his voice strong again.

She touched his forehead and smiled when she realized there was not the slightest hint of fever. Ignoring the strange glance he gave her, she picked up his wrist. His pulse was steady.

"Are you my doctor, Ashley?" he asked.

"I only helped, but I must tell you that I am afraid you shall live. It appears that those who say only the good die young are right."

He smiled as he took her fingers and brought them to his lips. "I am gratified to know that you were not worried about me, milady."

"Not a bit," she lied.

When he stroked her cheek, she leaned toward him. Before she could warn him not to strain himself, he brought her lips to his. His fingers wove into her hair, and he released her with reluctance when she drew away from him as he moaned. Not with passion, but with pain as he shifted his leg.

"Stay awhile, pretty one." A hunger in his voice matched the longing within her.

"Of course." She sat on a chair Ramsey pushed forward for her. "I know you want an accounting of all that has taken place in the past week."

"Do not worry about that. Jackie can tell me what I need to know."

"Jackie is gone." She glanced at Ramsey.

"I sent for you posthaste, milady," the old man said, guilt laced through his voice. "I did not pause to tell the laird anything."

Colin frowned. "Tell me what?"

"The marquess sent for the men from Castle Braeburn to join him in the battle against Montrose," Ashley replied. "They left earlier in the week."

Grimacing, Colin sat straighter as Ramsey went into the antechamber, clearly eager to avoid any anger aimed at him. "Left? Jackie is gone? Who has been looking after the castle?"

"By default, Jackie left me in charge."

Colin wondered if he still was within the maze of dreams created by his fever. That she called Jackie Kilbride by his given name was astonishing. And Jackie had appointed her as guardian of Castle Braeburn until Colin woke? Amazing!

He listened as Ashley reported what had occurred during the time he had been senseless. All he could do was nod and accept what had happened. It did no good to rant about his wound which kept him from joining his men in the fight to banish Montrose from the Highlands, but he could not silence a single curse.

"You shall have other times to battle your enemies," Ashley said.

He scowled. Was it just his pounding skull or did her voice sound odd? Noticing her wan face, he said, "Mayhap a toast to a victory over Montrose would be fitting."

"An excellent idea. Some wine will put some color back into your face."

"And yours."

She must not have heard him as she pushed herself to her feet because she said, "I am afraid the whisky is gone. We used it while Wynda sewed up your leg."

"Wynda?"

"She..." She put her hand to her head. She moaned once and crumpled into a pile on the floor.

"Ashley!" Colin cursed his weakness as he tried to stand. He fell back against the bench. "Ramsey, get in here!"

His servant raced in with Ella on his heels. Ella screamed, but Ramsey pushed by her and knelt beside Ashley.

Colin struggled again to stand.

Ramsey ordered, "Stay where you are, Laird MacLachlan. I cannot tend her if I must tend you, too."

Grumbling, Colin dropped back onto the bench. Ramsey was right. He peered around Ella. On the floor, Ashley's pale face was softened as if she were asleep.

"She has fainted," Ella said.

"What is that?" Colin stared at the cluster of what looked to be earthbound stars surrounding Ashley. The lights hovered around her like a coverlet, enveloping her in their soft glow.

"What is what?"

He tore his gaze from Ashley to look at Ella. Pointing, he said, "That. Can't you see it?"

"See what, my laird?"

Colin cursed again when he glanced back to see Ramsey lifting Ashley's limp form in his arms. The lights were gone. Putting his hand to his suddenly aching head, he wondered if the fever had burned insanity into him.

Instead of answering Ella, he watched as Ramsey set Ashley on a bench not far from where Colin sat. Colin pushed himself gingerly to his feet and limped to her. Ella settled a blanket over her lady.

"Has she been ill?" he asked.

Ella put her hands on his shoulders and pressed him into the chair where Ashley had been sitting. "Rest, my laird. She has strained herself caring for you. In the past week, she has gotten little sleep and eaten less."

"Why haven't you taken better care of her?" he demanded, then smiled weakly. "You tried. Trust Ashley to push herself so far. I suspect she never does anything half-heartedly."

"Fortunately for you," retorted Ramsey. "She saved—"

His words were interrupted by a soft groan. Slowly Ashley's eyes opened, then squeezed shut. Ella placed a cooled cloth on her forehead.

"What happened?" Ashley whispered.

"Shh, child. When did you eat last?"

"Last night I had some chicken pie."

Ella shook her head. "That was two days ago."

"Then I had some two days ago." Ashley ignored the gasps of disbelief. If only the room would stop whirling in its mad frenzy...

"Ashley?" Colin asked.

She recognized that deceptively calm tone. It meant he was furious. "Yes?"

"Take care of yourself. Have something to eat. Now!" When she started to protest, he added, "That is an order, Lady Ashley!"

"Colin, I—"

"I said it was an order!" He smiled, but she knew he was determined that she would obey him. "After all, if you do not take care of yourself, who shall oversee my recovery?"

His question was spoken in such a helpless timbre, she had to laugh. "I am sure you, Colin MacLachlan, shall be an irritating patient."

"The most irritating."

Pushing herself up to sit and holding the cloth to her still aching head, Ashley asked Ella to send for food for all of them. It was time for a celebration. Colin had survived the attack by his enemies. Now, mayhap there would be a chance for him to realize that she was not one of them.

But being his ally was not what she wanted, she knew, when she found herself staring at his lips. She wanted so much more. She was falling in love with a man who should have been dead centuries before she was born. A man who might not hesitate to use anyone or anything—even her love—to reach his goal of claiming Castle Braeburn.

# ELEVEN

Ashley bent her head into the night wind keening across the loch. Any hint of autumn had vanished into winter. As her cloak flapped around her and her gown twisted about her legs, she wished for her winter coat that was hanging in the back of her closet in Springfield. She might as well wish for summer.

Ice coated the rocks beside the water, and spray sliced into her face. Behind her, she heard a shout from the walls of Castle Braeburn. The watch was announcing the hour. She must complete her task and return to the castle because night was claiming the glen.

Carefully, she stepped up onto a rock. Balancing herself, she drew out the wrapped package she had hidden beneath her cloak. She bit her lower lip as she unwound the material around the knife. The wool fell to the ground, unnoticed, while she took care to hold the knife by its sheath. She could no longer deny what was right in front of her face. This knife spread evil like a sneeze spread a cold. Invisible and insidious and all-consuming in its sickness.

How many times had she heard someone say that Charlie McAllister must have gone daft to attack the laird like that? How many times had she tried to forget the delight in Colin's eyes when he had held this knife and spoken of how his enemies had died? How many times had it tried to ensnare her into its malevolence?

"No more!" she cried, flinging the knife out toward the ebony waters of the loch. "You will do no more evil."

It vanished with a soft plop.

Smiling, Ashley told herself she was probably just being silly, but she no longer trusted her common sense that told her that witchcraft was just something to scare people in horror stories. Common sense would have told her she could not be in this castle in this time, but here she was.

*Do not linger.*

She stiffened at the familiar voice, then waited for the comfort that always accompanied it. There was none.

*Do not linger. You must leave now.*

She had never heard panic in this voice before. She jumped down off the rock and winced when her foot slipped and her shin struck a sharp edge.

*Hurry. Do not linger. You must leave now.*

As Ashley turned to run back toward the castle, a low roar sounded from behind her. She looked back over her shoulder and gasped. From the waters of the usually tranquil lake, something dark was rising. Her first thought of the Loch Ness monster vanished when a fierce wave slapped over the rocks where she had been standing. Foam rushed up to where she stood. Through the thickening darkness, she could see another wave, even taller than the first.

She ran.

The wave caught her in its grip, sucking her back toward the loch. She screamed as she fought to escape. The water clung to her and dragged her back toward the loch. Gripping the earth, she fought to breathe.

It receded, and she clambered to her feet. She shrieked again when she heard the thunder of another wave approaching. She tried to run, but her soaked gown weighed every step.

"Help me!" she cried.

A hand caught hers, tugging her up the path. She collapsed as the wave dashed itself into oblivion inches from her feet. The concussion rocked through the ground like an earthquake.

"What was that?"

At Colin's question, Ashley looked up. He was leaning on the cane he had to use to help him walk. "I don't know," she whispered.

He helped her to her feet and tilted back her head. She yelped when his fingers brushed her chin that was raw from where it had been scraped. He looked past her, and she whirled to see another wave rising, but it fell back into itself with a heavy thump. The surface of the loch swallowed any hints of the turbulence. Above it, the sky was darker than any she had ever seen before she came to this time in the Highlands. The feeble glow from the candles within the castle did not seep far into the night.

"Whatever it was is gone," Colin said quietly.

"I hope so."

"Why are you out here at this hour?"

"I wanted to get rid of McAllister's knife." Ashley faltered. If she told him of her fear of it, he might laugh. Or he might believe her, and that would make the aura of witchcraft even more tangible.

"You chose a poor time to do that."

She glanced back at the loch. "I had no idea something like that would happen."

"It never has before?"

"No, not that I know of."

He reached for the ties on his cloak, then smiled and drew her against him, pulling his cloak over both of them. "You must not take a chill, Ashley."

"I don't want to bump your leg." She was frightened by the longings raging through her.

"Hush, pretty one," he murmured against her hair. "You cannot hurt me when you are so close to me."

His arm, which could be an iron bar when she tried to elude him, slipped around her waist. Her eyes shut as his lips stroked her cheek. When his mouth settled on hers, it posed a question.

Startled, she drew away. He had used his beguiling touch to persuade her to do his bidding. Now he was asking her to want him. Didn't he know how her craving for him haunted her thoughts? Her hand rose to caress his face. As she touched him, his heartbeat leapt like a horse breaking fast from the gate. He tilted her hand and placed a lingering kiss on each finger.

"Ashley, I had to do as I did."

She knew this was the only apology she would ever receive for being drawn into the lunacy of the false wedding. Not for a moment was he sorry that he had built upon Jackie's plan to bed her, for it had succeeded in ridding him of his enemies.

"I know," she whispered. "You shall never do anything but what you believe you must."

"In that, we are much alike, aren't we?" His fingers glided along her face in a whisper-light dance. "You are the most incredible woman I have ever met. Have you searched within my fantasies to become the woman of my dreams?"

His mouth over hers saved her from trying to think of a way to respond without betraying the truth. As he had on the hillside with the music of the rill washing over them, he enticed her into rapture. In his arms, her body pressed to his, she was swept away by currents of desire that were even more powerful than the waves rising from the loch.

When his fingers brushed her breast, her astonished cry of delight echoed in his throat. His tongue sought within her mouth. Her craving for him was becoming an ache that would not be ignored. As his mouth brushed the length of her neck, her fingers sought beneath his collar.

At her touch, he chuckled against her ear. "You tempt a man who can barely walk to swing you into his arms and carry you to his bed." His whisper sent a shiver of indescribable yearning through her.

"You shouldn't..." Her voice faded as she stared up into his glistening eyes. She longed to dive into their shadowed depths and let the heat boiling there sear her with pleasure.

"I should be honest with you, *belovit*." He brushed back the wet hair which had escaped from the bow at the back of her neck. "It would give me great pleasure to have you in my bed."

Ashley drew back before he could sense how much she wanted the same. She must not let this man lure her into his bed as readily as he had found a way into her heart. If she became his lover, what would happen if she was snatched back to her own time?

Yet, how much longer could she deny the hunger within her?

She loved Colin MacLachlan, even though there were so many things about him she did not like. When he was kind, as he had been since the disastrous wedding ceremony, she could forget his obsession to hold onto what he had won.

He brought her back into his arms as he whispered, "Let me take you back to the castle. You are shivering with the cold."

Not the cold, she wanted to tell him, but from the heat of his touch. "Yes," she whispered. "I think that would be a good idea."

"As I do," came a voice from behind her.

With a speed she had not guessed he could manage when he was recovering from his wound, Colin pushed her behind him and drew his sword. He lowered it as Wynda Thompson stepped forward and bowed her head toward him.

"You should take care," he growled. "Too many enemies surround this glen, so you could be mistaken for one."

"You are right, my laird." She raised her head, and her eyes glowed in the night like two dark beacons. "You have many enemies around you. Take Lady Ashley and return to the safety of Castle Braeburn." She turned to look out over the loch.

Ashley put her hand on Wynda's arm. "Do you know what happened here?"

"I know only that there is a danger for you here." Wynda glanced at Ashley's soaked clothes, then stared at the loch again. "I can tell you no more now."

"But if you know—"

"I know you must go with the laird *now*. Do not linger here."

Ashley flinched at the words that had rung through her head in the seconds before the loch erupted. The voice had not been Wynda's. Yet the words had been the same.

"Go," Wynda urged again. "Now."

Colin's hand on her arm drew Ashley back toward the wall. "She is right, Ashley. You must get out of these soaked clothes."

Wanting to argue, she knew it was useless. She could not convince Colin to stay without revealing the truth. She put her arm around him and helped him back within the walls.

Ramsey was waiting for his laird near the stairs by the great hall. The old man's scowl warned that he was greatly displeased that his laird had risked his recovery by going out into the cold night.

Glad not to have to explain anything, Ashley said with a strained smile, "I will leave you to Ramsey's care."

Colin caught her fingers as she turned to climb the stairs. "Ashley, you should—"

Her laugh could not hide her disquiet. "No, I should not. *You* should rest now."

"I would prefer to make tonight a most memorable one." He cupped her chin in his hand.

"You are asking too much of me."

"No, you are asking too little of me. There is so much I want to give you." He caught her hand between his and pressed it to his lips. "Soon, *belovit*."

She did not dare to answer as Ramsey helped him up the stairs, because the only answer her heart wanted to give him was yes.

***

With lookouts at each compass point along the wall and on the towers at the corners of the hall, Castle Braeburn waited for the war to invade the tranquil valley. Sparse messages sifted past the mountains from Jackie Kilbride. He warned that the war was turning in favor of the Royalists under Montrose.

Ashley wished she knew how the war would unfold here in the Highlands. King Charles was doomed, but what of Castle Braeburn?

She had little time to worry about that, because she was caught up in the preparations for Twelfth Night. Everyone in the castle was anticipating the revelry with excitement. After so many years of subjugation, they could celebrate their freedom along with the jests of the holiday.

With a list in her hand of tasks still needing to be done, Ashley hurried into the kitchen. She had been looking for Colin all over the castle. In the past week, he had mastered walking with his cane as he had mastered every other challenge in his life.

"Have you seen the laird, Beathas?" Ashley asked.

"Aye." The cook turned to check a pot on the closest hearth. "Donald mentioned seeing the laird not five minutes ago going out behind the stable."

"Out behind the stable? I wonder why he is there." She frowned. "If he thinks to ride before his leg is fully healed..."

Beathas chuckled gently. "Milady, you will never convince that man to heed good sense when he feels he is not fulfilling his duties."

"I know. Mayhap I can convince him, however, to delay them another fortnight."

The cold in the courtyard ripped away Ashley's breath. Her thick-soled shoes protected her from the frozen ground. Wrapping her shawl more tightly around her, she hurried toward the stable.

Ashley squinted and saw, through the glare of the sun on the snow, Colin walking toward the chapel. She called to him, but he must not have heard her.

A woman walked toward him, and they appeared to become involved with their conversation as they entered the cemetery of the families who had resided in this castle. Curiosity spurred her feet forward.

Ashley reached the low stone wall and paused to watch them go to an empty area of the graveyard. In amazement, she realized Gertie Graham was the woman with Colin. Why was Gertie here? They were arguing about something, she guessed, because their arms swept back and forth in wide gestures.

Gertie turned toward her, and Ashley flinched as the sunlight glinted off Gertie's bracelets, almost blinding her. As she rubbed her eyes, fury burst forth within her. It was too familiar and utterly alien. She fought to control it, but the wrath had the power of a hurricane. She flung herself through the iron gate. Its clank alerted Colin, who looked at her in astonishment.

Clutching her shawl to her throat, she stormed through the spitting flakes of snow. "What are you doing here?" she demanded. "This is the one part of my family's home you cannot take away from me. This is the proof that we have held this valley with our blood. Have you no decency, Colin MacLachlan?"

Colin scowled. "I have done nothing—"

"You have done nothing but kill all of those who acknowledge my claim to Castle Braeburn!" came the angry words she could not halt. "And I, who am the last of the Gordons, you seek to woo into your bed so you can complete your degradation of my family. Get out of here, Colin MacLachlan!"

Rage which matched what was holding her captive tightened his lips. He motioned to Gertie to leave.

Gertie bowed, flashed Ashley a smile, then walked away.

Colin put his hand on the closest tombstone. "How dare you order me about? I am the laird of Castle Braeburn, Lady Ashley. I thought you had accepted that."

"Do I have a choice? I must accept your tenancy here, but you need not disturb what remains of my family." She threw out her arms to embrace the uneven line of stones. Her fingers closed into fists as she fought not to speak the words that were not hers. *Help me!* She got no answer, and the only glitter was the sunshine on the snow. "Did you come here to gloat about claiming what should be mine?"

"Gloat?" The single word exploded from his lips to hang in the air between them.

Rounding the narrow stone, he seized her shoulders. At his touch, an ache swelled across Ashley's forehead. The fury released her. But whose fury was it? Not hers.

She shivered as she looked past the wall. Gertie was watching them, a smile still playing along her lips. Had Gertie done something to create this rage? *Witch*, Ella had whispered.

But that made no sense. Gertie had helped Lady Fia Gordon protect her child by sending Ashley away. Why would Gertie want to cause trouble for her now?

"I did not say what I meant, Colin," Ashley whispered, hoping she might heal the damage of the furious words. "I—"

Fiercely, he snarled, "You shall listen to me."

"You don't understand!"

"You say that too often. This time *you* shall understand!" When she tried to twist away, he shoved her to her knees. "Read it!" he commanded as he pointed at the gravestone.

"Colin, I—"

"Read it! Out loud!"

Her voice quivered as she obeyed. "In memory of Lord Livingstone Gordon, his wife, and the courageous men who served them. Rest in peace, brave warriors and beloved ones." She reached out to touch the cold stone. "Did you have this set here?"

Colin's expression was as frozen as the stone markers when he pulled her to her feet and led her from the cemetery. Although she asked him to listen to her apology, he said nothing. The pace he set, despite his cane, made her scurry to keep up with him.

Several people came toward them as they entered the keep, but Colin waved them away. Seeing the set of his features, they backed away silently.

In the great hall, Colin sat Ashley on a bench. Finally, he spoke. "I do not like being insulted before others, Lady Ashley."

His continued use of her title warned her of the depth of his rage. "I told you I did not mean what I said. Someone—I mean, something—I didn't know that you would—"

"What I did or did not do is unimportant. You think I wish to hurt you. You trust me with your lips, but not this castle!" Slamming his fist on a table, he snarled, "Damn you, Ashley Gordon."

She had to tell him the truth. He might think she was deranged, but that no longer mattered. He must realize that something or someone—Could it be Gertie Graham?—was controlling her somehow. She did not want to use the word witchcraft, but it refused to be dislodged from her thoughts. "Colin—"

"Begone!" he roared so loudly she was sure his voice would echo in every corner of the castle. "Begone from my sight!"

She stared in disbelief. "You must listen while I explain why I said what I did, Colin."

"You may call me Laird MacLachlan. Go to the kitchen."

"But I need to speak to you, Colin, about—"

"To you, Ashley, I am now Laird MacLachlan." His lips were taut, forcing each word past them. "You shall obey my orders without questioning them, just as the other servants do."

Ashley stood. When she put her fingers on his arm, he brushed them away.

"Please, I have to tell you this." Desperation strained her voice.

His smile burned with the evil which had taken over her thoughts. In horror, she took a step back. Was he infected with its rage as well? Or, and her heart cramped in mid-beat at the thought, did he hate her so much for injuring his pride?

"But you see, I do not have to listen to you," he replied. "I am Laird MacLachlan. You are only a prisoner who shall now earn her keep." Taking her by the arm, he steered her to the door leading to the kitchen. He called to a man in the passageway. "Dennis, take this woman to Beathas and tell Beathas to put her to work in the scullery."

"Lady Ashley?" Dennis asked, his brown eyes wide.

"She is *Lady* Ashley no longer." Colin walked away, his stiff shoulders displaying his anger.

Dennis cleared his throat, then said, "My la—" He looked away and gestured for her to precede him into the kitchen.

Ashley realized that, with Colin caught in the web of that fury, she must obey. Surely, he would come to his senses soon, escaping it as she had. Until then, she would speak to Beathas about the meals for the rest of the week.

"Milady!" Beathas cried as Ashley entered the kitchen. "What is wrong? Why have you been weeping?"

Ashley touched her cheek. It was wet with tears she had not noticed werefalling.

"I shall send for Ella," Beathas said as she drew Ashley to a table.

Ella bustled into the room as Beathas was putting a piece of cake in front of Ashley. "Milady, I heard—"

"Say nothing," Ashley whispered. Spreading the tale of Colin's unexpected anger might infuriate him more. She must take care what was said until she could persuade him to heed her. "It shall be all right. We have had disagreements before."

"Aye," concurred Ella. "Come upstairs, milady, and rest."

"I cannot. Colin sent me here."

"Mayhap I can talk to him."

Ashley grasped her hands, not wanting her maid to be the focus of this wicked fury. "No, Ella! He is very, very angry. This is not the time."

"If not to the laird, I shall speak to Ramsey. He will be able to convince the laird to see reason." She rose and patted Ashley's hand. "Enjoy your cake, milady. I shall return soon."

"Ask Ramsey to tell Colin that I truly am sorry. Tell Colin that he must let me explain."

"I shall." She rushed out of the kitchen.

Ashley smiled weakly at Beathas. The cook pushed the plate with the cake on it before her and urged her to eat. Sitting opposite Ashley, Beathas began to talk about any subject except the obvious one.

When silence swept through the kitchen, Beathas stood respectfully. Ashley looked over her shoulder, her spoon halfway to her mouth.

In the doorway, Colin stood like a vengeful god about to punish a disbeliever. His gaze settled on her, and she knew her hopes that he would escape the anger controlling him had been futile. She had never seen such rage on his face.

Slowly he advanced on her. Her spoon clattered to the floor as he jerked her to her feet. He pushed her away from the table and turned to speak to the cook.

"Beathas, is it normal to allow your scullery maids to eat the dessert to be served in the hall?"

"Scullery? My laird, 'tis Lady Ashley."

He cursed, then, taking a deep breath, raised his voice so everyone in the kitchens could hear him. "Lady Ashley exists no longer. If you wish to find her, you might wish to look in the cemetery she believed I desecrated." He pointed to Ashley. "Beathas, she is a scullery maid. Put her to work."

Ashley took a step toward Colin. "I have told you that I am sorry. If only you would let—"

He raised his hand. In disbelief that he would strike her, but knowing the strength of his fury, she leapt back, struck the bench, and tumbled to the floor. When she started to rise, he put the tip of his cane between her breasts, pinning her down.

"Heed me," Colin ordered, "or you shall find yourself expelled from Castle Braeburn."

"You cannot send me away! You vowed to let me stay here until we learn the marquess's decision."

"If you are not here when his messenger arrives, will anyone deny my tale that you were foolish enough to try to flee and were killed?" Lifting his cane away, he looked at Beathas. "I shall be expecting reports on how well your new scullery maid does her chores. Fail me, Beathas, and both of you will pay the price."

The cook's face was snowy pale. "My laird—"

"If you cannot do as I order, I shall find someone who will. Is that what you wish?"

Beathas glanced at Ashley, but shook her head. "No, my laird. It will be as you request."

"I thought you would see it my way." He added nothing else as he left.

As Beathas signaled to a lad to stand by the door to make sure Colin did not return, Ashley pushed herself to her feet. Beathas was wise to be cautious because Colin was crafty.

Handing Ashley the plate with the remaining cake, Beathas said, "I wish I could do more, but this is the best I can do. We must obey him."

"I know." She stared at the door leading toward the great hall and shuddered. What if he was not under some sort of spell? The grip of the fury within her had been short-lived. If this was not the same...She did not know what she would do.

# TWELVE

The first days Ashley spent in the kitchen passed quickly. Despite Colin's orders that she was to work in the scullery, Beathas asked her to help with the cooking.

Ashley tried to become accustomed to not using standardized measuring cups and spoons. Yeast, in this time a by-product of making ale, was not reliable, but she learned to bake dozens of loaves of bread at a time.

When she had asked Beathas for something else to wear instead of her brown velvet gown, Beathas had found a frock that was too long and too wide. With a borrowed needle and thread, Ashley tried to make it fit. Sewing had never been one of her favorite tasks, and she wore an apron to hide her crude handiwork.

By her third morning in the kitchen, she knew she must clear the air with Colin. She enjoyed working with Beathas, but there were things she had left half finished for the Twelfth Night celebration. With Christmas just two days away, she needed to get them done.

"I think it would be wiser if you stayed here," Beathas said when Ashley started for the great hall. The cook did not call her Lady Ashley or anything else.

"I shall be back in time to bake the bread. Beathas, I promise I shall do nothing to risk you."

"Me?" She laughed without humor. "You must be careful to do nothing to enrage the laird more."

Her mouth twisted. "I shall make every effort to avoid doing that."

Ashley climbed the stairs toward her rooms. When she saw a familiar form, she called out, "Ella!"

The old woman paused. Shaking her head, she held up her hands to warn Ashley to halt.

"Ella, what's wrong? Have you spoken to Ramsey?"

Ella started to reply, then whirled away faster than Ashley had thought possible. Ella raced toward the suite of rooms where

Ashley once had slept. Ashley was not surprised that the maid did not open the latched door when she knocked. Ella's actions warned her of the truth.

Colin had forbidden Ella to speak to her. She suspected if Ella did not obey the laird, Ashley would suffer. A quiver of fear ran more deeply than her frustration. His rage was lasting far longer than hers ever had. What if he was not under some sort of spell? She sighed, knowing she was no closer to an answer than she had been before.

A glitter caught her eye, and she looked up to see the sparkles swirling between her and the door. "Help me," she whispered.

*See the truth around you.*

"I can't!"

*See the truth around you. Look with your heart, not your eyes.*

Ashley ran toward the stairs. Her heart? It pleaded with her to believe that Colin was not himself. Yet, the facts were clear. Her odd fury had been like a firecracker—explosive, hot, but short-lived. He remained furious at her.

Her steps slowed on the landing when activity in the courtyard caught her eye. She paused by the window and watched Colin dismount. She gripped the sill when he staggered. He was still not completely steady on his feet. Why was he riding?

She moaned in despair when he turned to another horse that was coming into the courtyard. Lilias Lundy's dark gown was a splotch against the snow, but her golden hair glowed in the sunshine. Ashley's eyes burned with unwanted tears as Lilias took Colin's arm and pressed her full curves to him. Although Ashley wished she could turn away, she continued to stare as Colin pulled Lilias into his arms and smiled.

As he had smiled at Ashley just before he kissed her.

Ashley raced away from the window to seek a sanctuary far from everyone in the castle, in rooms that had been unused for years before she was born.

Born?

She should not be born for hundreds of years yet. Still, she was here and alive and with a heart that was breaking. She never had guessed that the nightmares she had suffered as a child would only get worse.

"I want to go home," she whispered.

\*\*\*

By the time Ashley returned to the kitchen, the bread had been baked and was waiting to be sliced. Beathas said nothing, and Ashley guessed everyone knew that Colin had brought Lilias to the castle.

Beathas walked over to the table where Ashley was slicing bread. "Come with me."

Putting the knife on the table, Ashley nodded. "What do you want me to do?"

"My—I mean, I would like you to work with Susan."

"My name is Ashley as it was when I worked here before. I should be glad to have a haven here as I did in the past."

Beathas clicked her tongue. "If it had not been for you, the laird would be dead."

"Colin could argue that he would not have been Charlie McAllister's target if I had been dead."

Beathas muttered under her breath as she led Ashley to a fireplace where a young woman was shelling walnuts. Her black hair glistened with bluish lights in the glow of the fire.

"Susan," said Beathas, "I have brought someone to help you."

Susan's eyes moved toward Ashley, revealing a white film which disguised their original color. She smiled, and her plain face brightened with welcome. "Lady Ashley, good day."

"You are new here, aren't you?"

Susan's brows lowered. "New? Milady, I have been in Castle Braeburn's kitchens since my mother brought me here to learn a trade years ago."

"Years ago?" Ashley searched her memory, but could not remember anything about a blind woman working here.

"Wynda Thompson was determined her daughter be able to take care of herself," Beathas said, smiling.

"Wynda Thompson?" Ashley almost choked on the name. Both Wynda and Gertie seemed to appear in the most unexpected places.

"Yes, milady," Susan replied.

"You must call me Ashley."

"Ashley it shall be. Sit here where it is warm. I know that it is said that if Candelmas Day is bright and clear, there will be two winters that year. I think we have the chill of two winters descending on us at the same time this year."

When Beathas went back to her work, Ashley took a bowl and began to pick the walnut meats from the cracked nuts. The steady sound of shells falling on the hearth created a comforting melody. She tried to concentrate on that sound instead of what might be happening elsewhere.

Colin and Lilias Lundy. The scene of him holding the blonde had scorched her heart. Were they laughing that Ashley had been foolish enough to introduce him to Lilias? At the time, Ashley had thought only of keeping him away from her. Now she wanted to be in his arms. She swallowed the sob rising through her.

"That sounds so sad," came a soft voice.

Ashley looked up to see Susan regarding her as steadily as if she could see Ashley's sorrow. Closing her eyes, Ashley tried to dredge up the courage to deny her sorrow. It was impossible.

"Ashley, I have heard you here." Susan leaned forward. "You treat us as if there were no difference between our rank and yours."

"There isn't," she whispered. "Not now."

Susan smiled sadly. "The laird cannot change what truly is. You are our lady. Do not despair. You are not alone."

"Thank you," she gulped. "You are being very kind, Susan."

Startling bitterness seared her answer. "I do not want you unhappy when you are the one who has been wronged."

"Col—the laird would not see it that way."

"Perhaps he sees too little. I believe he is afraid of you."

"Afraid of me?" Ashley laughed. "He is a warrior who has won this castle by defeating his enemies."

"Mayhap he is afraid of how he feels about you. I listen for truth in what I hear. The laird owes you much, and he may want to give you much in return, but that threatens his dream to hold Castle Braeburn."

She flinched. Susan's words echoed her own thoughts. The idea that Colin MacLachlan feared the desire growing between them disturbed her.

"Ashley?" Susan whispered. "May I touch your face? It helps if I can see with my fingers."

"Of course." Putting her bowl on the chair, she knelt beside Susan.

Her fingertips roamed lightly over Ashley's face, and a smile tilted her lips. "You must be as pretty as they say. They tell me your hair is like the heat from the fire."

Ashley sat in her chair. "I think they mean its color."

"I have embarrassed you."

"What do you mean?"

"Your voice is suddenly so soft. Does it mean I have said something wrong?"

"No, *you* haven't."

"You still think of the laird?" Susan asked.

"Yes." Ashley stiffened her shoulders. "But I shall be fine."

"We all know you will," she answered with such conviction that Ashley almost believed her.

Almost.

*** 

As Twelfth Night approached, Ashley worked with Susan during the day and slept next to her in a small storeroom that barely had room for their pallets. Christmas came and went. Instead of exchanging gifts, the residents of Castle Braeburn spent the day in quiet prayer.

The day after Christmas, the preparations for Twelfth Night began in earnest. Pies were made by the score. Ashley was kept busy taking them to the storage room where they would be kept cool. She liked the chance to be out of the kitchen and alone with her thoughts, even when they were not happy.

Let Colin think he had won! She did not care. Mayhap Ashley Gordon would be furious, but she was Ashley Babcock. Somewhere, in the midst of all this insanity, she had forgotten that. She must concentrate on a way to get back to her own time. Then Colin MacLachlan could have Castle Braeburn and Lilias Lundy. And he was welcome to both of them.

When Susan asked Ashley to help her to the gate where she would meet her mother and make plans to go home for Twelfth Night, Ashley was delighted to agree. Susan had made this banishment to the kitchen so much easier, helping Ashley laugh again.

The wind off the loch was unforgiving, pulling at them and scoring their faces as they walked into it.

They were halfway across the empty courtyard when an imperious voice called, "Girl, come here!"

Turning, Ashley saw Lilias Lundy's satisfied smile.

Susan whispered, "Ignore her, Ashley. She wants to gloat."

Ashley winced at the word Susan had chosen. That was what she had accused Colin of doing when this whole madness began. Gloating. "What do you want, Lilias?"

"Miss Lundy is what you servants are to call me," she said snidely as she swayed toward them.

"If I was to give you a title, it would not be *miss*," retorted Ashley. "I am sure you have never missed a chance to take what you want."

Lilias's face twisted with rage, then she smiled and plucked at her skirt to draw attention to the richness of her gown. "It's lovely, isn't it? A gift, of course, from my dear Colin." She laughed. "The laird is such a generous man and such a wonderful lover. Don't you think so, Ashley?"

"I would not know."

Preening like a satisfied cat, Lilias turned to Susan. "I find that hard to believe, don't you, lass?"

"If Ashley says that she does not know," Susan said quietly, "I believe her. Some people always tell the truth, instead of only when it suits them."

With a strangled snarl, Lilias raised her hand. Before she could strike Susan, Ashley grasped it and shoved Lilias aside.

"Leave us alone, Lilias!" Ashley retorted.

"Yes," added Susan. "Do not touch milady. You are a cowherder's daughter. She is a lady."

"She is," Lilias sneered, "a scullery maid."

"She *is* a lady, although the laird's orders sent her to the kitchen. When he tires of you, you will be sent away, too."

"Do not threaten me!" Her smile was aimed at Ashley. "The laird will not be pleased to hear of this."

Ashley folded her arms in front of her. This anger was all her own. "I am not afraid of you."

"Or of the laird? What will he make of your threats?"

She shrugged. "These are not threats, but simply the truth. Do you know what the truth is, Lilias?"

"You cannot fool me with your maidenly act. The laird told me about what you and he shared!"

Ashley laughed. She could not help herself. Lilias was lying. No matter how angry Colin was, he would never lie simply to besmirch her name. She wondered how much the blonde bragged about was untrue. Her amusement faded. One thing must be true. Lilias was Colin's mistress. As she took Susan's arm, she knew this betrayal of her heart was a pain she might never escape, even if she found her way back to her own time.

\*\*\*

Ashley hefted the half-filled tray of dirty dishes and walked to the next table in the deserted hall. She glanced up when her name was called. "What is it, Lacie?"

The young girl held up her tray. "I cannot put another thing on here. Can you bring the rest?"

"Of course."

"Do not forget to blow out the candles when you are done."

Ashley smiled. The penurious nature of the Scots might have begun at Castle Braeburn. If there was no one in a room, no candles must be left burning. She sighed. It was not to save time and pennies, but because it was so difficult to obtain any supplies. The war and the isolation of the castle in winter had cut them off from the rest of the world.

Humming, she reached for the trenchers. She interrupted herself with a chuckle when she realized it was a classic rock and roll tune. Not a classic in this time, she reminded herself with another ironic laugh.

When she heard footsteps, she looked up. She recognized the man as one of the soldiers left by Jackie to guard Castle Braeburn. She reached for the dishes on the table, paying him no attention.

Hands slipped around her waist, and she dropped the dishes onto the table. The wooden plates made a dull thump, and ale flowed among them as she tried to escape.

"Do not be in such a hurry to leave, Ashley." Moist lips touched her nape.

"Leave me alone!" She shrieked as the man's fingers cupped her breast.

He twisted her to face him, muting her scream beneath his mouth. She struggled, but he forced her back onto the wet table. Clawing at his face, she tried to elude his lips.

When he pinched her face between his fingers, she stared at his lascivious grin. "You do not need to fight me, Ashley," he murmured. "'Tis been so long since you shared the laird's bed. Aren't you lonely? Let Perkin ease that loneliness for you."

"Let me go!"

He reached for her bodice. Ashley's knee snapped up against him. His shrill screech echoed grotesquely along the high ceiling. She pulled away as he bent over in agony.

"Don't ever touch me again!" she ordered through clenched teeth. "If you do, I shall..."

She saw two people silhouetted in the wide doorway. Even from across the room, she saw Lilias's triumphant smile fading into dismay. This attack must have been Lilias's idea. She ignored Lilias as she stared at Colin. Her heart skipped in its fierce pace. He was walking without the cane.

How long she stared at him, she did not know. When he ignored her and continued along the passage beyond the great hall's door, Lilias chasing after him, the familiar sorrow welled up within her. He had had no sympathy for her, no reprimand for her attacker. He made his feelings, or lack of them, evident.

A groan from Perkin warned her to flee. Leaving the dirty dishes, she ran to the door to the kitchen. She blew out the last two candles, leaving the hall in darkness, but she could not escape the heartache of loving a man who despised her.

# THIRTEEN

Throughout the kitchens, the excitement grew as the morn of Twelfth Night dawned. Beathas became a martinet, ordering her staff like a general commanding a battlefield. From one fireplace to the next, she went. Each gingercake, each stuffed bird, each trencher of steaming haggis had to meet her high standards. When one lass dipped her finger into a bowl, she raised her ladle.

A collective gasp warned her not to let it fall. In a choked voice, Beathas said, "You must not taste the pudding before the laird, Ashley."

"You were going to strike me with that?" Ashley asked, looking from Beathas's suddenly pale face to the ladle. "Is that the normal punishment for such a crime?"

Backing away, the cook shook her head. "I shall not, milady. I shall not hit you, milady."

"Hush! If Colin—If the laird heard you, he will banish you from Castle Braeburn. You cannot risk your life for me."

"Aye," she said slowly. "I would gladly risk my life for you."

Putting her spoon back in the bowl, Ashley whispered, "Don't be foolish!"

Beathas dropped to her knees and gripped Ashley's skirt. Burying her face in the stained material, she cried, "You are Lady Ashley Gordon. Nothing can change that, Lady Ashley."

As Ashley gazed about in horror, the servants knelt with their fingers to their foreheads. Even Susan slipped from her seat by a hearth, revealing that her loyalty to Lady Ashley overwhelmed her friendship with Ashley.

"Rise," Ashley said.

They remained bowed before her.

She tugged her skirt out of Beathas's hands and grasped her cape off the hook by the door. She went out into the early darkness, hoping to find some coolness to ease the sickness inside her. Beyond the light oozing from the kitchen, she leaned against a stone wall.

It was starting again. The seeds of insurrection had not died with the men at the wedding ceremony. The madness was surging forth again.

Madness? Ashley stiffened. Was Gertie involved in this? She could not recall seeing the witch woman in the kitchen.

It did not matter. What mattered was that Colin should have known that sending her to the kitchen was bound to bring forth this dissent. Mayhap he did. Mayhap he was using her again to ferret out the rebels. If so, he was a bigger fool than his empty-headed mistress.

She tried to halt the tears bubbling into her eyes. She should not care with whom he slept, but she did. Just as she cared that rebellion would bring more death into the castle. Somehow she must convince Colin to listen to her.

"But how?" she whispered to the uncaring night. Colin's pride blinded him to the truth that she might be his most stalwart ally in Castle Braeburn.

If this was Gertie's handiwork, Ashley did not know how to help Colin escape it. If it was not, then Colin had used her to strengthen his hold on these lands. She gritted her teeth as she spat a curse. With a sigh, she vowed to help him stop the unrest before someone else died. He would have to compromise to receive her help, but he would not compromise her.

Shivering, Ashley turned to go back inside. She could not stay out when her dress and shawl were so thin.

Nobody spoke to her as Ashley sought out Beathas to find out what the cook wanted her to do.

In a hushed voice, the cook asked, "Would you mind working in the great hall?" Beathas's tone warned Ashley that the kitchen staff would no longer obey Colin's edict.

Pretending it had been an order, Ashley said, "Yes, I shall work in the great hall. Is there something you want me to take in there?"

"The tray of puddings must go, milady."

She closed her eyes in pain. If this mutiny continued, these people might suffer. She did not know how to stop it. If she ordered them to be less foolish, she would be admitting she was again Lady Ashley. Picking up the tray, she went slowly along the passage. After tonight, things would not be the same.

When Ashley walked into the great hall, a voice called out, "How does the greenery look, milady?"

She smiled weakly. It was not only the kitchen staff, but everyone in the castle. She could not ignore this problem and hope it would go away by itself. She must find some way to force Colin to listen to her. Putting the tray on a long table, she walked to where a young man was nailing strips of greenery to an archway.

"Donald, 'tis lovely," she said.

Loops of greenery decorated the high rafters and the wooden arches. Winter berries brightened the room. Huge candles burned in the iron chandeliers. Mistletoe hung in the darkest corners, and she smiled. It must have the same purpose in the seventeenth century as it had in her own time. Stolen kisses would delight shy lovers tonight.

But not her.

Ashley went back to place the pudding bowls next to the pewter platters on the table. As she had so often in the past weeks, she tried to concentrate on her task. She emptied the tray and refilled it. Many trips from the kitchen would be necessary to have enough puddings to put one at each place, along with steaming vegetables and fresh breads and pies. Casks of ale had been brought from the cellars and left overnight in the cold. Pitchers were poured to join the food on the burdened tables.

People drifted into the great hall and sat at the long tables. Music from pipers filled the room. Ashley poured ale into mugs as several men invited her to join them for the festivities. She avoided their eager fingers, wondering why they thought she was interested. Was this more of Lilias's scheme? If so, it was doomed.

"I am fine," she said when asked how she was doing. With a shocked glance, she looked from the spigot on the keg of ale to Ramsey's sympathetic eyes.

"Are you really?" he asked.

"I have been worse."

The elderly man's face was drawn with sorrow. "When you had to see an Englishman claim this castle?"

She nodded, although that had not been what she meant.

"I wanted you to know, milady, that I have tried to tell the laird how witless he has been. He does not want to see the truth."

She smiled. "You scolded him?"

"It is my duty to remind him of his obligations. His late father gave me that responsibility before his death." Ramsey sighed. "I have never seen him so stubborn. He refuses to heed me."

"Thank you for trying, Ramsey."

"If you need anything while I am here, come to me."

"While you are here?" She frowned. He would leave Castle Braeburn only if Colin did, but why would Colin be leaving? Had he been called to fight?

"I shall explain later, milady." He hurried toward the largest entrance to the great hall.

Ashley looked toward the door. There was a blare from the bagpipes as Colin and Lilias appeared at the door. Everybody in the room rose before dropping to their knees.

By the keg, Ashley did not move as she gazed at Colin in his most elegant plaid. It followed his muscular body, accenting his leonine strength. His white doublet contrasted with his raven hair. Suddenly she understood the meaning of breathtaking, because she could not breathe as she stared at him, wanting to be in his arms.

He turned, and his ice blue gaze locked with her eyes. She did not curtsy or look away.

Lilias placed her other hand on Colin's arm as he continued to stare at Ashley. She whispered in his ear. He frowned, but nodded. All the while, he continued to hold Ashley's gaze. He said nothing, but everyone in the room must be aware of the link between them.

When Colin blinked several times rapidly, he turned to escort Lilias to the raised table. Ashley's fingers tightened on the earthen pitcher. Mayhap she had been only fooling herself. Colin pulled out Lilias's chair and motioned for the others to rise. The silence was broken when Beathas brought out the roasted birds that had been decorated with feathers to resemble living creatures.

When the time arrived for the Lord of Misrule to be selected, hoots of delight filled the great hall as Davey Beaton held up the nut which had been in his slice of gingercake. It named him Lord of Misrule. For this one night, he would be the master of a domain within the hall's four walls.

A starched linen crown was placed on Davey's head. He was led about the room as everyone bowed to him. The lasses giggled as he neared them, for each one hoped for the chance to play the queen tonight. Finally he walked up to his throne, a chair covered with a purple velvet cloak.

"Welcome, my subjects, to the realm of the Lord of Misrule," Davey called. In his silly crown, he had an odd dignity that contrasted with his adolescent awkwardness. "My first command is for everyone to enjoy themselves tonight."

Cheers met his words. Throughout the hall, came shouts. "Pick your lady! Choose, Davey!"

"Milord is how you should address me!" he answered with a laugh.

"Then choose, *milord*!" called someone.

Again the lasses giggled, and Ashley smiled when one girl near her whispered that the one selected would be married to her heart's desire before the next Twelfth Night. Her smile widened as Davey walked through the crowd. When Beathas called to her, Ashley slipped away from the merriment to where the cook held out a piece of cake.

"'Tis not as exciting now that Davey has found the special nut," the cook said.

"It will taste good anyway." She started to take a bite, then paused when someone tapped her on the shoulder.

When she turned, Davey bowed deeply. "Milady, will you take your rightful place as Lady of Twelfth Night?"

Ashley hesitated. She did not need the ear-wrenching hush to warn her not to look toward the raised table where Colin sat.

Lilias's shrill voice severed the silence. "Colin, stop him! Will you allow him to crown that harlot as queen of Twelfth Night? You know only maidens can be chosen."

Ashley's mouth tightened. They had been forced to bend their heads to Lilias because she shared Colin's bed. Ashley fought back the pain at that thought. Instead she squared her shoulders. Davey was brave, risking his laird's rage. She must have courage to match his.

She whipped off her apron and tossed it on a bench. Holding her head high, she placed her fingers in Davey's hand. She dipped in the curtsy she had refused Colin earlier. "Your lordship, your lady awaits your command."

Cheers resounded. Ashley noted the uneasy expressions exchanged by those closest to where Colin sat. His face was set in an emotionless mask.

As Davey led her about the hall, the household dropped again to their knees. She glanced at Davey and saw his smile waver. The bows to him had been humorous. Tonight she was Lady Ashley again. Her reign would be short, for, like Cinderella, she soon would be amidst the ashes once more.

Davey seated her on the chair next to his. He looked at her expectantly.

She raised her hands and shouted, "On your feet, my friends. 'Tis time to dance."

She did not recognize who called out, "A toast to Lady Ashley!"

Pewter tankards clanked together before the ale was swallowed gustily. A fiddler began to play as another man picked up a flute.

Ashley leaned across the arm of her chair to whisper, "You dare much."

Davey grinned. "You are our lady. Could I have chosen another?"

"I hope Laird MacLachlan agrees with you."

"Tonight *I* am the lord, milady. There are many who think that you should be the lady of this castle much longer than one night." He glanced over his shoulder toward the raised table.

She patted his hand. Recalling the maid who had cried out when Colin had announced Ashley would be his bride, Ashley guessed that Davey would not be punished by his laird. The girl had been told only to keep her opinions to herself. That kind treatment had garnered Colin many allies. But that had been another Colin, a man who was fair in dealing with his people. This Colin...She could not guess what he would do, because she had not thought he would walk away and leave her to deal with Perkin Morton's lust alone.

When shouts came for them to join the dancing, Davey held out his hand shyly. Ashley smiled as she placed her hand in his, but her fingers trembled. This Colin might forgive Davey, but would he forgive her?

Together they walked to the center of the great hall. He bowed deeply. With a laugh, Ashley curtsied. He took her hands and twirled her about the room, stepping on her feet. He whirled her until she was dizzy, but she did not mind. For the first time in too long, she was enjoying herself.

The plaintive sound of bagpipes drowned out the flute and violin. The small hairs at the back of Ashley's neck rose as she recalled a piper playing a similar tune at the interrupted wedding. Did Colin want to remind everyone of that tonight? As she scanned the hall, she saw the dancers pausing and glancing toward the head table, clearly as unsettled and unsure as she was. The smiles had been replaced with fear and dismay.

Under the roar of the pipes, she asked, "Do you know this dance, Davey?"

"Aye, milady."

"Then dance!"

"But, Lady Ashley, if—"

"Dance, if you want to save Twelfth Night!"

Although he was clearly self-conscious, there was a grace in his movements which had been absent when he had danced with her. Ashley watched, clapping her hands with the rhythm of the music, as more and more of the men joined him. Her hands were grasped, and she was swirled into the pattern. She tried to copy the steps. As more women joined the dance, they formed a ring within the outer ring of men. Together they came, then whirled away to the next partner. All the time, their feet moved to the call of the pipes.

When the tune ended, applause and laughter filled the hall. Ashley looked at the piper who seemed abashed by the reaction. Davey called for more music, and the musicians smiled.

Ashley danced until her legs were tired, leaving her crown on the make-believe throne. Finally, breathless, she begged off and urged Davey to choose another partner. When he asked a young lass from the kitchen, she was not surprised. She had seen Davey and Effie talking in the courtyard. If things had been different, blonde Effie would have been the Lord of Misrule's lady tonight.

Ashley clasped her hands as she sat on her temporary throne. Things were not different, but she was not going to ruin the night by thinking such thoughts. It was impossible to keep Colin from her mind. He had not danced, and she wondered if his leg still bothered him.

When friends came to speak to her, soon she was laughing as someone put the crown back on her head. She watched the dancers spinning to the siren song of the pipes. The music's wild melody crawled into her blood.

Someone handed her a cup of mulled ale. Each time she emptied it, it was refilled. When the mulled ale was gone, her tankard was filled from the keg. As the strong ale warmed the coldness within her, she laughed along with the others.

Ashley paused in mid-word when the laughter vanished. Colin stopped in front of her and said, "Greetings, Lady of Twelfth Night."

The words reminded her of the day he had taken control of this castle and her. Tonight his triumphant expression was missing, replaced by a sadness which matched the emptiness in her heart. This night was not so different from that day. They had not learned to be anything but enemies.

"Greetings, Laird MacLachlan." She giggled. She had had too much to drink, but it did not matter. "Do you have a petition to be heard by the Lady of Twelfth Night?"

The music faded. From the raised table came the sound of hard heels beating the floor. Lilias pushed past the revelers. Colin ignored her, even when Lilias slipped her arm around him.

"Milady," he asked, "will you deign to allow one of your least subjects to approach your throne?"

"Do you speak for yourself, my laird," she returned coldly, "or for the one by your side?"

He drew Lilias's possessive arm from him. "Go back to your chair and wait."

"Wait?" Lilias demanded. "Wait for what? For you to pay court on a woman you want more than me?" She placed her hands on the full drapes of her skirt and glared at Ashley. "*Lady Ashley*! Do you know how many times I have heard him speak your name? And at times when you would think he would know it was not you!"

Colin grasped Lilias's shoulders and drew her away from the thrones. "Be quiet!" he ordered, then added, "'Tis I who would speak to you, milady."

"Come forward." Ashley's voice shook. She was trying to maintain her poise, but it was difficult when she feared that Lilias spoke of Colin mentioning Ashley's name in the bed he shared with his mistress.

Davey put his hand on Ashley's sleeve. "Milady, you need not—"

"'Tis all right." Her smile gentled as she patted his fingers.

Colin stepped closer, and her breath caught. No man should be this good-looking. Pulling her gaze from his, she could not keep from staring at his hands. Their touch brought her alive in ways she had not imagined. She clamped her fingers together in her lap. She must not let her own craving for him betray her.

He grimaced as he dipped to one knee, and she knew he had strained his leg. He raised her fingers to his lips, and that fire from his eyes swelled through her. "Most lovely sovereign lady."

"Ask what you will, my laird."

"Colin, my dear lady."

Her heart thudded. Was he seeking her forgiveness? "Ask what you will, Colin."

"Would you allow me to call Ella to take you to dress as a lady should?"

"Ella?" she squeaked with shock. She did not care about changing her clothes, but she had missed Ella and her gentle counsel. "You will let Ella talk to me?"

"Of course, Ashley. I have been wrong to deny you anything your heart desires." He signaled to Ella. As Ella came forward, her mouth round with shock, he brought Ashley to her feet. Raising her fingers to his mouth again, he turned to Ella. "Take your lady and prepare her to be the Lady of Twelfth Night."

Ella rushed forward, but halted when Ashley held up her hand.

Ashley pulled away from Colin. The ale had not dulled her wits enough to lure her into foolishness. She crossed her arms over her chest. When she wobbled, Davey's hand in the middle of her back steadied her.

"I wear the finest robes any lady could wear." Ashley touched her simple dress. "These are the clothes given to me by my friends. I am sorry if I have offended your sensibilities, my laird, but I prefer to stay as I am." She sat again.

"Ashley, be done with this nonsense."

"What nonsense? Tonight, I am the Lady of Twelfth Night. Tomorrow, I shall be a lowly maid." She leaned forward and laughed. "You can't take my pride from me."

"Ashley—"

"You are dismissed, my laird."

A gasp rose from the crowd.

Lilias pressed close to him and murmured, "Let the harlot have her fun tonight. Come, darling. We can have a bit more of that fine wassail and some fun of our own." She pulled on his arm.

Again he pushed her away. "Ashley, listen to me." When she turned away, he took her by the shoulders. "Ashley, listen to me."

"My laird, you overstep yourself." She plucked his hands from her. "Tonight I do not have to be shown how much you hate me."

"Ashley, I do not hate you. I love you."

"You what?" she cried as a flurry of comments raced around the room too swiftly for her to understand. Were the others pleased or upset at his pronouncement? Or shocked as she was? Colin *loved* her?

He drew her to her feet and into his arms. Her eyes closed as his lips touched her forehead. As her arms slid beneath his plaid to caress his back, he captured her mouth.

She answered his passion with her own for only the length of a heartbeat before she pulled away. "How dare you!" she whispered, too angry to speak louder. "Do you think that I will be fooled by another of your games, Colin? You are wrong! I will not believe your lies any longer!"

"'Tis no lie. I love you."

She smiled without humor. "Of course you love me. That is why you take another woman to your bed!"

Lilias ran forward to step between them. Putting her hand on Colin's arm, she tried to draw him away. No one else moved, not wanting to miss the drama, better than any mummer's play, being acted out before them.

"Take him, Lilias," Ashley said. "Take him, and be welcome to him." She threw the linen crown to the floor at Colin's feet. "Have everything my heart once wanted." She ran to the door leading to the kitchen. Nobody tried to halt her despite Colin's shout to stop.

Colin was shocked when Ella blocked his way. "No, my laird. Let her be. Haven't you hurt her enough?"

He stepped around her and ran along the passage, his leg hurting more on every step. No candles flickered in the kitchen when he entered. Only embers on a hearth lit the cavernous room. He did not need light to lead him to a table where a form huddled in misery. Gently he put his hands on Ashley's shoulders.

"Go away, Colin," she moaned. "You win. Whatever you were trying to prove, you have."

Wincing at the jolt in his leg, he straddled the bench and brought her head against his chest. When sobs shook her, he knew he had broken Ashley's fiery spirit. He wondered if she would believe him if he told her how he did not understand the madness that had engulfed him.

He had spoken words he should not have, words he did not mean. He had escaped only when he had seen Ashley's horrified face looking at him across the hall tonight when the piper had begun to play the same melody that had been part of the feigned wedding. How long had he been stuck in the miasma of rage? He must have been daft. Daft to invite Lilias to the castle. Even more daft to put Ashley from his side.

Would Ashley believe him when he told her that he had chosen Lilias simply because she was so unlike Ashley? Lilias was coy and dull, not like Ashley who was so forthright with him. When he held Ashley, he savored the fresh aroma of her hair and soft skin. The heavy thickness of Lilias's perfumes sickened him. He did not want Lilias and feared he had lost Ashley.

If not for Ashley, he would be dead and buried in the cemetery. Ramsey had told him that more than once. He had never seen his valet so angry, and he had kept Ramsey from leaving only with promises that he would find Ramsey another position as soon as the weather broke. It had been fortunate that the snows had been frequent and heavy. This damn castle had cost him dearly already.

But it was not gratitude which had urged him to tell Ashley the truth in his heart.

"Forgive me, *belovit*," he murmured in her ear. "I was cruel to you. Too cruel for the man who loves you."

She shook her head. "Stop it. You don't need to continue with that lie."

"'Tis not a lie." His hands framed her face to bring it up to look at him. In the dim light, the trails of her tears glistened like silver.

"No?" she asked bitterly.

"Ashley, listen to me." He had to make her see past the haze of her anger. "I know you have every reason not to believe me, but, if you never believe me again, know I am speaking the truth when I tell you I love you. I love your stubborn resistance to every word I say. I love your wit which cuts through me when you gaze at me with anger like amber fire in your eyes. I love everything about you."

Ashley did not know what to say. Every time she had dared to trust him, he found a way to twist her to his advantage.

When she remained silent, he said, "I know you love me as I love you." Gently he brought her lips to his. There was nothing tender about his hungry kiss which sliced through her, seeking the secrets hidden in her heart. "I know when I hold you and feel the fire blistering on your lips. Admit it, *belovit*. Tell me you love me, too."

"I do not want to love you, Colin!" she cried, leaping to her feet. "Go away, and leave me alone!"

He stood. She spun to race away. Before she reached the door to the stillroom, he pulled her into his arms. His fingers captured her face as he kissed her.

"What must I do to prove to you," he whispered, "that I do not want to hurt you? I want to bring you the joy that swells through my heart each time I see you."

"Each time?" she demanded. "Even when you watch another man attempt to rape me in the great hall and walk away saying nothing?"

"Have you seen Perkin Morton again?"

"No."

His face was grim as he said, "And you will not."

"Colin, did you—"

"No," he said with a sharp laugh. "No, I did not have him killed, although I was tempted. When he told me it was someone else who had planted the idea in his head, I found it better to send him to Jackie. Let him die with honor."

"Who would tell him to do something so horrible to me?"

"You know."

"Lilias?"

"No more talk now, *belovit*." His mouth teased hers to surrender to it. When she grew rigid, he snapped, "Dammit, woman, I love you!"

A chill raced along Ashley's spine. She had seen rage in his eyes. She had been taunted by his superior grin. This tenderness terrified her, for it enticed her to trust him one more time.

And was it real? They had been manipulated too many times by forces beyond anything she understood. Was this just another manifestation of some witchly spell?

She wanted his words to be true. She wanted him to love her as she loved him. It would be so perfect. All of the hatred between them could fade into the past as they shared the future together.

Future? Her future was hundreds of years from here, hundreds of years from now.

"No!" she cried.

"No?"

"Don't fall in love with me, Colin. I will not fall in love with you."

"Because you think I shall take you to my bed, then give you to the marquess's executioners?"

"Won't you if that is what he orders?"

He released her. "If that is what you believe, Ashley, I think you are right. There can be no love for you and me." She watched with dismay as he went to the doorway. There, he turned to say, "Milady, you need not sleep in the kitchen any longer."

He walked away, but she did not see him leave as she buried her face in her hands, knowing that he would never understand why she had denied her heart the love it longed for.

# FOURTEEN

Ashley woke in her own bed the morning after Twelfth Night, but it seemed strange. She did not belong here any longer. She was not sure where she belonged.

When she went to the kitchen, Beathas glanced up to see what had caused the wave of quiet. "Milady! I did not expect—I mean—"

Ashley sighed. She was an outsider here again. "I came to thank you, Beathas, for being so kind to me."

"You are our lady. I did as I should." The cook's stilted words could not cover her disquiet.

"Tomorrow, I would like to speak with you about the meals for next week. I thought we might change our time for discussing that to after the midday meal. I realize now that early afternoon is your quietest time." Ashley forced a laugh. "See? I learned some important lessons here."

Beathas chuckled. "In the afternoon will be fine."

"Will I disturb you if I speak to Susan?"

"Of course not, milady. Speak softly if you wish to avoid hurting the many aching heads here this morning."

Ashley laughed again, more sincerely. She crossed the kitchen to where Susan sat by her favorite fireplace. "Good morning, Susan. I was not sure if you would be back from your mother's cottage yet."

"Lady Ashley!" She smiled. "I wondered who was here when I heard the sound of velvet over petticoats. So it is true. Laird MacLachlan escaped the evil that enslaved him last night."

"The evil? What do you know of it?"

"I listen, milady. I hear what others might not. The laird's voice was harsh, not his own. 'Twas as if he were in the midst of an evil spell."

"Yes, but that is nonsense," Ashley said, although she was not so sure of her words. She did not want to speak of this where others might hear.

"Whatever it was, the change explains why Lilias Lundy has been sent back to her father."

Pulling up another chair, Ashley sat facing her friend. "She is gone?"

Susan's mouth twisted into a vindictive smile. "She was sent home with the sunrise. Waste no sympathy on her, milady, for it is being said that she already has made other arrangements to replace the laird."

"I am not surprised. Lilias is like a cat."

"Always looking for a new lover?"

Ashley chuckled. "I was thinking more about the way she always lands on her feet."

"On her feet is hardly where her new lover will want her." Susan giggled. "Forgive me, milady. My mother told me to tell you that all will come as you wish."

"Did she?"

"Yes, and my mother is seldom wrong."

Ashley wanted to ask the question burning on her tongue, but she held it back. If she was overheard asking Susan if her mother was a witch, both Susan and Wynda Thompson could be in danger from the witch-hunters.

"And you, my friend?" Susan asked. "What will you do now?"

She turned to look into the ever-changing flames on the hearth. "I don't know."

"I was told that he said he loves you."

"You do listen well."

Susan frowned. "You are trying to change the subject, milady."

"Colin has seldom been truthful with me."

"You know that is not true. He has often been honest with you."

"Except for..." She stood and gripped the back of her chair. "The problem is that I have fallen in love him."

Susan laughed. "Do not act as if you are revealing a secret, Lady Ashley. I know that you love the laird."

"How?"

"Even if my mother, who misses very little, had not told me, I would know. I do not need eyes to know how you glow when you speak his name. Your voice takes flight when it caresses his name as you wish him to caress you."

Ashley looked across the kitchen. She could not lie and say she was sorry she was no longer forced to stay here. Acting as the steward for the castle was the task she enjoyed most. If only she could be so sure of what was in her heart and in Colin's.

"Susan, I came here because I wanted to ask you—"

"No, milady."

"How can you say that when you do not know what I plan to say?"

"I know you want to ask me to work with Ella."

Ashley smiled. "You must have ears like a bat to hear what was spoken of in my chambers."

"Nothing stays unknown in this castle for long." Susan chuckled, then grew somber again. "I thank you, milady, but I wish to stay in the kitchens. Here I can serve as I can nowhere else."

"How did you get so wise?"

"Listening to others' mistakes!"

"If you change your mind—"

"I shall not." Susan's voice lowered as she added, "I shall miss you here with me."

"When spring comes, if I am still here, I want you to go riding with me. You have many horizons to chase, Susan."

"Aye, and you shall help me."

Ashley placed her hand on Susan's slender shoulder, then left the kitchen. It was time to continue with her life.

But that was impossible. Although most of those living in Castle Braeburn made an effort to act as if her banishment had never happened, Colin was as cool to her as if they were strangers. At dinner he acknowledged her, asked how her day had gone, and finished his meal as quickly as he could. As she watched him walk away, she knew Colin would not bend. He had offered her his heart, and she had hurt him as badly as he had her. She could not blame her actions on some unknown spell.

Could he? She was not certain, but she knew it was time to be honest with him. Yet, she could not when he gave her no chance to say more than good day to him.

Scanning the great hall, she smiled when her gaze met Ramsey White's. She was not surprised that he was trying to attract her attention. He pointed to the ceiling, and she nodded, understanding that he wanted to meet her in her rooms.

It was not easy to keep her feet from racing up the stairs, but she wanted no one to guess why she was in a hurry. Especially Colin. He might see her efforts to talk alone with Ramsey as plotting against him.

Ramsey was waiting in the largest chamber of her suite. "I am pleased that you understood me, milady." He barred the door behind her. "*Milady*. It is good to use that again."

She smiled. "I must admit I have enjoyed hearing it again, also. Will you be missed while we speak?"

"The laird is meeting with the captain of the guard and should not require my services for awhile."

Sitting, Ashley spread her full skirts around her. It seemed natural now to wear these voluminous clothes. "I am listening."

"The laird was speaking the truth on Twelfth Night," stated Ramsey.

"I wish I could believe that."

The white-haired man sighed. "I can understand your distrust, but he is telling the truth."

"I thought he was being truthful before." She counted on her fingers. "I thought he was being honest when he told me I had no hope of claiming this castle because he had sent word to the marquess before I could. I thought he was speaking the truth when he said I must marry him. I even believed him when he told me he had not wanted to use me as he did in that pretend wedding."

"He did not! The last, I mean." Ramsey dropped to a chair and clasped his hands until his knuckles bleached. "Milady, he rued having to risk your life to clear the castle of the ones who refused to accept him. Of the other things, I know nothing. What I do know is that he loves you."

"As he loved Lilias Lundy?"

"Her?" His face contorted into a grimace. "He loathed her. She hung around him like a lovesick calf until he found it easier to sleep on a pallet in my room."

Ashley gasped, "He did not—They did not—"

"'Tis you he wants, milady. He would go to her, but always drew away as if he fought a battle within himself."

"Oh." She dared say no more, because she could not reveal how she had fought those same battles herself against the evil that threatened to consume her.

"I think he kept her here as long as he did because he could not admit how much he loves you."

"He has a strange way of expressing himself." She stood and went to the window. Her fingers crushed the heavy velvet drapes.

"Do you love him, milady?"

She closed her eyes and sighed. Had Colin sent Ramsey to ask her this? She cringed at the horrible thought. When had she become so distrusting? That was not like Ashley Babcock. *Ashley Babcock!* She could not expect Colin to be honest when she hid the most important truth from him. The time had come for honesty.

Turning to Ramsey, whose face was long with unhappiness, she said, "Yes, I believe I am in love with him."

"And he loves you. He offered his heart to you. You refused."

"So the next move is mine?" She leaned on the windowsill and smiled. "You are wasted here, Ramsey. If you can heal the rift between Colin and me, you should be negotiating an end to the war."

He did not smile. "Look into your heart, and you shall know what you must do."

"I shall think about it."

"Aye, I know you will. Listen to the quiet voice which urges you to believe what you know is true."

*The quiet voice?* She almost asked that aloud, then realized Ramsey meant her love for Colin, not the soft voice that seemed to come out of nowhere and was accompanied by the sparkles. Swallowing roughly, she said, "Thank you, Ramsey."

"Thank you, milady." He stood and went to the door. "You have made my laird happier than he has ever been."

"And more miserable?"

"Don't they go hand in hand? Blessings and banes are part of the same whole. From the time he saw his family die and took the vow to regain their honor, he has thought of nothing but fulfilling that vow. Then he met you, and he has had to recall that a heart is supposed to hold more than hatred." As he opened the door, he added quietly, "The laird will be busy until at least the hour before midnight."

Ashley sat. She knew what Ramsey meant. Tonight, just before midnight, Colin would be returning to his rooms.

Ella did not seem surprised when Ashley asked for a bath to be brought. The maid went to arrange for it. Alone, Ashley leaned her head against the upright of her bed. The time had come to do what she knew was right.

She watched as her bath was filled, then closed her door and pulled off her gown. Sinking into the steaming warmth, she set her thoughts free, following them as she recalled her adventures in Castle Braeburn. Tonight she was set to embark on the latest. Before she had been tossed, without warning, into each experience. This time she would choose.

From the beginning, she had seen that Colin MacLachlan could be a stubborn, self-centered autocrat. But she was as stubborn as he was and as determined to do what she thought was right, no matter the cost. He would never change, and neither would she. Together, they had found misery...and rapture.

When Ella offered to help her get ready for bed, Ashley said, "I can manage. Go to bed if you wish."

"Milady, are you all right? Your face is flushed."

"The water was pleasantly hot. Go to sleep. Tomorrow we must update all the accounts which have been neglected."

"Aye, as you wish," she replied slowly. "Good night."

The door closed, and silence enveloped Ashley. As she pulled the lovely green robe around and buttoned it over the fine lace of her chemise, she did not look at the mirror. It stood like an accusing eye.

"Leave me alone!"

Whether she was speaking to the looking glass or to the uncertainty slipping out of her heart, warning her that she was a fool to trust Colin MacLachlan, she did not want to know. From the onset, she had tried to keep her heart from Colin. Now it was too late. It had been too late from the moment he had pulled her into his arms in the great hall and kissed her.

Ashley heard the night watchman call out the day's last hour. She eased out the door. The floor was icy beneath her bare feet. Few candles burned in the sconces on the wall. One of them sputtered and died with the heavy odor of burned wax. The others bounced with the vagaries of the breezes which refused to be kept out of the castle.

Ashley avoided the pools of light and clung to the shadows. As she walked past the stairwell, she could hear voices from the floors above and below her. Along this hallway, only quiet reigned. Her fingertips quivered as she reached Colin's door. She lifted the latch and swung the door open.

The room was empty. Candles brightened the antechamber's center and glistened off Colin's mighty claymore that was leaning against the chimney. It was waiting, ready, for whenever he might need it.

She went to the door to Colin's bedchamber. It opened with a soft squeak. When she closed it behind her, she leaned against the uneven boards with her eyes shut. She was here. There was no turning back. A rush of warmth thawed the last of her disquiet.

The glow from the fireplace chased the shadows to the corners. Her toes sank into the thick wool carpet as she went to the huge bed that had been her father's and was now where Colin slept.

The tester bed's carved columns were thicker than her arm. Animal faces were carved to peer out from what looked like a tree trunk. A crimson coverlet was spread across the high bed. From beneath the satin came the heat of a bed warming pan.

Ashley went to the fireplace. Rubbing her hands together, she held them out to the fire. The heat wavered around her, teasing her with the heavy fingers of fatigue. It must be reaching toward midnight. Uneasily, she stepped away from the lure of the heat and stifled a yawn. Tonight she did not want to be tired. As she moved back, her eyes rose to the portrait over the fireplace.

It was of her. Not of her, but of Lady Fia Gordon. The lady's emerald dress was the same shade as Ashley's robe and appeared luminous on the canvas. Yet Lady Fia's eyes were even more brilliant. Why had Colin brought this painting here from where it had been hidden in a dusty attic?

*You know the reason, bairn.*

Ashley slowly looked behind her. She held her breath when she saw the sparkles gathering by the window. Dampening her lips, she whispered, "Is that you?"

*It is I.* The sound of gentle laughter brushed Ashley with warmth. *Many said you were born to be my very image, and I can see they were not wrong.*

"Lady Fia?" She did not believe her own question, but everything about Castle Braeburn was unbelievable.

*You used to call me a different name.*

"So it is true? Everything Gertie Graham told me is true?"

*Gertie...Bairn, take care what—*

The sparkles vanished so swiftly that Ashley blinked. She started to call Lady Fia's name, but froze when she heard, "This is a wondrous surprise."

She whirled to see Colin closing the door. He crossed the wide floor between them, but did not touch her.

"Good evening, Colin," she said quietly. This was not how she had thought he would react when he discovered her waiting for him.

"To what do I owe this extraordinary visit?" His gaze swept along her.

She faltered. His voice offered no hint if he was pleased to see her here. In her fantasies, he had drawn her into his arms and kissed her before taking her to the lush thickness of his bed.

When she did not answer, he went to the cupboard and opened the door. His plaid fell from his shoulder when he unhooked the brooch holding it. Setting the brooch on a shelf, he turned back to her.

"Well, Ashley?" he asked. "I have given you a chance to devise a dozen lies to explain why you are here."

"Lies? Are those what you expect from me?" She fisted her hands on her hips.

"'Tis what I usually receive from you."

"If you want honesty, I will tell you that it was a mistake to come here. Therefore, I shall wish you a good night."

He stepped between her and the door. "It shall be a very good night, *belovit*, if you stop fleeing from the truth."

"The truth?" She laughed sharply. "When have you ever cared about the truth? Do you want to hear the truth? Tonight I came here because I love you." She shook her head. "I don't want to love you, but I do."

"The very words I thought you would never say." His broad fingers cupped her chin before his hands entangled in her hair.

"You are exasperating!"

"And you are beautiful." Slowly, a bare inch at each step, he drew her into his arms.

Her eyes closed as she leaned against him. She stroked his coarse doublet as he continued to tease her with gentle kisses. Butterfly soft, his mouth glided across her cheeks to sample her eyelids, her cheekbones, the crescent of her ear. Within her, embers became a flame. She grasped his head and brought his lips back to hers.

When he put his arm beneath her knees, he lifted her against his chest. The emerald silk of her gown came alive with the light from the fire, bathing them in its glow. As he placed her among the pillows on the magnificent bed, he whispered, "Tonight, you shall learn that I have spoken the truth when I tell you how much I love you. That truth you never need doubt again."

"Tell me later." Her voice was husky as she ordered, "Show me now."

With a moan of the yearning he could no longer contain, he pinned her to the bed. Her arms wrapped around his neck as she gave herself to the lure of his lips. As she gazed into his face, he drew back her hair and placed the tip of his tongue against her earlobe.

She closed her eyes as she swayed closer to him. Through the thin lace of her chemise, she sensed the pulse of his craving. Eagerly, her fingers guided his face back to hers. She tasted his rough cheeks and traced delight along his skin. When she laved the soft skin of his eyelids, his hands tightened on her.

Fiercely, he pressed her back into the pillows and leaned over her. His eyes glowed with azure frenzy, and he laughed when she gasped.

Her breath grew rapid as he taunted her mouth with rapid-fire kisses. When his tongue tantalized hers, she moaned. All gentleness disappeared from his demanding mouth as the swift pulse of his breath wafted through her. She pressed to him as his tongue led hers on an unrestrained dance.

She quivered when his lips etched a sparkling pattern of rapture along her neck. All of her was enmeshed in the delight left by his mouth following the modest neckline of her robe.

He undid the sash at her waist. He brought her up to her knees and made quick work of drawing the robe from her. She began to undo his doublet, but was hampered by the luscious kisses he placed against her shoulders as he dropped the lace straps of her chemise along her arms. Reaching beneath his gaping doublet, she stroked his muscular chest.

His voice rasped in her ear, "Do you know I have been waiting for this moment since I saw you? You were so brave, and your lips were so sweet."

"Kiss me now."

"My pleasure, milady."

She needed no urging to finish undoing his doublet. As she pushed it along his arms, she slanted into his chest. His skin tantalized her through her chemise. His swift heartbeat resonated into her. When the doublet rested atop her robe on the floor, her hands discovered the expanse of his chest. Touching him augmented the ache within her.

He lowered her back onto the bed and eagerly drew down her chemise. Then pausing, he said, "Stay here."

"Where else would I want to be?"

His kiss burned into her lips before he stepped away from the bed. She sat up, holding her chemise to her breasts as he went to the door and dropped the bar into place.

"Why didn't you do that before?" she teased as he returned.

He folded his arms on the high bed, so their eyes were level. Her throaty laugh was muffled as his lips wafted across her mouth before his hand caressed her breast. Her chemise fell away before his questing fingers.

He whispered, "It is not easy to know what you might do. I did not know if you had come here to discover rapture, or if you wanted merely to make me more insane with this ravenous desire."

"Both," she breathed as he bent to put his mouth against her bared breast.

When she gasped with astonishment at the wild urgings overtaking her, his muted chuckle tickled her. His tongue swirled a moist path along her. Her fingers clutched his shoulders as she fought to control the raging need within her.

"You make me feel so wonderful," she managed to whisper in his ear, then explored its ridges as avidly as he was her.

His gaze held her as he gave her that insolent smile, which at first had outraged her and now delighted her, before lowering her chemise farther. Gentle nibbles along her shoulder made her writhe. Drawing his mouth back to hers, she slid her hands along the varied textures of his chest to the waistband of his kilt. His groan of pleasure teased her to be more daring.

He tossed the last of his clothes aside and slanted her back into the coverlet that heated with the fire blazing through her. When he rose over her, she traced the masculine lines of his body which soon would be sharing hers. His moan was seared into her lips.

He gave her no time to savor his skin against hers. His mouth sought delight across her abdomen and up her breast. As before, he moved slowly until his tongue taunted the tip. With a greed that matched hers to touch him, he drew it into his mouth. She was consumed by a craving.

Her voice was unrecognizable in her own ears as she urged him to satisfy that need. If the savage hunger within her was not allayed, she feared she would be lost in torment. His hands stroked her legs as his mouth spiraled along her stomach, seeking to tantalize all of her.

Gasping out his name, she stretched to caress his hair as he explored her intimately, his tongue caressing her eager skin. His arm slipped beneath her shoulders to cradle her between his lips and the coverlet as he brought them together.

His hands splayed along her face, and she opened her eyes to see his so close. For once, she could see deep into their depths and was awed by the passion within them. She brought his mouth to hers, wanting to touch him with every inch of herself.

She matched the tempo he set and was swept into a wildfire that burned through her and him, making them one. In a fierce explosion of ecstasy, her joy was more splendid because he was with her as she never could have imagined.

*\*\*\**

Ashley's eyes slowly opened to see Colin's smiling face above hers. As he pushed an errant strand of hair from her eyes, she smiled and whispered, "That was wonderful."

"It was, wasn't it?" His mouth took hers to savor the last bits of passion.

"Aye," she drawled.

"I am so sorry, *belovit*."

"Sorry?" She drew back, shocked at the word she had not thought he would speak now.

His hands framed her face as he whispered, "Listen to me. Really listen for once, Ashley."

"All right."

"I am sorry for how I treated you the past few weeks." He closed his eyes and shook his head. "I look back on those days and wonder if my mind took leave of every bit of sense it possessed. There is nothing but a rage that was aimed at hurting you." His thumbs stroked her cheekbones. "I do not understand it, for it was a rage that was mine, but it was not mine."

"I understand."

"You do?" His eyes grew wide.

"It *was* a madness."

"Left by my fever?"

Ashley hesitated, wanting to be honest with him. How could she? She had no explanation that she could understand, and she feared he would denounce it as witchcraft. *What if it is witchcraft?* No, she would not let her thoughts go in that direction.

Running her fingers along his chest, she whispered, "The mind is mysterious, Colin. You must fight that rage and not let it govern you."

"You speak as if you know this rage yourself."

Again she faltered. To speak of that horror now might destroy the perfection of being in his arms. She wanted to keep tonight untainted by the hatred that had tried to tear them apart. Later... "I know that I do not want to speak of the past when I want to think only of this moment."

"Finally. Something we can agree upon." He chuckled and settled her in his arms, her head on his shoulder. When he kissed the top of her tousled hair, she laughed softly, pushing aside the darkness, so she could savor this delight.

Kissing the tip of her nose, he asked, "What is so funny, *belovit*?"

"I have always wanted to know what a Scotsman wears beneath his kilt. Now I know."

"You what?" He sat, shock widening his eyes. "Why would a lady like you—?"

Laughing, she said, "'Tis an old joke. A very old one!"

"I am not sure if I like to be part of an old joke."

"Would you prefer to be part of this new love?" She caressed his cheek and smiled as he turned to place his lips against her palm.

"As long as you are the other part."

His mouth over hers was a promise of the joys they had yet to share. As she ran her fingers along his stubborn jaw, she exulted in his touch. She had found ecstasy with a man who should have been only a shadow in the past. Even as his kisses enticed her back into pleasure, she wondered how long this stolen love could last.

# FIFTEEN

Ashley woke and stretched out her arms.

"Look out!" Colin chided.

Her eyes widened, and he knew she was recalling what they had shared in his bed last night. When a blush tinted her cheeks, he laughed again. Ashley could argue like an old chieftain, but she had been enticing in his arms. He touched her rosy skin with a single finger and smiled when she quivered with the anticipation that raced through him. He wished he could remain here with her. That could not be. He contented himself with kissing the curve of her throat and relishing her swift intake of breath.

"Good morning, milady," he murmured.

"Isn't that a bit formal?"

"Then how about this?"

She smiled as he pinned her against the pillows. His mouth's urgency matched her fiery caress along his back. When he raised his head, she locked her fingers at his nape and whispered, "That is much better."

"I want you to want my kisses every morning before we face the day to come." When he stood, Ashley ran her fingers along his hip. Desire thudded through him like a blow. With a laugh, he drew her up to her knees. "Do not add to my distress that I cannot linger with you any longer because I have tasks that must be completed today."

In the soft voice which had driven him to the very edge of reason last night, she murmured, "I do not want you to forget me as you go about your tasks today."

"That is about as likely as it is for a man to fly like a bird." When she laughed, he asked, "What is so amusing?"

"Nothing." She looked away, her smile disappearing.

Colin fought the frown tightening his lips. He recognized the tension along her. He had seen it too often, but he had no idea what caused it. This puzzle he did not want to solve today. He patted her bare bottom. "Get dressed, woman. 'Tis time you earn your keep."

"I thought I was."

With a laugh, he scooped up her clothes from the floor and dropped them over her head. He was closing his doublet when he realized Ashley still sat with her clothes in her hands.

"What is wrong?" he asked, wondering how anything could be wrong today.

"What time is it?"

He went to the window and shouldered aside the drapes. "Nearly midday."

"Colin, I cannot go out dressed like this in the middle of the day." When he chuckled, she added, hastily, "I mean in my nightclothes."

"Dress. I shall send Ramsey to bring you other things. Why don't you have Ella put your things in my cupboard?"

Ashley pulled her chemise over her head. As she slipped from the high bed, she tied the robe around her. She put her fingers lightly on his forearms. "You want me to move in here with you?"

"Why not? Do you wish to sleep alone?"

"Of course not."

"There is the room you first used, which Ella can have. I know it will be several days before everything can be settled."

Her eyebrows came together in bafflement. "What are you talking about? Several days until what?" Cold washed over her. "Do you mean until we hear from the marquess?"

"You do not remember!" He laughed.

"Remember? Remember what?"

He took her hand and led her back to the rumpled bed. Patting the pillow, he smiled. "Here is where my head was resting. Your head was against me. It was when I woke you just after moonrise. You *do* remember that, I assume?"

"I could never forget that." She smiled as she recalled his eager touch.

His kiss was deep, but swift. "But you have forgotten that I asked you to marry me then."

"You asked me to marry you?" she gasped. "What did I say?"

"You said, 'Hmm-mm-mm.' I assumed that was a yes. Was I right?"

Ashley stared at him. Was this another trick? Another bit of witchcraft to delude her? Stepping away, she went to a chair and sank onto it. She stared at a stain in the middle of the rug.

A single finger under her chin tilted her face to meet Colin's frown. "Did I mistake your murmur? I thought you loved me."

"I do!"

"Then you have another you wish to wed?"

She shook her head. "No one else."

Colin brought her to her feet and sat in the chair, pulling her onto his lap. He held her close to him. "Do you fear I am using you again?"

"I would be a fool not to have thought of that."

"True, but 'tis true as well that I want you as my wife."

Ashley looked up at his strong jaw, then back at the bed. "You do not need to feel obligated to wed me because of last night. If you think that you did me a dishonor in any way—"

"Dishonor?" He laughed. "I was quite *honored* to have you in my arms. I am obligated to protect those within this castle, Ashley, but 'tis only because of what is in my heart that I have asked you to marry me. I love you. You love me. 'Tis perfect."

"Yes," she said slowly. "It *is* perfect, isn't it?" Biting her bottom lip, she wondered how to explain why she was hesitating. Colin was being honest, but her greatest secret was still unrevealed.

Counting back the weeks, she was startled to realize how long she had been in the 17th century. She had no idea how to return to her own time. Her hands clenched against Colin's chest as she realized she might be able to find out. Gertie Graham could know, for her spell had sent the child Ashley Gordon from here years ago. She shuddered. The sparkles, which claimed to be Lady Fia Gordon, had been apprehensive when Ashley mentioned Gertie's name.

*What of Wynda Thompson?*

That thought was wholly her own. It was something she had to consider...later. For now, she wanted to think only of delighting in this love that should not exist. Let Gertie Graham fear that Colin was here to destroy Castle Braeburn and the last of the Gordons within its wall. It was time to listen to her own heart.

She looked into Colin's remarkably blue eyes. "Yes, I will marry you."

His smile shone as brightly as the morning sun. He let loose a shout which rang through her ears. Before she could react, he was whirling her about and kissing her with the same fervor.

A furious knock came on the door.

Colin placed Ashley on her feet just before Ramsey exploded into the room.

"My laird? What is it?"

"Surely you recognize *Fortis et fidus*," Colin answered with a feigned frown.

"Aye, I would know our clan's war cry anywhere, but, my laird..." His voice trailed off. "Good morning, milady," he said, as if it were the most ordinary thing for her to be here dressed in her robe.

"Good morning, Ramsey. Pay no attention to Colin." She grinned. "He is daft." When Colin held out his hand to her, she placed her fingers on it. "Tell him, Colin."

"See how she orders me, Ramsey." Colin chuckled. "What will it be like after we exchange our marriage vows?"

Ramsey's eyes crinkled as his broad grin threatened to crack his face. "'Twill be grand, my laird."

"Aye. Have Ella come with some clothes for Ashley. Later, the two of you can arrange for all of Ashley's things to be brought here." He squeezed her shoulders.

With a nod, Ramsey rushed to obey. He must have spread the news to everyone he met because, when Ashley went about Castle Braeburn to do her daily chores, she was stopped a dozen times and congratulated. She was startled when several of Colin's men offered their congratulations as well. The marriage would be more than a joining of their hearts. It would be a healing within the castle.

The excitement in the great hall during the evening meal was more high-spirited than during the Twelfth Night celebration. Cheers rose, and tankards were hefted when Ashley entered the great hall on Colin's arm. Music played throughout the meal, and dancing began before it was finished.

Colin kissed Ashley before he joined the men dancing to the bagpipes. She leaned on her elbows to watch him move with the grace he brought to everything he did. Although it seemed strange to see the kilted men dance alone, the movements of their plaids gave an added lilt to their steps. When the music faded, she leapt to her feet and applauded.

With a wave, Colin motioned for her to come to the middle of the floor. She ran to be enfolded in his arms. She pressed her face to his damp shirt, breathing in the musky scent left by the vigorous dance.

"A toast!" came a shout. "A toast to Laird Colin MacLachlan and Lady Ashley Gordon MacLachlan-to-be."

Her eyes glittering with joy, Ashley smiled at Colin. As the ale was downed about the room, he lowered his lips to cover hers. The merriment was muted by her heart pounding with jubilation.

\*\*\*

The wedding was set to be held in one week. Nobody mentioned the travesty of their first wedding ceremony, and Ashley believed that everyone had accepted this. Everyone but Gertie Graham, mayhap, but the old woman did not come to the castle.

For Ashley, the hours passed quickly. Her nights were luscious in Colin's arms. With their heads close together as they reclined on the rug before the massive hearth which warmed their bedroom, they spoke of their dreams for Castle Braeburn. If Colin noticed Ashley's withdrawal at odd times during their conversations, he said nothing of it. When he held her in his arms in their bed, she held back nothing from him.

Ashley continued to postpone the trip to Wynda's cottage. She did not want to be told how silly were her hopes of being assured she was in this century to stay. While she delayed, she could cling to her precious dreams. She tried to seek out Lady Fia, but the ghost seemed to have vanished.

Two days before the wedding, Colin startled Ashley by coming to the solar in the middle of the day. He seldom could steal time to take from training his men until the early twilight. His face was drawn with worry.

"What is it, Colin?" she asked, coming to her feet. She motioned the servants, who had been taking her orders for the day, to leave.

As the door closed behind them, he replied, "Montrose has attacked the marquess's camp at Inverlochy. With half as many men as Campbell had, he defeated them."

"Oh, how awful!"

"Aye," he said darkly. "The marquess and his closest allies sailed to safety and left their men to be slaughtered by Montrose."

"Jackie? What of him and your men?"

"That I do not know."

"Do you wish to postpone the wedding?"

He smiled and stroked her hair. "No, *belovit*. It may be weeks before we hear from Jackie. If he is alive, he will be chasing Montrose's men across the Highlands."

Suddenly she understood the wistfulness in his voice. "You want to go, Colin. No! I don't want you to die."

"You need not worry. This message repeated what I was told before. I am to stay here and keep this path of retreat open for whatever is left of Campbell's army." He balled up the paper and threw it into the fireplace. "Retreat!" he spat. "They should be thinking of gathering us together to destroy the Royalists."

Ashley was not sure what to say. She could not say she was sorry he would not be fighting to the death on some bleak hillside. To do so would be lying. She wanted him safe with her, but his bitterness hurt her, for she knew how important winning this war was to him. She put her arms around his waist and rested her face against his solid chest. Slowly his arms raised to allow her within his embrace. When his arm around her shoulders leaned her back, she welcomed his mouth.

Reluctantly he released her. "I love you, Ashley Gordon."

"I do not like seeing you so sad while you are imprisoned in Castle Braeburn. I know you want to be free, riding along the moors."

"Good idea. Let's go." He laughed and pushed her toward the door. "Go and change, my love."

"Change?"

"To go riding. Look out the window. The sun is shining. Shall we go for a ride?"

"Now?"

"Why not?"

With a laugh, she kissed his cheek. "I will meet you at the stable. Have my horse saddled for me. Not the sidesaddle, please."

He tweaked her nose. "I remember. Hurry."

"I will!"

As Ashley's light footsteps faded into the distance, Colin went to the bank of windows which looked south. There beyond the blue mountains lay England. He wished King Charles would keep his problems within his own borders. In the opposite direction, his men might be dying as they defended their country. Instead of joining them, he had been ordered to remain here. Jackie should send word within the next fortnight. No word would mean that the men from Castle Braeburn were among the ones slain in the debacle.

He strode out of the room. For now, he had to do as commanded. While he did, Ashley would convince him to think of other, more pleasurable things.

In the stable, Colin helped Ashley onto her horse, admiring her slim legs which were displayed halfway to her knees as she sat astride. She smiled as she drew her black cloak forward to cover them. The flush of desire rushing through him was stronger than it had been the night she had waited for him, giving life to his fantasies. Later, he could have her to himself in their bed. Now, he must think of other matters. Swinging onto his horse and flinging back his dark green cloak, he motioned for her to follow.

He kept the pace slow. Ice could appear anywhere and trip the most surefooted beast. About a mile from the castle wall, he turned his horse in among the bare trees. The way grew steep along the ridge. When they reached the top, he dismounted and helped her down into the windswept snow.

Colin took Ashley's hand and led her through the trees. He swept out his arm. "Here it is, Ashley. Here is what we fight for."

Ashley admired the purple mountains fading off in the distance, the sparkle of water from the stream cutting through these valleys, the hillsides which would be green with spring in a few months. It was wondrous, but not an inch of it was worth one drop of Colin's blood.

"Too many have died for this land already," she said.

"And their deaths must not be in vain."

"Such sentiments can only lead to more death."

"Would you let someone else take Castle Braeburn?" He laughed. "A silly question, for you challenged me for it." He turned her to look at him. "You know I am to keep this valley clear in case our allies need to retreat this far. Where they go, the Royalists will follow with their pillaging and savagery."

"I know."

He pressed something heavy into her hand. "Here. I want you to learn to use this."

"No! Take it back!" she cried in disgust as she stared at the long-barreled pistol. It could have been the one Jackie had pushed into her side to coerce her to marry Colin.

"You must learn to use it." Colin scowled. "The time will be coming when I must leave you to oversee the defense of Castle Braeburn. You must be able to protect yourself as well. You claimed these lands. Be willing to defend what is yours."

"I hate guns."

"But you must learn to use it." His fingers slipped beneath her cloak and curled around her nape. They brought her face up so he could see her unease. "I pray you need never touch another after today, but you must be prepared."

Ashley knew she was not going to change his mind. Raising the pistol, she examined the wooden butt. His fingers tilted the gun in a different direction as Colin frowned.

"The first lesson is simple," he said. "Never aim at anyone, except someone you intend to kill."

Her stomach twisted. When he put his arms around her to help her balance the pistol, he must have noticed her trembling fingers, because he said, "You may want to steady it with both hands."

"All right."

The pistol shook more, and he laughed. Taking it, he pointed at a rock. Easily he fired it.

Ashley cringed as the ball hit the outcropping.

He reloaded it with ease and he handed it to her. "Your turn."

She lifted the gun.

"Keep it low," he murmured. "Your hand will come up when you fire."

She drew back on the hammer. The explosion reverberated through her and ached in her arms. Her hands stung, and her eyes squeezed shut.

Colin laughed. "If you can hit the rock with your eyes closed, think how well you could do if you had had them open."

"I don't want to do that again."

His smile faded. "Ashley, you must not be afraid to fight for what is yours."

"How can you accuse me of that? Haven't I shown you that I will fight for what is mine?" She shoved the emptied pistol into his hand. "This is not my way of fighting."

"You choose other ways?"

Her eyebrows arched. "You have your ways. I have mine."

"Aye, and I like your ways." He laughed as he put the pistol under his cloak. "Shall we continue with our ride?"

"No more guns?"

"No more guns *today*."

She nodded reluctantly, knowing that he must have reasons which he had not told her to believe that she would need to know how to defend herself and Castle Braeburn.

Soon.

***

The next morning when Ashley knew she could no longer delay going to talk to Wynda Thompson, the wind was even stronger than it had been on the hilltop. Pulling on her heaviest cloak and wishing again for her warm overcoat, she went down to the kitchen. Susan might be willing to guide her to Wynda's cottage, because Ashley had no idea which one it was. Asking might bring questions she did not want to answer.

Beathas had lost her usual smile as she directed the preparations for the wedding feast which would last for two days after the wedding. Her frown deepened when Ashley asked if the cook could spare Susan.

"Susan?" Beathas asked. "Who do you mean?"

"Susan, the blind woman, who sits by the hearth."

"Milady, are you confused? There is no blind woman working in my kitchen."

Ashley opened her mouth, then closed it. She could not doubt the sincerity in Beathas's voice. Looking at where Susan usually sat, she saw no chair by the hearth. She put her fingers to her forehead, which abruptly ached. This made no sense. Beathas herself had assured Ashley that Susan had worked for years in the kitchen when Ashley could not recall the woman.

*See the truth around you.*

The words burst from her memory. But how could she see the truth when it came and went like a half-seen shadow?

"Milady, are you unwell?" Beathas asked.

Ashley shook her head and tried to smile. "Sorry, my mind is scattered in a dozen directions."

The cook relaxed. "Of course. I understand."

*I wish I did.*

Hurrying out of the kitchen, Ashley went out the gate and along the road toward the loch. She waved to some workers who were doing repairs on the walls, but did not stop. If she did, she would be tempted to ask them to point out Wynda Thompson's cottage.

The soft mist from the snows clung to the braes like thick cream on top of a milk pail. As it wafted on the wind, it appeared alive. Her fingers could not grasp it, for it turned back into drops and clung to her skin.

Ashley was not really surprised when, as she passed a stone cottage that resembled the others around the loch, a door opened and Wynda Thompson motioned for her to enter.

"Come in." The hand on her wrist seconded the request, which was truly an order. "Come in, milady."

"If I am not disturbing you."

"No one else is here, Lady Ashley. No one will know that you have come to me."

Ashley drew the shawl off her damp hair. Dropping it over the bench, which was the only place to sit in the room, she stared about. Herbs hung from the rafters, and something delicious was cooking on the hearth.

Wynda held out a cup. When Ashley did not take it, she smiled. "Fear not, milady. 'Tis only heated cider to take the chill from you on this damp day. I have no wish to hurt you. If you have sought me out, you know that my words are true."

"I know." Clasping the cup between her icy hands, she sat on the bench by the hearth. "I need help, Wynda."

"I suspected that."

"Tell me who Susan is."

She poured another cup for herself and shook her head. "I cannot."

"You don't have a daughter named Susan? About my age, dark-haired, blind."

"Milady, my womb withered too many years ago to have a child of your age." Sitting across from Ashley, she added, "That question I could not answer for you. Do you have others?"

"Yes."

Wynda smiled gently when Ashley added nothing else. "You need not fear, milady. I am an old woman, and I wish you no harm."

"You said you helped my mother."

"Aye." Her face clouded with sorrow. "I grieve every day for what she suffered, but I rejoice that she was able to send you out of harm's way until it was safe for you to return."

"Return?" Ashley dampened her arid lips. "Do you know where I was?"

"Far from here where no one could find you."

"Yes." Breathless expectation came out in her voice, but she could not ask the next question. It would betray too much.

Wynda put down her cup and took Ashley's hand between hers. "Milady, you have come here seeking guarantees that cannot be given. Who knows what the morrow will bring?"

"I marry Colin tomorrow. He deserves to know the truth that I was not always in this..." She jerked back her hand and pressed it over her lips.

"Fear not, milady. You have told me nothing that I should not know."

Ashley nodded, although Wynda's words were so cryptic she was unsure if the old woman knew the truth of how she had slipped through time or not.

"I do not have all the answers you need," the old woman continued, "but I shall search. Go back to Castle Braeburn. Marry your laird, if that is the way your heart takes you. When I have an answer, I shall send for you."

Ashley rose and drew her shawl around her. This had been a waste of time. She needed answers, not more puzzles. She needed to find *someone* who could give them to her. "Thank you."

"Do not do it, milady."

"Do what?"

"Put your thoughts into action." Wynda slowly came to her feet. "Do not go to Gertie Graham for advice. She is not your ally."

As she had before, Ashley said, "I know."

The wind pulled at Ashley's cloak as she rushed back within Castle Braeburn. It was no better within the walls, because the wind swirled in mini-cyclones, forcing people to bend into it even as they were buffeted from another side. Pulling her shawl closer to her face, she pushed through the main door and into the foyer beyond.

She flipped back the shawl and shook her head, her loosened hair slapping her in the face. She started to laugh, then froze at she stared at the woman standing directly in front of her.

Gertie Graham scowled as she closed the distance between them. "Are you deranged?" she snarled.

Seeing how the servants and Colin's men paused to listen, Ashley said, "If you wish to speak with me, let us do so in my solar, not here in the entry."

"Quite the fine lady you have become!" She shook her finger at Ashley, the bracelets on her wrist jangling like an off-key melody. "Is that what *he* promised you? That you could be the lady of your own family's castle? Is that why you let him bed you like a common harlot?"

"I do not want to speak of this here." She had to force the words past her clenched teeth. How dare Gertie try to humiliate her like this!

"As you wish, *milady*." She pushed past Ashley, but threw back over her shoulder, "Think well on the choice you have made. You know why you are here."

Ashley shuddered when the door closed behind Gertie. A serving lass hurried to her, asking if she needed something. Ashley thanked her and went up the stairs. Had she forgotten why she was here—why *Gertie* said she was here? To halt the greatest danger to Castle Braeburn. No, she had not forgotten. She simply could not believe that Colin was that danger. Their love was the way to help this castle, not destroy it.

Wasn't it?

As she supervised the many last-minute details of the wedding throughout the day and while she got ready for bed at the end of that long day, Ashley could not get Gertie's words out of her head. She wished she could speak to someone about this, but that would make things even more complicated. It would be better just to go to sleep and dream of her love tonight.

Brushing her hair, she tied it back as she did each night. It seldom stayed that way, for Colin delighted in it flowing through his fingers when they made love.

Colin strode into the room as Ashley was climbing into the high bed. "What are you doing here?" she gasped. "'Tis nearly midnight. You must not risk a curse on our marriage by seeing me before the ceremony."

"*Belovit*," he said, sitting on the bed, "what is this talk of curses? I have heard that word on your tongue too often in the past week. Are you frightened, Ashley?"

She did not look at him as she settled the pillows behind her. "I am a bride. Don't I have a right to be a wee bit nervous on the night before my wedding?"

He lifted her fingers to his mouth. Over them, his blue gaze tried to ferret out her secret. She had seen his curiosity so often and wondered if she could have been as patient while waiting to have the truth divulged. "Do you regret your decision?"

"To marry you?" When he nodded, she exclaimed, "Of course not, Colin!"

Tugging her into his arms, he kissed her. His fingers slipped along her arm as he bent to taste the skin above her nightgown. He placed gentle nibbles along her shoulder while he drew the sleeve down her arm before his mouth returned to capture hers in a wild rapture.

The call of the night watchman came from the wall.

"Go, Colin!" Ashley cried. "'Tis the midnight hour. You must not be here with me."

"Why not?"

"A groom should not—"

"Curses be damned!" He put his arm under her shoulders as he pressed her back into the bed. "You are mine, Ashley Gordon soon to be MacLachlan, as you have been since the day we met. I shall not be kept from you tonight because of an old wives' tale."

She tried to push him away. "Colin, please, it is not worth tempting—"

"You are worth tempting any fate, *belovit*, because you are so tempting."

Her protests were halted by his mouth on hers. It showed her more clearly than any words that he considered their love worth any curse. And, mayhap he was right.

Even so, later, when she rested beside him, listening to his soft breaths, coldness in the pit of her stomach burned like an ulcer. As she drifted off into her uneasy dreams, she clutched onto his arm with both hands.

# SIXTEEN

*They were within the walls.*

*Steel clashed. Men shouted, then screamed with their last breaths.*

*The little girl ran to cling to her mother's skirts. The mother's fingers trembled as they brushed the little girl's hair back from her face.*

*"It is time," the mother said.*

*A dark-haired woman kneeling by the window, her hands pressed together, interrupted her keening prayers. "Take care, milady. Before you begin, ask yourself if this risk is one you are willing to take."*

*As the mother bent to frame the little girl's face, she said to the other woman, "I must do this. They are here. They have killed my bairn's father and will suffer none of his blood to live. I will not stand by and watch them spill innocent blood."*

*"'Twill be your death to abide here a moment longer, milady," moaned the woman.*

*"My end is assured, for my death sentence was signed the day I wed. I will save my bairn."*

*"But you have no bairn."*

Ashley wanted to argue, but looked down to see the child had vanished. What was happening? She had thought she was the dream-child, the one lost in time. Now she was the woman? Why had her nightmare changed?

"Because," the woman by the window said, "you denied the truth of who you are and why you were drawn back to Castle Braeburn."

Staring at the woman, Ashley took a step away. It was Gertie Graham, wearing a triumphant smile. She glanced over her shoulder as she heard the pounding on the door. Death waited beyond it.

*"You have nowhere to go, Ashley Gordon, but the hell you have earned for betraying all of those who came before you by not slaying Colin MacLachlan."*

*"No!" she cried. "It cannot be wrong to fall in love with a man who loves me."*

*"He lies to you so that he might lie with you and mix his blood with yours to claim what the Gordons have held for generations."*

*Ashley shook her head, then put her hands over her ears. She could not shut out the sound of Gertie's laugh or the pounding on the door. Wanting to escape, she ran to a window. The courtyard below was scarlet with blood. Even if she survived the jump, she would be slain before she could reach the gate. She looked back across the room and saw Gertie reaching for the latch on the door.*

*"See your future, milady."*

*"They will kill me!"*

*"You will not die so easily when they have all of eternity to torment you."*

*"No!" she shrieked, running to pull Gertie from the door. She jerked back in horror when fire seared her fingers as she touched Gertie.*

*The dark-haired woman flung open the door, and darkness struck Ashley like a fist. It surrounded her, swallowing her in its fetid gut. She fought to breathe, to escape, to know she was still alive.*

*"Colin..." Her voice vanished into the oblivion around her. And she could not call him to share this hell that had found her. But she must warn him, because she feared he would be Gertie's next target. She needed help.*

*But who?*

*From deep within her, a cry that she had forgotten burst forth, "Mam, help me!" She feared the one she had lost for a lifetime would not be able to find her now.*

# SEVENTEEN

Ashley rubbed her aching eyes as they slowly cleared. Nothing was visible. It was as if a million flashbulbs had exploded at once. But she was free of the nightmare.

"Milady!"

Ashley stared at Ella who was walking toward her down a passage in Castle Braeburn. How had she gotten here? She must have been walking in her sleep. Odd, she never had been a sleepwalker before.

"Milady, where have you been?" Ella plucked at Ashley's sleeve. "You have traveled far by the looks of this gown and cloak."

She looked down at herself. She was wearing a simple dress with a dark cloak over it. Not the black one that she had donned when she rode with Colin, but a dusty brown one that she did not recognize.

Had it been more than a nightmare? Had she been pulled out of this time? When she had leapt through time before, no one had noticed. She must talk to Colin before she spoke to anyone else. Mayhap, if she told him the truth, he would help her understand. He could hold her in his arms and assure her that she was not still caught up in the madness of that nightmare.

"Where is Colin?" she asked.

Ella's wrinkled face lengthened. "In the courtyard drilling his men, milady, but you should not meet him there. Go to your rooms, and I shall bring him to speak to you privately."

"Why?"

"You left Castle Braeburn. The laird was unhappy with that."

Ashley wanted to ask how long she had been gone and what had happened since she fell asleep in Colin's arms, but she bit back those questions. She must ask Colin. Her heart contracted as she thought of his pain. He had dared to trust her, and she had vanished from his bed and his life. Without knowing the truth, he must think she had played him for the fool and was laughing up her sleeve at him somewhere. When she explained to him, he would learn he had not been the only one hurt by her sudden disappearance.

She hurried to the suite they shared. As she flung open the door, she came face-to-face with Ramsey.

His face was blank. "Good day, Lady Ashley. Does the laird know you are back?"

"Ella has gone to tell him. Oh, Ramsey, it is so grand to be back here." She could not hide her joy. "I have feared I would never be able to get back here."

"Is that so?" he asked coldly.

"Ramsey, what is wrong?"

He stared at her with the same horror Ella had when she scurried away along the corridor. Without a word, he pushed past her.

Ashley started to follow, then stopped. Ramsey was a barometer of his master's emotions. When Colin was pleased, the valet wore a wide smile. Clammy trepidation slipped along her back. How long had she been away?

Closing the door, she went to the bedroom. She pulled off her cloak and went to the cupboard. All her gowns hung there. Where had she gotten this black dress that was no different from what the servants wore? She hung the cape in the cupboard.

The door opened with a crash. Colin stood there, against the sunlight pouring through the antechamber's windows.

She ran to him. "My love, I—"

"Silence!" His fury halted her in mid-step. "You have decided to return, I see." He stepped toward her, and, involuntarily, she backed away as she had from Gertie in the nightmare. This could not be another nightmare, could it? Colin would not want to destroy her. She was not so sure when he went on, "You leave me the eve of our wedding, and now I am supposed to welcome you back two fortnights later with no questions."

"Two fortnights? I have been gone a month?"

"You have twisted my thoughts with your lies before, milady, but you cannot deny the passage of days."

"Colin, let me explain. It is not as you—" She winced as he grasped her arm. Pain erupted up it, although he did not hold it tightly. When had she hurt it? In the nightmare? She recalled how she had pulled back from Gertie. Had she hurt it then? None of this made sense. "I did not want to leave. You must believe me!"

"How did you sneak in here? The same way you crawled out?" He pulled her closer.

"Colin! Listen to me! Please!"

"I have heeded all the lies I wish to hear from your false lips." He cursed vividly. "Dolt that I am, I believed your assertions of love when all you wanted was to shame me."

Arguing with him when he would not listen to her would gain them nothing but more anger. She tried to push past him, but her gown caught on the brooch holding his plaid. It tore, revealing the lace of her underdress.

He laughed as she tried to hold her tattered dress together. "What, Ashley? Do you think you can play the reluctant virgin with me again?"

"If you would just listen to me," she whispered, trying to ignore the pain soaring through her at his furious words, "I shall tell you the truth."

"That might be a nice change."

She ignored his sarcasm as she snapped, "I did not go *anywhere*. I was in Castle Braeburn. I—"

"Castle Braeburn? Did you hide under the bed or in the cellars?"

"Listen to me, please." She hated the rage on his face. "You said you loved me. Is that the truth?"

"Aye."

"I told you I loved you, and that was the truth, too."

His eyes narrowed. "So I believed."

"If you believed that, then trust me to tell you the truth now."

He hesitated, his mouth working, then nodded. "I am listening."

Ashley took a deep breath. This was not how she had planned to reveal the truth, but she could not delay any longer. Slowly and knowing how absurd it sounded, she told him how she had come to Castle Braeburn and the journeys she had taken through her nightmares. It did not take long to explain, for he asked no questions. She saw his anger alter to skepticism, then to horror.

He whispered, "Witchcraft!"

"Mayhap, Colin. If it is, it is not at my hand." She gasped as he edged away from her. "Colin! Don't you understand? I love you! I want to be with you."

"Go back to your own time, Ashley or whatever you are," he ordered viciously. "I want nothing to do with black magic. You have tempted me with your devil-given beauty."

"I am not a demon!" she cried. "I am the woman who loves you more than anything else in the world."

"A mortal woman does not leap from one century to another." His eyes became sapphire slits. "Don't try to trick me with your charms. Go back to your master, witch."

"I cannot go anywhere. I did not plan to spend my childhood in another time. I never guessed that I once had been in this time and would be again." She put her hands on his arm, but he shook them off. "Colin, I want to be with you. Don't turn me away now."

He paid no attention to her outstretched hands. His eyes were the crystal blue of a winter sky seen through icicles. With his arms crossed on his chest and his feet planted on the floor, there was no chink in his fury. When he spoke, his voice was as frigid as his glare. "I do not want you!"

"You don't want me?" She clenched her hands. "Colin, you told me you love me. You asked me to be your wife. If you trust me with the truth of the love within your heart, why can't you trust me to tell you this truth?"

"The woman I love is not a witch!"

"I am not a witch."

"Then who created this spell?"

"I told you. Lady Fia Gordon." She took a deep breath, then whispered, "My mother."

He looked up at the portrait on the chimneypiece. "If she had a witch's powers, why did she allow Stanton to kill her husband and her and take Castle Braeburn?"

"I don't know." Tears tickled the corners of her eyes, and she fought to swallow. "Mayhap she knew she could not save all of them."

"So she saved you?"

She nodded. "I know it is hard to believe. I did not want to believe it, either, but I am here with you in this time and place. I will swear any oath you wish that what I have told you is the truth." Closing her eyes, she battered back hot tears. She opened her eyes and raised her chin as she whispered, "I swear it on the love we have shared, the love I hope is still in your heart as it is in mine. I love you. Tell me that you love me, too!"

Colin could not harden his heart to Ashley's plea. He yearned to believe her, but how could he? Her story was madness. Or was it? He remembered her odd actions and comments when he first had come to claim Castle Braeburn. They made sense if he accepted that she was lost in time. Either she was telling the truth, or she was as deranged as he had feared that day.

He could not halt his hands from closing around her elbows and bringing her closer. He stared into her glistening eyes. Even as he watched, a tear rolled from one to trace a damp path along her face. He might be as daft as she was, but he could not resist tasting her lips.

"Why are you crying now, *belovit*?" he whispered.

"Because you believe me." She leaned her head against his chest.

He was glad she was not looking into his face, for he was unsure if he could have masked his feelings. Her simple faith in him would be tarnished if he revealed that he could not shake his qualms. Of one thing he was certain. He wanted her. If she was a witch, it was an enchantment of love she had cast over him. This spell he did not want to break.

He laughed as he swept her up into his arms. Gently, he placed her on the bed. Many questions bubbled through his brain, but he did not want them answered. He wanted her.

While his mouth reacquainted itself with her lips, his fingers widened the rips on her gown and found the soft skin hidden beneath her chemise. Her hands combed through his hair as the tides of longing rose within him. With a moan, she undid his doublet.

"*Belovit*, you are eager today."

"I feared I would never be in your arms again." The tears returned to glitter in her eyes. "I was so frightened that we would be forever parted that I was sure I would go as mad as you believe me to be." When he started to protest, she silenced him with a kiss. "Love me. Let me know *this* is real."

Her request banished the last of his hesitation. As he drew the ripped gown away, his hunger matched hers. He gazed down at her supple curves, separated from him by only a few wisps of fabric and lace.

He caressed her as he pulled off her clothes and his. She stroked his back, then her hands glided lower to entice him until the pounding of his pulse was swifter than his ragged breaths. The fire in her middle was ready to detonate, but he continued to tantalize her until she moaned in eager surrender. When her eyes closed with pleasure as he touched the inner softness of her legs, the heated skin welcomed his touch.

As he merged himself within her, he sighed in indescribable bliss. This was what he wanted, to be a part of the body of this woman who was a part of his soul. With her mouth moist against his neck and his uneven breath stroking her ear, he gave himself to the ecstasy. The explosion fused him to her in rapture.

\*\*\*

At soft laughter, Ashley looked up into Colin's smile. Her trembling fingers outlined his cheekbones.

"I think you are a witch, *belovit*." When she stiffened beneath him, he chuckled. "Not an evil one, but one who spins webs of bewitchment with succulent kisses."

"You should not jest about this."

"Why not?"

"I know what you did—what you *do* to witches in this century." With a shiver, she whispered, "If someone believed you, I might be taken from you forever. I do not want to lose you again."

He kissed the tip of her nose. "Forgive me. You are right, and I did not mean to frighten you. Forgive also my angry words when I found you here." He stroked her cheek. "*Belovit*, I do not know why I said what I did."

"I may." She hesitated, then said, "You are right, Colin. I believe there has been a dark curse spread upon Castle Braeburn."

"By whom?"

Again she faltered, this time longer. She had lived with the fear of being labeled a witch since she had woken in this time. Although she was certain Gertie Graham had a hand in trying to foster anger between her and Colin, Ashley could not name her as a witch. No one should have to suffer like those poor souls in Salem, Massachusetts.

"'Tis just a feeling I have."

He nodded. "A feeling that you would be wise to heed."

"As you would be wise to heed what I told you. It was the truth. I lived in the future."

Lying beside her, he leaned her head against his shoulder. "I am trying to believe, Ashley, but it is not easy."

"It is not easy for me either." She tilted her head so she could see the portrait over the hearth. *Where are you, Mother? Why have you abandoned me when I could use your help now?* Her hope that the portrait would come to life died when nothing happened.

*See the truth around you.*

Again the words stirred from her memory. Looking up into Colin's eyes, she discovered a warmth as precious as when the sparkles had come to offer her comfort. The truth was that she loved Colin and he loved her, and she must not allow this love to be destroyed by the hatred around them.

Softly, she whispered, "One thing I have never doubted is that I love you, Colin."

"And I love you, *belovit*."

A knock intruded. When Ashley would have risen and reached for her clothes, Colin held her to the bed. Shaking his head in a warning to be silent, he called, "Who is it?"

"My laird, 'tis Ramsey. I was wondering—"

"Wonder later!" he shouted, stifling laughter as Ashley smiled. "Come back in an hour!"

A faint "Aye" came through the wooden door, then silence.

Colin rose on one elbow to see Ashley's face below him on his pillow. It was a vision which had haunted him through the long nights when she had been far from him. Farther from him than he had imagined.

He picked up a strand of her hair and rubbed it against his cheek. From it wafted her sweet scent. How Ashley had come to Castle Braeburn no longer mattered. She would have no chance to leave him again. From this point forward, she was going to remain at his side. His prisoner, but holding his heart in her own captivity of love. If this was a spell, it was one he wanted to last a lifetime.

"I am pleased that you are back with me," he murmured.

She smiled. "So I noticed."

"And you, *belovit*, are you happy to be here instead of in your own time?"

"This is my own time." Her smile widened, and she softened in his arms. "Yes, it is my own time. I never thought I would say that, but 'tis the truth."

"You did not answer me. Are you happy to be here?"

"I am so happy to be here with you. I was afraid I never would escape the nightmare that kept me from you."

"You *are* here, and that is what is important."

"Aye." She put her arms around his shoulders and drew his mouth to hers.

When the stolen hour passed too swiftly, Ashley asked Colin about what had happened while she had been away. She was pleased to learn that Jackie Kilbride and many of the men from

Castle Braeburn were reported to be alive and fighting Montrose. She also asked what would be said to the household about her absence. He told her not to worry and teased her with the silly stories they could tell about why she left Castle Braeburn for a month.

She understood what Colin's plan was when Ramsey returned with the end of the hour. If the white-haired man was shocked to see her sitting in a chair as she drew on her low shoes beneath her favorite, light green gown, he hid it well as he said, "My laird, there are understandably questions now that Lady Ashley has been seen in the castle."

Colin adjusted his plaid as if nothing bothered him. "Questions? 'Tis unfortunate for those asking that the questions shall remain unanswered. If anyone asks you, and they will, Ramsey, you need say only that Lady Ashley has been away, and now is she here where she belongs."

"My laird, they will think you mad." He glanced at Ashley, then said, "As they feared when milady vanished, and you thought that she had been abducted and threatened to tear apart every cottage and byre in the Highlands to retrieve her."

"Is that what you thought?" Ashley asked, coming to her feet. She curved her hand along Colin's cheek. "I am so sorry that you worried so."

"You are here and safe," Colin said gruffly, turning away, "and what happened before is past."

"My laird," Ramsey said, "they want to know—"

With a sigh, Colin faced his flustered servant. "*I* am satisfied with Ashley's explanation. That is all that is necessary." He smiled sadly. "For now, that is all anyone needs to know."

Ramsey nodded. "Aye, my laird. It shall be as you wish. The dinner hour has passed. Do you wish me to bring you a tray here?"

"I think Ashley would appreciate the chance to let the furor die down a bit before she faces the great hall."

Ashley barely tasted the food Ramsey brought. She wanted to convince Colin of the truth of her words. As she retold her story, she could see the disbelief he worked so hard to hide.

"Send for Wynda Thompson," she suggested. "She may understand this better than I do."

Slowly he lowered his half-filled goblet of wine to the table. He started to make the sign Ella had when Gertie Graham came to Castle Braeburn, but halted when Ashley gasped.

J.A. Ferguson

"I cannot send for her," he said, his hand fisting on the table. "She has been accused and tried for witchcraft. She dies on the morrow for her crimes."

She leapt to her feet. The heavy chair rocked back, crashing on the floor. "No, Colin! She is not a witch!" Even as she said the words, she was not so certain. One thing she knew without question. Wynda had been sincere when she said she would try to help Ashley find a way to stay here. With her gone... "Colin, this is all wrong."

"She was accused."

"By whom?'

"Gertie Graham."

Ashley knelt beside his chair and gripped his arm. "Gertie? You believed her? Oh, Colin, no!"

"She had proof."

Her mouth twisted. "I am sure. She devised something because she was afraid that Wynda would help me."

"Do what?"

"When I first came back to this time, Gertie Graham warned me that I had been brought back here for a reason. To keep Castle Braeburn safe from its greatest enemy."

"You should have been here when Stanton held these lands in terror."

She nodded. "I thought that as well, but Gertie believes that was not the castle's darkest hour. She hates you, Colin, because she believes you are the catalyst that triggered my mother's spell to return me to this time."

"Me? Castle Braeburn's greatest enemy?"

"That is what she believes."

He scowled. "That crone tricked me into believing she was my ally. She warned me of Charlie McAllister's treachery."

"And goaded him to rebel at the same time." She sighed. "She is a skilled manipulator." Taking a deep breath, she said, "I believe she has manipulated both of us to do and say things we would not have otherwise."

He tenderly cupped her cheek. "'Twas her putting words in our mouths in the cemetery."

"Yes."

"It was not a mind fever?"

She shook her head. "No. I am not certain how she is doing what she is doing, but I know she has put this rage into us, and the horrible words that fell from our lips."

"Why didn't you tell me this before?"

Sadly she smiled as she placed her fingers over his. "Would you have believed me?"

"No, but I think I am beginning to understand more about what has been happening here."

"Can you save Wynda?" Ashley rose and entwined her fingers together in front of her. "She is my friend, Colin, and she saved your life."

His eyebrows came together. "How?"

"Wynda came to help when you were shot. She stopped the infection which could have killed you."

Slowly he stood. "I think you are trying to convince me to do what I have already decided to do. Come with me, Ashley. They have her in the village."

"Is she hurt?"

He did not look at her as he pulled her ebony cloak from the cupboard. "She has been questioned, Ashley."

She quaked with horror as she recalled what that meant. Torture until the accused admitted to anything to end the pain. "Is she still alive?"

"I do not know." Colin held out his arm to Ashley. "Pull up your hood."

She understood his order. With her absence known throughout the glen, the situation would become even more complicated if rumor preceded them to where Wynda was being kept. He wanted to deal with one problem at a time. A wise decision, but, as they walked through the castle, she knew many were staring.

Her body ached with the need to keep her back straight as they went out of the keep and past the gate. He put his arm around her shoulders and leaned her against him, but said nothing.

Ashley fought not to run when they reached a small barn at the edge of the clump of cottages clinging to the loch. She wanted to rush to Wynda to give her solace. At the same time, she wanted to flee this atrocity.

A man holding a lantern stepped out of the darkness. "Begone." He flinched when Colin walked toward him. "My laird, I did not expect to see ye here tonight. Lady Ashley?" he choked.

Colin acted again as if there were nothing odd about seeing Ashley with him again. "Lundy, we wish to see Wynda Thompson."

Ashley bit her lip. She had not been able to see the man's face in the glare of the lantern. She should have guessed Lilias's father would be involved in this fanaticism. When she heard his muttered oath, she was glad she had not come alone.

"We would like to see Wynda Thompson," Colin said, slightly louder.

"Oh, aye." Lundy threw the door open and held out the lantern to Colin.

Inside the thatched byre, Ashley forgot Lilias's father. She cried out when she saw a beaten mass of cloth on the floor. Not cloth, but what remained of Wynda.

"What are you doing here?" asked Wynda, her voice surprisingly unchanged.

Ashley squatted so she could see Wynda's swollen face. "I just heard how you have been accused."

"Just heard?"

"I was...away."

Wynda moaned. "She tried again, did she? Fear not. She weakens with every evil she does. I go to my reward knowing, as you do, that I had no hand in the black magic which I have been accused of by the devil's mistress." Her blackened eyes widened. "My laird, you are here, too?"

He dropped to one knee beside Ashley. "I shall stop this, Wynda."

"Do not sully your name next to mine, for that is what she hopes you will do."

"She?" he asked.

"Milady knows."

Ashley nodded. "I know, Wynda. Can I do something to help you?"

"Do not fret, milady. I am an old woman. Soon, I shall be granted surcease of my woes." Her gaze held Ashley's. "I am glad to hear that you were not her victim, as your mother nearly was."

"What do you mean?"

"It no longer matters, milady. You know what you should know. You have sought the path of love instead of hate." She slid her wrinkled hand over Ashley's fingers. "Fear not. I have looked at the signs. For both you and the laird, there is love."

"Wynda, let us—"

She closed her eyes. "No, milady. Go back to Castle Braeburn. I shall cheat my executioners who plan to burn me alive at dawn, for I shall be gone by sunrise. There is nothing else I can do here."

Colin's hand tightened on Ashley's shoulders. As he drew her to her feet, she wept. She stumbled as he led her out of the barn.

"Wait here, *belovit*," he said. He went back to Lundy. In the lantern's light, she saw the flash of gold exchanging hands. She smiled through her tears. Colin was making sure Wynda had some comfort during her final night.

Colin dismissed her gratitude. "It is too late and too little. I should have stopped this witch-hunt, but I was too wrapped up in my grief to notice anyone else's."

"As Gertie hoped."

"Aye," he replied, sadly. He draped his arm over her shoulders. "That must be investigated."

"But not tonight."

"No, not tonight." He sighed. "I want real proof this time."

"More than what we have suffered?"

"Yes. She may have had a hand in it, but I cannot let my yearning for vengeance blind me to the truth."

"Do you believe me now?"

"I have from the beginning."

She pulled out from beneath his arm and faced him. "I thought you would be honest with me now."

"The truth is I *wanted* to believe you from the beginning. What has happened is over. Now we can get married as we planned."

She shook her head. "No, I will not marry you, Colin."

"What?" His eyes widened in the sparse moonlight.

"I cannot marry you, Colin. You must marry someone who will give you heirs, not someone who might disappear and never return."

"Ashley, you can be the mother of my heirs."

"No, I will be your mistress, but not your wife." Her laughter was brittle. "I love you, but I cannot marry you."

"If this is one of that witch's spells—"

"No, 'tis me speaking from my heart. It would be a mistake for us to marry now."

"Why?" he demanded, anger tainting his voice. "You have not given me one sensible reason."

"Don't you understand?" she cried. "When we were so happy before, I was taken from you." She put her fingers up to caress his face. "I love you, Colin. I will do nothing to risk losing you again."

"I am the laird. You understand what that means?"

Ashley closed her eyes to fight her savage pain. "You must have a son to succeed you."

"A legitimate one. No bastard can hold." He twisted her to look at him. "Do you want me to take another woman as my wife?"

"No! I mean, yes. I—I do not know what I mean."

He stroked her hair. "You are too distressed by all that has happened. You are not thinking clearly."

"Do not be condescending."

"Do not be foolish and ruin what we could have."

"I shall not—I *cannot* change my mind on this," she warned.

"Yes, you will!"

She walked away, then ran. Didn't he understand? She wanted to be his wife. She wanted to spend every day and every wondrous night with him. But her heart's desire might come at a horrible price.

Colin caught her at the stairs to the second floor and brought her into his arms. "Ashley," he urged, "do not be so hasty."

"I cannot marry you!" she whispered. "Will you force me again with a gun?"

"I want you with me forever."

Tears scorched her eyes as she kissed his cheek. "Don't you see I am doing this so we have a chance for that forever?"

"No!" His shout rang through the hallway. "I think you are too frightened to take the risks to gain what we both want."

"This is one thing I do not wish to risk."

"What one thing?" He released her so suddenly that Ashley rocked back to hit her heels on the riser. "We have nothing unless we are willing to fight for it."

"Is that your answer to everything? Fighting?"

"I am a warrior. I vowed to avenge my father's death, and I have."

"But this is not a battle to be fought with swords or pistols. This battle engages our hearts." Lifting her chin high, she wondered why he could not accept the truth. She had almost lost him once. Before she could say something she would regret, she started up the stairs.

"Ashley?"

With one hand on the banister, she looked down at him. Every plane of his emotionless face was sharper in the light from the candles burning along the wall.

"Will I see you at breakfast?" he asked.

She winced as if she had been struck. His words told her that she was not welcome in his bed tonight unless she acquiesced to his proposal. It was what she should have expected, for he was too proud to let anyone believe he was ruled by anything, even by love.

"Is this what you want?" she whispered.

"It is what must be." His voice was as dispassionate as his face.

"I pray your pride is worth this."

He climbed the stairs, but left several risers between them. "I pray yours is."

"My pride?"

"When you see that you are wrong about not risking what our hearts want in hopes of obtaining even more." He walked past her, not looking back.

She stared after him as she imagined the rumors which would soon be whipping through the castle. She wondered if anyone would guess that she no longer slept beside Colin, not because she did not love him, but because she loved him too much.

# EIGHTEEN

"Milady?"

In the solar, Ashley looked up from where she had been giving instructions to servants for the day's tasks. "Colin!" His name came out in a breathless whisper as she surged to her feet. His dark hair was burnished with blue fire in the sunlight coming through the tall windows. Mud clung to his boots, and she knew he had been out in the courtyard that was a mire from melting snow.

She halted, because his cool gaze was like a wall. From behind her, she heard a low rumble of dismay. No one in Castle Braeburn was unaware of the schism between the laird and Lady Ashley. Each day had become as dreary as her heart. It was as it had been before she and Colin had acknowledged their love. Colin never was the man she expected him to be. He was not a character from a heroic saga, but one who struggled with the barbarity of his time. She had wounded him. He had given her his love, and she had told him she could not accept the dangers of loving him.

"Milady," he said in the same impassive tone, "I thought you would want to know that I have just come from speaking with a courier."

She hoped no one noticed how her fingers quivered as she motioned for the servants to leave. They flowed around Colin as if he were a rock in the center of a stream. The last out the door closed it.

Motioning for Colin to sit, wondering why she had to act as if they were polite strangers, she went back to the bench where she had been working. She sat and asked, "Courier?"

"Yes, he came on behalf of the Marquess of Argyll."

"On behalf? He was from Harry Campbell?"

"Aye." He drew up a stool and sat.

"And he said?"

"So far, all he has told me is a confirmation that Jackie and the dozen surviving men from Castle Braeburn continue to fight for the Marquess of Argyll. Unlike so many of the others, they did not flee like frightened peasants from Montrose's treachery."

"How wonderful that he is still alive, Colin! Will they be home soon?"

"Mayhap within the month."

When he added nothing else, she could not stop the ache of a shiver that coursed up her back. Something was amiss. Something horrible. Her voice broke as she asked, "What did he say of me?"

"I thought you would wish to hear any further tidings yourself. He is waiting in my office."

She came to her feet. "What are we waiting for? Let's find out what he has to say."

Colin took her arm as she was about to rush past him. Gently he turned her to face him. He slipped his arm around her shoulders. Shock raced through her when his mouth captured hers. That amazement became dismay when she tasted his disquiet.

She pulled back, although she wanted to remain in his arms. "Colin, what did he tell you?"

"No more than I have told you."

"But you suspect—"

"That we will not know the contents of his message until we speak with him." He held out his arm. "Milady?"

Ashley let him draw her hand within his arm. His voice was cool once more. Did he regret kissing her when he had shut her out of his life?

Her heart pounded against her chest like fists on a wall as they entered Colin's office. The messenger, a short man whose clothes bore the signs of every mile he had traveled, bowed his head toward them. She saw how he watched Colin seat her on a padded bench.

Only then did the man step forward and hold out a rolled parchment. "Lord Campbell asked that this be delivered to you."

Ashley said nothing as Colin opened the message and read it carefully. He let it roll closed as he said, "Please tell the baron that Castle Braeburn will be pleased to host him and his companions when they arrive in a week."

"A week," Ashley repeated too softly for either man to hear.

"I shall take your answer to him, Laird MacLachlan," the messenger said.

As if it were of the least importance, Colin nodded. "I thank you for your quick delivery of this dispatch."

When the messenger left, Colin sat at his table and reopened the missive. His brow furrowed as he read it again, even more slowly.

Ashley rose. He let the parchment roll shut. What did he want to keep her from seeing? The stern set of his mouth warned her that she would be wasting time asking. He would tell her only when he thought she should know. That told her, more clearly than any words, that there was information within this message that angered him. Once, she would have known that would mean the marquess was deciding in favor of Lady Ashley Gordon's claim. Now...

"If we are to receive guests," she said quietly, "there are many tasks to be done."

"Aye."

She wanted to say something more, but she did not know what to say. Walking out of his office, she knew that Harry Campbell coming here forebode nothing but trouble. As she went to the kitchen to inform Beathas that guests would be within the walls next week, she knew it would be worse than trouble.

Disaster could be in the offing for everyone in Castle Braeburn.

*** 

Ashley was not surprised when Harry Campbell did not arrive the day he had told them to expect him. It was consistent with his egotism. She could not blame his delay on bad roads, for cold weather had returned, freezing them and making it much easier to travel.

She hid her opinions from Colin, for he would not be pleased to hear her belittle the nephew of his chieftain. For once, he was the naïve one. He had fought for this prize, but he had no experience with the political world that Lord Campbell adored. That world was populated with smiling hypocrites, determined to destroy those standing between them and power.

Ashley went to the tower on the northern corner of the castle. It gave her a view of the road dropping into the glen. With her cloak wrapped tightly around her, she withstood the blast of the wind and watched for Lord Campbell's entourage. She had not been there long before she heard footsteps.

"Ella told me you had come up here, but I did not think you would brave this cold to enjoy the view." Colin smiled as he swung his plaid around him to break the power of the wind moaning among the slits in the stones, but, she noticed, his eyes remained cold. He could not forgive her for refusing his proposal.

"Not the view," she managed to say past her chattering teeth.

Colin put his arm around Ashley and sighed. Nothing he said would comfort her. When she eased away from him, leaving a parapet between them, he sighed again. She refused to relent in her fear, instead of realizing that they should enjoy the nights they could share.

The few nights left...

His hands became fists on the stone. What had Lord Campbell's words meant? *Lady Ashley shall not be a burden for you much longer.* It could have been meant that the marquess was going to grant Castle Braeburn to Colin so the decision of Ashley's fate would be Colin's, or it could mean that Ashley was going to be put to death for daring to claim, because she so closely resembled Lady Fia, that she was Gordon's daughter.

He surveyed the lands which belonged to Castle Braeburn. The mountains ringed the loch like blue lace on a collar. It was everything he had dreamed would be his, but he wanted to share it with Ashley Gordon. No, that was not true. He wanted to share it with Ashley MacLachlan, his lady and his wife. In the months since he had arrived here, he had discovered he needed her honed wit as much as he needed her love. She was his match, and, one night when she again rested close to him in the warmth of their bed, he would convince her to be his wife. Her fear of being taken from this time must be put aside.

If only he could understand—and believe—her tale. She did, and Wynda Thompson had died believing it. But such a story made no sense. He had asked Ella if Ashley had suffered a brain-altering fever just before his arrival, but the maid assured him that Lady Ashley always enjoyed excellent health. But how could what she had told him be the truth?

Searching for words to ease the silence, Colin said, "In the spring, we shall return to our special spot on the brae. There, you can make me another of your delicious creations with bread and meat. What did you call them?"

"Sandwiches." A smile appeared and vanished so quickly he was unsure if he had seen it.

"Ashley—"

"Oh, no! Look!" She pointed toward the road.

At the same time Colin saw the dust rising from the road, a blast of a trumpet announced the sighting of Harry Campbell and his men.

"He is here," Ashley whispered. Beneath the scarlet left by the wind striking her face, her skin became as hueless as the snow. "Now, whatever you have not told me about will happen."

Colin cursed silently. He should have guessed her quick wit would discern that he had hidden the complete message from her because he dreaded what was within it. He turned her to look at him and was nearly staggered by the fear within her eyes. He stroked her icy cheek before he drew her lips beneath his. It was more than a kiss. It was a vow he would do all he could to see she was protected from a man who should be his welcome ally.

With a sob, she clung to him. He wrapped his plaid around her. If Campbell had come to take her from Castle Braeburn, the baron would soon realize he had made a grave error. Ashley Gordon belonged here with Colin MacLachlan. No man would take what was his.

Colin repeated that to himself as he stared over her head at the long line of riders. He swore again, this time aloud. Was this the retreat he had been told to prepare for? He could not guess why Campbell would bring so many men otherwise.

He steered Ashley toward the door in the tower. He paused to close it, because the damp air heralded snow.

In his rooms, Colin called, "Ramsey, call Ella to help Lady Ashley. Bring my *breacan-feile*. The baron has arrived."

"Aye, my laird." Ramsey rushed away to get his master's best kilt, but not before Colin saw his servant's shock that Ashley was within these rooms once more.

"Colin, I should go." Ashley took a step toward the door.

"*Belovit*, this is not the time to discuss what you should or should not do." He caught her hands in his, entwining his fingers through hers. He drew her into his bedchamber. "Ready yourself here to welcome Lord Campbell. You are safe here."

Ashley nodded, not trusting her voice. He need not say that he did not trust Harry Campbell. Nor did she need to say that she was happy for any excuse to be back here with him again. When his lips brushed hers, she fought not to surrender to tears. Tears of fright and tears of joy that she and Colin might resolve their differences.

Then he walked out, calling again to Ramsey, and she knew he did not trust himself to remain here with her when they must think of their arriving guest. Her hands clenched. She did not move from the center of the room as she stared at the ever-changing flames on the hearth. Not so many months ago, she had come to this time and tried to prepare for a life ruled by an arrogant beast named Colin MacLachlan. But he had not been a beast. He had been far kinder to her than she had had any right to expect as his rival for Castle Braeburn.

Harry Campbell would have no such compassion for her. The memories that came from her mother's spell forced her to recall how he had sneered at even Lord Stanton when he had been here last. And how she had denied him his pleasure by not letting him bed her. He would not forget that or forgive her. If Colin had not been here, Lord Campbell would have been able to exact his revenge on her now.

"No!" she moaned.

The thought of Lord Campbell's touch sickened her. She put her hand over her lips, trying not to recall his mouth on hers.

Ashley forced herself to relax. She was not alone. If Lord Campbell thought he could get his revenge on her by giving Castle Braeburn to Colin, then she would pretend to be shattered. The baron would leave, and things would continue as they should...if she could persuade Colin to believe what had happened to her.

"Milady, we must hurry," Ella cried, rushing into the room and unhooking Ashley's drab gown. Her maid said nothing else, but tension was a living presence in the room.

With a sudden smile, Ashley said, "Ella, I shall wear the red one."

"Red? But, milady, such a color will be offensive to the baron."

"I know. Let him know how I feel about him."

"I believe he knew that when you slapped his face."

"You saw that?" She could remember the moment in the stillroom beyond the kitchen when Lord Campbell had thought she would welcome his heavy-handed seduction.

"It has been my pleasure and my duty to watch over you as I promised your lady mother."

"My mother..." Ashley looked up at the portrait. She had not seen or heard anything of Lady Fia since the night she and Colin had become lovers. Was her mother displeased at that, or had she left because Lady Fia believed Ashley was now safe with Colin? She almost laughed at her assumption that a ghost was privy to the future. Colin would think she was completely daft, if he guessed that she had these thoughts.

It did not take long to dress in the elegant red gown. The fabric was startlingly brilliant against her auburn hair, making it vibrant gold. As she rose, she admired the lines of her gown. The square neckline was cut deep, but half hidden between the points of a wide collar. The narrow, pointed waistline flowed into the wide skirt draped back over her petticoats and trimmed with bright green. Ella bedecked Ashley's hair with the strands of pearls she had worn to the wedding which no one spoke of now.

When the door opened, Ashley turned to see Colin in his clan colors. It was the plaid he had worn when he had come to claim Castle Braeburn. A ruby brooch pinned it to his right shoulder, letting it sweep the heels of his boots as he walked. A thick, leather belt with a crested buckle held his kilt in place. It was draped to reach the center of his knee. Everything was perfect, even the *sgian dubh*, the tassel hooked to his stockings on his right leg.

His eyes narrowed when he looked at her, but all he said was, "'Tis time, milady."

The words tolled like a death knell in Ashley's ears. When he held out his hand, she placed her trembling fingers in it.

"Why are you so frightened, *belovit*?" he asked. "Hasn't the marquess shown his leniency toward you so far?"

"This is mercy? To be kept waiting week after week, never knowing what will happen to me?" She shivered. "After all this, he sends his despicable nephew here."

"Ashley, you remain alive." Colin touched her icy cheeks. "Do not let your fear keep you from seeing the truth. No one shall hurt you while I am laird here. We must not delay." He grimaced. "It is not meet to leave a guest waiting upon us."

"Stay close. I do not know if I can face the baron alone when..."

As he placed her hand on his arm again, he smiled. "I shall be with you always, *belovit*, for you are within my heart." He lifted her fingers to his lips. "We have much to speak of after the formalities of welcome are completed."

"I have missed you, too."

He chuckled. "You read my thoughts so easily."

She put her fingers over the center of his hard chest. "Because my heart listens to yours."

As they walked out of the room, Ashley's fears surged forth doubly strong. For months, this threat had been held over her head. Now she would know what the Marquess of Argyll had decided, but that was not what frightened her. That Harry

Campbell had chosen to deliver his uncle's verdict unsettled her more than she had guessed.

She was surprised that, when Colin led her into the reception hall, it was empty, save for one man. She had thought Lord Campbell would revel in proclaiming her fate before her household. He had been fond of theatrics during his previous visits. Mayhap the war had changed him.

No one spoke as she and Colin crossed the stone floor which was nearly as long as the great hall's. A few benches were pushed against the walls beneath the windows that were high up near the rafters. In the center of the room was a firepit with a carved table on either side of it. The fire within the pit did little to combat the cold.

The large man faced them. As always, Harry Campbell reminded Ashley of a hawk, for his sharply sculptured nose and piercing eyes marked him as a predator. Although his features were not as well defined as his uncle's stronger face, Harry Campbell was a young hawk, eager to establish his dominance. His long hair was as black as Colin's, but she knew he wore a fashionable wig. Last time she had seen him, he had had light brown hair.

His bearing and his tartan of the Campbells of Argyll proclaimed him as the representative of the *Ard-Righ*, the supreme chieftain of the clan. She was sure he relished this role. She saw his eager smile as his gaze roved along her and knew he had not changed. He still wanted her. She no longer worried that she never had met him, except in her memories. Her dual pasts were mingling into this single present.

When Colin bowed his head to acknowledge the envoy of the Marquess of Argyll, Ashley dipped in a curtsy. If there had been any way to avoid the motion, she would have. It galled her to bend her knee to this man she hated.

Her hand was taken, and she was drawn to her feet. Her gaze rose to meet Lord Campbell's dark eyes above his puritan collar. It did not surprise her that he now wore the Covenanters' uniform, even though he preferred fine feathers.

"Lady Ashley." He chuckled. "Yes, 'tis *Lady* Ashley you claim to be now."

"I claim only the truth," she replied.

"It is wonderful to see you again, no matter what you call yourself. You are, as always, a delight to the eyes."

"Thank you, Lord Campbell."

"How kind of you to wear this lovely gown for me!"

This was not the reaction she had anticipated, but she knew she must not reveal her surprise. "I am pleased that it pleases you, milord."

"My uncle is most solicitous of your health, milady. We wished to be sure you were provided for adequately. Have you been treated well?" Lord Campbell asked as if Colin were not in the room.

She wet her parched lips. Into her mind came memories of the time she had been banished to the kitchens while she had believed Colin was taking Lilias as his mistress. Over that memory came the fake wedding with Jackie threatening to slay her. Other recollections fled through her mind, but she answered, "Very well."

When Lord Campbell nodded with a secretive smile, she guessed he had a spy here and knew every detail of her life since Colin's arrival. He refused to release her fingers as he turned to Colin and smiled with fake gentility. "You have not found your duty of watching over this woman extraordinarily onerous, have you, MacLachlan?"

"Not extraordinarily." Colin's face was shuttered, revealing nothing.

Campbell chuckled. As if he were the host and they the guests, he gestured for them to be seated. He arched a single brow when Colin drew a bench forward and sat Ashley beside him. The chill was biting more than a few feet from the firepit, but the most fierce cold hung between the two men.

The baron began to pelt Colin with questions about any sighting of Montrose's Royalists near Castle Braeburn. Trying not to fidget on the bench, Ashley struggled not to blurt out her questions. Had a decision been made about the castle? Had it been made about her?

When Lord Campbell started to question her with the same pompous tone he had used with Colin, she wished she had been able to remain silent. He was interested in what had happened to any correspondence Lord Stanton might have left behind.

"Lord Stanton? Do you think he took *me* into his counsel on anything?" She laughed, then wished she had not when Lord Campbell glared at her.

"Come now, Ashley!" Lord Campbell argued. "You know more about what happened here than either MacLachlan or me. You cannot convince me that you did not seek a way to avenge your father's death."

"Milord, I would have been a fool to draw attention to myself by spying on Lord Stanton."

He snorted. "Do you think he was unaware of you? He bet me that he would bed you before my next visit."

"'Twas his misfortune and my good fortune that he did not live to attempt to win that wager," Ashley said quickly when she heard Colin's muttered curse. If the point of these pointless questions was to enrage Colin, she must put an end to them. She slipped her hand beneath Colin's plaid and stroked his arm, being careful not to look at him.

"But Stanton did not die before he finished some correspondence to King Charles. The marquess is interested in it. The last packet would have been prepared about the time he went to fight MacLachlan."

She followed Lord Campbell's gaze to Colin, who had made no comment to the baron during her interrogation. When her hand rose to touch Colin's, she drew it back. She did not want to betray herself. Swallowing to clear her throat that was clogged with fear, she said, "As I told you before, I do not know where Lord Stanton put his correspondence. If it was in his office, Colin would have found any letters."

"And I found nothing of the sort. Only ledger books and such," Colin replied calmly. "I do not see where your questioning of Ashley is doing any good, Campbell. She has told you that she has no knowledge of this."

"And you believe her?"

His eyes crinkled in amusement. "She only lies about important matters."

Lord Campbell seemed about to retort, but said, "Very well, Ashley. You may leave us. I shall expect you to join me in the solar for a game of chess this evening."

"Chess?" she asked, amazed. Chess was not the game she had guessed he wanted to play with her.

"You do still play, don't you?" He stroked his chin and laughed. "I often thought it amazing that a kitchen wench would play chess."

"Mayhap the talent came from her father, who was renowned for his military skills both on the battlefield and beyond," Colin said.

Ashley stared at him. He had expressed admiration for her father in the past, but usually to taunt her claim of being the laird's daughter.

"Ashley?" prompted Lord Campbell, not hiding his impatience.

"Yes, I would be honored to play chess with you this evening, Lord Campbell." It was a lie. She wanted nothing to do with him.

Rising, she did not look at Colin as she left. As soon as Colin learned the marquess's decision, he would tell her. Tonight, she would meet Lord Campbell and play a game that she had not played in years. She hoped she could remember the finesse chess required, for she did not doubt that Lord Campbell would be a challenging player.

As she walked along the strangely empty passage, she reviewed the basic moves in her head. So deep was she in her thoughts, she did not notice the men walking toward her until one stepped in front of her to block her way.

"Oh, pardon me." Seeing the Argyll tartan, she forced a smile.

When she would have walked around the taller man, she saw his companion was not going to let that happen. She smelled whisky on their breaths and knew their smiles meant that they wanted to create trouble for her. Trust Lord Campbell to have no interest in controlling his men. She could not believe he had given up his own drinking and wenching.

"We have been looking for Lady Ashley Gordon," drawled the taller man. "D'ye know where we might be finding the lassie?"

"I am sure Lady Ashley will be glad to speak to you when you are sober."

The men laughed as they slapped each other on the back, but there was nothing mirthful about the man's face pushed toward hers. "Lassie, we hear your lady sleeps with MacLachlan. Could do no better, I guess."

She said nothing. She was not going to respond to their drunken insults.

The man stepped closer toward her. She backed away. A gasp exploded from her as she bumped into a third man.

Knowing she must be bold, she said, "I assume your actions have been approved by the baron." If she showed any fear, they would be even crueler to her. "He will be sure to ask me your names. Do you want to make it easy and tell me, or shall I just describe your ugly faces?"

The men exchanged fearful glances. "She is bluffing," murmured one.

"Go!" she urged when they hesitated. "Lord Campbell is in the reception hall with Laird MacLachlan. Go, and ask Lord Campbell if he wants me to come to our chess game with the filth of his soldiers upon me."

At her insult, they grumbled, but stepped aside. She continued along the hallway. She did not look back. Fear trembled through her, but she suspected that the greatest danger waited for her with the coming of night and the game Harry Campbell intended to play.

# NINETEEN

Colin stood in the doorway of his rooms. No one took note of him. Ashley paced the sitting room while Ella sat and stared at her needlework. For once, her needle hung motionless from a thread. Ramsey wandered through the room, but did not look toward the door.

When Ashley paused in mid-step, she saw him and ran to him. She flung her arms around his shoulders and pressed against him. All thoughts of his irritation with Campbell vanished as he tilted her face and found her mouth. A hunger that had grown more voracious with each passing day that she was not in his arms raged through him like a fever.

He had kissed her so many times before, each one a separate delight, but never had it been like this. From the first time when he had held her in the great hall, he had thrilled at her eager response, but this was different. This time, she was kissing him as if she feared she never would have the chance again.

When, too soon, he raised his mouth from hers, her gaze did not meet his. She had softened in his arms, but grew rigid with fear again. His hands lingered on her as she moved out of his embrace. For a long minute, she stood with his hands holding hers, then stepped away.

His finger under her chin tipped her face back toward his. She sighed when his questing mouth caressed her cheek before brushing her lips. With a moan, she pressed to him again.

"I have been a fool to deny us this," he whispered against her hair. She quivered as his breath whirled about her ear.

"Aye, you have."

Colin was amazed when he could chuckle at her tart reply. Ashley might be convulsed with terror, but her wit remained sharp.

"I trust you will remind me the next time I am so foolish," he murmured.

Instead of retorting, she asked, "What did Lord Campbell say?"

He sighed and released her. Unbuckling his sword belt, he handed it to Ramsey. Gently he smoothed Ashley's hair back from her face. His jaw tightened. "One thing is clear. You need have no concerns about the baron wanting you dead."

"I guessed that."

"He hinted that Castle Braeburn would be mine if I did nothing to halt his plans for you."

"Which he made clear when he was here before."

Colin cursed, hating her calm tone. She would not just accept Campbell's edict, would she? When she glanced at him and quickly away, he knew she was not as serene as she wished him to think. "Of his exact plans, he is being very closemouthed."

"Which is unlike Harry Campbell!"

"Aye," he admitted. "'Tis most unlike him."

"He must know of our situation."

He laughed without humor. "Situation? You continue to amaze me with your choice of words, Ashley. Does he know you have shared my bed? There is no doubt of that, but he hints that he can take you away from me."

"He is the marquess's nephew. He has the power to do as he wishes."

"We shall see. It may be time for Lord Harry Campbell to learn a lesson about the boundaries of his power."

When she ran her hand along his arm, he caught it and turned it palm up so he could taste the luscious warmth of her skin. But her hand was icy cold as she whispered, "Be careful, Colin. After what happened to Carleton MacLaws when he stood in Lord Campbell's way, I know Harry Campbell is capable of any form of treachery."

"Aye," he repeated softly, "but he shall not win easily. I promise you that, *belovit*. He shall not win easily."

\*\*\*

When Colin told Ashley that he would offer her excuses to Lord Campbell for not appearing at the evening meal, she was grateful. It gave her time to prepare herself for the chess game in the solar. She had thought they would linger over dinner and talk, but the message from Harry Campbell for her to attend him in the solar came too soon, delivered by a very worried Davey Beaton.

"Milady, he wants to see you now." Loathing dripped from the lad's voice.

"One moment, Davey." Ashley turned to Ella. "Please, go to bed early. I know you do not feel well with your head stuffiness. If only Wynda was still alive! She would have an herb to help you."

The maid smiled weakly. "I shall be fine, milady. I will put out your nightclothes." She glanced at Davey, then looked back at Ashley. "I will put them out here."

"Thank you," Ashley said.

"'Twill be easier, for they will be waiting for you when you are done with the baron." Her voice quavered as she added, "Be wary, milady. He is a snake seeking a chance to strike."

"I know," she said softly. "Davey, shall we go?"

Walking beside the lad, she was disconcerted to see the corridors were empty. The smells from dinner could not blanket out the reeking fear. At the solar door, she thanked Davey. She reached for the door latch, but paused, startled to feel Davey's hand on her arm.

"Davey, what is wrong?"

"Milady, does the laird know that the baron has set his men to watch everyone in Castle Braeburn?"

"What do you mean?" She whispered as he did.

He grimaced. "The baron's men have taken the evening to position themselves so the men loyal to you and Laird MacLachlan cannot make a move against him. His men outnumber us two to one. I do not know if we can defend the castle against them when they are within the walls."

"Go to the laird, if you can do so without being seen, Davey. Tell him what you have told me."

"Aye, milady." His face was grim.

Ashley watched him walk away along the hallway before she reached again for the door latch. The sooner this game was started, the sooner it would be over.

Tonight would not be like when Lord Campbell had waylaid her in the stillroom. She was Gordon's daughter, rightful holder of this castle, not a poor kitchen maid who feared a baron. She would not give him the satisfaction of begging him to keep his hands off her. It took all her willpower to hide her thoughts as she said, "Good evening, Lord Campbell."

"Good evening, Ashley. Come in and sit here." He pointed to a chair opposite the settee where he lounged like a dissipate Roman. In his hand was a glass of whisky. That he did not rise when she entered warned her he did not intend to offer her any courtesy.

She thought back to the day when she had come into Colin's office and neither Colin nor Jackie had stood. She had recognized that as the insult it was. This was even more so, because now she was granted respect throughout the castle as her father's daughter.

He took a sip and asked, "Something to drink, Ashley?"

"No, Lord Campbell." She smiled coldly as she sat. "Whisky is a taste I have never acquired."

He chuckled. "'Tis a wise woman who knows her limitations. There are few things that you have not mastered, are there?" Leaning forward, he rocked the glass as his gaze grew intense. "Ashley Gordon, who claims to be the beautiful and intelligent daughter of a brave father and a legendary mother."

"I have done what I must to survive."

"Is that why you have charmed your way into MacLachlan's bed?"

A hot flush told her that her face was crimson. Trust Lord Campbell to discuss this personal subject so crudely. "Why I do what I do is my own business, milord. Have you given credence to the idea that I might love Colin?"

"You love the man who claims your father's castle?" His eyebrows arched toward the curls on his forehead. "I find that hard to believe."

"If you find it difficult to believe, then that is your problem." Standing, she went to the fireplace. She wanted to put some distance between them.

"So you have not been averse to the choice of MacLachlan for your jailer?"

"Jailer?" She faced him. "I did not realize that he had been given that duty. 'Twas a waste because I have no desire to leave Castle Braeburn."

"And MacLachlan?"

"I thought you came to Castle Braeburn to deliver your uncle's decision on the claim for this castle, nothing else."

"You have changed, Ashley. You are gentler." His gaze edged along her with studied, sensual urgency, making her blush again. "I must admit I like this change, for you were a very hard woman when last we met. I hope you will adjust to your new life as readily."

"New life? What new life?"

He rose and patted her cheek as if she were a child. When she started to draw away, he slipped his arm around her waist and tugged her closer.

"I think you forget we are to play chess," she reminded him tartly, putting her hands on his arms and pulling away.

"Is that so? I can think of other games to pursue with you."

"No kidding."

He stared at her, baffled. "What?"

Ashley walked to a table where a chess set waited for the game to start. The phrase had slipped out. She could not remember the last time she had spoken words from the future. "I tire of these word games."

He laughed. "I assure you that you will know soon what my esteemed uncle has planned for Castle Braeburn. Now, shall we play chess?"

She nodded, but not for a moment could she forget that Harry Campbell would do anything to get what he wanted.

At the chess board, Lord Campbell offered her the white chess pieces. Although she accepted this courtesy, she was afraid it was the only one he would offer her. When he was seated opposite her, he nodded for her to begin.

Ashley's fingers quaked when she reached for a pawn. She lifted the heavy piece and balanced it as she paused. As she placed it on a square, she felt a kinship to this small piece being sent out to be sacrificed.

The baron wasted no time countering her move. She smiled as she moved her next piece as quickly.

As his fingers hovered over the board, he eyed her. "You are confident, milady."

"This is warfare, Lord Campbell. One must not falter."

He smiled malevolently. "Stanton was a fool to let you live. 'Tis too bad that you have no more sense than your father, who died a martyr."

Ashley lowered her eyes, so he did not see her rage. She bit back her retort that her father had not left his men to be slaughtered while he fled to safety as Campbell and his nephew had.

Lord Campbell's barbed remarks did not cease as the game continued. Each comment made Ashley more determined to beat him in the only way she could. She could tell his mind was far busier trying to find a crack in her façade than in protecting his game pieces. Again and again, he turned the conversation to Lord

Stanton's letters, refusing to believe she had no idea what he was talking about.

At a knock, Ashley glanced up, hoping this intrusion would be help to end this intolerable game.

Colin opened the door. He did no more than glance at Lord Campbell before his gaze met hers. When he frowned, she knew, he, too, was tired of Lord Campbell toying with them.

She jumped up and went to him, but did not touch him. Again she knew Lord Campbell was watching intently. "Colin, I was hoping you would arrive in time to see me check Lord Campbell."

His laugh sounded genuine. "I am glad I was not delayed." He dropped his voice to a whisper, "Davey risked his life to tell me—"

"I so love playing chess. It is intriguing, and Lord Campbell has challenged me on my way to victory." She continued to babble as Colin murmured that the baron's men had taken control of Castle Braeburn, disarming their men.

"Why?" she asked as softly, taking a breath.

"I have not learned yet," he answered, turning her to walk back to Lord Campbell.

She fought to keep a serene expression as Colin crossed the room and sat her again at the table. He stood behind her and asked, as if it were the most important thing in his life, "How does the game progress?"

Lord Campbell answered, "She closes in for the kill."

"'Tis just as well Lady Ashley is our ally, is it not, Campbell?" Colin chuckled, but his hand fisted against her back.

Campbell's eyebrows came together in a scowl. "Your move, Ashley."

Moving one of her pieces, she said, "Check, Lord Campbell."

"Check?" he demanded. His attention returned to the board. He leaned back in his chair. "And checkmate after my next move?"

"Yes, Lord Campbell." She gave him a victorious smile.

"I concede to you. 'Twas a well played game."

"Thank you."

When Colin held out his hand, she took it and rose. His hand tightened around hers, and he turned her so he stood between her and Lord Campbell. He startled her when he bent to kiss her cheek and murmur, "Congratulations."

She did not have to look at the baron to know he was frowning. Colin was daring Lord Campbell to be as honest.

The chess pieces fell in a shower of broken alabaster. She whirled as Lord Campbell pointed at Colin. "You were told to watch over her, MacLachlan. Nothing else."

"I have done as ordered." Colin took Ashley's hand and squeezed it, wishing he could assure her that all would be well. He could not, not when Davey Beaton's warnings confirmed Colin's own observations. He kept his thoughts from his voice. "Ashley Gordon was kept here alive and unharmed while your uncle decided who should have claim to this castle."

"She was to be mine. My reward for my assistance to my uncle."

"You should have made your plans clear, Campbell. I had no idea you had other than a political interest in Lady Ashley."

"Political?" He guffawed. "Look at her, and tell me if you once thought of politics when you held her beneath you in your bed. If she is not going to be mine, then we must decide what will happen to her. She may well be a traitoress, a follower of our blighted Charles Stuart."

"You seek to have her prove her loyalty by marrying an ally?" Colin smiled as if the idea had just come into his head. "Then I shall wed her."

"Colin!" Ashley cried. "No!"

"No?" He looked into her shocked face. Anger exploded through him. Didn't she realize he was bargaining for her life? He understood her fear that, if she agreed to be his wife, she would be taken from him again. The situation had changed. No longer could she decide between being his lover or marrying him at the risk of being dragged from this century. Now she chanced dying by Campbell's order. Ignoring Campbell, he brought Ashley's face up. "Shall we make what we share permanent, *belovit*?"

"Marry her, MacLachlan," Campbell snarled, "and you may be deemed guilty, too."

"Guilty?" he fired back. "Of what?"

"The Gordons once welcomed Montrose here. Does she give them the secrets she has seduced from you?"

"Secrets? 'Tis no secret that not only has Montrose supped here, but the Campbells as well, both before Stanton destroyed the Gordons and after. Who fears the revelation of the facts, Campbell? I have nothing to hide. Ashley has been honest with you. That leaves only one person in this room who fears the truth."

"Ashley?   Honest?" Campbell sneered.   "She has never spoken a truthful word in her life."

"Yes, I have!" she retorted, recklessly.   "I abhor you, Harry Campbell.   That is the truth!"

"Ashley."   Colin drew her closer to him.   "Take care."

The warning came too late, because Campbell's rage was refocused on her.   She knew he was furious that she would have chosen Colin, whom he saw as upstart laird, over the nephew of the Marquess of Argyll.

"Did you tell your lover where you were during the month you disappeared from Castle Braeburn?" the baron asked.

She swallowed roughly and glanced at Colin.   His steady gaze strengthened her.   "Yes, Lord Campbell, Colin knows where I was."

"And where was that?"

Colin answered, "She was here in Castle Braeburn.   An illness took her far from us for a while.  Because we feared panic within the walls, we suggested that she had left.   I thought her friends here would rather be hoping for her return than fearing her death.   She recovered and 'returned.'" His eyes narrowed in what Ashley recognized as his most dangerous expression.   "If I had known which person here was your spy, Campbell, I would have been happy to share the truth."

"Damn you, MacLachlan!"   He glared down his long nose.  "You were raised in a hovel, and that is where you should die.  Unfortunately, that would be too difficult to arrange quickly.  So..."   He shouted an order.

Several soldiers in Campbell tartan rushed into the room.  Ashley cried out in horror as she was yanked away from Colin and shoved toward the baron.  Colin tried to halt them, but he was pummeled to the floor.

Grabbing her arm, Campbell shouted, "Take him to the dungeon and put him in a cell there while I speak with *Lady* Ashley."

"No!" she cried.   "You cannot order that."

"No?"  Campbell laughed.   "I believe I just did."

Colin pushed himself to his feet.   "I am laird of this castle!"  His voice was not raised, but its closely restrained fury was more threatening than Campbell's raving.   "I have followed the marquess's orders, and this is my reward?"

"Reward?"  He laughed.   "You have had your chance to play the laird, MacLachlan.  Now you will learn the justice dealt to traitors."

"You cannot blame Colin for your mistakes!" Ashley cried. "He never would have abandoned his men to be butchered by his enemies."

Campbell's face turned scarlet with rage. "I have yet to decide which of you to punish first. Do not force me to choose you, Ashley."

As Campbell raised his hand, Colin jumped forward and seized it. Campbell's shriek brought his men swarming over Colin again. Ashley tried to stop them, but she was thrust aside.

"Do not hurt yourself," Colin said, rising to his knees. He wiped the back of his hand against his bloody lip. "Trust me, *belovit*."

Ashley started to protest, but her own thoughts were drowned out by a smaller voice, coming as if from a great distance.

*See the truth around you.*

Was that her mother returning from wherever to help her or her own thoughts? Either way, she must heed the advice. She could not let Campbell kill Colin here. A few hours in the dungeon might save Colin's life, for Davey Beaton must not be the only one who had seen the truth of what was happening within Castle Braeburn. Surely, Colin's men were already scheming some way to defeat Campbell's soldiers.

This was an uneasy path they had to follow. If they slipped once along it, Campbell would slay them.

"Take him away," ordered Campbell, then he called, "Wait."

His men stared at him in astonishment.

"I believe *Lady* Ashley—" He continued to put the snide emphasis on her title. "—will wish as chatelaine of Castle Braeburn to see where her lover will spend his last hours."

"Campbell!" shouted Colin, struggling against the men who held his arms. "Do not make her a part of your brutality."

"Brutality? I wish only for her to see what the cost of not obeying my orders will be for her." Campbell put his arm around her waist. When she jerked away, he pulled her back closer. "She can start by cooperating now."

Ashley wanted to spit in his face, but acquiesced. He did not have to voice his threat. She knew it. If she did not do as he ordered, Colin would die. Nice and simple, although she suspected Colin's death would be anything but nice and simple.

The corridors were as quiet as a mortuary. As they reached the door leading to the stairwell down into the dungeons, Colin startled everyone by turning and putting his arm around Ashley's waist.

"The stairs are uneven, and I do not want her to fall," he said before Campbell could snarl an order.

"Mayhap you wish to push her to her death." The baron laughed tersely. "Then she cannot betray your complicity in her schemes."

"'Twould be a good idea if there was a need. There is not." He lowered his voice. "Do what you can to keep yourself alive, *belovit*."

"And you," she whispered.

"Do what is possible."

Ashley stiffened. He believed saving his life was impossible. Although she wanted to tell him that she would not let him die simply to save her own life, she said nothing as they followed one of Campbell's men down the stairs. She must not let Lord Campbell discover how close she was to shattering into tears.

At the bottom, Colin paused. "I assume you have selected quarters for me."

With a snarl, the baron swept out his arm. "Pick whichever you wish, MacLachlan. This is, after all, your castle, as you are so fond of reminding us."

Colin grabbed one of the torches held by Campbell's men. A surprised shout echoed through the catacombs. With his arm still around Ashley, he swept her along as he peered into the various rooms. "Here will do."

With a guffaw, Lord Campbell ordered the door opened. He cursed when Colin turned Ashley against his chest and bent toward her.

"Release her, MacLachlan!" he bellowed. "This is not another chance for you to seduce her." He reached out a hand to drag her away.

The flames made a whooshing sound as Colin brought the torch down between Campbell and Ashley. Colin's eyes burned as brightly as the brand. "Take care, Campbell, or we shall see which burns more quickly. The wool of your coat or the wool on your head."

Sputtering, Campbell ordered his men to disarm MacLachlan. One guard started to step forward, but scuttled back when Colin swung the torch once more. The others looked at their leader for further orders.

"Promise me that you will not hurt Ashley," Colin stated. "Give me your vow on your uncle's name."

Lord Campbell glared at them. His fingers lingered over the butt of the pistol he had pulled from beneath his short coat.

Suddenly he laughed. "I give you my vow on my uncle's name that she will be alive to witness your death, MacLachlan."

"Go with him," Colin said quietly, handing the torch to one of Campbell's men.

"But, Colin—"

"Go with him."

Blinking back tears, she nodded. She had to trust Colin, for he knew this time far better than she did. He must know a way to save his life and hers. She wished he would give her a hint how, but she could not ask. Not with Campbell and his men listening to every word.

Colin gave her a push toward Campbell, then whirled her back into his own arms. His fervent kiss sent need and pain through her, for she knew he was kissing her good-bye. She gripped his arms, not wanting to let this moment end.

She moaned when her shoulders were grasped, pulling her away from him. Putting her hand over her mouth, she tried not to be ill while she watched Colin shoved into a cell. It closed with a clang that ached through her heart.

Campbell's arm encircled her waist. "Come with me, Ashley."

"I prefer to spend the night here."

"That can be arranged." His face was macabre in the flickering light. "But you would soon be calling for me to free you from your cell."

"Never!" she spat.

"We shall see." His smile chilled her to the pit of her stomach.

Ashley tried to look back as she went up the stairs, but the darkness had already claimed Colin's cell. She wondered if he was thinking, as she was, of the death awaiting them at Lord Campbell's pleasure.

It would not be easy. It would not be quick.

# TWENTY

"Papers?" asked Ella and Ramsey at the same time.

"Letters that Lord Stanton would have written." Ashley pulled open another drawer in Colin's desk and emptied it onto the floor. Lord Campbell had given her an hour to find Lord Stanton's correspondence with the king. She suspected he was enjoying more of Castle Braeburn's whisky, but did not care what he was doing as long as he was not here watching her panicked search.

"There is nothing like that here," Ramsey said. He halted her from reaching for another drawer. "The laird would have had it destroyed if it had been."

Sinking to the floor, Ashley sorted through the papers. "There must be something. Lord Campbell is desperate to find it."

"Because it implicates him in that Royalist plot," Ella said quietly.

Ashley's head jerked up as she stared at her maid. "Ella?"

"Have you forgotten what was whispered through the castle in the months before the war reached Scotland?" Ella knelt and folded Ashley's hands between hers. "Milady, you heard the rumors, too."

"Of how Lord Stanton wished to obtain the king's pleasure by wooing some of Argyll's men away." Her eyes widened as the memory drifted from the mists of her terror. "The first one he sought to turn was Harry Campbell."

Ella nodded. "Aye. Lord Stanton was an evil man, but not a stupid one. He knew that if he could persuade the baron to align himself with the king, others would follow, leaving the marquess with just the shadow of an army."

"If Lord Stanton put that in writing to the king..." Ashley sighed. "Lord Campbell will slay us if we do not find it. He will

slay us if we do, because he will know we are privy to what was
within it."

"Mayhap not." Ramsey held out his hand and brought her to
her feet. "The English lord would have sealed his letter with wax
and his signet ring, so it could be opened only by the king. If the
letter is brought to Lord Campbell with the seal unbroken, he will
know you have not read it."

"But where could it be?"

"I have no idea, milady," Ella said.

"Or even if it still exists." Ramsey clasped his hands behind
his back and scowled.

Ashley refused to listen to his dreary tone. She had not told
either servant where Colin was, for she feared Ramsey would not
be stopped from going to Colin's rescue. The old man would die
before he could reach the dungeon.

Sitting in Colin's chair, she leaned her head back and closed
her eyes. She had to think like Lord Stanton. What would the
Englishman have done with letters he wanted to safeguard
because he had not had a chance to send a messenger with them
to King Charles?

"He would not have left them in his office," she said,
standing again.

"Then where?" asked Ella.

"How big would such a packet of papers be?" Ashley looked
from one servant to the other.

Ramsey spaced his hands about an inch or two apart.
"Mayhap this thick. I suspect, from seeing other reports that the
laird has found hidden throughout these rooms, that Lord Stanton
would have included many pages to impress his king."

"So big?" When he nodded, she grabbed Ella's hands. "The
table in the bedchamber of the rooms I was using had a drawer
jammed with papers."

"I recall it."

"Lord Stanton would have known that his rooms would be
suspect if he did not return. He might have trusted his wife to get
the papers to the king."

"Only she fled even before news of his death." Ella smiled.
"If those papers are the ones you seek, the baron may take them
and leave without delay."

"Yes, yes," she lied. Harry Campbell would not be willing
to leave until he had satisfied his pride by destroying her and
Colin, but mayhap by giving him what he sought, she could

persuade him to go and leave them alive. "Can you find them, Ella?"

"I shall now."

"Ramsey," she continued, "we should not be defenseless. Colin had a pistol."

"I know where it is, milady. Shall I bring it?"

"Yes, as soon as you have helped Ella see if those pages are what we seek."

"I shall go now with her, and then I..."

Ashley looked over her shoulder to see one of Campbell's men in the doorway of the office. Shoving Ella back into the room, he stepped aside to let the baron enter.

Campbell swaggered to her and gripped her face in his hand. Paying no attention to Ramsey's low growl, he asked, "Do you have them, Ashley?"

"We have not found them yet," she struggled to say as he squeezed her face.

"Your hour is past."

"I know. If you will give us a bit more time..."

"You may have more time, but MacLachlan does not. I told you an hour."

"The laird?" cried Ramsey. "What have you done with him?" He leapt forward, but was knocked to the ground by Campbell's man.

"Ramsey!" Ashley bent toward him, but was pulled back by the baron.

"Come with me, *Lady* Ashley. I want to see if I can help you remember where Stanton put his papers."

"I know where they might be."

"I do not want a might be. I want an answer." He put his face close to hers. "Do you understand?"

Ashley looked at his narrowed eyes and saw the truth. He did not want her to have found the papers yet. He was enjoying this chance to govern her through her fear for Colin. For the first time, she wondered if he was fleeing his uncle, who might have guessed that Harry Campbell was a traitor. She dared not ask.

"Ella, keep looking," she cried as Campbell drove her out the door ahead of him.

"Aye, milady." Sobs followed Ella's answer.

Ashley muttered Colin's favorite curse under her breath as she walked out into the hallway beside the baron. She was not surprised when she was led to the door to the dungeon.

J.A. Ferguson

In spite of her determination to be composed, she could not halt her feet from rushing her into Colin's arms when she saw him standing in front of his cell door. She brought his mouth down to hers, wanting to savor each kiss, knowing she might never kiss him again. As his arms came up to enfold her to him, she did not care why Campbell had brought her here. She only wanted to be in Colin's arms. She was startled when his lips brushed her earlobe. A quiver of rapture rippled through her.

"What are you doing?" she whispered.

"After all this time, you don't know?"

"Do not tease me!"

He kissed her cool lips lightly. "I want to show you how much I love you, *belovit*."

"Then hold me. Hold me, and never let me go."

All humor left his voice. "Aye, Ashley. I shall hold you in my heart forever."

"Isn't this sweet?" snarled Lord Campbell.

Her fists knotted against Colin's nape as she moaned softly. Panic caressed her, tempting her to surrender to it.

In a whisper, Colin ordered, "Whatever you do, *belovit*, do not lie to protect me." Turning to face his enemy, he said smoothly, "Yes, Campbell, to tell you the truth, Ashley's kisses are sweet."

"Bring them!" the baron ordered, stamping deeper into the dungeon's maze.

When one of the soldiers stepped forward to pull Ashley from his arms, Colin pushed her behind him. "We shall come, but I shall not have her sullied by these filthy hands. Call them off, Campbell, or—"

"You cannot threaten me, MacLachlan!"

"That is strange. I thought I just did." He took Ashley's hand and placed it securely on his arm. "Let us get this over with." He gave Campbell that cold smile which had so cowed Ashley when they first met. Now knowing Colin, she knew she had been right to be terrified by it.

Lord Campbell faltered, and she guessed he was as daunted as she had been. Glancing over her shoulder as they followed the soldiers, she saw the baron's eager anticipation return. He intended to make Colin pay for every insult.

When they were shoved through a door into a surprisingly well-lit room, Ashley cried out in dismay. Manacles hung from the wall, and a rack stood in one corner. Metal instruments she could not name were stacked along the wall. She looked back again and saw Lord Campbell's superior smile. Too late, she understood what he had been doing for the past hour. He had been preparing this torture chamber.

"Stop this before it goes any further," she begged.

Campbell reached out for her, but Colin pulled her away. Her fingers covered his hands on her arms. Just touching him helped her face the threat embodied by Harry Campbell.

"If you choose not to respect Colin's claim to Castle Braeburn," she said with quiet dignity, "then accept mine as Lady Ashley Gordon of Castle Braeburn. You have long been welcomed here, and—"

"Shut up!" he screeched. In the light of the dozen torches on the wall, his choleric face was scarlet.

He was scared. That made him more dangerous. Lord Stanton's correspondence must be even more damning than she had guessed.

He signaled to his men. She screamed as she was ripped from Colin's protective embrace.

"Bring her over here." Lord Campbell was smiling again. "You know what to do with MacLachlan."

Ashley struggled to escape as she watched Colin's wrists being hooked into a set of manacles hanging from the wall. Her screams of protest went unheeded, save for laughter. A memory burst, unbidden, through her head. Lord Stanton had used these torture devices with delight. Now Lord Campbell would.

She moaned when a man laughed and grasped the back of Colin's collar. His doublet was split so it hung from his arms. Another memory refused to be ignored. The memory of Lord Stanton whipping a man to death in the courtyard.

"Please stop this, Lord Campbell," she pleaded.

"Ashley, do not beg him for clemency," Colin shouted. "He will not give it to you, even while he makes you pay its price."

Lord Campbell smiled as he took a whip from one of his men. He let it slip to the floor to slither over her thin slippers. As he moved it gently, it seemed to come alive.

She wretched, knowing she would be sick if this continued. When he stepped closer, she flinched away from his eager fingers.

"You can tell me now, if you wish, Ashley."

"Tell you what? I told you that I do not know where the letters to—"

"Silence!" Viciously he twisted her head so she could not see Colin. "You can stop this, Ashley, by telling me where what I seek is."

"The letters—"

"I said, 'Silence!'" The sound of his hand striking her face was louder than the clanking chains as Colin tried futilely to escape to help her. As Campbell's face contorted to spit out an order, she knew she had to do all she could to help Colin.

Except lie. She had promised not to do that. Nausea roiled through her as she thought of what that vow might cost him, but she would not break it. Colin trusted her. She could not betray that trust.

"I told you, Lord Campbell," she said. Putting her fingers on his ebony coat, she brought his attention back to her. "Give me a chance to find what you seek."

"I gave you a chance. My patience grows thin."

"I might be able to find them if you give me more time."

"Where?" he demanded. When she hesitated, his dark eyebrows became a straight line. A tic at the corner of his left eye threatened to mesmerize her. "Tell me, Ashley."

"I would if I could."

"I know." Because he was smiling, she did not expect him to whirl and raise the whip. She shrieked as it struck Colin's bare back. A bloody welt appeared instantly.

"Tell me, Ashley!" he demanded. "Tell me, or..."

He raised the leather strap again.

Even as the whip was biting into him, Colin shouted, "Do not lie, Ashley! Do not lie to save me!"

"I told you, Lord Campbell," she cried. "If you will give me a chance, I shall find what you seek."

"Too late, Ashley." He laughed, and she knew that, even if she handed him the letters now, he would not relent.

With her knuckles pressed against her lips, she shuddered as the whip was raised again and again to cut into Colin. Not once did he cry out, and, except for that first, involuntary shriek, she was as silent. The only sound was the whistle of the whip severing the air and hitting Colin.

Lord Campbell threw down the whip. He gripped her face, and she moaned as his fingers dug into her sore cheek. He looked from her to the whip and then to where Colin sagged against the wall. "Mayhap I should have you change places. MacLachlan would do anything to protect you."

Ashley ignored him as she stared at Colin. The sight of his blistered back streaked with blood sickened her. She took a step toward him. "Colin, oh, Colin, can you hear me?"

Campbell shouted something, and strong hands pulled her away from Colin. Somehow she got her arm free. She swung her fist wildly and winced when it hit her captor's jaw. The man released her. She spun to go to Colin.

"Move, and I shall thrash him until he is dead!" Lord Campbell bellowed.

Ashley froze before turning to face Lord Campbell. "He is halfway there now. There is no need to continue this when I have told you already I will cooperate with you."

She flung up her hands to cover her head and cowered as she heard the whip snapped, striking the floor in front of her toes.

"Cooperate, Ashley?" Lord Campbell laughed. "Mayhap it is time for you to show me how willing you are to cooperate."

She hid her trembling hands in her gown. "How?"

With the handle of the whip, he pointed to the floor. "Beg, Ashley. If you want him to live, beg for him."

"I have. You have not heeded me."

"You may find me more amenable to your pleas now. You need only know what to beg me for."

"For you to be my lover?" She could barely speak the words.

"That would be a good start."

She shook her head. "No!"

"If that is how you feel..." He raised the scourge once more.

She gripped his wrist, and the long whip tumbled harmlessly to the ground. She saw the hunger in his eyes and knew she had no choice. From the corner of her eye, she glanced at Colin. He had not moved since the torture had halted. She was not sure if he was even conscious. The steady trickle of blood from one of the deeper cuts in his back was slowing, but his skin was an abstract design of crimson stripes. Never again would his skin be smooth beneath her fingers as he brought her to ecstasy. Each time she touched Colin, the memory of this moment would taint their joy.

"Well, Ashley?" The baron's hand crept along her arm with the disgusting sensation of a multi-legged creature.

She sank to her knees. All around her, she heard derisive laughter. She ignored it. Colin's life was worth more than her pride. "I beg you, Lord Campbell."

"You beg me to do what?"

"Save Colin's life."

"Why should I?" He grasped her hair, bringing her head painfully back to look up into his triumphant face.

"Because I offer you myself in exchange for Colin's life."

Campbell coiled the leather whip around his arm, then tossed it to another man who caught it easily. Raising her to her feet, he brought her into his arms. As he stared down into her eyes, he began slowly to undo the hooks along the back of her gown. She flinched at the murmur of anticipation among his men.

Her fingernails bit sharply into the her palms as she fought to restrain her revulsion. Knowing it was useless to pretend, she did not hide her hatred. His fingers slipped beneath the opened gown to caress her rigid back through her chemise. She feared she would not be able to keep from being ill.

"No protests?" he taunted. He pressed his mouth against the side of her neck. Slowly he drew the neckline of her gown downward to reveal the curve of her breasts above her chemise. "You will really trade yourself for that worthless excuse for a man?"

"Stop this torment and let him live, and I will do whatever you want."

"A generous offer, Ashley." He ran his finger along the lace covering her breasts. "Whatever I want will bring me much pleasure. My tastes are varied, as I know you have heard."

Her face became icy. She *had* heard of the perversions he enjoyed. She *had* heard of the women who had never been seen again or had been left dead or mad. Again she raised her chin as she glanced at Colin. She had promised not to lie to save him, but she had not promised to refrain from selling herself to Harry Campbell. If this was what it took to allow Colin to live, she would do it.

When her face was twisted back to meet Lord Campbell's lascivious eyes, she fought her panic. The battle was not yet lost. Like in the game of chess, there were many pieces to help the weakened king. Somehow, she had to alert Colin's allies to help *now*.

Quietly, she said, "I shall do as you say if you vow two things. First, you must promise me you will not hurt Colin again. Then, secondly, he must be taken care of so his wounds do not fester."

Lord Campbell stared at her. "You dare to negotiate with me?"

"I thought that was what we were doing. Reaching an agreement on the value of Colin's life."

"Damn you, Ashley Gordon! You do not give orders—" Suddenly a cruel smile tilted his lips as he gazed at her. "Why not? MacLachlan should live to see you give yourself to me. I shall do as you ask, and I shall expect you waiting for me in a half hour in MacLachlan's rooms."

She dipped in a shallow curtsy. "Yes, Lord Campbell. As you say, so shall it be."

*A half hour?* She hoped it would be enough time, for she knew she would not be able to halt the baron from raping her this time.

\*\*\*

Ella screamed as she saw her bedraggled lady shoved through the door of the laird's suite. When she stepped forward to aid her lady, one of the baron's men raised his pistol and aimed it at her.

With a snarl, he stated, "Hush, old woman, or I shall have your tongue ripped from your mouth."

Ashley whirled away from the man, holding her gaping dress over her breasts. "Get out! Take your threats and get out of here."

"'Tis the baron's orders that we stay here with you, milady." He grinned. "Seems he does not trust you not to play him false."

Knowing it was useless to argue with this well-trained cur, Ashley took Ella's arm and led her to the bedroom. The man did not stray from his post by the door.

"Get my robe," she said, wincing as each word she spoke hurt her aching cheek. "Did you bring what we talked about?"

"The pistol is beneath your pillow, milady."

Ashley glanced at the bed and gasped. Hanging from around its top were the strands of rowan and ivy that had decorated her bed. She realized that Ella and Ramsey had brought it here in hopes of a reconciliation between her and Colin.

Blinking back tears, she whispered, "Thank you."

Ella nodded, then said, "As far as the other things—" She glanced at the door. "We have not been allowed to leave to search for them."

"Where is Ramsey?"

"Trying to sneak out."

"Good." She grimaced again as the single word sent pain bolting through her.

"Lord Campbell struck you?" Ella gasped, reaching into the cupboard.

"Yes."

"The laird allowed this to happen?"

"Colin is hurt far worse."

Ella moaned a prayer as Ashley drew on her robe and let her ruined dress fall to the floor. Quickly she told Ella what had happened since Lord Campbell escorted her from these rooms.

The old woman put her hand over her breast and sank into a chair. "He ordered the laird flogged? How does the laird do, milady?"

"I do not know." For the first time, fear made her falter. She could see the whip slicing into Colin. She could hear its high squeal and the dull thud as it struck him.

"He is strong, Lady Ashley. If the wounds do not become infected by evil humors, he should survive."

"Lord Campbell promised Colin would be tended as long as I welcomed him here."

It had not seemed possible that Ella's face could grow more ashen, but it did. In a voice thick with despair and disgust, she whispered, "He knows you are the laird's lady."

"Do you think such a small detail would matter to Harry Campbell?" She wrapped her arms around herself. "He cannot wait to tell Colin that he forced me into Colin's bed."

"May the devil come to take that man!"

"Your wish comes too late, Ella," came a voice from the doorway.

Ashley whirled and stared at Gertie Graham's smile. Hearing Ella's frantic prayer, Ashley folded her arms in front of her. "I should have guessed you were part of this, Gertie. Harry Campbell needed a spy here, and you were glad to serve the part."

"It has had its rewards." She held up her arms which glittered with gold bracelets instead of the silver ones she had worn before. Touching one, she murmured, "A simple suggestion to the baron to have the laird's men sent to die on the battlefield and keep the laird here where the baron could enjoy watching him die gained me this one. It was as it should be. *I* did not forget that you were to be here to protect Castle Braeburn from its greatest enemy."

"You?"

"No, milady. Someone else within this room."

In disbelief, Ashley stared. Gertie had persuaded her that Colin was Castle Braeburn's greatest threat, the reason Ashley had been snatched from the future to continue her life in this time. Colin fought all his life to avenge his father's death and obtain the right to claim this castle as its laird. Now Ashley understood what Gertie truly believed. The greatest threat to Castle Braeburn was Ashley Gordon. Ashley wanted to protest, but mayhap she *was* the doom that Gertie had foretold, for the castle and for Colin. Her arrival back in the 17th century had led to this moment.

"What are you doing here?" Lord Campbell asked as he strode into the room.

Ashley glanced at Ella who tilted her head so slightly toward the bed. That was where Ramsey had hidden the pistol. If Ashley could reach it, she might put an end to this. She inched toward the bed, trying to silence her frantic heartbeat. She must not let Harry Campbell think she was eager to be in that bed with him.

"Milord," Gertie said with a smile, "my help to you is not complete."

"I have no need of you, witch woman. Ashley is mine now."

"Do you believe that?" She motioned to Ella. "Leave us."

"I shall not leave milady with you," Ella retorted stoutly.

"Leave us," repeated Lord Campbell, "or your lady shall watch you die."

"Go," whispered Ashley, taking another small step toward the bed. When Ella hesitated, she repeated the order.

Lord Campbell closed the door behind Ella. "What is it you can do for me, witch woman?"

Ashley tried to avoid Gertie's fingers, but Gertie grasped the chain holding the locket with the miniatures. Raising it up, she twirled it so it twinkled in the candlelight.

"Lady Ashley will do whatever I tell her to do if she stares at this." Gertie chuckled.

Pulling her gaze from the locket, Ashley put her hands over her eyes as she edged toward the bed again. She had not guessed that Gertie had hypnotized her with this legacy from her parents. That explained how, at the most inopportune moments, she found herself saying things she had not wanted to say. Post-hypnotic suggestion! That would seem like witchcraft at this time.

"She is under my spell, milord," Gertie continued, "and I have used it to keep her from succumbing to the spell the laird spun for her with his touch."

"Not well," growled Lord Campbell. "He bedded her first."

"Unfortunately, I was busy with other matters at the time."

"Trying to banish me from Castle Braeburn and sending an innocent woman to die!" cried Ashley. How much farther was it to the bed? The room seemed to have grown as wide as the loch.

"Innocent?" Gertie laughed. "Wynda Thompson *was* a witch! She wore many guises to keep you from me—the old woman and the young woman who befriended you in the kitchen."

Ashley gasped, unsure what to say. Just when she had convinced herself that there was no witchcraft here, that it was nothing but carnival tricks, Gertie said this. Was it the truth? She did not want to believe it, but she could not deny that she had no memory of Susan before she was sent to the kitchen, and Beathas did not recall Susan being in the kitchen at all. Had Susan been simply a manifestation of Wynda's attempts to protect her, as the old woman had said?

"I can make her do whatever you wish, milord." Gertie chuckled. "You need only ask."

"Do not believe her!" Ashley cried, stretching out her hand to touch the bed. Now she had to find the pillow and the pistol under it without them being the wiser. "She thought she had rid the castle of me, but I came back. She does not want to admit that the love Colin and I share is stronger than her evil."

Ignoring Ashley, Lord Campbell said, "I would like to see proof of this, witch woman."

"Gladly, milord." She pointed to a bench by the foot of the bed. "Have her sit there."

Ashley moaned as she was pulled away from the head of the bed when her fingers had been so near to the pistol. Shoved to sit on the bench, she closed her eyes.

"Open them," ordered the baron, "or I shall have MacLachlan whipped to death."

"No, do not hurt him more," Ashley whispered.

"Then obey me."

She nodded. *Mother...Mam, help me.* The name came from her deepest memories. *Mam, I cannot battle them alone.*

*You are not alone. See the truth around you.*

Gertie stepped in front of her and ripped the locket from around Ashley's neck. Holding it up, she spun it slowly as she whispered something.

*See the truth around you.*

"Look at the locket," Lord Campbell ordered. "If you value MacLachlan's life, look at it."

Ashley did look at it, then past it to the portrait of her mother. She gazed into the eyes smiling down on her, knowing that the others would think she was watching the locket. As Gertie spoke to her, telling her to close her eyes or to raise her arm, she obeyed.

"She is in my spell, milord," Gertie said with a triumphant laugh.

"Prove it."

Gertie laughed again. "Kiss the baron, Ashley."

Although her stomach turned and she wanted to shout that no one would do under hypnosis what they would not do normally, Ashley rose and went to Lord Campbell. She pressed her lips to his. When his arms held her so tightly to him she could not mistake his arousal, she knew the danger she was courting. She had no other choice. The truth around her was that she would risk anything to save Colin's life.

Lord Campbell laughed as she stepped back on Gertie's command. "Unbelievable. How long will she stay like this?"

"As long as you wish, milord." Gertie fingered the gold bracelet on her arm. "As long as *I* am pleased with the arrangement."

"You will be, I assure you." He laughed victoriously. "Wait here."

The baron rushed out of the room, shouting something that Ashley could not understand through the half-closed door. She wanted to turn, so she could hear more easily, but she must not let them guess she was not Gertie's puppet.

More noise came from the outer room, but Gertie ordered her to sit on the bench again. Ashley tried to swallow her curiosity as she lowered herself slowly to the bench. She continued to stare straight ahead.

Her ploy nearly failed when Colin was pushed into the room, his hands in manacles. She fought to keep her face blank. Her fingers trembled, and she hoped no one took note, for that shaking could reveal she was not hypnotized.

When her shoulders were grasped, she was jerked to her feet. She clamped her lips closed, so her groan of despair did not escape when she was turned to face Colin. His shoulders were bent with pain, but pride remained on his face while his eyes blazed with fury.

"So you do not believe me, MacLachlan," taunted the baron, "when I tell you that Ashley will do anything I wish?"

"What have you done to her?"

Ashley's heart ached as she wished she could soothe Colin's anger and fear that this was true witchcraft. If she did anything to comfort him, Lord Campbell would be so furious at her trick that he would order Colin slain here.

"I?" The baron laughed. "She is as she is because of Gertie's skills."

"Witch!" Colin snarled. "I should have had you put to death weeks ago."

"You let Ashley Gordon persuade you to wait." Gertie's triumphant laugh matched the baron's. "She is a gentle-hearted fool, and you are the greater fool to do her bidding."

A hard object was shoved into Ashley's hand. She did not dare to look down at it, but, as her fingers were closed around it, she realized, with horror, that it was a pistol.

Smiling, Lord Campbell said, "I shall prove to you how completely she is mine, MacLachlan, as this castle soon will be. Tell her, Gertie, to kill MacLachlan."

Gertie gripped Ashley's face and twisted her head toward the witch woman's cruel smile. "Kill Colin MacLachlan, Ashley. Now." She shoved Ashley forward a step, so the end of the long barrel was only a finger's breadth from Colin's chest. "Kill him. Now."

Ashley took a steadying breath. There would be only a single ball in the pistol. She must use it with care. Slowly she raised her eyes from the center of Colin's chest. Surprise flickered through his eyes when her gaze locked with his, and she knew he must have seen her despair and realized she was feigning this trance.

"Kill him. Now!" Gertie's voice rose with impatience from where she stood beside Lord Campbell.

"Why hasn't she shot him?" the baron asked.

"It is not easy to make her do what she would not customarily do." Gertie snarled something, then said, "Ashley, he is the doom for your father's castle. Your mother sent you away so you might survive until this moment when you fulfilled your fate. Kill him. Now!"

Ashley stared up at Colin. He did not need to speak, and neither did she. *See the truth around you.* The truth was that her enemies were his enemies, just as her heart was his.

She whirled and aimed the gun at Lord Campbell's middle. His face blanched as did Gertie's. She had but one shot. She drew back the hammer, remembering to aim low. The greatest danger to Castle Braeburn was not Colin MacLachlan. It was not Ashley Gordon. It was not even Harry Campbell.

She reaimed the gun. The greatest danger to Castle Braeburn was Gertie Graham. She fired.

Screams came from all around her. Shouts sounded everywhere, but Ashley saw only Gertie racing toward her, blood spewing from her.

"Run!" cried Colin. He tried to step forward, but the chains caught on his legs. He swore as Gertie shoved Ashley to the floor.

"You fool!" Campbell shouted, pulling out his own gun.

A shot fired, and Colin cringed, waiting for the pain of the ball cutting through him. In amazement, he saw shock on Campbell's face. The baron looked down at the blood flowing over his fingers from the hole somewhere in the middle of his abdomen. When he lurched toward the door, he fell forward to the floor.

Jackie and a dozen other men ran into the room followed by Ella. The maid rushed to the bed and pulled out a pistol.

"Leave milady alone, you witch!" she cried, aiming it at Gertie who was pressing Ashley to the floor.

"Don't shoot it!" Colin shouted. "You might strike Ashley."

Jackie grabbed the gun from Ella's hand before unlocking the manacles on Colin's arms. He grinned. "Just in time, my laird."

"Aye." He did not smile while he pushed through the crowd to where Gertie was being pulled off Ashley. The witch woman was dead, he realized, as he squatted beside her. He paid no attention to the pains lashing his back as if Campbell's whip struck him anew, making every motion a separate agony. Putting his hand on Ashley's shoulder, he shook her gently. "*Belovit*, it is over."

Her eyes did not open.

He held his hand over her lips. The soft pulse of her breath caressed them. Had she been shot? No, he realized quickly. The blood on her was the witch woman's. Again he shook her. "*Belovit*, wake up." He looked up. "Ella, I cannot wake her."

The maid dropped to her knees. "She is not dead, my laird, but I fear Gertie has had her final revenge. She is in some sort of sleeping trance. We may have lost her forever."

"Or," he whispered, sickness eating at his soul, "*to* forever."

# TWENTY-ONE

*They were within the walls.*

*Steel clashed. Men shouted, then screamed with their last breaths.*

*The little girl ran to cling to her mother's skirts. The mother's fingers trembled as they brushed the little girl's hair back from her face.*

*"It is time," the mother said.*

*A dark-haired woman kneeling by the window, her hands pressed together, interrupted her keening prayers. "Take care, milady. Before you begin, ask yourself if this risk is one you are willing to take."*

*As the mother bent to frame the little girl's face, she said to the other woman, "I must do this. They are here. They have killed my bairn's father and will suffer none of his blood to live. I will not stand by and watch them spill innocent blood."*

*"'Twill be your death to abide here a moment longer, milady," moaned the woman.*

*"My end is assured, for my death sentence was signed the day I wed. I will save my bairn."*

*A hand cupped Ashley's face, and she looked into eyes so much like her own. "Mam," she whispered.*

*"My bairn."*

*Ashley realized she was no longer a child, for suddenly she could meet Lady Fia's gaze evenly. "What am I doing here again?"*

*"You were sent from where you were. We brought you here from the darkness, so that you might understand."*

*"We?"*

*Lady Fia turned to the woman by the window. Slowly the woman came to her feet, her dark hair now a silvery-white.*

*"Wynda!" cried Ashley. "But Gertie Graham was the woman who was in my dreams."*

*"Your nightmares, bairn," Lady Fia corrected gently. "I had intended that your dreams would remind you of the truth of your*

*past, but Gertie Graham intruded here where I thought she could not. I had thought I was so careful, making certain that you would be loved in the future by a family who needed you as you needed them. I even created an enchantment so that everyone within Castle Braeburn would believe that you had never left."*

*"The memories that I have of a life I didn't live?"*

*Lady Fia smiled. "The memories of the life that you might have had if we had been foolish enough to succeed at hiding you from your father's enemies. I did not dare to risk that, for I knew Lord Stanton would not be satisfied until you were dead, too. So I knew I must send you to another time." Her smile disappeared. "Yet, even as I, in my arrogance, was sending you to safety, Gertie Graham was spinning an incantation of her own that tried to make you forget what you were by turning those memories into an evil that haunted you as nightmares. Neither Wynda, who has taught me what I needed to know to save you, nor I guessed that Gertie's hatred of our family would be so strong that she could come here and make you forget what I urged you to ne'er forget."*

*"Why does she hate me so much?"*

*"You are the granddaughter of your grandfather, bairn. Gertie tried her arts on your father's father, hoping to become his mistress, but they failed, for love will always be stronger than evil's ways. Spurned, she vowed to betray us all. In this time, she has helped Lord Stanton come within these walls."*

*"And that is why you had to send me to the future, so I would not be her victim after you..."*

*"Died." Lady Fia smiled as brightly as the sparkles had twinkled each time she had spoken to Ashley. "You can say it, my beloved bairn. I have been dead for too many years to fear death."*

*"But you stayed here to watch over me."*

*"Aye." She glanced at Wynda.*

*Ashley put out her hands to take the old woman's gnarled ones. "And you stayed, too. You and Susan." She hesitated, then asked, "Are you Susan?"*

*"I am who I needed to be to protect you and guide you, milady, away from Gertie Graham's evil."*

*"But you were slain by the witch-hunters."*

*"When you trusted the laird to be your ally against the hate which sought to destroy you." She raised Ashley's hands to her forehead. "It has been my duty and my pleasure to serve you."*

*"Ella said that! Are you Ella, too?"*

*"No, milady."* Wynda chuckled. *"I thought Ella might recognize me, but she was too overwrought to notice her old mam coming to help the laird."*

*"But you are..."* She looked from one woman to the other before whispering, *"You are a witch?"*

*"I am not the evil I have been denounced as,"* Wynda replied. *"I have learned and studied the old ways and the healing ways and have taught what I could to Lady Fia, for I saw the dark times coming when she would need the old knowledge. The spell I gave your mother was meant to bring you back at the proper time."*

*"And when Colin arrived, it became time because he was the partner I needed to fight those who would destroy me."* Ashley hugged her mother, then Wynda. *"Thank you for telling me all of this. Now, mayhap, Colin will believe me when I explain it to him. I hate to ask you to return me to Colin's and my time when there are so many more things I would like to ask you."*

*"Of your family?"* Lady Fia asked.

She nodded. *"Of my family here and in the future."*

*"As I told you, your mother and father in the future needed you as much as you needed them."* Tears misted her eyes. *"If not for you, they would never have had the love of a child who loved them."* She brushed Ashley's hair. *"That gift you gave to me and your father as well as to those who were with you in the future."*

*"How did you know where and when to send me?"*

Wynda smiled. *"There are ways of knowing that you have yet to learn, milady. Some things you now can only believe with your heart."*

*"You have learned to trust Colin MacLachlan,"* Lady Fia added. *"That you believed with your heart."*

*"Colin!"* Ashley moaned. *"Please send me back to him now. He has been badly hurt."*

Again Wynda and her mother exchanged a glance, but without a smile this time.

*"That may not be so easy,"* Lady Fia said.

*"But you brought me here."*

*"Aye,"* Lady Fia said. *"We brought you here, but Gertie Graham sent you away from Castle Braeburn. She knows a hint of the evil that comes from selling her heart to Satan. We cannot return you from here."*

*"I cannot go back?"* She sank to a chair. This time, she could not halt the tears that had been burning in her eyes. All that she had done, all she had dared, all might now be lost. A finger touched her face, wiping away her tear.

"Why won't she wake?" Colin asked again as he wiped a tear from Ashley's face. With care, he lifted her into his arms.

"Let me help," Jackie said.

"Step aside."

"You are hurt, my laird." Jackie held out his arms. "You could injure yourself more by carrying her."

"I know that! Now step aside." Colin fought his pain as he carried Ashley to the bed and placed her gently amid the pillows. The pain came not just from his lacerated back, but from within his heart. He could not speak to Jackie of how Gertie Graham had tried to send Ashley from here before. Had she succeeded this time?

While Jackie had the corpses dragged out and cleared the room of servants and soldiers, Colin stared at Ashley's waxen features on the ivory pillowcase. Her auburn hair and pink lips were the sole bits of color on her face. He touched her cheek where a single tear rolled.

"Ashley? Wake up, *belovit*! Come back to me."

She did not stir.

He knelt beside the bed and pressed his forehead to her limp hand. "*Belovit*, forgive me for letting my pride turn you away when you were here with me. I will love you forever. Wherever you are, whenever you are, know that I am waiting here and now for you. Ne'er forget that, *belovit*. Ne're forget."

She quivered, and he raised his head. What had he said? *Ne'er forget?*

"*Belovit*," he said, "ne'er forget that I love you. Ashley!" he gasped when her eyes slowly opened.

She did not look at him as she rose to her knees and reached up to the bed curtains. "This," she whispered, touching the rowan, "is the mountain ash for which I was named, the symbol of Castle Braeburn's past." Her fingertips brushed the ivy twisted through it. "And this is for Castle Braeburn's future when it is held by the MacLachlans. This castle is my home. I belong here in this time and in this place. I am home." Sitting back on her heels, she framed his face with her hands and brought his mouth to hers. She smiled when he drew back.

"Where have you been, *belovit*?"

She touched his face as if trying to assure herself that he stood before her. "I was where I had to be to learn the truth. I was not brought here, Colin, from the future to halt the greatest danger to this castle."

"You said that was what you were told by..." He glanced at the floor where blood still pooled.

"Gertie lied to me. My mother explained." She looked up at the portrait. "I was sent from here to be safe until the time came for me to marry the rightful laird of Castle Braeburn." She touched his face again. "You, my love."

"So will you marry me?" He laughed as he sat beside her. "I have asked you twice before, and I have heard that the third time is charmed."

Before she could answer, the door crashed open. Ramsey rushed in, his doublet tattered and his plaid covered with dust and debris. He waved a handful of papers. "I found them, milady."

"Found Stanton's correspondence?" she asked.

When he handed the packet to her, she broke the seal and read the top page. She gasped and handed it to Colin. The damning words were inked there. Harry Campbell had not been lured into a Royalist plot. He had been the instigator, hoping to gain wealth and prestige and get out from beneath his uncle's shadow.

With a curse, Colin threw the pages onto the fire. They sizzled and curled, then vanished in the flame. "Let the marquess mourn his nephew's death without knowing of this betrayal. This could rip apart the rebellion against the king." He turned to his man. "Thank you, Ramsey, for retrieving these."

"'Twas not easy." He patted his round stomach. "I am not as able to slip in and out of narrow windows and half-closed doors as I once was." He bowed his head. "If you need anything else, my laird, milady, call."

"Thank you," Ashley whispered before Ramsey went out and closed the door. She looked at Colin. When he limped as he walked toward her, she exclaimed, "You should be resting!"

"Aye, but first..." He took her hands between his. "*Belovit*, you have not answered me."

"Yes," she said, "I will marry you and live with you here in Castle Braeburn." She looked past him as he was about to kiss her and smiled to see small lights glittering near the hearth.

He turned. "Those sparkling lights! I have seen them before."

"As I have. My mam's heart might have ceased beating, but her love could not be banished from this castle. I suspect we shall always have a ghost or two within these walls. Mayhap even Gertie Graham, although her power over us is gone, now that we know her for what she was."

"I do not want to think of any spells but the one you have cast over me, *belovit*." He drew her into his arms and leaned her back again into the pillows.

As his lips covered hers, she discovered anew how love was like an unending shadow, dangerous and mysterious, lush and caressing...and forever.

# ABOUT THE AUTHOR

J. A. Ferguson is the best-selling lead author of Regencies and historicals (Ballads, Precious Gems, and Splendors) for Kensington writing as Jo Ann Ferguson and Rebecca North, paranormals for ImaJinn (writing as J.A. Ferguson), and historicals for Berkley (writing as Joanna Hampton), Harper, New Concepts Publishing, and Tudor. She writes inspirational contemporaries for MountainView Publishing (writing as Jo Ann Brown). She sold a historical suspense to M. Evans and contributed to an encyclopedia published by Garland on the English Regency period. Her work has been honored with award nominations by ROMY, *Romantic Times,* Rom/Con, and *Affaire de Coeur,* and has been showcased on Amazon.com. *The Counterfeit Count,* May 1997 Zebra Regency, won the 1998 ARTemis Award for Regency from Romance Writers of America. She is the editor of *Now That You've Sold Your Book. . .What Next?* and wrote the clause by clause explanation of publishing contracts included in it.

She is the current national president of Romance Writers of America and is the recipient of the Emma Merritt National Service Award, the highest honor for volunteer work from Romance Writers of America. She also has received the first Goldrick Service Award from the New England Chapter/Romance Writers of America. She was awarded a Massachusetts Art Grant to teach creative writing, and she established the romance writing course at Brown University.

She lives in Massachusetts with her favorite hero—her husband Bill—her three children, one very arrogant cat and an outrageous kitten.

J. A. Ferguson enjoys hearing from her readers. You may contact her at:

J. A. Ferguson
PO Box 843
Attleboro, MA 02703
email: jaferg@erols.com
http://www.joannferguson.com

# DON'T MISS
# *Dreamsinger*
### by
## J. A. Ferguson

## Nominated for the
## 1999 PEARL Award

### (Paranormal Excellence Award in Romantic Literature)

#### A WORLD LOST. . .
First Daughter Nerienne, heir to the Tiria of Gayome, faces the destruction of her world when her mother's enemies kill the Tiria. Nerienne is left with just her magic and with Bidge, a strange, shelled creature that speaks only to Nerienne. She is rescued by Durgan Ketassian, leader of the rebels in the northern woods, but can she trust this man whom her mother condemned to die?

#### A DREAM FOUND. . .
Durgan knows he cannot trust Nerienne, for the Tiria has been his enemy since she began slaying dreamsingers, those skilled musicians who sing the future through one's dreams. He has vowed to see his people free of the Tiria's domination, never guessing the Tiria's daughter could awaken parts of his heart which he shut away.

#### A SONG WITHOUT END. . .
To save Gayome, Nerienne and Durgan must work together to defeat their common enemy, but to become allies opens them to the greatest threat of all. . .falling in love.

SEE ORDER FORM IN BACK OF BOOK

# 2000 RELEASES FROM IMAJINN BOOKS

**February 2000:** *Mad About Max*
by Holly Fuhrmann - Fairytale romance

**March 2000:** *Cupid: The Bewildering Bequest*
by J. M. Jeffries - Mythological romance

**April 2000:** *Timeless Shadows*
by J. A. Ferguson - Time travel romance

**May 2000:** *Midnight Gamble*
by Nancy Gideon - Vampire romance

**June 2000:** *Etched in Stone*
by Dimitri Fitchett - Time travel/reincarnation romance

**July 2000:** *Hold Onto the Night*
by Shauna Michaels - Shapeshifter romance

**August 2000:** *Dreamshaper*
by J. A. Ferguson - Fantasy romance

**September 2000:** *Cupid: The Captivating Chauffer*
by J. M. Jeffries - Mythological romance

# MORE
## 2000 RELEASES
# FROM
# IMAJINN BOOKS

**October 2000:**   *Arabian Knight*
   by **Tracy Cozzens** - Fantasy/Time Travel romance

**October 2000:**   **Midnight Redeemer**
   by **Nancy Gideon** - Vampire romance

**November 2000:**   *Magic for Joy*
   by **Holly Fuhrmann** - Fairytale romance

**December 2000:**   *Glass Slipper.com*
   by **Rebecca Anderson** - Fairytale romance

# ORDER FORM

Name:_____

Address_____

City_____ __

**State**_____ **Zip**_____**Phone\***_____

| QTY | Book | Cost | Amount |
|---|---|---|---|
| | Dreamsinger | $8.50 | |

| | | | |
|---|---|---|---|
| **Total** | | SUBTOTAL | |
| **Paid by:** | | | |
| ☐Check or money order | | SHIPPING | |
| ☐ Credit Card (Circle one)  Visa Mastercard | | MI Residents | |
| Discover  American Express | | add SalesTax | |
| _____ | | TOTAL | |
| Card Number | | | |

_____

Expiration Date

_____

**Name on Card**

Would you like your book(s) autographed?  If so, please provide the name the author

should use._____

\*Phone number is required if you pay by Credit Card

**Mail to:    ImaJinn Books, PO Box 162, Hickory Corners, MI 49060-0162**

**Visit our web site at:         http://www.imajinnbooks.com**

**Questions?  Call us toll free: 877-625-3592**